How Miss Rutherford Got Her Groove Back

How Miss Rutherford Got Her Groove Back

Sophie Barnes

AVONIMPULSE

EPub Edition FEBRUARY 2012 ISBN: 9780062190321

Print Edition ISBN: 9780062190338

10 9 8 7 6 5 4 3 2

To my two boys,
whose sunny dispositions brighten up my days,
and to my husband,
whose love and support have made this story possible.

Prologue

Hardington, 1811

There was nothing but blue skies for as far as the eye could see as Emily Rutherford made light, brisk steps along the dusty road. She had been out much of that morning, as she oftentimes was whenever the weather allowed (and when she was free to do so), working on her landscape painting. There was a quiet spot not far from the cottage—up on a hill—from which she had a splendid view of the village of Hardington with its quaint stone church, winding streets, and colorful gardens that lay like neatly arranged postage stamps behind the houses.

To the right of the village lay Coldwell Manor, a wide stone building that sat heavily upon the English countryside. Emily had been there on a number of occasions as a child, when her parents had still been alive.

James Rutherford, the Viscount of Hillsbury, and his wife, Anna, had been one of the most celebrated couples in the area, their acquaintance sought after with great effort, as they always held the most spectacular and talked-about parties.

But that was then and this was now. Emily's parents had both passed away five years earlier in a boating accident. To the great misfortune of Emily and her sisters, Claire and Beatrice, there had been no will. Their parents had been young and had in all likelihood imagined that there would be plenty of time for that later. Thus, they had been left with next to nothing, since the majority of their parents' fortune had passed to the next male heir, their cousin Edward.

You see, when Emily's grandmother had passed away, their grandfather had remarried a widow who had brought her own son, Jack, into the family. Jack had left home as soon as it had been possible for him to do so, and had hastily married a young woman named Elizabeth. She had died no more than a year after the wedding while giving birth to Edward.

Even though the Rutherford girls and their parents had always treated Jack and Edward as if they were blood relations, Edward had always been painfully aware of the fact that he did not belong. So it was with great satisfaction that he discovered that he'd inherited Lord Hillsbury's fortune, simply because Emily's grandfather had secretly adopted Jack years earlier, in the hopes of strengthening his and Edward's ties with the rest of the family.

Emily and her sisters had been shocked to find that they'd been left without the right to anything, save for the modest cottage that their cousin had, out of the supposed goodness of his heart, purchased for them to live in. They *were* family, *after all.* But they would be expected to find themselves suitable husbands to support them and, it was hoped, become less of a burden to their distant relative.

And so it was that Emily had accepted a position at the nearby school in order to help make ends meet. She was not one to be blown over by the difficulties life had to offer, but was instead determined to make the best of any given situation. And, besides, she loved her students, who gave her a sense of purpose and always filled her with good cheer.

The three sisters were striking, with petite figures they'd inherited from their mother, though Emily was the only one blessed with her famous green eyes.

As the eldest of the three sisters, Beatrice had been the one to take charge of the household. She had put her heart and soul into ensuring that they were well cared for, and she had done it well, and without a single complaint, ever.

But it was clear that they could not go on like this forever. Husbands had to be found for all three of them. The trouble was that having had it all and then so graciously fallen, they needed to find suitors who could restore them to their former glory—no small task.

At present, the only one who had the chance to restore each of them to their rightful station was Emily. She had since childhood been a close friend of Adrian Fairchild, Viscount Carroway's son, of Coldwell Manor. In fact, they had been best friends and still saw each other regularly. Marriage between the two seemed inevitable.

Chapter One

Emily clutched her canvas and easel tightly under her right arm as she quickened her step, her box of paints held firmly in her left hand. She realized she must look terribly awkward as she struggled along, trying desperately not to drop anything.

As the rustic little cottage with its climbing roses spread across its façade came into view, Emily hurried ahead. She was eager to return home for there was much to be done today. She and her sisters had been formally invited to attend the yearly ball at Coldwell Manor. It had of course been Adrian's doing, for nobody would have thought to invite them otherwise.

The invitation had arrived a little over a week ago, and the three sisters had talked of nothing else since. It was the only invitation that they had received in the last year, as it had been the only one they'd received the year before that, and the year before that. And since it was only once a year that they were invited out, it had become the occasion they looked forward to with unparalleled eagerness and anticipation.

Bursting through the front door of the cottage, Emily immediately set down her cumbersome load on the floor to rest against the wall. She untied the green ribbon of her bonnet and removed it, running her fingers lightly through her hair. She was all jitters, she knew—something that would suit a young girl but hardly a fully-grown woman. So she took a moment to calm herself and smooth over her dress before quietly opening the door to the parlor.

Claire and Beatrice were both seated within, animatedly conversing with a guest that Emily recognized immediately. "Kate!" she exclaimed, forgetting herself and her composure as she rushed forward, her arms spread wide. "How good of you to have come! I've missed you terribly, and not a day has gone by where I haven't wondered about you. How long has it been?"

"Far too long, I suppose," Kate replied. She was a stunningly beautiful woman with a tall, shapely figure and light blonde hair. Her eyes were the clearest blue, her lips full and rosy. She and Emily had spent much of their childhood together in one another's company, though they'd seen less of each other in recent years now that Kate's family had moved to Stonebrook, the estate that her father had inherited from his brother.

At present, Kate had just returned from her annual two-week visit to her aunt and uncle. As they happened to live in London, Kate thoroughly enjoyed her visits.

"Tell me about your stay, Kate," Emily said, as she took the last remaining seat. "It must have been thoroughly splendid. Was it?"

Kate gave a slight nod followed by a broad smile. "It was

indeed. I was just telling Claire and Beatrice that Aunt Harriet and Uncle Geoffrey took me to the theatre a number of times. We saw Tchaikovsky's *Sleeping Beauty* on one occasion and very much enjoyed *Romeo and Juliet* on another. And the parties! Oh Emily, you would have loved it . . . all the lovely dresses, the music, and the dancing."

Claire and Beatrice both raised an eyebrow. "The dancing?" Beatrice asked. "Did you happen to meet any young gentlemen who sparked your interest?"

It was no secret that the main reason Kate's parents encouraged her to visit London was in order for her aunt and uncle to introduce her to the *ton*. Her parents hoped that she would find herself a suitable husband there. She was, after all, approaching her twenty-fourth year. Still, she had returned from her visit earlier than intended, in order to attend the Carroway ball that evening.

Kate giggled shyly as a bright pink hue flooded her face. "I must admit that there was one particular gentleman who . . ."

A squeal of delight filled the air, cutting her off, and before Kate knew what was happening, Emily had sprung out of her chair and was throwing her arms about her in a tight embrace. "That's wonderful news! You must tell us everything at once! Who is he? Are you engaged?"

"As a matter of fact, we have formed an attachment." Kate peeled herself away from Emily, her cheeks even redder than before from all the attention. "However, I did intend for this to be a quick visit. After all, there are a lot of things that need my attention before the ball this evening. I understand from your sisters that you shall all be attending?"

Emily's face brightened at the mere mention of that evening's event and found it impossible to hide a brilliant smile. "Oh, absolutely," she said. "We wouldn't miss it for the world."

"Then I shall tell you everything later," Kate said, looking at each of them with a secretive smile. "Now, I really must be off." She rose to her feet and reached for her bonnet.

"Well, it was lovely to see you again," Emily told her. "I shall look forward to seeing you this evening and finding out more about this elusive gentleman whom you plan to marry."

"As shall I," Kate told her with a small smile as she gave Emily a quick hug.

Emily and her sisters stood in the doorway and watched her walk away. She turned once to wave to them, still tying the ribbon of her bonnet below her chin.

"Her parents must be relieved," Beatrice remarked as they went back inside. "Considering her looks and the fact that her mother is the Duke of Bedford's sister, I'm surprised it took her this long to form an attachment."

"She's a romantic," Emily said. "She believes in true love and a happily ever after just as much as I do. Finding that can take time."

"At least you don't have to worry about that, dear sister," Claire said with a teasing smile.

Now it was Emily's turn to blush. Her sisters were both aware of her undying love for Adrian. She had in truth pined away endless hours, daydreaming of what her future would be like if she were married to him.

"When do you suppose that he will offer for you?" Claire

now asked. "From what you have told us, it seems that the two of you have some sort of understanding?"

"Yes, we do," Emily said with a thoughtful smile. "I do not know if he is *in* love with me, as I am with him, but I do not doubt that he loves me in some way or he would not have suggested that we should one day marry."

"I've told you too many times to count, surely he must be *in* love with you if he suggested as much," Beatrice told her. "How could he not be?"

Emily regarded her sister for a brief moment. The concern was clear in her eyes. She was clearly worried that Emily would end up unhappy in her marriage if Adrian didn't love her wholeheartedly.

"Oh, Bea," Emily said, wishing she could wash away her sister's fears. "You do so worry about us, don't you?"

"It is my job to worry about you, and I do believe that it has kept you safe from harm thus far."

"Well, Adrian would never hurt me. He has been my truest friend for as long as I can remember. I do not mind if he is not *in* love with me. I should find myself fortunate indeed if I became his wife, and I should be thoroughly happy. Aside from the fact that I can think of no other man that I would rather spend my life with, do you not see what my marrying him would mean for us?"

"Of course we do," Claire told her. "We just don't want you to give up on finding true happiness on our account. Emily, you must not agree to marry him just because it will reinstate us to our rightful positions."

Emily gave an exasperated sigh. She knew how much

her sisters loved her, but they were taking this too far. "Do you not see?" she asked them. "Marrying Adrian would be a dream come true for me—it would be *true* happiness. I love him with all my heart and I know that he loves me."

"Then by all means, let us hope that he will soon honor your agreement and offer for you," Claire told her.

"Yes, let's," Beatrice agreed with a warm smile. "Who knows? Perhaps you and Kate will both be married before the year is out."

Chapter Two

Emily and her sisters spent the rest of the day readying themselves for the evening ahead. They had laundered their dresses the previous day and now took turns pressing them in the kitchen, where the oven kept the irons hot.

At three o'clock, they paused for tea. They had just sat down in the parlor when Beatrice spotted Mrs. Hughes through the window. She was a short, plump woman in her fifties, with short, curly hair that had recently begun to show signs of grey.

"I daresay," Beatrice exclaimed. "I do believe that Mrs. Hughes intends to pay us a visit."

Claire immediately turned her head in order to have a look for herself. "Well, I hope we shall not be too delayed by this. After all, we still have to bathe and dress and . . ." she trailed off with a sigh. "You know how much the woman loves to talk."

It was true. Mrs. Hughes was a veritable gossip who could be very difficult to get rid of if they encouraged her to stay for tea.

"We cannot be so rude as to turn her away," Emily said. "Especially not when we are just now sitting down to tea ourselves. It would be very poor behavior on our part."

"Yes, of course we must invite her in," Beatrice said as she rose to her feet. "I shall go and greet her. Claire, stop scowling."

A moment later, Mrs. Hughes was sitting in their parlor on a chair next to Emily. "I'm terribly sorry if I caught you at a bad time," she began, still drawing heavy breaths from her quick walk. "I presume you must be readying yourselves for the ball this evening."

"Well . . . we . . ." Claire began.

"We were just taking a break from all of that and allowing ourselves to enjoy a cup of tea," Beatrice cut in, quickly interrupting any inappropriate remark her sister might have been about to make.

"Would you like a cup?" Emily asked.

Claire groaned, and Emily and Beatrice both glanced at her reproachfully, in response to which she gave an exasperated sigh. There was no telling how long Mrs. Hughes planned to stay.

"I would love a cup" was the reply. "If it's not too much trouble," she added, looking around.

"No trouble at all," Emily told her as she went to fetch another teacup from the china cabinet. She set it on a small round table next to Mrs. Hughes's chair and proceeded to pour tea into it. She then offered her a biscuit, which Mrs. Hughes eagerly accepted.

"What brings you here this afternoon?" Beatrice asked with a friendly smile. "I am guessing that there is something that you wish to tell us."

"Well," Mrs. Hughes began as she took a bite from the biscuit and followed it with a sip of tea. "There are two issues which I thought might be of interest to you. Firstly, I have been led to believe that the young Mr. Fairchild is inclined to choose a bride this season."

Emily almost choked on her tea. "Adrian?" she virtually sputtered.

"Why, of course," Mrs. Hughes told her, as if that was the silliest of all questions. "His brothers are already married, are they not?"

"Why, yes, I suppose they are," Emily agreed.

"If I am not completely misinformed, I do believe that you must have some inkling as to whom his chosen bride shall be. Is that not so, Miss Emily?" Mrs. Hughes regarded her kindly as she sipped her tea.

Emily's bright red blush was hard to miss. She was thankful that if she should blush so, then it was amongst only those who had her best interests at heart. "We do have an agreement," Emily confessed. "But nothing has been set in stone. Perhaps he has other intentions."

The mere thought of Adrian planning to marry someone other than her made her immensely nervous. What would she do if that happened? Her heart would surely shatter into a thousand pieces.

"Honestly, my dear, there really is no need to fret about such things. You have an agreement and Adrian is above all else a true gentleman. Everyone in Hardington knows how much he adores you," Mrs. Hughes told her as she placed her hand on Emily's and gave it a reassuring squeeze.

Emily let out a small sigh of relief. She knew what she was

being told was true, but it was still nice to have it confirmed. Adrian was, as Mrs. Hughes had said, a true gentleman. He was kind and generous, but above all else he was honorable.

"So as you see, you must prepare yourself, my dear. He will undoubtedly broach the subject with you this very evening. If I am correct in my assumptions, you may find yourself to be engaged no later than tomorrow morning," Mrs. Hughes told her.

That had Emily's nerves playing havoc all over again. Would Adrian really propose to her that very evening? Her stomach fluttered at the mere thought of it. However would she keep herself together until he did? She was sure she would be a total wreck by the time she saw him that evening.

"You mentioned that there were two things that might interest us?" Claire suddenly asked, breaking Emily's spell. "What was the other?"

"Oh, I merely wished to inform you that Francis Riley, the Earl of Dunhurst, is visiting Coldwell Manor this week and possibly even next, as well. As I recall, he is also a friend of yours. Is he not?"

Emily groaned inwardly. It was true that she had met Francis on numerous occasions while growing up. He was Adrian's cousin, sharing the same maternal grandparents, but all similarities ended there.

Where Adrian was fair-haired, Francis was dark. Where Adrian was open and warm, Francis was forever brooding. One could always count on Adrian for a good laugh, but Francis . . . Emily wondered when she had last seen him smile.

She seemed to recall that he hadn't always been that way. Hadn't they all enjoyed playing together as children? They'd all been happy back then, including Francis. In fact, Francis had been a closer friend to her then than Adrian had been, but somewhere along the way he had changed and Emily couldn't help but wonder why.

"Francis!" Emily heard Claire exclaim. "But he's positively dull!"

"That's a terrible thing to say," Beatrice scolded her sister. "I really wish that you would learn to keep such statements to yourself, particularly when we have guests."

"Oh, it's quite all right," Mrs. Hughes told them. "After all, everyone knows that Lord Dunhurst has a somewhat stern demeanor. However, I do not think he is unkind."

"I never suggested that he was," Claire said pointedly, as Beatrice and Emily cringed at her rudeness.

"In any event, it is hardly our place to judge him," Beatrice concluded in an attempt to smooth over her sister's last statement. "I am sure that there is a valid reason for his being the way he is. In any case, it is his business and not ours."

Emily gave a slight sigh as she smiled at her older sister. "You always were a diplomat, Bea," she said. "But in this instance I really must agree with Claire. Francis *is* an absolute bore. On top of that, he's stern to the point of rudeness. I understand he wasn't always this way, but what matters is what he has become."

Beatrice didn't respond. Her reprimanding glare told Emily just how disappointed she was in her. Must she always behave properly then, flattering even those who did not deserve flattering? But she loved her elder sister and had no wish to embarrass her in public.

"Oh, I daresay," Mrs. Hughes suddenly remarked as she

strained her neck to peer out the window. "It does appear as if the gentleman in question has come to call upon you."

"Who? Francis?" Claire exclaimed, turning in her seat in order to have a look.

"It would appear so, yes," Mrs. Hughes remarked as she raised her spectacles to her eyes. "He's securing his horse to your fence as we speak—beautiful creature, I must say. Then again, Lord Dunhurst always did have impeccable taste when it came to horses."

Beatrice hurried to the door, straightening her apron as she went. If she was put out of sorts by receiving more guests in one afternoon than they usually received in the course of a whole week, she hid it exceedingly well. Emily was quite impressed with her sister's ability to remain calm and undeterred by it all. Even if none of them were particularly fond of Francis, he was an earl after all.

When he appeared a moment later in the doorway, Emily was incapable of ignoring just how stiff and awkward he looked. In fact, there was something about him that suggested that this was truly the last place in the world he wished to be.

Yet there was one thing by which she was somewhat taken aback. Francis was far more handsome than she remembered him. It was perhaps two years since she had seen him last, and it was quite clear that her mind had chosen only to remember the faults that she had found with his personality. When it came to looks, he certainly had no equal. Not even Adrian could measure up to him in that regard, though Emily felt a twinge of disloyalty for thinking it.

But Francis was a fine specimen: tall and lean with broad

shoulders. His thick black hair, cut short, still retained an untidy look that Emily found oddly appealing. His eyes were dark, as though filled with concern and sadness; his nose perfectly straight like that of Michelangelo's *David*. He was clean-shaven to expose a chiseled jaw line and a mouth that mirrored the look in his eyes.

"Miss Emily, Miss Claire," he said as he glanced at both Claire and Emily in turn, giving each of them a curt nod. "Mrs. Hughes."

"Lord Dunhurst," they each said, returning his greeting.

"Would you like to have a cup of tea?" Beatrice asked as she pushed her way past him in the doorway, already heading for the china cabinet.

"Oh, no, please don't trouble yourself on my account, Miss Rutherford," he told her as he carelessly beat the tip of his riding crop against his brown leather boots. Emily guessed that it must be some form of habit, brought about when he was agitated about something.

"Then by all means, please tell us how else we may be of service to you," Beatrice said, her voice a little more tense than usual. Perhaps his presence here had rattled her a bit after all.

The situation was ridiculous. They had all known each other since they were children. They had run about in the garden, called one another by their given names. Yet here they were behaving more formally than ever. A slight smile played upon Emily's lips as she contemplated how fun it would have been if he had simply marched in and said "Beatrice, Emily, and Claire—I happened to be stopping by and thought you might like to catch some frogs with me, for old time's sake . . ."

Yet here they were with the formal addresses, acting as if they barely knew one another.

"Adrian tells me that you will be attending the ball this evening," Francis said with a hint of dryness in his voice. "It will be quite a distance for you to walk in all your finery. Perhaps you would like for us to send a carriage?"

"That is indeed very generous of you," Beatrice told him. She looked across at her sisters who both appeared eager to accept. It would at least ensure that their white muslin gowns would still be clean upon arrival at Coldwell Manor. "We accept your offer, with many thanks."

Francis gave her a curt nod before regarding the other women present. "It is settled then. You may expect the carriage at seven thirty."

"Thank you very much indeed, Francis," Emily replied. She'd had enough of formalities. Besides, Lord Dunhurst needed to loosen up a bit, though he didn't seem quite as stiff as she remembered.

His dark eyes settled on her when she spoke his name, narrowing slightly as he regarded her solemnly. Emily couldn't help but smile slightly at provoking him. It was very clear he found her form of address far too familiar. She couldn't help but wonder if it was because she and her sisters were no longer of the same social rank as he.

Of course it was.

Emily's smile faded as she suddenly saw the situation from Francis's point of view. He was an earl. How embarrassing it must be for him to have to come here on such an errand. If it hadn't been for Adrian's thoughtfulness . . . well, thank goodness for that.

"Well, I shan't detain you any longer," Francis told them, his eyes still on Emily. "I look forward to seeing you all this evening."

"Mrs. Hughes," he then said, giving the woman yet another curt nod. He then addressed each of the three sisters in turn, made a gracious bow, and turned on his heel and left.

They watched through the windows as he swung himself up into the saddle and started off at a canter.

"Well! He is far more handsome than I recalled," Claire remarked, breaking the silence that he had left behind.

"And he wasn't nearly as stern as I remembered him, either," Beatrice added. "Though I daresay he was a bit put out by the liberty you took, Emily, in addressing him so casually."

"Oh, fiddlesticks," Emily exclaimed as she rolled her eyes heavenward. "It was obvious that he had no desire to be here. I merely meant to provoke him slightly."

"And a fine job you did," Beatrice told her with a sigh.

"Oh, Bea, the man is insufferable. We were friends once—close friends, but now, ever since Mama and Papa died and our situation is no longer what it used to be, he suddenly expects us to address him formally. Well I shan't, Bea, and if that irks him, well then he is indeed a far greater snob than I ever would have imagined."

"Emily, please do try to make an effort this evening. At least for my sake, and for Claire's. I do not wish for you to cause a scene simply because you've suddenly decided to thwart the rules of society."

Emily sighed deeply as she regarded her sisters thoughtfully. "Very well," she finally said. "I shall call him Lord Dunhurst for your sakes alone, but I shall do it very begrudgingly." She added the last part with a sulky expression that instantly lightened the mood.

"Whatever the case," Mrs. Hughes now told them. "It does appear that he is a very eligible gentleman indeed. Perhaps you might consider this, should he invite you to dance with him this evening."

Beatrice and Claire both chuckled, reddening with embarrassment, while Emily groaned at the prospect of having Lord Riley as her brother-in-law for all eternity.

Chapter Three

The night was warm, the air filled with the scent of honeysuckle, as the sisters walked down their garden path to the carriage that awaited them. In the distance came the sound of frogs croaking—a sound to which Emily had a sentimental attachment. It reminded her of the rare summer evenings when, as a child, her father would take her and her sisters outside to stargaze. She smiled at the memory. Those had been happy days for all of them.

The carriage rolled along at a steady pace, lurching only slightly whenever it hit a bump in the road. Claire's eyes sparkled with joy at the experience. It had been a very long time indeed since they had had the pleasure of enjoying a carriage ride.

"So far this has been a wonderful evening," she exclaimed to her sisters, who returned her enthusiasm with warm smiles. "I do wish that we could do this more often."

The driveway's gravel crunched beneath the horse's hooves as they drove up to the front door. A smartly dressed footman set down the steps, then helped each of the sisters alight. They then made their way up the stone steps toward the grand foyer of Coldwell Manor.

"Beatrice, Emily, Claire! How good of you to come," a gentle voice exclaimed, the minute they made their entrance.

They all turned toward the tall, slender figure that approached them—beautifully dressed in a richly embroidered gown trimmed with lace and ribbons.

"We wouldn't have missed it for the world. Thank you so much for inviting us, Lady Carroway," Emily smiled. "We've been looking forward to this evening ever since we received the invitation."

"You look lovely, all three of you. I hope you shall enjoy a few dances before the night is over. There are a number of gentlemen who are very eager to make your acquaintances. I hope you do not mind my introducing them to you?" she asked, looking suddenly worried that she might have done something inappropriate. Taking Beatrice's arm, she steered the three sisters toward the ballroom.

"Not at all," Beatrice grinned. "We shall welcome all gentlemen who wish to speak with us. How else are we to find suitable husbands?"

Although Beatrice had said it jokingly, Claire still managed a faint groan at her sister's remark. Was it really necessary to be so frank about the fact that they were actively looking? It made them seem nothing short of desperate, a view that deeply colored her cheeks from sheer embarrassment as she looked about to ensure that no one else had heard.

Picking up on her mortification, Lady Carroway made a quick attempt to soothe her. "It's quite all right, Claire—your secret's safe with me."

Obviously it had the opposite effect and did nothing but deepen the color in her cheeks. What a horrific moment this was turning out to be.

"Well," Lady Carroway continued. "I was wondering if you would mind it if I took a quick turn about the room with your sister. She and I have much to discuss," she said pointedly as she turned her gaze on Emily.

"Not at all," Beatrice remarked.

"Then let us go before Claire dies of embarrassment, which she seems just about ready to do at any moment." Lady Carroway gave a small chuckle as she took hold of Emily's arm and guided her away from her sisters.

Light, wispy notes of music began to rise from the orchestra, signaling that the first dance was about to commence. When Emily craned her neck to ensure that her sisters were all right, she saw that they were already deeply immersed in conversation with a number of old acquaintances. She therefore allowed herself to give Lady Carroway her full attention.

"You know that I have always been very fond of you, Emily—*and* your sisters," the viscountess was now saying. "I know that you have had a difficult number of years. Losing both of your parents at such a young age was very hard on you, I know." She paused momentarily as she glanced out over the dance floor, her posture as regal as that of any queen.

"I have always considered you to be a part of this family, Emily, and have had the pleasure of watching you grow into the fine young woman that you are today—kind, nurturing, and full of joy." She stopped as she pulled Emily to the side, where a large bay window overlooked the park-like grounds. She lowered her voice. "You have always been a loyal friend to

Adrian. The way in which you look at him has not gone unnoticed, either. I know that you love him."

"I . . ." Emily began, but Lady Carroway raised her hand to stop the explanation that she knew was coming.

"It's quite all right, Emily. I am only too pleased that my son is fortunate enough to be loved by you. And I know that he loves you in return. That is what I wish to speak to you about," she said with a brilliant gleam in her eyes. "Adrian has told us that he intends to marry. He would not elaborate on the matter, but I am certain that he intends to ask you."

Emily could barely contain her excitement, and yet, she couldn't help the growing sense of unease that was gradually taking hold of her. "You are sure of this?" she asked.

"I know that he adores you, Emily. I can't think of anyone else that he might even consider. Can you?"

"I suppose not."

"Then don't worry. It will all be settled very soon." Lady Carroway put her hand reassuringly on Emily's arm. "You shall make him very happy indeed, Emily, and as for us . . . well . . . we shall soon have a daughter."

Emotion flooded Emily's body so rapidly at this final remark that she knew not whether to laugh or cry. As it turned out, she did both. How fortunate she was to be shown such love and acceptance from Adrian's mother. On impulse she gave her future mother-in-law a hug, which was returned to her wholeheartedly.

"Emily!"

The familiar voice made her heart leap with joy as she pulled away from Lady Carroway's embrace. Both women turned to find Adrian striding toward them with a radiant

Kate on his arm. They made a handsome couple indeed, Emily thought. It made her feel all the more lucky that she had his love and friendship.

"Adrian," she gasped with a smile, still taken aback by his strikingly handsome features, even after all these years. "It's been a while since I last saw you."

"Too long," he agreed as he tilted his head to kiss her on the cheek. It was a familiar gesture that he had adopted when they were children, and although it was done in a brotherly fashion, it had always filled Emily with warmth.

"I see that you have wasted no time in attaching a beautiful lady to your arm," Lady Carroway teased her son.

Kate blushed ever so slightly at the remark. She knew that Mother Nature had endowed her with looks that were easy on the eyes, yet she was always embarrassed whenever it was brought into conversation. "It is a pleasure to see you again, Lady Carroway," she said in a muted voice.

All Emily could think was how desperately she longed to drag her friend away to a private corner and insist she tell her everything about her trip to London and the gentleman who'd won her heart. But it would have to wait.

"I suppose you wish to steel Emily away from me, Adrian. The two of you probably have much to discuss," Lady Carroway commented as she gave her son a knowing look.

"We do indeed, though I am afraid that it must wait, for I have just promised Kate that I would dance the next set with her."

"I'm terribly sorry," Kate managed, looking slightly flushed and embarrassed. "The truth of it is that Adrian has been quite the gentleman. He saw me standing alone after

Papa and Mama had gone off to talk to their friends, and well . . ."

"I insisted that she accompany me until you arrived."

"I hope you do not mind too much, Emily. In fact, I've been eagerly waiting for you myself. We really must finish the conversation that we were having earlier."

"It's quite all right," Emily told her friend with a broad smile. "Why don't the two of you go and enjoy yourselves. I can dance with Adrian afterward, and then you and I can have a little chat."

"That's what I love about you, Emily—you're always so agreeable," Adrian grinned. "Ah, I hear the music starting as we speak. Come on, Kate, let's show them how it's done."

As Adrian hurried away, pulling a stumbling Kate after him, Emily watched them go. Something about it didn't sit well with her, though she couldn't quite figure out what it was. She shook away her misgivings.

It's just a dance.

When she turned, she spotted a momentary look of regret upon Lady Carroway's face, and then it was gone.

"Come, my dear." Lady Carroway pulled her along but said nothing more. It was clear that her thoughts were on something else entirely.

When they joined her sisters again, Claire could barely contain her curiosity. "Why is Adrian dancing with Kate instead of with you?" she whispered.

"I wasn't here when he asked her," Emily explained. "Adrian had already offered to dance with Kate before I arrived, and it really would have been badly done if he didn't honor his prior engagement." It was a simple explanation, yet something about the whole exchange still bothered her.

"He should have waited." Lady Carroway's voice was filled with irritation. "He should have waited and danced with you first. I'm sorry about this, Emily; it's terribly rude of him."

Emily wasn't one to get too caught up in etiquette. She merely shrugged. Why did it matter whom Adrian danced with? They were all friends after all, and Kate had known him just as long as she had. Emily had never been the jealous type, and she was determined not to start now. On the contrary, it pleased her to know that her two dearest friends could get along.

At least, that's what she told herself.

Her thoughts came tumbling to the ground when she felt a sharp nudge in her ribs. It was Claire. "Emily," she whispered. "Lord Dunhurst is asking you if you would like to dance the next set with him. He is still waiting for your reply."

It was all too familiar to her. She had always had a tendency to daydream. As a child, her tutors had sometimes had to tap her shoulder with a ruler to bring her back to reality. At such moments it always seemed as if she had been absent for far longer than was probably the case. She now looked flustered as she noticed Francis standing before her, an eyebrow raised as he awaited her answer.

"Please excuse me," she told him with a faint smile. "But I must regretfully decline as I shall be dancing the next set with Mr. Fairchild."

She couldn't help but notice a brief flicker of annoyance pass behind his eyes. It did nothing but aggravate her.

"In that case, I shall disturb you no longer," he said as he took his leave and walked away, his eyes dark and his jaw clenched tightly shut.

Emily followed him with her eyes as she let out a deep sigh of relief. Why did he always have this effect on her? She wondered. There was just something about him that she found to be rather unpleasant. She turned toward her sisters. "He makes me feel most uncomfortable," she noted.

"You were rather cold toward him, Emily," Beatrice told her. "In fact, I daresay you were quite rude."

"*I* with *him?* Is he not the one who never manages to smile? And how rude of him not to invite one of you to dance after I informed him that I'd be dancing with Adrian."

"Honestly, Emily, he was really quite polite in asking you. Perhaps he noticed the look of disappointment on your face when Adrian chose to dance with Kate instead. There's no need denying it—you did look rather put-out, though you made a brave attempt not to. So if you ask me, I think Francis was rather thoughtful and kind when he asked you. Naturally he would not ask anyone else once you had so flatly refused him."

Emily had seen no such thing. Was Beatrice right? But why would Francis ask her to dance anyway? It was no secret that he disliked her company. Perhaps Beatrice was right. Perhaps he'd merely been trying to help. Emily sighed once again. She suddenly felt as if she had wronged him in some way.

Perhaps she ought to apologize.

But the next thing she knew, Kate and Adrian had returned, both talking amidst bursts of laughter as they walked up to her.

"You appear to have been enjoying yourselves immensely," Lady Carroway observed with a strained smile.

Kate looked suddenly flushed. There was that embarrassment again.

"We have been, indeed," Adrian said. "Now, dear Emily, I do believe that it is your turn."

Emily couldn't conceal her happiness as he took her by the arm and led her toward the dance floor. From behind her, she could hear Claire making a quiet remark, which was swiftly followed by a string of giggles. She was confident that a joke had just been made at her expense, but all she could do was smile at it. This truly was the best night ever.

Chapter Four

As Emily and Adrian faced one another across the dance floor, she knew that she had never felt happier. How handsome he looked, all dressed in black and white—so elegant. She felt her heart skip a beat. And when he gave her that winning smile of his, it all but took her breath away.

And yet it was as if he wasn't quite present. It seemed as if something was distracting him. Of course it was, she thought. Marriage and marriage proposals were a serious business. He was probably trying to decide on the best way in which to broach the topic.

As the music started up, they stepped lightly toward one another, meeting for a brief moment in the middle of the floor, hands barely touching, before stepping apart once more. When they met again, they turned quickly about, his hand resting ever so gently upon her waist. "You have no idea how much I've missed you," he told her.

Her heart leapt with joy at those reassuring words. "As I have you," she assured him.

"I would like an opportunity to speak with you . . . in private," he whispered. "Once this dance has ended."

Her stomach fluttered. He intended to ask her tonight after all. She was suddenly rendered speechless, her nerves playing havoc with her body. She simply nodded in agreement.

As the music faded, he grasped her hand in his and pulled her along with him, away from the crowded ballroom, through French doors that had been flung open and outside onto a terrace overlooking the garden.

The air was sweet with a faint scent of jasmine as they paused here momentarily. Adrian squeezed her hand lightly as he glanced about. Nobody else was out here. Everyone was inside enjoying the festivities.

Spotting a low bench, he dragged her toward it. She sat down immediately, gracefully, and expectantly as he took the seat next to her, still holding her hand in his.

"How long have we been friends, Emily?"

"Since the beginning of time." She managed to keep her tone even, though it was barely louder than a whisper.

"I've decided to marry," he told her abruptly.

Emily caught her breath as tears of joy began to gather in her eyes. Finally!

"I realize it may come as a surprise to you, though it shouldn't really. I've always said that I wanted to marry before I turned thirty. I know that there is plenty of time yet—for as you know, I am but seven and twenty—but it seems so right, Emily."

"Does it?" she asked faintly, her heart beating so erratically she could barely concentrate on what he was telling her.

"You and I have always been close. That's why I want you to be the first to know . . . I've asked Kate to be my wife."

Everything slowed to a halt, and her heart felt like it had suddenly stopped. She sat perfectly still, motionless as if she were frozen in time. Had she heard him right? Had the man she'd been in love with for all eternity just told her he would marry her friend? Not her, but *Kate*?

"I saw her in London, while she was there visiting her aunt and uncle . . ." Adrian was saying, but Emily had stopped listening.

She looked down at her hands. He was still holding them in his. How quickly the significance of his touch had altered. No more than a second ago, she had taken it to be a sign of his love for her. Now, she saw it for what it was: one friend reaching out to another for approval. She felt her heart beat once and then again as her throat tightened and her eyes began to burn. How could she have been so naïve as to think that he would ever have considered making her his wife?

She was suddenly acutely aware of everything. It was unbearably clear that there had been no understanding after all. In all likelihood he didn't even recall the conversation they'd had six years ago. "I'm not ready for marriage yet," he'd said. "But when I will be, there's nobody I'd rather marry than you, my dearest friend."

He had kissed her gently that day, beneath the cherry blossoms behind her cottage. It now dawned on her that he had done it all on a whim. He might have meant what he'd said for the briefest of moments, but that was all it had been to him. To her however . . . her heart was breaking apart, piece by piece, at an agonizingly slow pace.

She had to get away from him with her dignity still intact. He mustn't see her unravel as she knew she was about to. It was enough of a humiliation that the entire town would soon know that she was not to be his bride. Not now, not ever, even though that was what everyone had thought. That was what everyone had told her. And she had believed them. . . . She had hoped. . . . Oh God, what a fool she had been.

Very slowly, as if worried that a sudden movement might cause her to shatter, she withdrew her hand. She then raised her eyes to meet his and gave him the most dazzling smile that she could muster. Then, fighting against the pain in her throat, she did her best to speak in a smooth, calm voice. "I am so happy for you, Adrian. You have made a wonderful choice in Kate, and I just know that she will make a brilliant wife. You are really very well suited for one another."

"So you approve? I'm so relieved. You have no idea how nervous I was about telling you. Your opinion matters more to me than anyone else's. Thank you, Emily—you really are a true friend," he told her sincerely. "I knew I could count on you for support."

Was this a nightmare? Emily wondered. Would she wake up any minute to find that it had all been nothing but a dream? That the gut-wrenching sadness she felt right now was unfounded? No, this was not a dream. She *was* in fact sitting here, telling the man she loved more than life itself that he had her blessing to marry somebody else.

You are a true friend. The words echoed in her mind, viciously stabbing at her heart.

"Are you all right?" she heard him ask.

Panic spread erratically throughout her body. How much

longer could she maintain her composure? Already the tears were welling in her eyes. Emily was thankful for the darkness of night that masked her true emotions. She nodded vigorously in response to his question, then managed to choke out, "Yes, I'm fine. Like I said, I wish both of you the best, Adrian." Rising to her feet, she steadied herself, willing herself to remain calm for a moment longer. "Goodbye."

"Goodbye? What the devil . . . where are you going, Emily? Are you quite sure you're all right? You're not ill, are you?"

"As a matter of fact, I think I'm about to be quite ill indeed," she told him sharply, her pain transforming into anger. How could he pretend to be so ignorant of her feelings? How could he act as though he hadn't the faintest idea of how she felt about him? It suddenly infuriated her that he had been so careless, so selfish, and so unfeeling. It wasn't like him . . . or was it? Had she just not seen how thoughtless he could be?

"I have to go, Adrian—I'm sorry. Please excuse me." Snatching her hand away from his, she fled, her mind set only on getting away from him, Kate, and the rest of Hardington's inhabitants.

Adrian watched as she ran down the steps and disappeared into the garden. He wondered for a moment if he should run after her. After all, she had said that she was feeling ill. Then again, for whatever reason, it seemed as if she wanted to be alone. He got up slowly, his eyes unwillingly searching for her in the darkness, but she was gone.

As he walked back inside, light notes of music floated out to greet him. He studied the ballroom for a moment, looking for Kate. Instead he located his mother and Emily's sisters, who appeared to be deep in conversation with one another.

"Ladies," he greeted them, interrupting their conversation. "I merely wish to inform you that Emily appears to have taken ill. She wished to be alone for a while and, well . . . in fact, I believe she may have gone home."

"Dear God, Adrian!" his mother exclaimed. "And you let her leave, just like that? You should have offered her a carriage."

"I would have, Mother," he said, his voice betraying his annoyance. "However, she hurried off before I had the chance to suggest it."

"And why was that, Adrian?" Lady Carroway asked, her eyes narrowing as she studied her son.

"How the devil should I know?"

"You mean to tell me that you didn't even ask her why she was suddenly unwell? After all, she was fine before she left to dance with you. In fact, she was radiant . . . no sign of impending illness whatsoever. What did you tell her, Adrian?"

Adrian held his mother's gaze. "Just that I have asked Kate to marry me. I wanted her to be the first to know," he said as all three women drew sharp breaths and stared at him in horror. "She congratulated me and wished me well, as unlike you—as it is becoming increasingly clear—I know that I can always count on her for support."

"You're a damn fool, Adrian," his mother snapped. "Beatrice and Claire, I must apologize for my son's obvious lack of tact. Come quickly . . . we must find Francis. He'll know what to do."

"Perhaps I could . . ."

"Thank you, but I do believe that you've done quite enough." Without offering her son another word, Lady Carroway turned on her heel and hurried off. Only Beatrice managed a quick goodbye, though her eyes now seemed to be filled with anything but compassion for him.

What the hell is going on?

Adrian watched them go. He'd be damned if he ever understood what went on in women's brains. It all seemed to be one big muddle to him. With an exasperated sigh he glanced around once more in search of Kate. Finding her, he picked up a glass of wine from a tray held by a waiter, then made his way over to where she was standing.

They spotted Francis in the card room, where he was having a friendly game of bridge together with Lord Hutton, Mr. Birkley, and Lord Carroway, the latter being his partner. Lady Carroway quietly requested that Claire and Beatrice wait for her by the door. She then approached her husband.

Beatrice and Claire watched Lord Carroway's reaction as his wife spoke to him, her voice but a whisper, close to his ear. As she straightened, he ran a hand through his hair. He made no attempt to hide his obvious concern as he threw his cards down onto the table. "Gentlemen, it appears that we are done here. Lord Dunhurst, please go with my wife. There seems to be a pressing matter that needs your immediate attention. . . . She will explain it to you."

Without the slightest display of emotion, Francis finished the remainder of his cognac. He then rose to his feet, gave a polite nod to his companions, and followed Lady Carroway from the room.

"How may I be of service?" he asked. He had followed the

women into the parlor, where they had each taken a seat. He had remained standing, his elbow resting against the mantle of the fireplace. The three women clearly looked disturbed by something. He couldn't help but wonder what it might be, though he was sure that he was about to find out.

"I'm terribly sorry to trouble you with this, Francis, but it's a delicate matter that needs handling with some care," Lady Carroway began.

"Emily's run off," Beatrice blurted out, her voice filled with distress. Lady Carroway placed a staying hand upon her arm, held her gaze for a moment, and then turned once again toward Francis.

He appeared unmoved by the information, save for a slightly raised eyebrow. "Why does that worry you?" he asked. "She may have been tired and decided to leave early. Perhaps she simply wished to get some fresh air and will be back at any moment."

Beatrice's eyes ignited with fury. "How can you treat the situation so lightly, sir? Clearly we would not have troubled you unless we had good reason to."

"My apologies, Miss Rutherford, but given the fact that your sister is to be engaged to Adrian—I'm not completely oblivious to the goings on around here, you know," he said as he saw that his aunt was about to protest. "Would it not be more fitting if you asked him to ride about in search of her? Besides, if she is seeking some time alone, I very much doubt that I would be a welcome companion for her."

Beatrice's first reaction was to retaliate, but she knew that he was probably right. He would be very unwelcome indeed. However, it was late and the sky was already showing signs of rain. She knew how devastated Emily must be, and she couldn't help but worry about her being out there on her own, even if she was on her way home.

"The situation is as follows," Lady Carroway said. "It appears that Adrian has misled us all as far as his true intentions are concerned, though I cannot believe that he would do something like this without a word of warning to any of us. But apparently he has already proposed to Kate and has just asked Emily for her blessing." Francis's eyes seemed to darken, his jaw clenched ever so slightly. "My son, it seems, never felt anything more than friendship for Emily, but what is truly astounding is how ignorant he seems to be of her feelings toward him. I just don't understand how we could have been so wrong in our assumptions. And I cannot imagine why Kate's father has not broached this subject with my husband. I must speak to him and Adrian about this, but that's neither here nor there. The point is that Emily became ill, so to speak, and ran off as a result of Adrian's desire to share the delightful news with her."

"I take it she did not find it so delightful," Francis murmured, his face set in stone.

"Indeed, we may be quite certain that she did not," Beatrice said, her voice filled with resentment. Then in a more agreeable tone she added, "We would be forever grateful if you would please find her, my lord."

"Let us not waste any more time then," he said, his voice filled with steel as he strode toward the door. "Remind me to have a serious talk with Adrian once I return."

With that, he was gone.

Chapter Five

A misty drizzle filled the air as Francis swung himself up into the saddle and kicked his five-year-old gelding into a furious gallop.

He cursed his cousin beneath his breath for his idiocy. He never should have allowed Emily to leave in such a state. Why had he not run after her and insisted that she take a carriage, if indeed she had wished to go home? Walking about on country roads in this weather—and clad in a light summer dress—was pure madness.

It wasn't the first time he'd been forced to clean up one of Adrian's messes, he recalled as his jaw tightened. This would be the last, he vowed. Nothing was more disagreeable than having to come to the rescue of a woman who so clearly resented his very existence.

How had it come to this? They had been friends once. Now, she could barely stand the sight of him.

The drizzle became a sudden downpour, and Francis's eyes narrowed as heavy drops of water ran down his face. He was soon soaked through, his cloak doing little to keep him dry. Emily . . . he thought for a moment of her cheerful smile and infectious laughter. Some people just weren't meant to suffer, he thought, as he pushed her image from his mind and rode on.

He saw the cottage emerge through the darkness, the rain beating loudly as the wind threw torrents against the walls. Tying his horse loosely to the fence, he ran up the muddy path and proceeded to hammer on the door as water cascaded down his back. Not a single sound answered him. . . . There wasn't even the faintest glow of light coming from within, as there should have been, had she been home.

His alarm rose. Where could she be? He knew he hadn't passed her on the way. Cursing her recklessness, he paused to think, ignoring the cold, wet fabric of his clothes.

A faint memory came to mind. "This is my favorite place in all the world," she had once told him. It had been many years ago . . . before her parents had died. He had gone to the estate that had been her home and that now belonged to her cousin. He'd wanted to see if she wanted to go rowing. Beatrice had told him where to find her.

With eyes as dark as the night sky and his mouth drawn tight in anger, Francis reared his horse around and set out once more. If anything bad had happened to Emily as a result of this . . . so help him God, he'd have a fine time beating some sense into Adrian himself.

Leaving the road behind, he made a sharp turn out into the fields. The soft swell of the hills rose in the distance, silhouetted against the gray clouds that thundered overhead. Wiping the rain from his face with the palm of his hand, he paused for a moment to look around. He soon spotted the outline of a partially torn-down farmhouse, resting below a towering oak. Francis nudged his horse onward.

When he reached the top of the hill, he sighed inwardly as he rode around the dilapidated stone building. She didn't appear to be there either. Dismounting, he walked toward the house; the walls were still partially in place, though the roof was mostly gone, and the windows and doors gaped blindly at him through the darkness. Stepping carefully over some fallen bricks as he steadied himself against the doorframe, he entered.

The minute he spotted the slight figure, huddled against the far corner of what had once been the sitting room, Francis rushed forward. His chest contracted as he knelt beside her, wrapping his cloak around her delicate frame. Her hair hung in wet streaks around her face, her mud-stained dress clung against her body. She trembled slightly as he scooped her up in his arms, turning pain-stricken eyes toward him.

"How could you have been so stupid, Emily?" His voice harsh with fear for her.

He expected her to lash out at him, to berate his anger as had become a habit of hers over the years, but she didn't respond. She merely twined her arms around his neck and rested her head against his chest. There wasn't a fight left in her, he realized with sudden panic, as he briskly carried her back outside and set her on his horse.

Arriving back at the manor, he lifted her gently down, and wishing to draw as little attention as possible, entered through the kitchen entrance. Emily registered nothing. She appeared to have fallen into a deep sleep, her head lolling slightly from side to side as he walked.

"Please have two hot baths drawn immediately," he told a maid in passing. Then, addressing a second maid, he said, "Follow me."

After setting Emily down on a bed in one of the spare bedrooms, Francis left the maid to undress and care for her as he himself made his way back downstairs to the ballroom.

Beatrice drew a sharp breath, then reached for Lady Carroway's wrist when she saw him striding toward them. He was soaked to the skin, his hair plastered against his forehead and water dripping from his clothes as he walked. And yet, in spite of it all, he still looked outrageously handsome, though his eyes were fierce with a mixture of anger and concern.

"I found her inside that small farmhouse at the top of the hill," he said, addressing Beatrice. "She's soaked and will in all likelihood get quite sick as a result of this."

"Where is she now, my lord?" Beatrice asked, her voice far quieter and more calm than she felt.

His eyes moved to Lady Carroway. "I took the liberty of taking her upstairs to one of your spare bedrooms. A hot bath is being prepared for her, and one of your maids is caring for her."

Lady Carroway looked at Francis with grateful eyes. "Thank you. You did the right thing, Francis. She will stay here until we're sure that she's well. I hope that's all right with you, Beatrice?"

"I'm extremely grateful for your concern and for all of your help," Beatrice replied with a heavy sigh. "Thank you, Lord Dunhurst, for finding her and bringing her back to us."

"It was the least I could do," he said, his face betraying

no emotion, though every fiber of his being was in turmoil. "Why don't you go and see to her, Miss Rutherford? Take Miss Claire with you. If she's awake, she will need comforting. Just turn right at the top of the landing—it's the third door on your left."

Beatrice gave him a grave but thankful smile as she took Claire's hand and led her away toward the stairs.

"I wish to have a word with Adrian," Francis remarked when they were out of earshot.

Lady Carroway nodded pensively. She had meant to speak with him herself, but had been busy attending to the rest of her guests. Besides, perhaps it would be best if Francis did it. "Very well . . . why don't you take him to the library? You won't be disturbed there."

Wishing his aunt a good evening, Francis went in search of Adrian. He finally found him, accompanied by Kate, who appeared to be having the time of her life. "A quick word, if you don't mind," he said, looking Adrian squarely in the eyes.

"But of course . . . where should we . . ."

"Through here," Francis replied in a tight voice. "We'll go to the library." He raised an eyebrow at Kate, then paused as though he expected her to disengage herself from Adrian and vanish.

"It's all right if she comes along," Adrian declared. "You may say what you wish in her presence."

"Very well," Francis muttered. "Two birds with one stone, I suppose . . ."

Once inside the library, Francis made straight for the side table, picked up a glass, and poured himself some scotch. "Would you like some?" he asked Adrian with a cold glare.

Adrian hesitated a moment, then shook his head as he sat down in a deep, brown leather armchair.

"How about you, Lady Kate?" Francis went on, taking a swig of his drink as he turned toward her. "Would you like something to wash away the guilt?"

A look of confusion came over Kate's face. "I cannot imagine what you might be referring to, Lord Dunhurst."

"I'm sure you can't," Francis sneered.

"What the devil . . . Francis, I have to say that I do not like your tone." Adrian sprang to his feet, ready to take Francis head-on. "Just what exactly is the meaning of this?"

"As if you don't know." Francis glared at Kate and Adrian in turn. "You certainly make a fine pair."

Kate stared back at him as if he'd gone mad. He was clearly riled about something, though she couldn't begin to fathom what it might be.

"Would you please tell us what the blazes you're talking about?" Adrian asked.

Francis looked over at his cousin, incredulous. "Do you seriously wish me to believe that you are so blind that you really have no idea about how much pain you've caused this evening?"

Adrian replied with a blank stare that spoke volumes and Francis realized that his cousin was a bigger idiot than he ever would have thought him to be. He sighed deeply, taking yet another sip of his scotch. He then took a seat in the armchair facing Adrian's. "Emily is in love with you, you fool." His words were calm and simple. Once they were out, Francis leaned back in his seat and waited for their full effect to take place.

There was a short silence, then a sudden roar of laughter

that filled every corner of the room. Francis merely looked on with the utmost ease as he waited for it to fade.

The laughter came to a sudden halt when Adrian realized that nobody else had joined him. Eyeing Kate, he saw that his bride-to-be had suddenly turned rather pale. "You . . . you cannot possibly be serious?" he asked as he brought himself under control. "Emily's like a sister to me. . . . I mean, come on, Francis! For God's sake, even she knows that."

Francis lifted an eyebrow. "Does she?"

"Of course. Why wouldn't she? She's my best friend. . . . I mean . . . it would be ridiculous to think . . ." The words trailed off as Adrian pondered the idea.

The last words had sparked fresh anger in Francis's veins. He clenched his hand around his glass as he glared across at Adrian. "Ridiculous? Just what exactly is so ridiculous about it? Isn't she good enough for you, Adrian? She was good enough to be your friend, but when it comes to making her your wife, the thought of it is ridiculous to you? You should be ashamed of yourself, Adrian."

"I didn't mean it like that . . . I . . . Kate, did you know about this?"

Kate shook her head with incredulity. "We haven't talked about you in years. . . . I didn't think . . . I mean, I just assumed that her feelings for you had been a passing fancy. It never occurred to me that she still hoped to marry you." Tears sprang to her eyes. "Please, Dunhurst, you must believe me when I say that I never intended to hurt Emily in any way."

"According to her sisters, she was under the impression that she and Adrian had an understanding," Francis ground out.

"An understanding? But I . . ." Adrian racked his brain for an answer, but it was as if a thick fog had settled. His eyes narrowed in concentration, and then out of nowhere there was a glimmer of a faint memory that caused his eyes to widen as he took a deep breath. "Oh, dear Lord," he exclaimed.

"What? What is it?" Kate asked as she turned toward him.

"It was a long time ago . . . six years, perhaps. We'd spent most of the day together when she began talking loosely about what she hoped for her future. She mentioned that she would love nothing better than to spend the rest of her life just as we had spent that day.

"I told her that if that was the case, then perhaps I should offer for her one day . . . as long as she promised that she would say yes when I did. I mentioned something about not wanting to bruise my ego by holding out for her, only to have her say no. She promised, we laughed about it, and then I kissed her . . ."

Kate's hands flew to her face. "You kissed her?"

"Just a friendly kiss—nothing more. As for everything else . . . it was just some childish fun, really."

"I don't think she saw it that way," Kate murmured as she wiped the tears from her eyes. "She's been waiting for you all these years, and when she heard that you planned to propose, she must have thought . . . damn it, Adrian. . . . Emily is my friend . . . or *was*, at least, until tonight."

They had known each other most of their lives . . . had shared innermost secrets with one another. Emily had always been there whenever she had needed a friend to talk to, a shoulder to cry on, or somebody to laugh with. And this evening, she had unwillingly betrayed her in the most horrific way possible. She had crushed Emily's dreams of marrying the man that she had loved.

"I'm such a scoundrel." She paused for a moment before turning a sharp eye on Adrian. "Do you think we ought to call it off?"

"What? Our engagement? Absolutely not, Kate. You and I love each other . . . I cannot imagine my life without you by my side."

Kate gave him a weak smile. "I love you, too—with all my heart."

"Then what sense would there be in denying our own happiness?"

Francis studied the pair behind serious eyes. Should they not be allowed to be together if they both loved one another? Should they have to suffer to spare a friend's feelings? It didn't seem fair, and yet he didn't want them to get away unscathed.

"You acted without thinking," he berated them. "And as a result, you've hurt someone who didn't deserve to be hurt. Emily feels everything with enormous force, whether it be joy or sadness. She wears her nerves on the outside, her heart unguarded, and you . . ." He pointed at both of them. "You spared no consideration for her feelings."

He wasn't sure how or why, but somehow, he suddenly felt as though he knew Emily Rutherford inside out. It no longer seemed to matter that they hadn't been on good terms for years. For some unspeakable reason, Francis just couldn't bear the thought that she'd been hurt. "It was badly done . . . badly done, indeed. I only hope that your actions haven't torn her completely to pieces." Then, in a more quiet tone, as if he was talking to himself, he continued. "She's not like the rest of us. I fear you may have broken her."

Chapter Six

Emily sighed deeply as she opened her eyes. How many times had she opened and closed them now, drifting in and out of sleep, she wondered. Each time she woke, she cursed the fact that her body was stronger than she had thought it might be. Why did she keep on waking up?

A quiet knock sounded before a maid entered. She walked briskly across the room to the window and with rapid tugs, opened the burgundy drapes, allowing bright light to flood across the floor. Emily groaned, rolled over, and hid her head beneath the sheets. When she heard the door close, she let out a sigh. Thankfully the maid had decided to leave her alone again, even if she had disturbed her in a most irritating way. Closing her eyes once more, Emily attempted to clear her mind in the hope of returning to a happy sleep, when from out of nowhere, a male voice spoke to her.

The tone was firm and direct, one that commanded authority and expected to be obeyed. "Enough is enough, Emily," he told her severely. "You've been cooped up in here for four days now. It's time you got out of bed and joined the world of the living."

Her eyes sharpened as she threw back the covers to glare across the room at Francis, her nostrils flaring with sudden anger. "How dare you belittle my pain?" She yelled as she hurled a pillow at him.

Francis stepped easily out of the way as the missile sailed past him. Clearly, the fact that he had entered her bedroom uninvited was not the main cause for her concern. A wistful smile tugged at the corner of his mouth. Sitting there with her hair a mess, her eyes shooting daggers at him, she really was a sight to behold. "It's up to you, Emily. You can come willingly, or I can come over there and personally drag you out of bed."

A look of horror swept over her face. "You wouldn't dare," she said, her voice faltering.

"Oh, but I would," he assured her as he took a step toward her. "You must remember that you're a guest here, and though my aunt has ensured me that you may stay for as long as you wish, I think it would be quite fitting if—seeing as you are capable of getting out of bed—you would return to your own home."

"You're kicking me out?" Her voice was a sad little whisper that couldn't help but tear at his heart.

"Emily, manners, etiquette, and adhering to what is and isn't done has always been your forte," he told her kindly. "Just because you yourself have been wronged does not mean that you now have the right to take advantage of other people's kindness. So please, hop on out of bed, get dressed, and meet me downstairs in say . . . half an hour? We'll have some breakfast before we go."

Without giving her the chance to say anything else, Francis quickly escaped back out into the hallway, shutting the door firmly behind him. He stood there for a moment, wondering if he was about to make a monumental mistake. There was still time to change his mind. With a heavy sigh, he left the bedroom door behind him and wandered downstairs to wait for her.

When she appeared in the dining room doorway, she was wearing a light pink summer dress cut fashionably low to show off the swell of her breasts. Stopping for a moment, she glanced about with an uneasy gaze, wringing her hands together in front of her. Then, drawing a nervous breath, she walked toward Francis, pulled out a chair, and took a seat at the end of the table, right next to him.

"Tea?" he asked as he reached for the pot. She nodded her head slightly as she followed the movement of his hand with her eyes. She looked pale, he noticed, but her eyes were no longer puffy as they had been four days ago. He almost wished that they were, for the emptiness within them wrenched at his heart. And yet, she'd never looked lovelier to him. What a damn shame, he thought, as he poured the steaming tea into a fragile cup.

"Eat something," he told her. When she failed to respond, he picked up a basket with warm buns and held it toward her.

"Thank you," she said.

When she didn't acknowledge the food, he slowly set the basket back down, understanding that she was thanking him for something else entirely. "Don't mention it," he said quietly.

"I'm sorry about earlier . . . I . . ."

Instinctively he reached out and placed his hand on hers, squeezing it gently. It was meant as a form of reassurance, a way of letting her know that she wasn't alone, that she had friends around her, willing to cheer her up and help her through this.

She snatched it away immediately, her eyes rounding on him with sudden anger. "What are you doing, Francis?" Her voice was harsh.

For a moment she had him thrown, but he quickly recovered, his eyebrows knitting together in that all-too-familiar frown of his. "What do you mean?" he asked, his hand still resting on the table next to her plate.

"You and I aren't friends. We haven't been for years, so there's no need for you to pretend." She fixed him with a level gaze as she calmed her voice. "I'm deeply indebted to you for what you did the other night, though I wish you would have left me to die."

"How can you say such a thing?" he asked, his voice rising in anger. "How can you be so damn selfish, Emily, to even think such a thing? I realize that it must be your emotions talking, but still, think of how much pain your death would cause . . . of how many people would be affected."

"Ha!" she laughed in a mocking voice as she tilted her head back to gaze up at the ceiling.

If there had been any tears left in her, she would have cried them then and there. But her tears had run dry, so she just squinted instead, sensing the familiar pain rising in her throat. "I've just discovered that the two people whom I used to think of as my closest friends weren't my friends at all. I was happy, Francis. I've always found a way in which to be happy. Even after my parents died, I found happiness and comfort in knowing that Adrian loved me—in knowing that whatever troubles I might come across, Kate would be there to help me through them.

"She and I used to be closer than I've ever been with Claire or Beatrice. But guess what . . . ? It wasn't real." She continued, her voice cracking. "Why wasn't I good enough? Why did he pick Kate over me? He must have known how I felt. . . . Kate certainly did, though it's been a while since we've discussed it. But to tell me like that . . . do you not think it was cruel? Or did I truly deserve it? Because honestly, the way I've felt for the last few days . . . I wouldn't wish it on my worst enemy.

They tore out my heart together, and then they crushed it, without even thinking twice about it."

Emily's eyes met Francis's. She couldn't read any sign of emotion in them—just the same, familiar grey coldness. "For whatever reason, I know you don't particularly like me, and to be fair, I'm not too fond of you either. We've had our differences, though I'm not even sure why anymore.

"We used to be friends," she whispered, her voice full of regret. He knew she wasn't just talking about the two of them, that her thoughts included Adrian and Kate. Her smile was gone, and with it, her love for life. Somehow, without fully understanding why, he planned to change that, though he hadn't a clue how to even begin.

"I don't want your pity." Her voice was suddenly strong and determined. "I don't want anyone's pity."

"Fair enough," he told her seriously. "Then you shan't have

it. However, I would recommend that you eat something before we set out. It will be a while before you eat again."

Unsure of whether or not this was the right thing to do, the decision had now been made. There was no turning back. She always managed to annoy the hell out of him, though he didn't understand why. He was even more unsure as to why he wanted to have anything to do with her right now. She was clearly emotionally unstable and would probably be better served if she didn't have to put up with his constant presence. Hell, *he* would probably be better served if he stayed clear of *her*. He always managed to spark her temper, particularly now, after everything that had happened. But perhaps his urge to help her could be attributed to the fact that he had always been the only person in existence who managed to bring a scowl to her otherwise happy face. And now that someone else had been the cause of her unhappiness, he wanted to wring their necks, both of them, for causing her so much grief.

Her eyes narrowed with suspicion. "What are you talking about?"

"I'm taking you and your sisters to London for a while. A change of scenery will do you a world of good."

She gaped at him in astonishment.

"You need to . . ."

"You have no idea about what I need, Francis," she blurted out, except that he did. Getting away from this place was exactly what she needed.

She needed a chance to forget everything that Hardington reminded her of. But to go on a trip to London with Francis . . . it hardly appealed to her at all. He was constant doom and gloom, nothing but frowns—the most unlikely person in the world to turn her mood around.

"You mentioned that Beatrice and Claire will be coming along also?" she asked.

He nodded slowly.

"And where exactly do you propose that we all stay during our visit? We cannot live with you . . . three single women living with a bachelor . . . we' be ruined before we made it through the front door."

"I realize that, Emily." His eyes held hers as he leaned back in his chair. "Which is why you and your sisters shan't be staying at number seven, where I live, but at number five instead." As if to clarify, he added, "Both properties belong to me."

"I see." Emily stared back at him with a large degree of skepticism. "And it is completely vacant?"

Francis nodded his head. "Nobody has lived there since my father died, though I have invited my great-aunt Genevieve to join us." His mood seemed to brighten a little at the thought of the old lady. "She's really quite lovely—my grandmother's younger sister, to be precise. I'm certain you'll enjoy her company." He reached for his teacup. "So as far as propriety goes . . . I daresay that nobody will bat an eyelid."

Emily regarded Francis with a great deal of thoughtfulness before giving him the briefest of nods. "Thank you for the invitation," she finally said. "I accept."

It was impossible to read his emotions as her eyes met his for a brief, uncomfortable moment. What a shame that he'd forgotten how to smile. She couldn't help but wonder what had happened to have caused such a change in him.

Thinking of herself for a moment, she couldn't resist the slightest of smiles. He looked at her quizzically as it faded once more, leaving nothing but sadness upon her face. "I was just thinking that we'll make a perfect pair among the *ton*," she said.

He raised a quizzical eyebrow.

"I believe we shall be known as Mr. and Mrs. Miserable in no time at all."

His eyes twinkled helplessly with momentary amusement, though his lips remained tightly drawn. What surprised him was that he rather liked that she had referred to them as a pair. He'd no idea why such a thing pleased him, when only days ago, the mere suggestion would undoubtedly have horrified him. The thought of exploring such a possibility was suddenly very intriguing. "Then we had best not disappoint," he told her as he stood, held out his hand, and helped her to her feet.

"I was worried that I would have to face Adrian this morning," Emily admitted as she sat across from Francis in the carriage. They were on their way to pick up her sisters, who, she was certain, would be eagerly awaiting her. "Thank you for ensuring that I didn't have to."

He didn't respond, merely gave her his trademark nod, telling her that he acknowledged what she had said. He was content with not talking. The less people said, the less likely they were to complicate things.

He'd long since gotten used to keeping his own emotions bottled up and therefore had no particular desire to know what other people felt. The truth was that he wasn't even sure of what *he* felt anymore. He'd become so used to the wall he'd built up around himself—constructed from so much anger, pain, and frustration that it would be impossible for anyone to scale. And yet . . . he steeled himself for a moment . . . there had been the beginnings of hope today.

It didn't take spectacles to see that Emily could barely abide him, and yet for some peculiar reason, amidst her pain, she had managed to inch *him* a little bit closer to happiness.

Looking at her now as she gazed out of the window, her eyes blind to the scenery around her, he could almost hear her inner voice screaming. Stray wisps of her dark hair flowed in the breeze, framing her pale skin. It would be good to get some color back in those cheeks, he thought. Even her mouth seemed to have lost its hue. He had always admired how pink her lips could be without the application of makeup, yet now as he looked at them, they appeared faded.

He knew that their falling out had been entirely his fault. He had changed and it hadn't been gradual. Something had hardened him, made him bitter and constantly angry. He had taken it out on his friends on numerous occasions, sparking arguments for no other reason than to satisfy his own rage. It was no wonder that Emily hated him.

The feeling had always been mutual, however. She had been his antagonist—the chirpy, constantly happy, nothing-could-shake-her-love-for-life girl that enforced his bitterness. He had grown allergic to her bubbling laughter that did nothing but remind him that there was nothing to laugh about.

He had always expected to be gratified to see her lose that spark. The sweet revenge of years' worth of torment. Yet here he was, angry—not at her, but at those who had so thoughtlessly wronged her.

If Adrian and Kate were right for each other, wanted each other, then that was one thing. What he couldn't accept was the way they had both handled it, as if Emily's feelings meant nothing to them.

Pulling up to the cottage where Beatrice and Claire awaited them, his mind returned to the present. As Emily turned toward him, her eyes locking onto his, he caught his breath.

He wanted to make her happy again. He knew that this had been his reason for inviting her to London in the first place. But it was more than that. He wanted to keep her close. For some inexplicable, illogical reason, he wanted Emily Rutherford more than he had ever wanted anything else in his life.

Perhaps it was rooted in the friendship they'd once shared. Kate could keep her dazzling looks, for all he cared—it was Emily who had always been his favorite. They'd been able to talk about anything back then. They'd shared a freedom with one another . . . the knowledge that they could just be themselves. And of course, the comfort of always having each other to turn to for help and support.

But when it came to that first love, it was Adrian who'd captured her attention instead of him. He couldn't blame her, of course—after all, it was difficult to hold a candle to Adrian's charm. Still, the way she'd stared after Adrian and hung on his every word had irritated him to no end. And then, when the accident had happened, he'd found it impossible to share it with anyone—not even Emily. Instead, he'd pushed her away. To this day she didn't know the truth about what had happened. He'd wanted it that way. He'd needed to get away from it all, and by the time he returned, he'd completely given up the fight for Emily's heart.

But perhaps he could try again now. Thank God Adrian had turned out to be a complete and utter idiot. Now all he had to do was make Emily like him again—not an easy task by any means he acknowledged, but then again, he did enjoy a challenge.

Chapter Seven

London

The carriage drew up to Francis's Mayfair home on Berkeley Square at some point in the early afternoon. A balding, older gentleman whom Francis introduced as Parker opened the door for them at number five. "Parker is my butler, both here and at Dunhurst Park," Francis explained. "He will see to it that you are all well settled."

"How many are there?" Claire asked in wonderment as she looked about with big round eyes. Being only eighteen years of age she was more easily taken by all the extravagance of the upper class home.

"There are two maids, a cook, and a scullery maid who are here at all times. Parker, Jonathan Rosedale—my secretary—and Thomas—my valet—travel with me back and forth. Jonathan had an errand to attend to, but will be joining us later this evening." Francis paused for a moment as if hesitating about whether or not to elaborate. "In truth, Jonathan is more than just an employee; he has been a close friend of mine for many years, even before I hired him—we went to Oxford together. I'm fortunate to have him around."

"Will it not be terribly difficult for them all to run back and forth between the two houses?" Emily asked with marked concern.

"Erm . . . not really," Francis muttered, suddenly looking nervous. He quickly composed himself before offering the three sisters a brief bow. "It would not be seemly for me to accompany you inside. Parker is very capable—I shall leave you in his care. Good day."

Emily stared after him as he headed up the steps toward number seven, opened the door, and disappeared inside. "Is it just me, or did his behavior just now seem rather curious?"

Beatrice shrugged. "I thought he was quite polite, actually. Shall we go inside?"

As soon as the front door closed behind them, they spotted Francis entering the hall from another direction.

Emily's eyes narrowed. "I thought you would be staying next door."

"And so I shall. However, I did think it time to mention that there is a door that connects the two houses—it's in the library."

Beatrice and Emily both gasped while Claire just started giggling. Emily stopped her with a quick nudge to her side. "You deceived me," Emily said. "You deceived us all."

"I have to say," Beatrice added. "This is highly irregular."

"There's nothing for it," Emily said, her voice filled with disappointment. "We have to leave."

Francis stepped forward. "Look—I realize that this is by

no means ideal, but I didn't think you would have come, had you known."

"You would have been correct," Emily snapped.

"However," he continued, seemingly unfazed by Emily's remark. "As far as anyone will be able to tell, we shall be living in two separate houses. My aunt shall be living with you as an appropriate chaperone and nobody need be the wiser. Besides, it will allow us to socialize without the unnecessary bother of going out and coming back in."

"But *we* will know," Emily protested.

"I daresay that you are quite right, my lord," Beatrice suddenly said, effectively silencing her sister. "Nobody need be the wiser—we shall be happy to remain, provided your aunt is here, as you say."

Emily turned to her sister in disbelief. "Beatrice, you cannot possibly mean to . . ."

"We've come all this way for a change of scenery, Emily, and I for one have little desire to endure another three hours by carriage in order to return to Hardington." She lowered her voice to a whisper. "Besides, I daresay you'd have little issue with the matter if it were Adrian rather than Francis who was living next-door with an adjoining doorway."

Emily could say nothing to that, so Beatrice merely returned her attention to Francis. "So . . . when might we have the pleasure of meeting this aunt of yours?" she asked.

"I am certain Lady Genevieve will be with us shortly," Francis said. Then, removing his hat and handing it to Parker, he ran his fingers through his thick hair, ruffling it slightly. Emily stared at him for a moment, stunned by the change in his appearance. Gone was his sleek and carefully groomed look that she had grown so used to. He still looked handsome, but in a roguish way that made her stomach flip as she sucked in a breath.

Shifting his gaze, his eyes locked onto hers, taking in the look of confusion on her face. Something drew her in—his dark eyes captivating—as a slight shiver ran down her spine. Narrowing his eyes, his expression seemed to change. Gone was the hostility, so that for the briefest of moments, he looked as if he understood her. Then, like a candle being snuffed, the moment was gone.

It was absurd. Of course it was. She could barely stomach Francis for more than a few minutes at a time.

A loud thump brought her back to full awareness. Turning slightly, she spotted an elderly woman with silver hair coming toward them at a crooked gait. Her frame was tiny, but her posture was perfectly straight, her head was held high, and her eyes were so piercing that she could very likely strike fear even in the most courageous of men. Had Francis really described her as lovely? Militant would be a more apt description.

"Aunt Genevieve," Francis remarked with a slight bow. "How good of you to join us."

Silence followed as Genevieve's eyes slowly drifted from one face to another, scrutinizing each and every detail about all of them. When she was done, she nodded with great satisfaction, her slim lips widening into a warm smile that instantly lit up her face. The cool façade had completely vanished by the time she stepped forward to welcome the sisters. "It's so lovely to finally meet you, my dears," she said. She cast a quick look at Francis. "I see now why my presence here is required, Francis. Shame on you for not telling me how pretty these ladies are."

"Well, I didn't think that . . ." Francis began, while Beatrice, Claire, and Emily, their faces quite flushed with embarrassment, performed a series of awkward curtsies.

"Tut, tut." Genevieve wagged an admonishing finger at her nephew. She then leaned forward against her cane and served Beatrice the most inquisitive of stares. "When did you last eat?"

"I . . ." Beatrice glanced sideways at her two sisters. "I mean, we . . ."

"When?" Genevieve repeated, her eyebrows meeting in the middle.

"This morning, my lady."

Genevieve leaned back a little. "Well, that really won't do." She turned to Francis. "These ladies are as skinny as my cane. You did well in bringing them here, though I daresay we'll have our work cut out for us if we're to fatten them up in time for the next ball."

Francis couldn't help but notice the look of despair on the sisters' faces. He decided that it was time to jump to their rescue. "Aunt Genevieve, I really don't think that . . ."

"I hope you don't take this the wrong way, Francis," Genevieve remarked. "But I really don't give a rat's bottom for what you think right now. If these ladies are to attract the proper attention, then it's imperative that they show themselves off to their best advantage. Some ample bosoms are what we need—mark my word."

A shocked silence followed.

It was Beatrice who eventually spoke. "I know that you have our best intentions at heart, my lady, but we didn't come here in search of husbands. And even if we did, I would certainly hope that they'd be drawn to our character rather than our looks."

"Humpf . . . it's no wonder that you haven't married yet." Genevieve waved her hand dismissively. "Never mind. There will be plenty of time for us to work out a strategy. Now, Parker . . . I will leave it to you to speak to cook. I'm off to bed for the evening."

"But it's only five o'clock," Francis put in. "Won't you join us for dinner?"

"No, no . . . I'll take my dinner in my room—Parker will bring up a tray for me, won't you, Parker?"

"As you wish, my lady," Parker replied.

Sweeping past all of them, her cane thumping loudly as she went, Genevieve climbed the staircase and disappeared out of sight.

"She's rather forthright, is she not?" Beatrice eventually remarked.

"My apologies," Francis muttered. "I hope you didn't take too great offense."

"Not at all," Claire exclaimed. "We love eccentric relations—is that not so, Emily?"

Emily gave her sister a sharp look of warning before turning to Francis. "I think your aunt is absolutely charming," she said. "I have no doubt we'll get along splendidly with one another."

"Good." His tone was curt, but the flicker of appreciation

in his eyes did not go unnoticed. It was gone as swiftly as it had appeared.

"Not to rush you, sir," Parker interjected. "But perhaps we ought to follow her ladyship's advice—I asked cook to prepare a snack in time for your arrival. This way, if you please."

They all followed the butler into the parlor, where some cucumber sandwiches, cut neatly into triangles, had been carefully piled onto a couple of plates.

"It isn't much," Parker told them with an apologetic smile. "But there really isn't long until dinner. This is just to tide you over."

"Thank you, Parker," Francis told him. "You made the right decision." Then, pausing for a moment, he turned to halt the retreating butler. "We shall be ready for dinner at seven."

"Yes, my lord." Parker then ducked through the door and vanished in order to take the guests' bags to their prospective rooms.

Beatrice picked up a sandwich and took a small bite out of one corner as she wandered over to the bay window together with Francis. "Thank you once again for hosting us," she said as she looked out over the garden. "It really is most kind of you."

"Not at all," he replied. "I merely thought it might help."

"I'm sure it shall," Beatrice assured him as she glanced toward Emily. "We were very worried about her, you know. We still are."

For a while they stood there, side by side, taking in the view of the rhododendrons that were in full bloom throughout the garden.

"I hope you will not take offense to what I am about to tell you," he suddenly told her in a muted tone. Beatrice said nothing. She merely waited for him to continue as she dusted her hands free of crumbs with her napkin.

"I intend for the three of you to enjoy your stay here," he explained. "You shall be my guests at the theatre and at all of the balls that you wish to attend; Jonathan will show you the invitations tomorrow so that you may begin your selection.

"However, it's a few years since you've attended such formal events. I don't believe that Claire ever has, seeing as she's only eighteen, and I daresay, neither has Emily. Am I correct?"

Beatrice gave a small smile. "Yes, you are."

"But I'm sure that you must have," he continued with a frown as he turned his head to look at her directly. "Then you know that you shall require new gowns." A pained look flashed across her face. "I'm sorry, Beatrice, but you know that I'm right. But," he continued, his tone lightening. "You must not worry about the expense. I will see to it that you are adequately dressed."

Her eyes shot up at him. "We cannot possibly allow you to . . ." Her voice had initially risen, but she instantly dropped it to a low whisper as her eyes darted frantically across at where Emily and Claire were sitting.

She was too proud to accept so much, he thought. He was adamant about wanting to do it, however, so he played the one card that he knew would work. "It was my aunt's suggestion, actually. She believes it will help Emily." He paused momentarily before continuing. "If we take her out to some extravagant events and let her be seen, she will soon have a long line of suitors following in her wake. Even if it turns out that she isn't interested in any of them, it will at least take her mind off Adrian. He's lost to her forever and it's important that she sees that there are plenty of other options available to her. But you will all need to fit the part. Thus, you will need a decent wardrobe. Consider it a favor."

Biting down on her bottom lip, he saw that she wished to say yes. And yet she hesitated. He understood her completely; she'd always managed to keep her sisters dressed and fed without ever asking for help from anyone.

Taking a deep breath, he decided to play his second card. "You have to forget about your pride for a moment, Beatrice," he told her. Her eyes narrowed into a frown as she opened her mouth to protest, but he plowed on. "Think of what is in your sisters' best interest. This is the opportunity of a lifetime for them—the chance to find the eligible husbands that I *know* you've always hoped for them to marry. You have to let me help you."

Breathing a deep sigh, she nodded, her eyes flooding with thankfulness as if he'd just pulled her out of a crevasse. A smile crawled across her lips. "All right," she said as her nod grew more self-assured. "All right, Francis, I accept . . . though I have no idea how I will ever repay you or Lady Genevieve. Thank you."

Francis opened his mouth as if to say something just as Claire came over, putting her arm around her sister and resting her head against her shoulder. "What's the conspiracy about?" she asked as she gave Francis a cheeky smile. He merely drew his eyebrows closer together and held her gaze. "The two of you look as thick as thieves," she explained as she gave Beatrice a slight pinch. Beatrice shrieked and reeled away from her sister. "Come on then. I'm desperate to know!"

"Shall we tell her?" Beatrice asked, eyeing Francis.

"Hmmm, I don't know if we can trust her," he said with extreme severity. "What if she gives us away under torture?"

"You're quite right," Beatrice said with a slight giggle, her serious expression beginning to slip. "In fact, I *know* she'll crack under torture."

"Is that so?" Perhaps we ought to put it to the test."

Stuck between them, Claire had no time to escape before Francis held her still and Beatrice fell on her, tickling her until she squealed with laughter and was begging them to stop.

From her corner, seated on a toffee-colored velvet sofa, Emily regarded the scene with growing interest. For the five minutes or so that it lasted, it was as if she found herself transported back in time. They were all children again, horsing around the way they had once been so used to. They were happy, devoid of any worries or concerns for the future—content to know that they were well taken care of by their parents, who loved them. It was bliss and it was fun and for just a while, Emily forgot.

The fun drew her in and swallowed her up. She forgot that her parents were dead, that their cousin had taken everything from them, including their mother's jewelry collection. In short, he had left them with nothing by which to remember their parents. Most importantly, she managed to forget the pain that came from losing both Kate and Adrian.

As the hurt and the anger dwindled with each of Claire's

squeals, Emily found herself truly smiling for the first time since Adrian had told her he would marry Kate. Jumping to her feet, she immediately hurried to join in the fun.

Claire's eyes grew big when she saw that they were now three against her, except she suddenly heard Beatrice screech. Emily had joined her side, she realized with relief. They were now evenly numbered, though Francis still counted for two in terms of sheer strength.

Beatrice screamed again as Emily squeezed her sides in a rough tickle. Using her as a shield between themselves and Francis, Claire and Emily both half-hid behind their elder sister, holding on to her firmly so she couldn't attack them. Their breath came raggedly as they peered out to find Francis coming toward them with a vengeful grin painted upon his face.

"We'll have mercy on you if you join our alliance," Emily whispered in Beatrice's ear.

"And if I don't?"

"We'll tickle you until you're blue in the face."

Beatrice gulped as if truly frightened by the prospect, and then nodded her head definitively. "You have a deal."

Seeing Beatrice released and the same smug grin on all three faces, Francis halted in his tracks. He began backing away. "Treachery!" he called out as he fled, putting the toffee-colored sofa between them. "Beatrice," he stammered in an exaggerated tone of disappointment. "How could you? I trusted you!"

"They made me an offer that I simply couldn't refuse," she said with a smirk.

As Emily and Claire made their way around each side

of the sofa, Beatrice guarded any escape route that Francis might contemplate taking.

"OK," he said, feigning desperation. "I surrender."

"Oh no, you don't," Emily chided him, with a playful twist to her mouth. "You're not getting off that easily this time."

"Oh?" He didn't smile, but his eyes held a warmth that she had long since forgotten he had in him.

And then they were upon him, grabbing him by the arms and tackling him to the floor. He probably could have fought them off easily, had he tried, but why ruin the moment for them?

"Don't think we don't remember where your weakness lies, Francis," Beatrice giggled as she reached for his feet. His eyes grew wary, then truly worried.

Oh no . . . not my feet.

He tried to kick them away but it was futile. They'd managed to gain the upper hand.

Pinning him down, the sisters wasted no time in removing his shoes. Then, showing no mercy whatsoever, they proceeded to tickle him.

Within seconds Francis was roaring with laughter as tears welled in his eyes. "Do you surrender?" Emily demanded.

Francis coughed, attempting to stifle yet another laugh, and managed a choked "yes."

Helping him to his feet, they handed him back his shoes. He lowered himself onto the sofa, wiping at his eyes with the back of his hand as he straightened his jacket and began putting his shoes back on. "Remind me never to take the three of you on again," he said. "At least not singlehandedly. You're stronger than I remember."

Claire looked most triumphant. "We're not little girls anymore," she smirked.

"I know," he muttered with a frown. And just like that, all the amusement was unwillingly gone. They had gotten carried away and acted completely inappropriately. He was a grown man and they were women to whom he wasn't even related. What had he been thinking?

When he glanced back up, he caught Emily looking at him with a bemused expression, a trace of mischief still in her eyes. She had seen him let down his guard and show that he was capable of something other than a stern glare. And yet, the very fact that she now appeared to see right through him set his forehead in deep furrows. She looked away, but not before he noticed that the glimmer behind her eyes had dulled. Only a hopeless sadness remained.

"So?" He heard a voice ask. It was Claire. "What's the big secret?"

"What big secret?" Francis asked with a grin.

Claire rolled her eyes as she sighed with exasperation. "Do I need to tickle you again, Francis? Or is it enough if I remind you that you lost. I think I've earned the right to know."

"Let the poor girl out of her misery, Francis," Beatrice declared. "Unless of course you want me to tell her."

"I suppose you're right. Go ahead then, tell her."

"Very well," Beatrice said as she straightened her back. "Francis has graciously given us the opportunity to attend the most important balls of the season." Claire let out a squeal of delight, which Beatrice silenced by raising her hand. "In order for us to do so, however, we must dress appropriately. Francis has generously offered to cover all costs, and I have accepted.

So, both you, Claire, and you, Emily, will be making your debuts this season amongst the very elite that society has to offer. It's a gift that mustn't be passed up."

Her last words were stern, taking on a demanding tone. She held Emily's gaze as she spoke them, for she knew that her sister would protest with every fiber of her being. Emily was suffering and she wanted space and time in which to do so. She didn't want to accept what she would surely term "charity" from anyone, least of all from Francis.

Beatrice understood her sister's reasoning, of course. But Francis was right. Beatrice had no idea why he was being so helpful and so kind, but she knew that the chance was unlikely to present itself twice. She would have to be firm, she realized, but she was confident that Emily would eventually do as she was asked. She would simply have to tell her younger sister how much this might affect all of them and that she mustn't say no—if not for her own sake, then for Claire's.

Chapter Eight

Attempting to hide his surprise to the best of his abilities, Jonathan regarded his friend and employer hesitantly. "Do you have any idea how much time and effort will be involved? Not to mention the expense . . ." He let out a sigh as he shook his head in bewilderment. "What were you thinking, Francis? Taking three grown women under your wing like that . . . it's completely out of character."

Francis eyed Jonathan suspiciously. "What are you saying? That I'm not capable of being charitable and kind?"

"I merely . . ."

"I know what everyone thinks of me, Jonathan," Francis said, cutting him off. "Don't you dare try and sugar it over for me. Not you, of all people. It's what I value most about your friendship—your unfailing honesty and your loyalty. You're never afraid of saying it as it is . . . I wish more people would be that way."

"Very well then," Jonathan told him firmly. "No, I don't think you're capable of being that charitable or kind, unless there's some reason behind it that I'm unaware of. So . . . what's your angle, old friend?"

Slumping down into a brown leather armchair, Francis's hand caught his chin as he rested his elbow against one of the fat side arms. He let out an exhausted sigh. "I don't know," he muttered, glancing across at Jonathan as he spoke.

Jonathan echoed his sigh and rubbed the brim of his nose between his thumb and his index finger. "Have you had any thoughts as to who might be able, and, more importantly, willing to sponsor them for the duration of the season? Your aunt won't do—she's much too old to take on such a strenuous task."

"I didn't think . . ."

"Clearly!" Jonathan remarked as he let out another exasperated sigh, shaking his head in frustration. It was fortuitous that he and Francis had known each other for as long as they had, or he might have been looking for a new job that very instant. But that wasn't the case. They were like brothers, so when Jonathan occasionally happened to give Francis hell, it never amounted to anything more than friendly banter.

"Just for the sake of asking," Jonathan continued with a sudden look of hope upon his face, "is there any chance at all that you might be tempted to tell these women that you've had a change of heart?"

Francis's expression grew dark. He was a man of his word and he intended to keep it. "None," he said flatly.

"I didn't think so." Jonathan paused for a moment. Resting his elbows on the armrests of his chair, he arched his fingers below his chin. "So who could sponsor them? Doing it yourself is completely out of the question—I hope I don't have to explain that much to you."

Francis frowned as he ran his fingers over the brim of his glass. Jonathan was right. It would be most unseemly for a gentleman to escort unmarried women about town when he wasn't even related to them. And while Genevieve would ensure that nobody would frown at the fact that they were his houseguests, Jonathan did make a valid point—he couldn't expect her to stay out until the early hours of the morning, when even he considered this to be somewhat grueling. But if not her, then who? For Claire and Emily, it would be their coming-out balls. They would need a woman of some degree of social standing to take them under her wing. He had given it some serious thought, and had decided that he had just the right person in mind. He turned his eyes on Jonathan. "Baroness Giddington," he said.

Jonathan gave Francis an immediate smile of approval, though it was tinged with a mischievous smirk. "You don't think she'll plow them into obscurity? The woman has a lot of presence."

"I know what you're getting at, Jon, and I must admit that I did think about that possibility quite a bit myself."

"And?"

"And I've decided that she's still the best option. She's a close friend of mine—with no children of her own—who loves to shop. She would jump at the opportunity, turning this into her very own pet project, I can assure you."

"Oh, I don't doubt you for a minute, old friend. The woman takes great pride in being one of the most talked-about socialites in London. She attends every ball there is, never wearing the same gown more than once. One is truly inclined to pity her poor husband."

"Why? Lord Giddington is quite content with having a wife as lovely and charming as Veronica. And besides, she does her part, too, in order to finance all of those lovely gowns of hers. If it weren't for her and her natural ability to connect with people, I'm quite certain that Giddington's ventures wouldn't thrive as well as they do."

Jonathan tilted his head to the side as he scrunched up his mouth, raising an eyebrow as if attempting to visualize Baroness Giddington escorting Beatrice, Emily, and Claire about town. "All right. Baroness Giddington it is," he said firmly. "You ought to call on her as soon as possible to discuss the situation with her. What if she refuses?"

Francis ignored the question as he picked up a random leather-bound book from the bookshelf and began leafing through it. "Why don't you stop by her house tomorrow and invite her to join us for tea? The sooner we get started on this, the better."

"You look nervous," Francis said as he took in the scene. He had just come into the parlor to find the three sisters sitting stiffly, side by side on a scarlet chaise longue. "She doesn't bite, you know."

"It's Baroness Giddington," Beatrice barely managed to get out. "Everyone has heard of her, even we who have been secluded in the countryside for the past six years. Of course we're nervous."

"Don't be," he told them. "She's a lovely lady and I'm sure she'll be quite fond of you. However, you do conjure up the image of disobedient schoolgirls unhappily waiting to be scolded." His attempt at lighthearted humor wasn't lost on Emily, as she looked up at him with growing curiosity.

Pretending not to notice, he rested his hand gently against the back of a cream dupioni silk chair. "Beatrice. Would you please come and sit over here? And Claire, why don't you pick up your needlework from the basket over there. It will give your hands something to do besides twisting at the fabric of your dress."

As they rearranged themselves in an attempt not to appear affected by the Baroness's visit, the sound of the doorbell chiming suddenly froze them all in place. "It appears her ladyship has arrived," Francis remarked, breaking the strained silence. He cast a quick glance about the room. "Take a deep breath, ladies, and just relax. Oh, and Emily, do try to smile a little. You look positively glum."

The remark had no other effect than to aggravate Emily even further. Following her conversation with Beatrice, she had finally agreed to join her sisters at least once during the upcoming season. Not for her own sake, but for that of Beatrice and Claire, who had stubbornly refused to go without her. She had very rationally concluded that, since she had no intention of securing a husband for herself, all the money spent on gowns for her would be a ridiculous waste.

Now, Emily suddenly had the urge to leap from her seat, run upstairs, and lock herself in her room. Her eyes were already navigating around the furniture in search of the fastest escape route when a shrill voice interrupted her train of thought.

"Francis!" Veronica made her appearance with outstretched arms in a dress and bonnet that Emily wasn't likely to forget, ever. It was bright blue in color, trimmed with scarlet ribbons. Over it she wore a Spencer jacket in a deep shade of green. Her bonnet was dressed with matching ribbons and feathers so fluffy that Emily immediately likened her to a peacock. Even her cheerful greeting sounded like a squawk, now that she thought about it.

"Let me introduce you to the three Rutherford sisters," Emily heard Francis say.

A pained expression passed over Veronica's face as she held out her hand toward Beatrice. "I knew your parents quite well . . . quite well, indeed," she said. "What a tragedy."

"You are most kind, my lady," Beatrice replied as she gave her a polite nod.

Stillness followed as a heavy blanket of silence settled over them, each of them thinking—with the appropriate amount of respect—just how tragic the loss of Lord and Lady Hillsbury had been. But something about Lady Giddington's attire and voice—coupled with her solemn demeanor—just looked too much like a parody for Emily to take seriously. She couldn't help but find herself biting down on her lower lip in an attempt not to laugh.

But then suddenly it happened all the same, in spite of her efforts.

It began with the twitch of her lower lip as it took on a life of its own, rippling outward to the corners of her mouth and forcing them upward into a helpless smile. She instantly clasped one hand over her mouth in a frantic attempt to silence the sound that was coming from her throat. The result was that she half-spluttered, half-coughed, her eyes painfully wide as she desperately wished a hole would emerge in the oriental carpet and mercifully swallow her up.

Fortunately, she had appeared to be choking rather than concealing an onset of laughter, thus supplying a very fortuitous excuse.

"Are you quite all right?" Veronica asked, turning her attention on Emily.

"Yes, quite," Emily managed, adding a cough in order to prevent the urge to smile. "Please excuse me. I believe I must have gotten a speck of dust caught in my throat—it happens sometimes."

Thankfully her eyes had also begun to water, adding to the plausibility of her lie, but as she looked about, she caught Francis giving her a stern stare. It was as if he'd caught her in a terrible act and was silently admonishing her for it. Embarrassed, she quickly averted her eyes to look at a potted plant in the corner of the room.

How was it possible for him to make her feel so rotten about herself? She had never cared about his opinion in the past. Yet at that very moment, the look that he had given her had made her feel so very small.

Of course it wasn't that she thought there was anything the least bit humorous about her parents' deaths. She loved her parents and had spent two years in full mourning as opposed to the standard one. Not a day passed without her thinking of them, yet there had been something very comical about the way in which Baroness Giddington (or Mrs. Peacock, as Emily presently thought of her) had looked as she raised her eyes toward heaven and let out a small sigh. One might even be tempted to think that she had rehearsed the scene at home in front of a mirror and was now merely acting it out. Emily's mouth twitched again at the idea.

How strange to have that sudden urge to laugh again, Emily thought. She hadn't laughed in a whole week, which was so very unlike her. It felt good, though—like a burden had been lifted from her shoulders and she was finally able to relax. Oh, but she mustn't laugh now, not again. Out came yet another croak.

"Oh, for heaven's sake," Veronica exclaimed. "Would somebody please get this poor woman some water?"

Francis quickly poured a glass from the decanter sitting on the table. Some of it missed, splashing onto the polished wooden surface. He quickly brushed it away with the palm of his hand to prevent it from leaving a permanent mark—something that his mother had always made a point of.

Thrusting it forward, the water sloshed from side to side, almost spilling onto the top of Emily's dress as she reached for the glass and steadied it. "Thank you," she muttered, looking everywhere but at Francis, who she knew would be regarding her disapprovingly.

"This is Emily," Francis said as he addressed Veronica with a tight smile that wasn't really a smile at all. "She's the middle sister, Beatrice being the eldest and Claire the youngest."

"It's a pleasure to meet you," Beatrice told Lady Giddington kindly.

Thank God for Beatrice, Emily thought as she worked on mastering some form of self-control. It was proving difficult, but not impossible, even though Francis seemed to be in an increasingly bad mood. Emily didn't doubt for a minute that it was because of her. She closed her eyes briefly in order to rid herself of "the giggles," as she termed it—likening her fits of laughter to a disease of sorts. She then took a deep breath, opened her eyes again, and managed a brilliant smile that didn't appear to be nearly as fake as it felt.

"Well, I daresay," Veronica remarked as she loosened the ribbons of her bonnet and removed it. "You are all as lovely as Francis told me you would be. This shan't be difficult at all!"

"Liar!" Emily wanted to yell. If there was one thing that she was sure of, it was that Francis had never used the word "lovely" to describe her or her sisters in his life. She was willing to bet her life on it if she had to. But she kept her smile steady, appearing at least outwardly to be having a jolly good time indeed. The truth, however, was that she had no desire to be there at all. She would so much rather be shoveling manure in Mr. Hughes's pig sty back in Hardington, but refused to think of it lest she suffer yet another onset of "the giggles."

As it turned out, Baroness Giddington wasn't nearly as pretentious as Emily had first thought. In fact, the rest of the afternoon passed surprisingly well with a large degree of amicable conversation. And yet, as Emily had recently come to discover, things were more often than not too good to be true.

"Did you happen to hear that Mr. Adrian Fairchild is in town?" Veronica asked as she raised a smug eyebrow. She was certain that she would be the first to deliver the news, for she had just happened to pass Lady Carroway in the street that very morning. "He is a friend of yours, is he not?"

Emily almost spat out the tea that she'd been drinking,

biting down on her tongue instead as she clamped her mouth shut. Her eyes darted nervously toward Beatrice, who was inscrutable as she carefully picked up a plate of biscuits and offered it to the baroness. "Indeed he is," she replied coolly. "In fact, we saw him just a little over a week ago. We really had no idea that he would be coming to London, but perhaps Francis knew . . . they are after all related to one another."

"Ah yes." Veronica appeared as if she was attempting to figure out the exact relationship between her friend and Adrian.

"I did not," Francis told them bluntly, a dark shadow flickering behind his eyes. "What brings him to London?"

A bright smile spread across Veronica's face. It was quite clear that she was pleased with the opportunity to tell them all just exactly why Adrian had come to town. Emily shifted slightly in her seat, her nervous demeanor destroying all attempts she was making at looking indifferent. "Well," Veronica told them, then paused for dramatic effect as she looked at each of them in turn. "He has come to town to make a formal announcement of his engagement to Lady Kate Clemens. It will happen at the Carroway ball, which, because of this new development, is sure to be all the talk of the town—in fact, it is sure to be an event that we must not miss at any cost."

At that Emily did choke on her tea, setting off yet another bout of coughing.

"Perhaps you ought to see a doctor about that cough of yours, my dear?" Veronica suggested with an appropriate amount of concern. "We don't want you spraying fluids on people when we're out in public."

"I'll be just fine," Emily managed to retort with a sharper

tone to her voice than she had intended. She couldn't, however, guarantee that she wouldn't die of embarrassment. People were bound to talk—after all, gossip was the top priority amongst the *ton*. She could hear them whispering even now, wondering why the woman who had been the closest friend of both the bride and groom was in such a foul mood on such an otherwise happy occasion. They might even go so far as to say that she had ruined the evening for everyone. And those who knew why she wasn't smiling would be wondering why she had bothered to come at all.

She had been reluctant to participate in Francis's attempt at making her and her sisters presentable enough to appear at public events. But once she'd been convinced, she'd begun to let the idea of it excite her—if for no other reason than that it stopped her from thinking about love lost. Who would have thought that one of those events—strike that, the most important of those events—would be Adrian Fairchild's engagement party?

Emily was suddenly in a thoroughly sour mood. She had come to London to escape from Adrian and Kate, yet now she was about to find herself being dragged off to a ball that was intended to celebrate their love for one another, the happiness of their spending the rest of their lives together—a life that she had so abruptly been excluded from.

Emily dropped her head in her hands with a groan. This was turning out to be a very long season indeed. Quite frankly, the sooner it was over, the better, Emily decided.

Chapter Nine

"Might I have a word with you?" Francis asked as he addressed Emily with an even expression that told her nothing of what he might be thinking. Still, she had a faint idea.

They had just seen the back of Baroness Giddington's bright blue dress and feathers exiting the door, though not before settling upon a mutually agreeable time for the sisters to join her at the dressmaker's. The dreaded time was set for Friday morning at ten. Beatrice, Claire, and Emily would meet her there and afterward they would go to lunch. In the afternoon they would have a look at all the invitations together in order to decide upon which to accept.

Before any of this was to take place, however, there was still the small matter of Francis to deal with. And though Emily couldn't be completely certain, she was still fairly sure that he was extremely annoyed with her. She groaned inwardly as she followed him through to his study, not because she cared if he was annoyed with her or not, but because their conversation promised to be an annoying deterrent from the quiet walk she'd been looking forward to. Partaking in small talk over tea and biscuits with Baroness Giddington had fairly depleted Emily of that day's pent-up resources for social dialogue. Now she wanted nothing more than to be alone with her thoughts, if for no other reason than to digest the absurdity of attending the Carroway ball.

"Please close the door behind you." Francis broke the hushed silence. His voice was calm, but lacked emotion—perfectly suited to his character, Emily thought, as she gently pushed the door closed, leaving it slightly ajar for the sake of propriety. Turning around, she saw Francis disappear through a wide doorway, the doors to which had been swung completely open. She followed him, realizing with sudden apprehension that they must have wandered from one house over to the other. Steeling herself, she glanced around the room she was now in, noticing with some interest that Francis had a rather impressive collection of books.

"Have a seat," he told her as he gestured toward one of two brown leather club chairs in the corner. It squeaked ever so slightly as she did as he had asked. "Would you like something to drink?"

"Would you like to get to the point?" she asked dryly, surprising even herself with her rudeness.

Francis merely raised an eyebrow, put down the carafe that he had just picked up with the intention of pouring himself a cognac, and walked over to the other chair. "Very well," he said as he sat down next to her, facing her at an angle. "Would you mind explaining to me what the hell it was that you found to be so amusing that you could barely contain yourself in front of Veronica?"

"Veronica?"

Francis gave an impatient wave of his hand. "Baroness Giddington." He had forgotten that she had been only formally introduced. "Honestly, Emily, if I didn't know better I would have thought that you were laughing at her."

"I was," Emily told him flatly. If she had ever had the intention of shocking Francis Riley, she had, with this declaration, succeeded quite well.

Though he didn't reveal just how surprised he truly was—not only because she had openly laughed at one of the highest-ranking socialites in London, but because she'd openly admitted to it—his mouth did open slightly and his eyes did take on a look of wonder. It was as if he was seeing her for the very first time. She had always struck him as being the very definition of kindness, yet she had just now displayed a streak of cruelty that he couldn't understand, let alone like.

"May I ask why?"

Emily gave a slight sigh as she smoothed her dress across her lap. "It's impossible to explain," she said, suddenly sounding terribly awkward.

"Indulge me." His calm tone had slipped, letting a harsher one through. There was no point in pretending—she had truly begun to annoy him.

"It was a case of the giggles," she told him as seriously as she could manage.

"I beg your pardon?"

"It happens to me occasionally," she explained. "I can't help it. Sometimes I just have an uncontrollable urge to laugh, even though my brain might be telling me that there really isn't anything to laugh about. It was badly done of me. I'm sorry, Francis."

He looked at her curiously. Who was she? He had never in his life imagined that Emily Rutherford was a lady who was capable of being so forthright. Something had changed. What was it?

And then he realized something. What surprised him wasn't her demeanor, but how relieved he was to have figured it out. Emily hadn't laughed out of cruelty. For some inexplicable reason, she simply hadn't been able to help herself. It didn't mean that she didn't like Veronica, or that she even thought that there was something funny about the lady that welcomed a joke at her expense. She had plain and simply had a case of the giggles and it was, as she had plainly put it, impossible to explain.

"Veronica is my friend, Emily," Francis told her gently. "I will not allow you to laugh at her. Do I make myself clear?"

"But I wasn't . . ."

"Do I make myself clear?" He repeated the question as his eyes bore into hers, as stern as they could be.

"Perfectly," she muttered, meeting his eyes with equal severity.

"Are you looking forward to attending your first ball?" he suddenly asked, changing the subject one hundred and eighty degrees. He had leaned back in his chair and appeared, to her surprise, rather relaxed. It was impossible to tell that he had been chastising her a mere moment ago, and it did take a second, possibly two, for her to get her bearings straight.

Taking a deep breath, she let out a rather dramatic sigh, and deciding she might as well forget about her walk, kicked off her shoes and curled her legs up underneath her on the seat. Francis shot her a look that she immediately judged to be disapproving, so straightening her back she primly asked him, "What?"

"Nothing," he replied. But the tone was there, the tone that implied that it wasn't *nothing* at all, which of course gave her the immediate need to explain. "My feet often swell," she muttered. Then, with a more assertive voice, "It's more comfortable like this, all right?" When he failed to supply her with anything other than a blank stare, she was compelled to elaborate, though heaven only knew why.

"I'm a petite woman. These sort of chairs are made for men—men like you, for instance—who are capable of filling them out. I always feel as if I'm drowning in them, and I cannot slouch back against the back of it—my corset simply will not allow it. Besides," she continued, "we've known each other for years, you and I. I hardly think it makes much difference how I sit."

A faint smile had begun to tug at Francis's lips as he envisioned a miniature Emily sprawling about on a giant chair, which was exactly the imagery that she had evoked. But then she had mentioned her corset, and just like that, his mind had stopped, zeroing in on that single word, unable to move beyond it. Still, he looked ready to smile at any moment, except his eyes had taken on a peculiarly distracted look, which in turn made him look like a bit of an idiot.

"Francis?" she asked.

He inhaled sharply at the sound of her voice, then pressed both hands against his eyes, rubbing slightly as if to wipe away the image.

"Are you all right?"

"Yes, yes, I'm fine," he told her in a slightly irritated tone of voice.

"Perhaps I should go," she told him, but he immediately stopped her with a sharp "no" that surprised her.

"I think I'll have a scotch. Are you certain you don't want anything?" he asked as he rose to his feet and strode across the room to pluck a half-filled bottle off a table.

"Perhaps a small sherry . . . if you have some," she replied cautiously. Was she actually about to have a drink with Francis Riley, the one person in the world that she always strove to avoid? It had seemed that he had been on the brink of smiling earlier. She couldn't imagine why. Surely what she'd said hadn't been all that amusing. Then again, perhaps it had. At any rate, the thought of making Francis smile somehow intrigued her. The idea that he almost had must surely mean that he wasn't as mean as she thought. Only happy people with a positive outlook on life smiled. And since he had almost smiled, then maybe, just maybe, he wasn't nearly as bad as she thought.

The notion startled her so much that she let out a loud gasp, which in turn startled him. He spun around, spilling the sherry that he was in the middle of pouring, to give her a quizzical look.

"I'm sorry," she said, "I just . . . well I . . ." Darn it! Why was it so difficult to think of a plausible excuse? For lack of anything better, she settled on something completely inappropriate. "I just remembered that I mentioned my corset to you earlier, and well . . . it was really very inappropriate of me. You see, I was babbling on and on, and well . . . I'm sorry."

"And yet you brought it up again," he scolded, his hand frozen in midair as his mind turned once again toward that word. Once again that ridiculous urge to hold her that he'd felt in the carriage on their way to London swept over him. If only the woman didn't happen to be Emily Rutherford.

And yet she had changed. He had noticed it before, and wondered what had brought it on.

Upon reflection, he realized that he need only look in the mirror to find his answer. Pain had changed her. It had wiped away the wishy-washiness that he had always deemed to be her greatest flaw, and made her more direct . . . more blatantly honest. Emily Rutherford had been jaded, and for some peculiar reason, he liked her new personality—in fact, he preferred it. It added a sense of depth to her and made her stand out amongst all the other women who always did and said what was proper. Emily Rutherford had begun to speak her mind, and he was intrigued.

"I completely forgot what we were talking about before you spilt the sherry," she said in a voice that told him that she was annoyed by the fact.

Walking over to her, he handed her the glass and she took a careful sip, the strong liquid, tinged with sweetness, swishing about her mouth before she allowed herself to swallow. She put the glass down on the round table that stood between their chairs.

"I believe you were telling me about your corset . . ." Francis lifted his glass to his lips in hopes of hiding his smirk as he sat back down. There it was again . . . the image of her corset playing havoc with his mind.

"No, no . . ." She waved her hand dismissively. "Before that."

"Before that you were saying something about your feet."

"Oh, don't be daft, Francis," she exclaimed with some

degree of annoyance. "You know perfectly well that I'm referring to what we were talking about even before that."

Catching the slight look of surprise on his face, she bit her bottom lip. "Sorry, that was rude of me."

"Hmmm . . . I rather think I ought to be flattered that you feel you know me well enough to call me daft," he smiled.

He didn't make an attempt to hide it this time, and as he watched the look of dismay spreading across Emily's face, his smile broadened even further. He never would have thought that talking to Emily Rutherford could have forced such a change in him. He was suddenly at ease . . . not exactly happy, but at ease enough to smile, and it felt good . . . really good. "What?" he asked her.

She shook her head in bewilderment. "I've known you all these years," she said. "And yet I feel as though I'm seeing you for the very first time. Odd how much a smile can change your entire appearance. I've missed that smile, Francis." She said the last bit more to herself than to him, yet it made him glad nonetheless. Glad that he had somehow managed to alter her impression of him. And it had been such a surprisingly easy thing to do.

"I asked you if you were looking forward to attending your first ball," he said. "That's what we were talking about before you mentioned your feet."

She stopped for a moment to think. "Oh yes, you're quite right."

"Well, are you?"

"I suppose I am in a small way . . . all the excitement of it . . . you know?" She paused as the smile slipped from her face. "But I had hoped I'd be able to enjoy it more. The Carroway ball has taken all the fun out of it. I'm already trying to come up with the perfect excuse not to go."

"Don't you dare!" Francis exclaimed. "Emily, you won't feel better by avoiding the issue." He leaned forward in his chair and set his glass on the table next to hers. "You need to face both of them, to show them that they don't have the power to break you."

"How can you possibly presume to tell me what I *need* to do?" She rose to her feet and turned toward the door, her voice even, yet suddenly cold. The spark he'd seen in her earlier had dimmed. Instead she looked tired and worn out—defeated. "What makes you such an expert?"

"Oh, for heaven's sake, Emily," he grumbled as he got up. He wanted nothing more than to shake some sense into her. In fact, he intended on doing just that as he reached out, grabbed hold of her arm, and spun her forcefully toward him.

She let out a small gasp—complete surprise evident on her entire face, from her wide eyes to her slightly open mouth.

And then he just stood there, not knowing what to do. He looked down into her deep green eyes, only to discover that they weren't entirely green—they were brown toward the center . . . golden brown. How could he not have noticed this before, he wondered. Then again, he'd never had the opportunity to look this closely.

A few strands of her hair had come loose, dangling mindlessly against her cheek. Lifting his hand, he carefully brushed them away and tucked them behind her ear as she sucked in her breath.

He could feel the warmth of her skin beneath his hands, flowing up his arms and outward, until it filled his entire body. His immediate instinct was to pull her closer, to kiss her deeply and passionately on that delightful mouth of hers.

But the timing was all wrong. If he kissed her now, he'd be rushing it, and for some peculiar reason (he couldn't quite comprehend why), it seemed important that he take his time with Emily. Something deep within him warned him not to kiss her at that very moment, but to wait. So instead of pulling her toward him, he straightened his back, let go of her, and lowered his arms to his sides. "You *will* attend that ball, and you *shall* do it with your head held high. You won't cower in a corner or on a bench at the side of the dance floor. You shall dance, Emily Rutherford, and you shall have a bloody good time doing it. Is that understood?"

Emily nodded numbly, both confused and slightly disturbed, though she wasn't quite sure which sentiment dominated her current mood. Had he said those exact same words five minutes earlier, she would undoubtedly have snapped at him. However, she was incapable of an appropriate rejoinder at that very moment, for her mind had become cloudy and foggy. In fact, she couldn't recall ever being so befuddled before in her life.

It had almost looked as if Francis had intended on kissing her, right there in the study, in the middle of the afternoon. Francis, whose somber attitude she had barely been able to tolerate only a few days ago. Yet somehow, the world as she knew it had managed to unhinge itself and topple sideways. All of a sudden, Adrian, with whom she had been in love for years, was engaged to someone else—that someone else being none other than her best friend Kate. Kate, who'd had to suffer all of Emily's incessant chatter about Adrian to such a degree that her ears must have started to bleed. And now, to top it all off, she was beginning to think that Francis might actually like her in more than merely a friendly sort of way, that in spite of how badly she'd treated the poor man over the years, he might actually like to kiss her.

There was no other explanation than the most obvious one of all: she was completely delusional! No, she was mad . . . mad about Francis—no, no, no! She wasn't—she just thought she might be. She was vulnerable and easily susceptible to any man's charms. She had been spurned, and therefore (she rationalized), it was only natural that she might (subconsciously, of course) try to interpret a man's way of speaking or looking at her as a sign that he might be interested in her.

And yet, her whole body had responded to the way he had looked at her. Her heart was fluttering, her stomach was in upheaval, and she felt as if she'd lost her knees somewhere between him grabbing hold of her and then brushing aside her hair. Surely such things didn't occur from something she had just imagined . . . or did it?

Whatever had happened, she didn't understand it, and she didn't even try to, for it made no sense to her whatsoever. She knew only one thing, and that was that she deeply wished he would have kissed her.

Chapter Ten

Emily stared into the mirror in front of her as she carefully ran her hands over her pale green gown. Her long hair had been braided and coiled into a bun at the nape of her neck, the shorter strands at the front curled, ever so slightly, in order to frame her face.

She took a slow, deep breath. This was it—the evening that she had been dreading had finally arrived. She had already attended three other balls together with her sisters, including an evening at Almack's, where they had each received Lady Hawthorne's permission to waltz. Emily had taken to waltzing immediately, though Beatrice had on more than one occasion insisted that she not smile quite as much as she did—it would give people the impression that she enjoyed her partners' closeness more than was deemed appropriate.

Emily did try to follow her older sister's advice—not because she herself cared a farthing for what others might think, but rather to prevent Beatrice from keeling over from sheer embarrassment. It was, after all, Beatrice who had been responsible for their upbringing following their parents' deaths. Any inappropriate behavior or lack of etiquette would be construed as nothing more than a testament to Beatrice's failing attempts at educating her sisters properly.

Lady Giddington had accompanied them on each occasion as their chaperone. It was odd, really. Upon meeting her again (after that dreadfully embarrassing incident where she had behaved so rudely that she wondered why Beatrice hadn't admonished her also), Emily had wondered what on earth had prompted her to laugh in the first place. Veronica had been most kind and helpful toward all of them. Not only that, but it seemed that she actually possessed an extraordinary sense of which dresses suited them best (in spite of the unfortunate blue one that she herself had worn when they had first met). And, she had looked nothing short of stunning in each of the gowns that she had worn since.

Emily looked analytically at her face as it stared back at her from the mirror. Adhering to fashion, she always stayed out of the sun, and therefore had the same pale complexion as everyone else she knew. Yet there was a line to be drawn between fashionably pale and looking sickly, and she rather fancied herself as appearing to be quite sickly looking indeed.

It must be nerves, she thought as she pinched her cheeks in hopes of adding some color. In fact, if she had to be altogether honest, her stomach was completely unsettled and her skin had begun to crawl with anxiety. She felt faint and reached out to her vanity in order to steady herself. This was a bad idea. She knew without a shadow of a doubt that it was quite possibly the worst idea in the world for her to attend this ball. She ought to stay at home, curled up in bed where she belonged. But . . . Francis wouldn't allow it. He had said as much, and when she had had the chance to, she hadn't argued the point. And so, here she was on the verge of collapse, ready to head on out to a ball she was sure to hate.

She sighed one last time, then straightened her back, and turned toward the door.

Gracefully resting her hand on the banister, Emily made her way down the stairs toward the murmur of voices coming from the parlor. Pausing for a moment with her hand on the door handle, she pushed the remaining nerves under a magnificent mask of composure. Then, turning the handle, she nudged the door open and entered.

Francis was in deep conversation with Jonathan, who was always invited to join them. They seemed to be discussing a few of Francis's investments.

"Perhaps you ought to forget about your other ventures," Jonathan was saying. "And increase your stock with the East India Company."

"Perhaps," Francis agreed with a thoughtful frown. Then, seeing the door open out of the corner of his eye, he turned his head and immediately caught his breath.

How could Adrian have been so stupid? That was the first thought that came to mind as he saw Emily standing there, framed in the doorway with the hallway light glowing behind her. She looked positively stunning.

He had tried to hold his growing feelings for her in check since their meeting in his study. That was almost two weeks ago now and he had managed the feat in spite of how difficult it had been for him.

He had wanted to get to the bottom of his own emotions—to find out if making his intentions known to her would be worth the risk. After all, in spite of their past disagreements, Emily was a sweet girl, so he didn't want to play the rogue and tarnish her otherwise spotless reputation. If he were to kiss her, he would only do so if he was sure that he might be able to follow through with a proposal of marriage, and marriage was definitely not something to be taken lightly.

And then of course there was *her* opinion to consider. Would she even care to entertain the thought of kissing him, let alone marrying him? He was willing to bet his life that she wasn't. Not yet anyway. Therefore, he had made up his mind. He had devised a carefully thought-out plan, its sole purpose being to eventually ensure Emily's hand in marriage. And he would do it the old-fashioned way—through trickery.

If indeed she happened to be a woman like any other, he knew she must have been thinking of him since he had held her in the study, wondering why he hadn't kissed her. He had caught her a number of times since then, thoughtfully regarding him as if trying to figure him out.

Even now as her gaze swept across the room, it seemed she made a deliberated effort not to look at him. But then of course curiosity got the better of her, and her eyes found him. The corner of his mouth drew upward in a crooked smile. Color flooded her face, she looked away, and just like that, he knew that she'd been thinking of him. The thrill of it (though it didn't show) rippled through his veins. It was all the encouragement he needed in order to pursue her. With a satisfied inward smile, he turned back to Jonathan to finish his conversation.

Emily stood, stranded with her whirlwind of emotions. Had she imagined it yet again? She was sure that he had looked at her with desire in his eyes, and yet he had turned away with an otherwise unmoved expression. It left her feeling rather deflated.

All that nervous energy that she had built up was suddenly gone, and that was when she realized that it had all been for him. She hadn't thought of Adrian when she had readied herself for the ball. She had thought of Francis, wondering—no, hoping—that he would approve of the way she looked. Yet he had barely given her any attention at all.

The disappointment frightened her. Why would she care about Francis's opinion? Why did it matter what he thought of her? Once again the cloud of confusion that had become all too familiar over the past couple of weeks washed over her. She turned to Beatrice and Claire, seated on a bench by the window.

"You look particularly lovely this evening." Trust Beatrice to say something like that. There was no doubt she meant it—Emily just wished that Francis would have said it instead. There she was, thinking of him again. She hated the fact that she thought of him at all. "Thank you," she replied in the cheeriest voice she could manage. "So do the two of you. Your hair is beautifully styled, Claire, and Bea, your dress complements your complexion perfectly. Well done!"

The two women smiled, clearly pleased with the compliment.

"Did Francis tell you?" Claire asked as she almost bounced up and down on the bench with excitement.

"Tell me what?" Emily's eyes moved from one sister to the other, trying to read the expressions on their faces.

"He plans to dance with all three of us this evening. Can

you imagine? Francis dancing!" Claire's eyes grew wide. "It must be centuries since anyone has seen him dance. I wonder if he even remembers how to."

She whispered the last part as Beatrice quickly hushed her. "You mustn't say such things," she admonished. "Least of all in his own home—not to mention his presence. Have you no sense of decorum at all?" But the suppressed giggle was present in Beatrice's eyes, even as she made the stoic attempt at sounding severe.

"Claire does have a point, Bea," Emily cut in, to the immense satisfaction of Claire, who grinned at her sister's unexpected show of support. "I certainly can't remember Francis ever dancing at any of the events where we've seen him."

Claire's grin withered, and Beatrice suddenly looked stricken. Emily went on, determined to remember some of Francis's faults, in the face of her recent and extremely confounding feelings toward him. "He always stands as far away from the dance floor as possible. That's of course unless he's in the game room playing cards, which, judging from my observations, I think is where he feels far more comfortable. One does tend to wonder, however, why a man with such strikingly good looks is never seen in the company of a lady. Then again, his glum demeanor is hardly to his advantage. If I'm not mistaken, I do believe the majority of young women fear him."

"And here I was, thinking that it was just such a demeanor that most young women were drawn to—the troubled rogue that melts their hearts with a dark and brooding stare."

She recognized the voice immediately, a slight shiver running down her spine, her body trembling as heat rushed into her face. She knew she needn't worry about looking too pale anymore. No mirror was required to tell her that her face had turned scarlet.

Her eyes squeezed shut as she bit down on her lip—embarrassment seeping out of every pore. Taking a deep breath, she turned to face him.

He was closer than she had expected—so close that she could feel the warmth of his breath against her face. She looked up into those dark and mysterious eyes of his. "I . . ." was all she managed before he cut her off.

"Are my looks really that striking?" he asked with a mischievous undertone.

"What? Er . . . well . . . you see . . . the thing is . . ." Emily stammered. Good God, he smelled good, standing there so close to her. She wanted nothing more than to drown in his aroma. Her head felt dizzy with it and it was clearly impairing her ability to string a coherent sentence together. "I'm sorry," she finally managed to get out. "That was insensitive of me. I hope you'll forgive my rudeness."

"Well . . . that depends." His voice was close to a whisper. She could have sworn that everyone else in the room had vanished in that instant—nobody else seemed to exist as long as he stood there staring into her eyes, the heat there warning her that this was more than a straightforward conversation. He was publicly flirting with her—she was now certain of it—and it excited her in a way that nothing else ever had.

Francis arched an eyebrow as he lowered his head toward her. "Would you do me the honor of letting me show you that I do indeed remember how to dance?"

Emily sucked in a breath and pretended to ponder the

question with a great deal of thought before finally saying, "I would be delighted, Francis."

He then offered her his arm. "Shall we? I believe our carriage awaits."

"Well, if you are to escort Emily, then I shall have the pleasure of attending to her sisters," Jonathan grinned as he offered one arm to Beatrice and the other to Claire. "Really, old friend! It seems that I have, yet again, made the better deal."

"I hardly think so," Emily heard Francis mutter, as he guided her out of the room. A warm feeling wafted through her—delight over his apparent pleasure at having her hand resting upon his arm. Perhaps it was finally time to realize that there was more to life than Adrian. And Francis may be just the man to show her what she'd been missing.

Chapter Eleven

He tried desperately not to look at her as they sat across from one another on their way to the Carroway mansion on Grosvenor Square. Yet every now and again, his gaze found her, his eyes drawn helplessly toward the luscious rise of her breasts as they swayed slightly with each and every jolt that the landau made.

It was ridiculous, really, to take a carriage such a short distance. His house was no more than a five-minute walk along Mount Street and then up Charles Street. However, one could never be sure if it might rain, and besides, it was night. Even if they were in Mayfair, as opposed to in the center of town, it would be highly unseemly for young ladies to have to walk more than ten feet in their evening attire.

Francis's thoughts turned once again to Emily, his feelings for her churning inside him like a raging sea in a storm.

How did this happen?

God help him, Emily Rutherford was the last person on earth he would ever have thought would awaken such desire in him. For years now the feelings he'd once had for her had been carefully removed to a distant corner of his mind and forgotten, but seeing her every day for the past two weeks had tormented him, her honesty drawing him in like a fish hooked on a line.

With each day that passed, he wanted her more. She remained constantly in his thoughts . . . thoughts that were becoming less and less pure. For pity's sake, he wished she would have brought a shawl to cover those beckoning breasts so that he might hope to think of something else. He cursed beneath his breath as he turned to look out of the window.

"Don't worry," Beatrice said, addressing Emily. "We'll be right by your side."

"Do I look worried?" Since climbing into the carriage, Emily's mind had returned to Adrian and Kate. The last couple of weeks had been impossibly difficult, and yet, Francis and her sisters had miraculously managed to turn her mind to other things—particularly Francis.

Nevertheless, knowing that she was now approaching the Carroway ball made everything come crashing back down on her. Her newfound confidence began to shrivel. She would have to face the two people who had completely betrayed her trust. They had gone ahead and made their future plans without the slightest word of warning.

It was more than that, though. She had loved him—*had* being the operative word. And yet, she could not bring herself to hate either one of them. Perhaps that was the worst part of all. If she could only hate them for what they had done, she might be able to find some release by lashing out at them.

However, it was impossible for her to hate anyone, least of

all someone she had been such close friends with, regardless of what they might have done. No, Emily Rutherford didn't hate Adrian or Kate. What she felt was far worse. She felt pain and overwhelming loss. Closing her eyes against the tears, she lowered her head to look at her hands.

"You look as if you're about to cry," Claire told her.

"Claire!" Beatrice muttered. "You mustn't draw attention to that sort of thing. Emily is in a fragile enough state as it is without you highlighting the point."

"Sorry." The apology was low and almost went unheard, but it was sincere.

"Claire's right, though," Emily said as she put on a brave smile and looked up, her eyes glittering. "I feel miserable. I fear that this was really a very bad idea indeed." She allowed herself to glance over at Francis, but he appeared to be caught up in his own thoughts. Besides, what would he say? Knowing him, he would probably just make her feel worse for not having the ability to spurn her friends for hurting her.

She let out a wretched sigh as the carriage jerked to a halt.

Jonathan jumped to the ground, straightened himself, and then extended his hand in order to assist Claire. Moving to follow her sister, Beatrice rose from the bench, only to find herself deterred by Francis, his hand holding on to her wrist. "Beatrice, would you allow me to have a moment alone with your sister?" he asked her, a grave look upon his face.

"I'm not entirely sure that it would be proper, Francis," she replied in earnest, though with the slightest hint of regret.

"Perhaps if you were to wait just outside the carriage?" he urged. "We shall leave the door ajar," he added. Beatrice paused a moment, seemingly contemplating the issue. "It will take but the fraction of a heartbeat," he promised her, his eyes meeting hers dead-on.

"Very well then," she agreed. "I shall wait outside. Do be quick about it, though—we wouldn't like to cause a stir—particularly since other carriages are arriving as we speak." Her white satin dress rustled about her as she reached out to take Jonathan's hand, leaving Francis and Emily alone to face one another.

Having no desire to waste the precious time that Beatrice had allowed him, Francis hurried across to seat himself beside Emily. She gasped as her eyes widened, bewilderment etched deeply in her delicate features.

"I know that you are troubled by having to come here this evening," he told her seriously in a rush of words. "Don't worry, though. You shall not be left alone with either one of them for a second, I assure you. However, should you decide that it is too difficult for you to stay, then I doubt if anyone would blame you for having a sudden headache."

"Thank you, Francis," she told him with the faintest of smiles. "You are most considerate."

Without waiting a moment longer, he put his arm around her waist, pulled her toward him, and lowered his head, his lips gently grazing hers in the sweetest of kisses that Emily could ever have imagined.

Nothing she had ever experienced came close to this. Even Adrian's kiss fell short by comparison.

This was sensual. It had a softness to it, with a yearning behind it that sent shivers of excitement down her spine.

Heat flooded her, from her head to her toes, as she savored the feeling of his lips against hers.

Forgetting herself, she raised her hand to grab on to him, to draw him nearer, yet before she could manage to do so, he had pulled away.

"Hopefully, that will give you something else to think about," he told her with a sly shadow of a smile.

Though he acted unperturbed, she couldn't ignore the heated gaze with which he now looked at her. She clasped her hands to stop them from trembling. Her heart was still racing, her skin prickling. She almost wanted to ask him to kiss her again, but before she could muster up the courage, he had left the carriage and was now standing on the ground below, waiting to assist her.

With a dreamy look upon her face and a lightheaded sensation of walking on clouds, she stumbled down the steps to take his arm and enter the manor.

A hush fell across the ballroom as their names were announced. Everyone knew about the Rutherford sisters and the untimely deaths of their parents. Since this was the first that the *ton* had seen of them in six years, necks now craned and heads twisted in attempts at catching a look at them.

Emily gripped Francis's arm tightly, the sudden attention unnerving her. He couldn't help but smile to himself—it was immensely satisfying to know that she had turned to him to help her through it. Placing his right hand upon hers, he gave it a gentle squeeze of reassurance.

Then, as if by magic, it seemed as if she strengthened her resolve. Her back straightened, her chin rose and she took on an admirably regal look. She felt safe with him, and the discovery of it squeezed his heart and filled him with such warmth. How rewarding it was to know this. He wondered if she knew it herself.

As they descended the stairs, they were met by both Veronica and their hostess, Adrian's mother.

"Lady Carroway, Lady Giddington," Francis and Jonathan said in turn as they greeted the two women with a slight bow.

"Lord Dunhurst and Mr. Jonathan," the two women chirped in reply.

"How good of you to come," Lady Carroway said to them with a smile. Then, turning toward the three sisters, her smile broadened. "Beatrice, Emily, and Claire—I can't tell you how pleased I am to see you."

"You are most kind," Beatrice told her. "It was really very good of you to invite us."

"I wouldn't have had it any other way."

"Pray tell us, how is the happy couple doing?" Emily found herself asking, much to her own surprise.

Everyone else looked equally shocked, which naturally brought a smile to Emily's lips. She somehow enjoyed the effect she'd had on them. Only Francis knew that she was not nearly as composed as she would have them all believe. The knuckles of the hand that gripped his arm had turned white.

"Emily, it's very kind of you to ask, but really, we needn't talk about them if you'd rather not," Lady Carroway told her gently.

Emily steadied herself, then thought of the one thing that

would help her get through the evening. Blood rushed to her head as she thought of Francis kissing her in the carriage.

"I'm sorry," Lady Carroway said as she saw how red Emily turned. "I've embarrassed you."

Francis turned his eyes on Emily. He knew immediately that her blush had nothing to do with what Lady Carroway had said. *This will give you something else to think about,* he had told her. He smirked, trying to bite back a grin. How satisfying it was to see the effect he'd had on her, and in full view of the entire *ton*. It took tremendous restraint to stop him from laughing out loud.

"Not at all," Emily told Lady Carroway. "I'm quite all right, really. If I hadn't wished to be confronted with the issue, I could have pleaded a headache and stayed away. However, I am here to offer my congratulations to both of them. That is why I inquired as to how they are doing."

Beatrice's heart swelled with pride at her sister's words. Taking her free hand in hers, she leaned toward her. "Well done, Emily," she whispered in her ear. "Well done indeed."

"Would you care to dance?" Emily suddenly heard Francis asking her. He had no intention of waiting for his aunt to tell them about Kate and Adrian's welfare. His arm had become thoroughly sore, but aside from that, he had a compelling need to have Emily to himself for a while.

"I . . ." She hesitated as an array of different thoughts filled her mind . . . some of them (in fact, an alarming majority) were not at all proper for a young unmarried woman to be thinking. If she accepted, would she be accepting more than just a dance? Her heart was still in tatters. Her better judgment was telling her to turn and run. But the tiniest of voices in her head was urging her to accept. Troubled by indecision, she remained quite still.

"Emily?" she heard his voice like a far-off call.

Then Beatrice nudged her. "Lord Dunhurst is awaiting your reply," she murmured. She then added in a low whisper that only Emily could hear, "You mustn't refuse him, Emily—not publicly, no matter what your feelings are. Now pull yourself together."

With a little shove, Emily found herself being pushed toward Francis, her feet almost landing on top of his as she stumbled. He caught her gracefully, holding her steady with practiced ease and without batting an eyelid.

His face was most serious as he regarded her, those dark eyes of his drawing her toward him. Oh, she could easily forget everything else around her when she looked into those eyes. And his strong jaw line, his sensual lips that were now drawn tight in expectation. She now knew what it was to have those lips pressed against hers as she gazed upon them reverently, unable to look at anything else as a sudden wave of heat washed over her. *Pull yourself together.* Beatrice's voice echoed in her head, returning her to the present with the same effect that a bucket of ice water might have. "As I told you earlier this evening, I would be delighted," she managed to get out, surprised by the smoothness of her own voice.

All seriousness vanished from his features at her acceptance. Emily couldn't quite believe the effect that she had apparently had on him. He looked positively happy for the first time in years.

By the time they had made their way to the dance floor, the first notes of the waltz were already sifting through the air.

Francis pulled Emily close up against him, placing one hand firmly behind her back as he held her hand with the other. Then, with unparalleled poise, he led her about at an even pace.

Startling new sensations overwhelmed her. She couldn't help but notice the firmness of his chest, the strength of his arms that held her with such care. The scent of him . . . dear God, it was heavenly—a musky aroma that blended delightfully well with his cologne. She was giddy with intoxication. How could it be that she'd never noticed before? Francis was the very definition of masculine vitality. He should have had endless lines of mothers hammering at his door, eager to see their daughters wed him.

They must have found fault with his demeanor just as much as she had. Would she have allowed her daughter to marry a man who never once smiled? Who always seemed cold and callous? Probably not. But something in the last couple of weeks had brought on a gradual change in him. He looked different, as if a burden had been lifted, and to her astonishment, she found that he was handsomer than ever before, though she couldn't imagine how that was possible.

And then there was the kiss. What in the name of all that was holy had prompted him to do that? He had completely shaken her universe to such an extent that the world as she knew it had dropped off its axis and was now bouncing around in complete mayhem. She decided that she might as well stop speculating and simply ask.

As they came about a third time, the skirt of her gown whooshing against her legs, she leaned her head closer to him. "Why did you kiss me when we were alone in the carriage?" she asked in a whisper.

She felt a slight shift in his shoulders at the question. "Would you rather that I had kissed you publicly?"

"What?" She was aghast. "Of course not!"

"Well, that's why I kissed you in the carriage."

She leaned back slightly in order to see his face. He was grinning down at her, his eyes light with amusement. If they hadn't been in the middle of the dance floor, she would have pummeled him. Well, perhaps not, but she liked to think that she would have, as she lowered her gaze to hide her smile.

"You know perfectly well that that's not what I was asking," she muttered.

The music faded and Francis turned toward her with a bow while she made a slight curtsey. She then placed her hand lightly on the arm he offered her. "Well?" she insisted as they walked away from the next set. He waved over a waiter with a tray filled with champagne flutes. They each took one, continuing toward the perimeter of the room where the heat was less stifling.

She watched him closely as he sipped his drink, a thoughtful expression lurking behind his dark eyes. "I told you already. It was meant as a distraction, to help take your mind off more upsetting matters. When you find yourself confronted by Adrian and his bride-to-be—as you shall, for there they are right now, coming our way—I want you to look unaffected and to carry yourself like a queen."

Emily looked out over the crowd, spotting Adrian and Kate immediately, steering straight toward them, just as Francis had said. Her pulse quickened and she felt suddenly out of sorts.

"That's all it was?" she asked Francis quickly, her eyes

darting between him and the approaching couple, gauging the time it would take for the pair to reach them.

"It was a simple kiss, Emily, not the works of Shakespeare," he told her coolly. "There's no reason for you to analyze it to death."

The bluntness of his words shocked her, but really, what had she expected him to say? This *was* after all, Francis, the man who hid away from everyone behind his harsh, glowering façade. Then why did she feel so thoroughly disappointed? She knew why. Of course she did. She thought she'd managed to penetrate his wall of steel, as if he'd given her a glimpse of who he'd once been and of who she hoped he would one day be again.

And then Kate and Adrian were upon them, banishing all other thoughts from her mind.

"Emily—it's so good of you to have come," Adrian told her smoothly as he came to a stop right next to her. He took her hand in his and gently brushed his lips against it. Biting down on her lower lip, Emily tried to focus on the pain, rather than on Adrian's touch.

There was no denying it. She felt as though she was the center of a monstrous joke. After all, the man she'd always loved and her closest friend—to whom she had confided everything—had fallen for each other. As if that wasn't enough to send her head spinning, she was now finding herself drawn irrefutably toward the last person in the world with whom she ever would have thought to get involved—the glum and brooding Lord Dunhurst. Forget Adrian. Her mind was now filled to the brim with Francis—his face, his words, his kiss. They might as well be standing in the middle of Bedlam instead of in the Carroway ballroom, as far as she was concerned.

And when she looked up and caught Francis rolling his eyes at Adrian's greeting, Emily knew that she was in for another case of the giggles. She quickly snatched her hand away and covered her mouth with it to feign a cough, concealing all evidence of her impending laughter, or so she hoped. But her eyes had betrayed her, and having seen her in the same predicament once recently, Francis raised a knowing eyebrow, a faint smile tugging at his lips.

"Francis," Adrian continued with an acknowledging nod, unaware of anything unusual.

"Mr. Fairchild," Francis replied, the formality of his greeting highlighting their now strained relationship. "Lady Kate." He made no attempt to kiss her hand, his own clasped firmly behind his back.

"You look well," Kate said, her comment directed at Emily. There was concern in her voice, but Emily ignored it. She had lost Adrian, but she would not give up her dignity. Everyone expected her to collapse in a puddle of tears. She was now more determined than ever not to let that happen.

In spite of what Francis had just said, she needed him now to help her through this. She clenched and unclenched her fingers, considering whether or not to grab hold of him somehow. But before she was able to decide, his hand found hers, squeezing it ever so gently in reassurance. Her eyes darted upward to be met by the most supportive of gazes. Giving her an almost imperceptible nod, he nudged her onward.

"As do you," Emily replied, relief flooding her. There was something to be gained from confronting her fear—a sense of finality. "I trust that the wedding preparations are coming along well."

"Emily, I . . ." A pained look tore at Kate's beautiful features. She was without a shadow of a doubt filled with guilt.

Emily waved a dismissive hand in the air. "Everything is forgotten, and besides . . . this is your engagement party. I forbid you from not enjoying every moment of it."

"That's very kind of you, Emily," Kate told her warily, as if she feared Emily's calmness more than she would a nervous breakdown. *She probably thinks I'm plotting my revenge as we speak.* Emily stifled yet another laugh. Francis squeezed her hand and she wondered then if perhaps he was able to read her mind.

As it happened, he thought that she was handling it quite well thus far, in spite of her apparent urge to giggle at each and every word that was spoken. He watched her fondly as she addressed the friends that had so deeply wounded her.

Then, before his very eyes, she suddenly transformed. Her back straightened even further, she lifted her chin slightly, and then she looked both of them squarely in the eye without flinching. "I will say this, however. You were my closest and my dearest friends. I loved you more than you shall ever know. Quite foolish, really, since neither of you cared for me at all."

Adrian opened his mouth to speak, but she silenced him with her hand. "You, Adrian, led me to believe that we had an agreement—perhaps I was too eager and hasty to draw that conclusion. But it is impossible that you never noticed how I felt about you when everyone else did. If you had cared, Adrian—if you had cared at all—you would have known that kissing me meant more than the world to me. It saddens me to think that it meant so little to you.

"And, Kate. I poured out my heart to you. It was a long time ago, I'll grant you that, but for you to spring something like this on me without a single word of warning . . .

"You were my dearest friends, both of you, but you broke my heart, truly you did. The worst of it is that I know—I think even *you* know—that I would never have treated your hearts so carelessly.

"You are marrying for love, and for that I cannot be anything but happy—grateful even—for at least the loss of your friendship has not been for nothing."

Kate looked at her in bewilderment. "Surely you don't mean to tell us . . ."

"That is exactly what I mean to tell you," her voice slicing through the air like steel. "I will remember our friendship fondly, but such a friendship is based on trust and respect. You have failed me in both. I'm afraid that it is over."

Without another word, Emily turned her back on them forever and walked away, her dress swooshing about her ankles. Francis followed in her wake, his heart swelling with pride—she was most assuredly not the same Emily that he had known as a youth, the giddy little thing that always shied away from any conflict. Instead, she was a woman of unbelievable strength, courage, and resolve.

A woman that he now wanted entirely for himself.

Chapter Twelve

"I believe that I am presently overstaying my welcome," Emily told Beatrice as she sidled up next to her sister and drew her slightly away from Ladies Carroway and Giddington. "I ought to leave."

"Did you have a quarrel?" Beatrice asked, her eyes big and round with worry.

"No. I merely told Kate and Adrian exactly how I feel." Emily looked out over the throng of people. "Where's Claire?"

Doing her best to hide her concern, Beatrice nodded her head in the direction of the dance floor. "Lord Camden asked her to dance."

"How wonderful!" Emily exclaimed. "And you? Do you not wish to dance?"

"Nobody has asked, as of yet," Beatrice told her with a brave attempt at hiding her embarrassment—Francis was after all within earshot.

Realizing her blunder, Emily gave her sister an apologetic smile.

"I was actually hoping that you might dance the next set

with me." Francis's eyes shone with a sincerity that made Emily want to throw her arms around him in a grateful hug.

Beatrice smiled at him thankfully. "That is indeed most kind of you," she said. "However, I believe that I am quite happy here in conversation with your aunt and Lady Giddington. However, if we must leave, then by all means, let me bid our hosts a good night."

"I'm sorry to see you leave on my account," Emily told her.

"Claire will be most disappointed. I believe she has taken a liking to the young lord," Beatrice said.

"Emily," Francis cut in. "There's really no need for your sisters to leave. I can escort you home and then send the carriage back to wait for them."

Beatrice beamed with delight, so pleased that she entirely forgot how inappropriate it would be for Francis and Emily to share a carriage together without a chaperone. Unwilling to complicate things any further, Emily decided to ignore the issue. Instead, she moved over to where Lady Carroway was standing. "I fear I must take my leave of your company, my lady. I wish to thank you for your hospitality. You have always been kind to me. For that I am grateful."

Lady Carroway eyed her thoughtfully as if trying to determine what had brought about such an early departure. "I have always valued our friendship and I always shall." Her words spoke volumes and were indeed a comfort to Emily.

"Lady Giddington, I shall see you on Friday?"

Veronica smiled at Emily and gave her a short nod. "Indeed you shall."

"Very well, then, enjoy the rest of the evening, ladies.

"Beatrice, I believe that I will turn in early, but I will

see you in the morning." She gave her sister a cheeky look. "I expect you to tell me everything about Claire and Lord Camden."

Beatrice grinned, shaking her head at her sister's lust for gossip. Then, taking Francis's arm, Emily glided away toward the stairs. With a final backward glance, she just managed to see Jonathan ask Beatrice to dance, and she couldn't help but let out a sigh of relief.

Emily and Francis sat in silence as the carriage rocked from side to side, the whispering wind streaming in through the open window, caressing their faces and playing with their hair. Recognizing Emily's need for fresh air, Francis had asked the driver to take a longer route home.

Emily leaned forward to look out of the window as they drove up Duke Street, turning right onto Oxford. She loved the clippity-clop of the horses' hooves against the cobblestones in the hushed night air, coupled with the dim, yellow glow of the gaslights. Both created a dreamlike atmosphere that swept all worries from her mind.

The touch of Francis's hand upon her knee startled her. "Emily?" she heard him say.

"What is it?" she asked, surprised by the level of annoyance in her voice. Turning away from the window, she looked over at him, her heart almost skidding to a halt as she did so.

She had been so caught up in her own thoughts, mesmerized by the lights and buildings that they had passed along the way, that she had forgotten all about Francis.

How was it possible for anyone to be so disarmingly handsome? Even now, with his typically serious expression, she could feel the blood rushing to her face. Her heart fluttered and her stomach flip-flopped while he remained seemingly unperturbed. It wasn't fair. She didn't like him, she reminded herself. She hadn't liked him in years, yet here he was turning her insides to mush. What in God's name was going on?

She leaned back toward the window again. It had suddenly gotten ridiculously hot in the carriage. She needed the breeze to cool her down. "I'm sorry." She was relieved that her voice at least sounded normal. "I was caught up in my own thoughts. I didn't mean to balk at you. You startled me, that's all."

He regarded her thoughtfully for a moment, his eyes seemingly boring into her. She shifted on the bench, uncomfortable by the way in which her skin prickled at the nape of her neck.

"I was just trying to tell you how well you did back there." His voice was low and husky.

As her eyes roamed across his face, taking in each and every detail, her face heated once again as her mouth went dry. She licked her lips and moved her eyes skittishly to the corner of the carriage.

Don't look at him, don't look at him.

She had become all too painfully aware of the effect that he'd begun to have on her. This was the last thing she wanted—getting emotionally involved with Francis Riley. He would never be capable of returning any feelings she might develop toward him. How could he? It required a soft heart to love, and his was as solid as a lump of lead.

Yes, he had surprised her on more than one occasion recently, but that wasn't enough to wipe away ten years of . . . of what? She couldn't claim that he had ever been unkind, but he lacked something that was vital to her very existence: joy.

Why was she even worrying about this? She had no intention of falling in love with the man. There was no denying that she found him attractive, but so would any other level-headed female. But love? She almost laughed at herself for even thinking it.

Throwing an imaginary bucket of ice water over her head, she straightened her back and moved her eyes to meet his squarely. "It had to be done. I'm just happy that I came away with my head held high."

"You did indeed. It can't have been easy."

She let out a deep sigh. "You're right," she smiled. "I wasn't sure that I would make it out of there without collapsing in a fit of tears."

"Emily . . ."

"They were my friends, Francis!" Her voice was fierce with emotion. "Had they just treated me with a bit more care, they could have had it all: each other and my friendship. Why did they have to make a mess of it?"

"Love does the strangest things to people's minds," he muttered.

Letting out another sigh, she paused before continuing. "I'm sorry to burden you with all of this, but . . . Beatrice worries too much about me as it is, and Claire . . . well, Claire's Claire. She'll just say something inappropriate in an attempt to take my mind off of it."

"Do you not like it when people try to help you by making you think of something else?" he asked, a smoldering heat suddenly very much present in his dark brown eyes.

Emily sucked in her breath, her heart fluttering uncontrollably as her mind went straight back to the kiss they'd shared earlier that evening. "That depends." Why did she say that? She should have said "no." Why hadn't she?

"Oh?" he asked with sudden interest "On what? If you don't mind my asking."

"On who that person is and on their efforts," she replied. Good Lord, was she actually sitting in a carriage, flirting with Francis? Her skin prickled as heat surged through her from the top of her head to the tips of her toes. She needed more air.

Francis was enjoying himself immensely. Toying with Emily and making her squirm was quite possibly the most amusing thing he'd done in years. Apparently she wasn't as immune to him as she liked to appear. Yet she seemed oblivious to his own growing desire, his urge to pull her onto his lap and smother her in kisses. To feel her slim thighs rubbing against his legs, her breasts pressing against his chest.... He wanted her in his bed, yet he willed himself to push that thought aside. He needed to wait. After all, she had nothing but reservations toward him. And rightly so. Seducing her would take time and lots and lots of patience. He wondered if he was up to the challenge, but then again, what other diversions did he have?

Willing himself not to take the bait, he smiled at her casually. "Emily, I realize we've had our differences, you and I, but if you ever need to talk, I really don't mind listening. In fact, I hope that you consider me your friend, and in so doing, realize that I will do what I can in order to help."

She swallowed hard and thanked him, turning her gaze

back toward the street. They had just turned onto Piccadilly and would be arriving at Berkeley Square within the next five minutes. But even that would not be enough time for her to get her feelings under control.

Francis had somehow managed to bring something that had been deeply hidden within her to the surface. She couldn't have found the words to describe it if she had tried, but it was something new—a primitive urge to do things she never would have had the courage to think of doing before.

Her knowledge of what went on between a man and a woman was not entirely lacking. She understood the basics, and the more Francis continued to look at her with those fiery eyes of his, the more she found herself wishing that he would be the one to show her.

She silently admonished herself for her indecent thoughts, though that was of no avail whatsoever—it only made them more prominent.

Looking up, she saw Francis's back disappearing through the door. They were home again and he was holding out his hand to her in order to help her down.

Chapter Thirteen

"Would you care for a drink?" he asked as he handed his cloak over to Parker. As had become the custom, they'd each entered by their own door before rejoining in the hallway at number five.

Emily paused in the process of removing her satin gloves, pondering the idea. "I think I would," she told him with a decisive nod as she pulled her hand free from the second glove and handed the pair over to Parker.

She didn't quite catch the look of surprise on Francis's face. He thought she might have refused his company—she clearly had a lot of thoughts and emotions that needed resolving, but he was glad to find that she didn't mind being alone with him. He was making progress after all.

"Come along then," he told her in an easy tone as he led the way down the corridor and into his study. He strode over to the side table. "What would you like then? Sherry?"

She swallowed hard as she watched him uncertainly from the doorway. Perhaps this wasn't such a good idea after all. Her feelings toward him were becoming anything but friendly camaraderie. She wasn't used to it—particularly not with him—and it absolutely, positively unnerved her to the very core of her being.

With a sudden sense of panic, she realized how frightened she was. What if he tried to kiss her again? How would she stop him without offending him? After all, she'd allowed him the liberty once already—surely he must now believe that he had the right to do it again. Her pulse quickened at the very thought of his lips touching hers again.

Another, more terrifying notion urged her to take a small step forward. What if he didn't try to kiss her again? She'd barely been able to think of anything else all evening, and as much as it galled her to think that her mind would stray to such . . . such sinful pleasures . . . something deep within the core of her being desperately wished to be held by him again.

"I'm not a mind reader, you know."

She shook her head, ridding herself of her reverie. What had he asked her? "Sorry . . . uhm . . . no, thank you. I think I'll have a brandy, if you don't mind."

He arched an eyebrow as he studied her with a certain element of surprise twinkling in his eyes.

"What?" she asked as she cocked her head to one side, regaining her composure and striding confidently over to the same armchair that she had used the last time she'd shared a drink with him.

"I wouldn't have thought you could stomach the stuff," he told her, his voice telling her that he wasn't at all convinced she'd chosen the right drink.

"I don't make a habit out of it, but occasionally I do make an exception." Her eyes misted slightly as she continued. "My father loved a glass of brandy in the evening. I wouldn't necessarily say that I'm particularly fond of it myself, but the smell and the taste remind me of him. It helps me bring him a little bit closer."

She smiled sweetly, obviously caught up in the memory of the man that Francis also remembered quite fondly. Lord Hillsbury had always had a pleasant air about him. He'd been exceedingly patient, not only with his own children, but also with all of their friends'. In fact, it had been Emily's father, rather than his own, who had taught him how to carve a horse out of wood and how to fish. His own father had always been so incredibly busy.

A dark shadow crept over his face as he thought of his parent. What he wouldn't have given to have had a father like Emily's.

Shaking off his sudden change of mood, Francis poured Emily's drink for her and set her glass on the table next to her chair.

She looked up, her mind returned to the present. "If you could travel to any place in the world, where would you go?" She asked without warning.

Francis stopped pouring his own drink in mid-stream, so surprised was he by her question. Most women he knew had no conversational skills that extended beyond gossip or fashion. What a refreshing change this was. He turned slowly toward her, obviously giving great thought to the question. "I believe I should like to go to Egypt," he finally told her. "They say that the pyramids are quite magnificent."

You're magnificent.

Good grief! Why would she think such a thing? Thank God she hadn't said it out loud.

"What did you say?" His eyes sparkled with great curiosity.

Lord help me, I did say it out loud.

"Hmmm?" Her voice took on a nonchalant ring to it. "Oh, I agree—they're magnificent."

His frown told her that he wasn't entirely sure he hadn't just been hoodwinked. Eager to take his mind off of it, she charged ahead. "Well, I should like to visit Greece—the source of civilization. To walk through the Acropolis, perhaps up the very same steps that Plato once climbed . . . to feel that unity with some of the greatest people history has ever seen . . . it would thrill me beyond compare."

Stunned by her revelation, Francis was all but able to hide his astonishment. "Most women I know wouldn't care a fig about dusty ruins and ancient philosophers. Why the interest?"

Emily shrugged as she took a sip of her brandy, the warm liquid leaving a simmering heat in its wake as it passed down her throat. "The real question is how you *cannot* be interested." Emily met his eyes with sharp accuracy. There was something new in them that she hadn't seen before. What was it? "Everything that we cherish, including the moral backbone of our society, has come from Greece." Emily shifted slightly in her seat. "Do you mind if I take off my slippers? My feet are unbearably uncomfortable."

"By all means," he told her. He didn't in the least bit mind seeing those dainty little feet of hers again, even though it was with stockings—one day he hoped she might allow him to remove those stockings for her—but that would have to wait a while yet.

"Have you ever read *The Apology of Socrates?*" she now asked.

Francis shook his head. "I've heard of it, of course, but I've never read it. I take it you have?" he inquired, his voice filled with wonderment.

"I have—along with many of the other dialogues.

"Both my parents were avid readers. They had a huge library that I frequented quite regularly." She giggled softly, then smiled to herself. "I must admit I did develop a partial fondness for the dusty smell of books—quite an oddity, I suppose, considering most people can't stand it."

How odd this was, Francis thought. He was having a conversation with Emily Rutherford and he wasn't the least bit bored—quite the contrary, really. How could he have forgotten how interesting she was? These were real topics for conversation—topics that mattered far more than finding out who was courting whom. These topics had some meat that one could sink one's teeth into.

He suddenly wondered if she was enjoying herself as much as he. He certainly hoped so and found himself searching for other topics that she might like to discuss.

"I highly recommend it," she said, still talking of the Socratic dialogue. "The way in which he defends himself would put any contemporary barrister to shame. Then, once sentenced, one cannot but marvel at his reasoning for not fearing to die. It's so simple, yet so obvious—I must admit that I don't think very many of our present-day writers, if any, can hold a candle to it."

Her eyes sparkled with such enthusiasm—such passion—that he could not look away. She was stunning, absolutely stunning as she sat there, so elegant in her evening attire. And she was displaying a mind more complex even than many men of his acquaintance could lay claim to. How he would love to pass each and every day in her company, just listening to her speak.

He was enraptured by each and every part of her. There was no denying that he wanted her with every fiber of his being, so much so that he wondered at his own ability to stop from throwing himself at her feet. So painful was his need to kiss her, to touch her, to become a part of her. It was like a madness that was consuming him, a passion so strong that he was beyond all help and reason.

There was nothing for it. He would make her his—so strong was his resolve that he felt as if his life depended on it. But what if she didn't want him? The frightful thought crossed his mind, lingering as if to mock him.

She had already reacted to some of his gestures—and to his kiss. But it wasn't more than what any other warm-blooded woman would have felt. No—he needed to know if her blood burned as hot for him as his did for her.

Carefully setting his glass down on the table, Francis rose to his feet and stepped toward her. She looked apprehensive as she leaned back in her seat, as if shying away from him. Then, kneeling before her, he took her hand in his. "You are an exceedingly interesting woman," he whispered as he pressed a kiss against her hand.

She did not pull away, though she stiffened at his touch. Her eyes darted toward the door, which still stood ajar. "We must not, Francis—what if someone sees us?"

When he looked up at her, he immediately saw the blush that had risen to her cheeks, the expectant look in her eyes. Oh yes, he had an effect on her all right, but more important than that, she wasn't attempting to flee, no matter her apprehension. "There's no need for you to worry about that, Emily," he whispered. "Genevieve has been asleep for hours, and Parker has retired to his quarters. As for everyone else . . . they're still out. So you see . . . we're quite alone." Holding her hand gently, he turned it over and pressed another kiss against her wrist. A small gasp escaped her lips.

Ripples of heat flooded her body as his hot lips burned against her skin. It was as if her heart had stopped the moment he kissed her hand, then taken flight at an alarming pace as he lifted his eyes to meet hers.

His eyes were hot with desire as they roamed over her, taking in each and every part of her, from her succulent lips to the dip between her shoulder and her collarbone.

When his eyes finally settled on the rise and fall of her breasts, feasting on the way they swelled beneath her bodice, delightful tingles spread like wildfire—from the tips of her toes, darting straight up to her nipples.

He looked like a hungry wolf watching a lamb—so hungry for her that her mouth went instantly dry. She licked her lips, all sense of time and space fleeing from her mind. Never before had she felt so alive, so wanted by another person, so wrought with passion and urgent desire—it thrilled her to the bone as delightful shivers ran up and down her spine.

And there was simply no denying it. She wanted this pleasure, this moment of impulse. But it was more than that. She wanted him; oh God, how she wanted him. At that very moment, nothing else mattered. There was no room in her head for logical thought or common sense or anything else that wasn't Francis.

Keeping his eyes on her, he let go of her hand, placing it gently back in her lap. And that was when he knew that she yearned for him to do so much more to her than just hold her hand. The look of loss and disappointment that filled her eyes strengthened his resolve.

Before she might protest, before she might see reason, he leaned toward her, capturing her head with his hands, and kissed her fiercely on her luscious pink lips. She gasped like a swimmer coming up for air when he moved away, trailing soft kisses along her exquisite jawline and down her lovely neck.

"Dear, sweet Emily," he murmured as his lips brushed gently across her skin. Her breath came in quick bursts that set his soul on fire. So sensitive was she to his touch that when his hand pressed down against her thigh, he felt her body tremble.

"So beautiful," he whispered as he placed small butterfly kisses on the mounds of her breasts, paying tribute to each of them with great reverence.

He waited for her to push him away—certain that she would shy away from his obvious intentions. But instead he felt her fingers raking through his hair and pressing him toward her. Dear God in heaven—how was he to control himself when her passion so ardently matched his own?

As a gentleman, he had no desire to ruin her, but as a man, he didn't give a toss about the consequences. She was like a sweet piece of fruit, just ready for the picking. A strong sense of responsibility loomed in the distance. He determined to do the right thing, but not before allowing himself one final delicacy.

Moving his hands up along her sides, he ran his thumbs heavily against her breasts, forcing them upward, her ripe nipples popping out from beneath her bodice. His eyes blazed as they gorged on the crimson buds. Then, all other thoughts swept aside, he buried his face against her.

She moaned with pleasure as he drew her into his mouth, sucking lightly, his tongue soft and gentle against her skin.

Pulling away with unparalleled willpower, he looked up at her. Her eyes were dizzy with longing—a longing he recognized as that carnal need to sate an unrelenting desire to mate.

He wanted nothing more than to satisfy both of their cravings, but an inner voice called for him to stop—though not without allowing himself one last kiss.

As he brushed his lips against her, she wrapped her arms tightly about his neck, drawing him closer. She wished he would have lingered longer at her breasts. Never before had she felt such eager yearning for something that she did not fully comprehend. An ache had settled between her thighs and she knew that only Francis had the means by which to placate it.

Yet as he nibbled on her lips and ran his tongue across them, all focus went to her mouth. He teased her lips apart, then pushed his tongue inside to tangle with hers. There was a potent flavor of brandy on both their breaths as they each explored the inside of the other's mouth with fervent pleasure.

Francis suddenly paused, pulled back, and glanced toward the half-closed door.

"I thought I heard something," he said with some degree of frustration.

She stilled and held her breath to listen. A peel of laughter suddenly reached them, coming seemingly from the front hall. "Oh God," she exclaimed. "It must be Beatrice and Claire returned home."

With agile dexterity, Francis leapt away from her, rose to his full height, and adjusted his waistcoat. He looked rather stiff and awkward as he tried to find a place for his hands. He eventually clasped them behind his back, standing at attention, before realizing that he was not the only one doing so. Without further ado, he promptly sat down on the chair closest to him, and quickly crossed his legs. Then, casting a glimpse in Emily's direction, his eyes widened as he saw that her nipples were still protruding from behind her gown. Voices grew louder as they approached. He spoke her name, but she failed to hear him—too flustered, no doubt, to notice. Exasperated, he stomped his foot loudly on the floor. Her eyes shot toward him. With a quick nod of his head, coupled with an elaborate wave of his hand, he made her aware of her indecent exposure.

She had only just managed to make herself presentable and placed her glass of brandy to her lips in an attempt to conceal all evidence of their kiss, when Beatrice pushed through the door, her elegant gown swooshing about her ankles as she entered the study with a marvelous smile. "We saw that the light was on so we thought we might join you. Are you all right, though? We heard a loud thud just a moment ago."

Francis cleared his throat in hopes of hiding his smile. He wasn't sure that he'd be able to help Emily, though. Her eyes were already creased with signs of laughter as she peaked out from behind the brim of her glass. "Yes, yes, we're quite all right. I merely dropped a book—clumsy of me, really—please, do join us."

"What was it?" Claire asked as she made her way past Beatrice. Jonathan followed her inside and made his way straight to the side table.

"Hmmm? What was what?" Francis asked, distracted by Jonathan, who was making a racket out of inspecting all the bottles.

"The book, of course," Claire insisted. "The one you say you dropped."

"Oh that—it was *The Apology of Socrates,* I believe." A muffled sound was heard coming from Emily's direction as she did her best to choke back the laughter that threatened to spill out of her.

"I love that book," Beatrice commented. She then frowned. "It's not very big, though—hardly big enough to make such a loud sound. Are you sure that it was indeed *The Apology of Socrates* that you dropped?"

Why in God's name he was having this harebrained conversation was beyond him. Nevertheless, it seemed as if he was unlikely to escape from it, so he straightened his spine and ploughed on. "Well, it was actually a compilation of all the Socratic dialogues—including the apology—thus making it a large enough book to produce the sound you heard." Taking a brief breath of air, Francis continued like a runaway coach—not allowing anyone the opportunity to interrupt. "So, how was your evening? Splendid, I take it, judging from your smiles. These affairs can be quite taxing; in fact, I generally find myself exhausted by the time the season draws to an end. But it doesn't seem to have taken a toll on either of you yet. You look as if you've just had the time of your life."

The sisters immediately launched into a detailed description, while Francis let out a slow sigh of relief and touched his hand to his forehead. The topic had been changed. He looked over at Emily, sending her an admonishing scowl for her lack of self-restraint. She replied with a merciless smile that had his insides tied up in knots within a heartbeat.

She was truly remarkable, and she had let him kiss her. It was as if part of his heart had softened and opened, allowing her in. But aside from the kiss, he had thoroughly enjoyed their conversation. Not only had she told him something that he did not already know, but she had also given him something to think about. He wondered what else he might learn from her, given the time and assuming that she would be happy to talk to him again. With an impish smile, he wagered that she would.

"Claire danced two more sets after you left." She nodded her head in Jonathan's direction. "Mr. Rosedale was kind enough to take pity on me and so I also enjoyed a waltz."

"Really, Miss Rutherford, if anyone took pity on anyone, then you were surely the one taking pity on me. I was so nervous when I asked you, for I was sure that you would say no."

Emily wondered, was that a blush in Beatrice's cheeks? It certainly looked like it. She had never in her life known Beatrice to color with embarrassment or self-awareness—or for any other reason, for that matter. She would be sure to ask her about it later.

"Would anyone care for a drink?" Jonathan asked as he raised a carafe in the air to highlight his question.

"A sherry for me, if you don't mind," Beatrice told him.

"And for me too," Claire added, then turned sharply toward Emily. "So, what have the two of you been up to all this time?"

Brandy sprayed from Emily's mouth as she coughed and sputtered.

"Oh dear, Emily," Beatrice exclaimed, rushing to her sister's side and relieving her of her glass before she did any more damage to the silk carpet. "Are you all right?"

"I'm so sorry," Emily muttered, wiping her mouth and chin with the handkerchief Claire had produced for her. "Please forgive me. I'm not usually this unladylike—how embarrassing."

"Don't concern yourself too much about it, Emily," Francis told her in a soft voice. "We're all friends here." He had also had to fight for control at Claire's words. Emily had thankfully managed to grab everyone's attention so that none of them saw the cheeky gleam in his eyes or the smile that played upon his lips. "Though perhaps Veronica was right in suggesting that you see a doctor—it seems you have rather an alarming tendency to choke." He sent her a wink, to which she responded with a glower.

"Well, if you will please excuse me—I wish to retire for the evening. It's quite late and all this excitement has thoroughly worn me out," Emily said as she got up from her chair.

"I'm sorry to hear it. I hope you shall be better rested next time, so that you may fully enjoy all that such an evening has to offer," Francis told her with a devilish smile. The implication could not have been clearer. Yet had she missed it, the roaring fire in his eyes told her that he was not referring to exerting oneself on the dance floor, or participating in amicable conversation.

Heat rose to her face as she flushed with color. She could do little more than send him a look of annoyance as she ignored the warmth that tugged at her belly or her knees that were suddenly weak like pudding. Damn the man and his roguish looks, his Corinthian physique, and his masculine scent . . . she would have none of it—at least not for now. "Good night, then," she said as she gathered strength and fled the room.

Breathless, she leaned against the closed door in her bedroom, her palms resting against the smooth, cool surface. *At least not for now* . . . the thought reverberated in her head. He had awoken something in her—a dormant passion she'd never thought she possessed.

As much as she had wanted to remove all thoughts of Francis from her mind, all possibility for that had been dashed away that evening. Each and every corner of her mind was filled with him, relentlessly tormenting and teasing her.

He was like an oasis in a desert where she was parched from thirst. Nothing would satisfy her until she allowed herself to partake in all he had to offer.

All he had to offer.

She trembled slightly, a rush of heat filling her as her thoughts strayed to . . . she gasped in horror. Good Lord!

He must think me a complete Cyprian to have carried on with him the way I did.

She felt mortified, and quickly determined not to let herself get so easily carried away the next time she happened to be alone with him. For some peculiar, unimaginable reason,

Francis's opinion of her had suddenly become vitally important. Something had changed in both of them, she felt, and she didn't want to ruin it by acting like a demimondaine. Besides, if she allowed him to kiss her like that again, things were sure to get out of hand. She knew she'd wanted it in the heat of the moment, but now that the moment was gone, she was able to think more rationally.

If she allowed Francis to take her innocence, she feared that she might lose her head over him, and that was something that she wasn't prepared to do. She'd been hurt enough by Adrian already—falling for Francis (as unlikely as it seemed) would be no better. He was not the kind of man who might return her affection, particularly since he wasn't very affectionate in any way, whatsoever. He was moody, brooding, and stern, though she did acknowledge that he had smiled more in the past couple of weeks than she'd seen him do in the past ten years. It was no matter—her mind was made up—she would not allow herself to fall in love with him.

Chapter Fourteen

Emily woke feeling lighthearted and giddy as she replayed her kiss with Francis in her mind. Though she had come to terms with the fact that it would never be more than just a kiss, she still felt a strange, newfound sense of connection with him. She wondered if he felt the same way.

Getting up, she threw on her dressing gown and seated herself in front of her vanity table to carry out her morning routine. A maid assisted her with her hair, after which Emily attended to her more personal needs. She then dressed in a light pink muslin dress with small embroidered roses at the hem, finishing with a spray of rosewater across her chest.

It surprised her how quiet the house was. There were, after all, five people living there in total—not taking the staff into consideration. When she entered the dining room, however, she found that nobody else was there, and that the plates on the table were untouched. She was—not entirely to her surprise—apparently the first one to have risen.

It was quite pleasant in a way, she realized. She would finally be able to sit and read the paper in peace as she savored her breakfast. Bacon and eggs had always been her favorite. She'd been most fortunate to indulge in them throughout her stay in Francis's home. Once the cook had found out how much she loved them, she'd insisted that Emily have them every day.

Pouring herself a cup of tea, she rang for Parker, who arrived within minutes, carrying her food with him on a tray "Good morning, Miss Emily," he told her with a strained smile.

"Good morning, Parker," she replied. "I'm sorry to point this out to you, but it seems that there's a place missing." The butler regarded her blandly. She would clearly have to spell it out for him. "We are five and there are only four places set."

"You're quite right, Miss Emily—so there are."

There was a long, pregnant silence as he stood watching her. "Well, why on earth is that, if I may ask?" Emily's voice was filling with aggravation at the butler's all-too-butlery persona. She wanted answers.

"His lordship has gone out of town. He will not be dining at this table for the next few days. That is why there are only four places set instead of five."

Emily could scarcely believe it. Francis had left, just like that, without a single word of goodbye to her.

Lifting her chin in hopes of hiding the tremendous disappointment that welled inside her, she thanked Parker for the piece of information, then turned her attention toward her plate. There she sat—long after Parker had left the room—staring at her untouched food, her mind a whirlwind of thoughts and questions.

Why did she suddenly feel so damned wretched? She told

herself that she didn't even like the man. Then why did she care? She knew the answer to that one: she cared because she was lying to herself in thinking she did not like him. The truth was that she had come to like him very much . . . too much.

She felt that somehow they had bridged the gap that had lain between them for so many years, and had finally begun to get along. But it was so much more than that. It was as if she'd glimpsed the real Francis—the Francis that had hidden himself away beneath layers of anger, sorrow, and pain. She had found that his eyes could still sparkle and that his lips could still smile, and she realized then—with a pang of guilt—why she had despised him for so long.

When they were children she had loved that smile—the way one corner would edge upward into a cheeky smirk before spreading into a wholesome grin. They had been two of a kind back then—boisterous, teasing, and full of joy for everything that life had to offer. Adrian and Kate had both been more reserved somehow, often embarrassed by Emily's sudden bursts of laughter or Francis's playful mockery of everyone and everything.

A sudden smile pulled at her lips as she recalled how scarlet both Kate and Adrian had turned when Adrian's cook had prepared a caramel pudding for them. The plates had arrived, each with a plump mound of a pudding that had been thoughtfully adorned with a single cherry on the top. "Well, I don't think I need to tell you all what that looks like," Francis had exclaimed with marked amusement as Kate's hand automatically flew to her breast. "I'm sure you can see it for yourselves!"

The truth was, he had been the only one who had truly understood her, and now he had abandoned her, leaving her alone with a sense of humor that no one else would ever understand or appreciate as well as he had—not even Adrian.

And then another pang hit her. Had she thrown herself into love of Adrian in order to battle her own grief at the way in which Francis had suddenly changed? It was absurd. But what if it was the truth? She'd never understood what had caused such a drastic change in his personality. It wasn't for lack of asking, but he'd grown gruffer each time she'd brought it up, slowly withdrawing from the world around him until he was just a shadow of the boy she'd known and loved.

Loved.

Emily's heart leapt at the very idea of it. She'd hated him—despised and loathed him—for shutting her out and turning her away. And over the years she'd forgotten the source of her hate until all she'd known was how little she liked his company, his mere presence, and very existence. And it was all because she'd felt betrayed—because she had loved him.

Emily gasped in horror at the self-admission. What the devil was she to do now? This wasn't at all what she had planned for.

There was only one thing for it—Francis must never know how she felt about him. He was not one who would ever offer her his heart and soul—he was too gripped by whatever darkness it was that held him. Though he had kissed her—and quite passionately at that—she knew she ought to take it for what it was: a momentary lapse in his better judgment. She would not allow herself to think otherwise. That sort of stupidity had hurt her once before. In a way, she thanked Adrian. He had shown her that a kiss need not, by any means, lead to the altar.

A sudden bubble of laughter spread to her limbs as she pictured a sour-looking Francis speaking his marriage vows as he silently regretted ever having kissed her. She had best keep her thoughts and feelings to herself, for she had no intention of trying to leg-shackle a man who until recently seemed to detest the very sight of her.

"Have you been up long?" Beatrice asked as she entered the dining room, her hair neatly wrapped in a tight bun at the nape of her neck. She wore a plain white linen dress, accented by a yellow ribbon that glowed about her waist.

"I suppose so," Emily replied as she looked at the cold food upon her plate. "I suppose I was brooding."

Beatrice arched a brow as she took a seat across from Emily. "About anything in particular?"

"Not really." She waved a dismissive hand. "It's not important." Then, taking a sip of her tepid tea, "Did you sleep well?"

"Blissfully so." Her sister smiled, a dreamy look still heavy in her eyes.

"And Claire? I trust she's still fast asleep?"

"Oh yes," Beatrice chuckled. "Heaven knows that girl is a renowned sleepyhead. I'm sure she'll be down soon though."

"Good morning, ladies," Jonathan said as he made his appearance.

"Oh, good morning, Mr. Rosedale," Emily smiled as her eyes strayed to her sister's flushed cheeks. Beatrice merely nodded an embarrassed greeting from behind her teacup while Emily did the best she could to contain her curiosity.

"It appears that Francis has gone out of town," Jonathan told them. "He left a note for me—doesn't say when he'll be back."

So it *had* been a spur-of-the-moment idea, Emily thought. She couldn't help but wonder if it had anything to do with her, but she soon determined that was ridiculous and pushed the thought aside. "Did he say where he went or why?" she found herself asking.

"He went home," Jonathan told her. "To Dunhurst Park. He didn't say why."

"Oh," Emily whispered, so softly that nobody heard her. "Do you know when we might expect him?"

"I do not, though I imagine that he shall return as soon as possible. He would not leave his guests alone for an extended period of time, I assure you."

As Jonathan left them again in order to return to his work, Beatrice lowered her teacup with a shaky hand.

"Why, Bea, I do believe that you are smitten," Emily told her.

"I've no idea what you're talking about," Beatrice muttered. "I simply like the man—that is all. He's . . . nice."

"The whole world can see that that is clearly not all," Emily expressed. "I can't imagine anything ever being as red as your face was when he said good morning."

"Dash it all—was I that obvious?"

Emily laid her hand on top of her sister's and gave it a reassuring squeeze. "Not to worry. I don't believe he noticed—he seemed rather caught up in Francis's sudden departure."

"A bit odd, that . . ." Beatrice mused. "I wonder what the hurry was."

"Me too," Emily told her.

I do hope that it wasn't because of me.

Chapter Fifteen

"Where is she?" Francis's voice was filled with rage as he flew up the steps of his home at Dunhurst Park. He had ridden without pause after receiving the urgent message, finally arriving three hours later.

"In the drawing room, sir," the housekeeper told him in a fluster as she rushed to keep up with him. "She's been shouting all manner of abuse at the servants. A number of them won't have it any more—they've threatened to leave—and I . . . well, I'm inclined to follow their lead, though I do beg your pardon, sir."

"For the love of God, Mrs. Reynolds, how long has she been here?"

"Since yesterday afternoon, sir—she slept in the library," Mrs. Reynolds told him, looking thoroughly perplexed. "We tried sending her away, but she wouldn't have it—insisted we contact you immediately, or else. I didn't know what else to do, what with Parker being away and all."

"One day and half of my staff is already threatening to resign? I never took her for anything less than a cankerous shrew, but . . ." His words trailed off. "She must have been trouble, indeed, if even you have become eager to leave."

"I do apologize, sir. I surely hope it will not come to that."

"As do I, Mrs. Reynolds, as do I," Francis bit out as he strode down the hall and into the drawing room.

"What do you want?" Francis's voice sliced through the air as he regarded the woman who sat so elegantly on the silk brocade chaise. Her auburn hair was knotted at the nape of her neck, while fashionable ringlets framed a face that was, indeed, quite pretty. She wore a white dress with wildflowers embroidered along the hem and a hat on her head, adorned with a green satin ribbon.

Francis's eyes were cold as ice, his mouth drawn tight over gritting teeth. Oh, how he longed to be rid of her.

If she detected his wrath, she pretended not to notice as she smiled at him sweetly. "Ah, Francis—at last. I have so been looking forward to seeing you again. Please, won't you come and join me?"

He walked toward her, the hatred fierce in his dark eyes. Yet she held his gaze, unflinching—that pleasant smile still pasted on her lips—such an image of kindness. But to him she represented anything but. In his eyes, she stood for everything that he had lost. This creature that sat before him was by no means a lady. On the contrary, she was a cold and calculating bitch, and he must not allow himself to be ensnared by her pretenses.

"How have you been, Francis?" she asked, her eyes gleaming with curiosity.

"I don't believe you came here to ask about my well-being,

Charlotte," Francis sneered. "In fact, I very much doubt that you give a damn."

Charlotte's eyes narrowed slightly at the comment. She puckered her lips, then rose to her feet in a stately fashion. "You're quite right, my dear." Her voice was silky soft as it drifted through the air. Francis flinched slightly at the endearment, his eyes darting instinctively across the room to where they settled on a painting on the wall. He loved that painting, and he looked at it now, imploring it to help him get through this horrid affair.

A beautiful woman stared down at him, her big round eyes filled with happiness. Her hair was dark blonde, falling in loose tresses about her heart-shaped face, and her eyes were the brightest blue. Elisabeth Riley—the beloved woman who had raised him—looked truly enchanting in her portrait.

He had never seen her cry—not once—though she certainly would have had ample reason to. But no, she had smiled and laughed and played with him throughout his childhood. She had raised him well, implementing in him a joy for all the little wonders of the world around him . . . the sound of leaves rustling in the treetops, the way a heartbeat could convey emotion. It tore at his heart and his soul to know how unhappy she must have been beneath that façade.

"She was so weak in character, you know." Charlotte's words slashed at his heart.

He whipped his head around in her direction. "Watch your mouth, Charlotte," he warned.

"Or what?" she asked as she tilted her head. "Come, Francis. We both know you can't touch me. I have the upper hand—remember?" Her voice was taunting to his ears as she leered at him from behind those fluttering lashes of hers. "I'll never forget how she begged for her husband to come to her at night instead of to me . . . the look of despair in her eyes when she saw that I was far more tempting. Pathetic, really!"

"This is still my house, Charlotte, and as such, I will ask you as nicely as I can to refrain from mentioning my mother." His voice was so sharp it would have felled an army, yet Charlotte remained seemingly unperturbed. Her words, however, had set his blood boiling. His hatred for her ran deep. In time he would find something . . . some way in which to make her pay.

She gave a small, bubbling laugh as she clasped her hands in front of her in rapt amusement. Then she shook her head. "Oh, Francis," she mused. "Dear, dear Francis." She paused for a moment as something within her shifted. He had seen it happen before and knew that her act had finally come to an end. Coldness descended upon her like frost on a winter's morning. The warmth was gone from her eyes, replaced by an icy glare. "*I* am your mother. Don't think for a minute that I intend to let you forget that."

"You are mistaken, madam," he told her coolly as he pointed toward the painting of Elisabeth Riley. "*She* was my mother—my true mother. *You* are nothing but a bit o' muslin, a Cyprian, a demimondaine—I'll let you pick the term you find most fitting, shall I?" His eyes mocked her relentlessly.

"And you, sir, are nothing but a by-blow," she scoffed.

The words were like a slap across his face, though he did not show it.

How he longed to wring the vile woman's neck, but by

some miracle he managed to restrain himself. He would not see himself incarcerated on her account.

He would never understand how his father could have kept her as his mistress for all those years, but then again, she was a fabulous actress who had no doubt captivated him with a wonderful performance.

He strolled over to the window and looked out over the garden. The sunny day with cloudless skies was in stark contrast to his mood. Finding no solace in it, he turned away. "I would be much obliged if you would please get to the point," he told her. "I assume you've come to get more money. Am I correct?"

Her countenance was once again as sweet as a five-year-old girl in pigtails. "Why, Francis, that's just the thing. How clever of you to have figured it out," she drawled.

"How much?"

"Oh . . . shall we say . . . five thousand pounds for now? I think that sounds fair." She nodded affirmatively.

"Fair?" Francis's voice reverberated through the room. His eyes were knit close together in apparent outrage. "It's not fair by any means, Charlotte. It's madness! Do you have any concept of money whatsoever, or did you just throw a random number out there in hopes that I wouldn't question it?"

The insult struck her unawares. She took a sharp breath as heat rushed to her cheeks. Few things rattled her, but clearly his implication that she was intellectually handicapped was definitely one of them. Francis saw her push her uncertainty aside, determined instead to focus on his weakness.

"I believe you have forgotten the letter that I have in my possession, Francis," she declared. All emotion had vanished from her face as her unfeeling eyes met his. "Five thousand pounds, Francis—that is the price that you must pay if you wish for that letter to remain a secret. If you don't pay it," she smirked, "then you shall be as ruined as I, for I will indeed publish it for the entire world to see. Don't doubt for a minute that I won't."

He let out a ragged sigh as he bent his head in contemplation.

There must be a way out of this mess, he thought.

How can I get rid of her? I'll be paying her off for years to come as long as she's holding that damn letter over my head.

But for now, he would have to give her the money, he reckoned, and then he would sit down and try to think of a more permanent solution.

His face was grim as he looked back up at her. "Very well," he nodded. "You may come and collect it tomorrow. Now get out of my house before I have you thrown out."

"That's better, my dear," she purred as she strolled toward him. She clasped his chin in her hand, then, leaned toward his cheek for a farewell kiss.

He pushed her away so vehemently that she twirled about, stumbling over her own feet, yet she managed to retain her balance. "Why, Francis, darling," she said as her hand rose to her cheek in a look of surprise that was fairly overdone, even for her. "Don't tell me you do not love your own mother. I'm not sure if I could bear it."

Her tone was so sarcastic that it gave Francis the urge to beat her over the head with a mallet. "Madam, if it were up to me, I would have you drawn and quartered. Now, I bid you good day." Turning on his heel, fully intent on leaving her presence if she would not leave his, he headed for the door.

"Not to worry, my dear," she called after him. "I will always love you, Francis—even if it is only for your money!"

A wild cackle spread through the air, following him like wildfire as he rushed to get away from her. Seeing her again after so long . . . speaking with her . . . the touch of her hand on his chin . . . Francis shuddered. He felt much the same as he would have, had he just been covered in fecal matter. He needed a bath, immediately, and then he would go for a ride to clear his head.

Chapter Sixteen

Francis spent the next three days in his own company. He had been forced to meet with Charlotte again in order to hand over the five thousand pounds—something he had done with great reluctance. But he didn't want his family name tarnished, either—least of all by a woman like her.

His mood was darker than it had been in a while. It had been just over two years since Charlotte's last visit, and he had grown comfortable, ignoring the fact that she would inevitably call again once her funds ran out.

If only there were a way for him to get his hands on that blasted letter, he thought, as he marched across the moor, his fists clenched tightly by his sides. A gust of wind picked up, blowing the tails of his coat out behind him and catching hold of his hair.

So much anger and pent-up rage coursed through his body, tensing each and every muscle so tautly that he was sure his head would fly off from all the pressure. He needed an outlet, some means by which to release so many years of harbored pain. Looking around, he saw nobody. He had ridden out onto the moor, haphazardly flying across the billowing blanket of lilac heather, with no other thought than to get away from it all. Dunhurst Park would be at least five miles away.

Standing there now beneath billowing clouds, his horse tethered to a tree, he basked in the feeling of the wind, whipping against his face. Then, having filled his lungs to the limit, he expelled the air in a beastly roar that would have sent any lurching demons scampering back to hell.

Just then, the clouds broke above his head in a heavy downpour that had him soaked within a minute. Clasping his hands to his shoulders, he looked upward as the water washed over his face. He felt depleted, yet somehow better than he had in a long time. For the first time since his arrival, he finally felt as if he might be ready to return to London.

Until then, he had known that he would have been terrible company. He feared that he might take his anger out on Emily and her sisters. Indeed he knew that he would, for it had happened before, and it was not something that he wished to see happen again. He was a gentleman, after all, but it was more than that. He finally felt as if he was making progress in bettering Emily's opinion of him. Emily . . . her face shone in his memory like a beacon of hope, and he realized then not only that he missed her, but how much he suddenly needed her.

All those years he had shied away from her, jealous of her happiness, her joy—hating her for it. He had sought refuge with his demons in a cold and lonely place, wallowing in self-pity and anguished contempt for the world that surrounded him.

Yet now it was as if he'd been given fresh sight. He had happened to see her at her worst—suffering and hurt, her heart broken in a thousand little pieces. But then, like a trampled flower, he had watched her regain her strength, rise up again, and fell her opponents with a few words of kindness and regret. He was in awe of her—if any such thing were possible—and indeed, he knew that it was from the way he now felt.

She had proved to be a better person than anyone he had ever known—more righteous, more honest, and braver. And then, after all the years where his constant anger had divided them, she had allowed him to re-enter her realm of happiness again. They had talked, and though he hadn't quite laughed, he had come closer to freeing himself in her presence than he'd ever come before.

Just looking at her enchanted him. The way one could see the laughter in her eyes before it ever reached her lips. And then, when she finally did laugh, the uninhibited delight that she embodied was so infectious that none in her presence could help from laughing, either—regardless of whether or not they knew the original cause behind it.

More than that was his discovery of how insightful and well read she was. He was slightly ashamed at how surprised he had been to find that she had been capable of conversing on topics other than women's fashion plates, or other such nonsense. As children, their focus had been more on play than on serious dialogue, and so it had never been an issue. But he was immeasurably pleased to find how knowledgeable and well educated she'd become. In short, he was exceedingly proud of her, but more than that, he admired her tremendously.

His thoughts went to the kiss they had shared. He shouldn't have done it—he knew it had been wrong—but he couldn't help himself. And then, it had felt so right, so perfect, and she had kissed him back. His heart soared at the thought of it. Emily Rutherford had not pushed him away by any means. She had clung to him, run her fingers through his hair, and shared in the passion of the moment as his equal. And when he'd grazed her breasts with his lips, she'd sighed and moaned—a sound so pleasing to his ears that his blood had caught on fire.

There was no turning his back on it. Whatever problems he had with Charlotte, nothing was going to snuff this light that had been rekindled in his soul. He wanted Emily and he would be damned if anyone was going to stand in his way.

It was late afternoon when he returned to Dunhurst Park, leaving puddles in his wake as he darted up the front steps. The rain had subsided, allowing for rays of sunshine to break through from between the clouds. An eager pair of robins emerged from their nest and took flight, darting across the sky.

In his room, Francis quickly removed his wet clothes, managing quite nicely without his valet, whom he had left behind in London. He then pulled on a fresh pair of beige leather breeches, a crisp white linen shirt—the neck of which he wrapped in a cravat—and a pair of light brown hessian boots. Donning a white waistcoat, he threw on his black coat, picked up his kidskin gloves, and headed out the door.

Chapter Seventeen

It was nearly midnight by the time Francis arrived at his home in Berkeley Square. Stepping inside, he was faintly surprised by the dim glow of light coming from his study down the hall. Perhaps Jonathan was working late, or merely enjoying a quiet glass of port before returning home. He wouldn't mind a glass himself, he thought, as he pulled off his gloves, laid them inside his hat, and placed the hat on a side table for Parker to tend to later. Unbuttoning his coat as he went, he made his way toward his study, managing to unfasten the last button as he reached the open doorway.

With a deep breath, he wandered inside, relieved to be back in the warm evening glow of his favorite room in the house. Looking about, he immediately caught his breath as he regarded the slight figure neatly curled up in one of the leather chairs.

There, fast asleep, her lips slightly parted in slumber, lay Emily. She had been right about the chair being too big for her, he thought with a smile as he watched her nestled on the seat, her feet tucked up beneath her. At the foot of the chair lay a book. Francis picked it up to find that he was holding a brand new copy of *Sense and Sensibility* by a certain Jane Austen. Curious of its content, he scanned the back of the dust jacket, only to conclude that it must belong to Emily. Ever the romantic, he thought musingly, as he laid the book carefully on the table next to her chair.

He stood for another moment, watching her rest, his eyes drawn hypnotically toward the rise and fall of her breasts as they strained against her bodice, swelling lusciously at the neckline. His stomach tightened as a wave of heat rushed over him, settling deep within his loins. His urge to reach out and touch her was overwhelming, yet somehow he managed to avert his gaze. One touch would never sate his appetite—of that he was certain. Instead, he proceeded to turn off the lights. Then, with a conscious effort to think of anything other than Emily's warm and pliable body, he stooped to gather her up in his arms.

Fresh quivers ran down his spine as her scent, a soft fragrance of roses in bloom, enveloped him. He cursed beneath his breath at his apparent lack of self-control. What was he thinking, getting this close to her? She shifted slightly in her sleep, her head tilting backward in a pose that beckoned for him to brush his lips against the delicate curve of her neck. With an inward groan, he tightened his hold on her for fear that he might otherwise drop her right there on the stairs. Taking a deep breath, he tried to focus on each of the steps he took as he approached her bedroom.

Fumbling with the door handle as he juggled her in his arms, he finally managed to open the door and enter the room, kicking the door shut with the heel of his foot. He then crossed the room to her bed and gently settled her on top of the golden brocade bedspread.

Turning on the light next to her bed, he straightened himself to look at her, wondering if he ought to cover her with something. His own body came to mind, but he quickly trashed that thought with a mounting degree of annoyance. He was, after all, a gentleman—he tried to remind himself.

Clenching his fists, he turned away from temptation, intent on fleeing the room before he happened to change his mind.

"Francis?" Her voice was music to his hears. Oh how he'd missed it for the past few days. He ought to ignore it, to pretend he hadn't heard her and just leave, but his feet were somehow glued to the floor.

"You fell asleep in the study, Emily," he told her in a soft whisper as he turned his head to look at her. She had turned onto her side, partly risen as she rested on one of her elbows, her eyes still drowsy from slumber. His eyes roamed over her. Her hair was tousled, her bodice askew, yet he'd never thought she looked more beautiful.

As she moved slightly on the bed, he watched in silent disbelief as one of her breasts rose over the neckline, showing off a pink nipple, so ripe that Francis's mouth went dry and his pulse quickened to a deadly pace. "I should go," he told her in a hoarse voice, wishing he had the power to look away from her inviting body. She wasn't even aware of what she'd just displayed for him as she lay there, the hint of a pleasant dream still upon her face.

"I was hoping perhaps we could talk," she told him as she got up and came toward him.

"Emily," he murmured as he put up his hands to stop her from coming any closer. "You don't know what you're asking."

She paused in mid-stride, a pensive look upon her face as she licked her lips with the tip of her tongue. Francis felt the all-too-familiar throbbing as his manhood strained against the seam of his breaches. Never in his life had he been so aroused from just looking at a woman. . . . Hell, she wasn't even naked!

"Francis? Are you all right?" she asked. "You look unwell or as if you're somehow in pain." She looked genuinely troubled. "Is there anything that I can do for you?"

Francis groaned. Her questions were so innocent. If only she knew that she was the cause of his torment. *Yes*, he thought, *there is something you can do for me—throw yourself on your back and let me explore you; let me ravish you with kisses and taste every inch of your divine body.*

Instead he just stood there, not knowing what to say or what to do. Well, that wasn't entirely true. He *knew* what to do, what he ought to do, but he didn't want to do it. He didn't want to leave, to turn around and walk away. He wanted Emily and he wanted her to tell him that she wanted him too.

"I'm glad you're back," she told him suddenly, without warning.

"Oh?" His voice was curious, his eyes dark and searching.

She thought she detected that same simmering heat that she'd seen the other day in the study when he'd kissed her, but she wasn't sure. She'd been thinking about nothing but that kiss ever since he'd gone away. How she longed to be kissed like that again, somewhere where they would not be so easily interrupted. Somewhere like right here, right now.

She knew that she ought to be ashamed to think such things; it just wasn't proper for a lady to have such impure thoughts. And her thoughts about Francis were *very* impure. What made it feel less indecent, however, was that she was becoming increasingly certain that he'd been having the same impure thoughts about her—and nothing excited her more.

But how would she broach such a delicate subject? Perhaps if she didn't look at him, talking about it would be easier. She turned away from him, her hand resting against the foot of the bed. "I was wondering why you went away," she said.

Silence filled the room and for a moment she thought he might not tell her, but then he did. "There was a personal matter that I needed to attend to. It's a rather delicate situation, really. I'd prefer it if we didn't discuss it right now—perhaps tomorrow, or the day after that. In fact, there's a lot that I need to tell you, Emily. I've kept it all inside for years, and I believe it's time that I spoke to somebody about it. And truth be told, there's nobody I'd rather share it with than you."

On his ride back to town, he had realized that the only person to whom he wished to divulge his secrets was Emily. Emily, the one person who had always urged him to tell her what was on his mind—at least in the beginning, before she grew tired of being constantly rebuffed. But there was a time and a place for everything, and this was most definitely not the time or the place for him to bare his heart to her.

"So it had nothing to do with the kiss?" Her voice was so low that he had to strain to hear her.

"Of course not," he heard himself saying. "Why would you think that?"

"Why indeed?" she sighed, the hint of mockery barely present in her voice. "Because you left the very next morning, without any explanation or even a goodbye. What was I to think?"

"Like I said, I left because there was a personal matter that needed my attention. It had nothing to do with you, or the kiss."

"Did you like it then?" She gasped as soon as the question left her lips, horrified at her own candor.

"If you're referring to the kiss, then yes, I did, Emily. I liked the kiss a great deal." He paused, watching her with great intensity. He could almost feel the heat that was flushing her face, for it was surely the same as what filled his own.

And then she turned to face him and he looked into her eyes, the hunger there mirroring his own. "Would you like to kiss me again?" she murmured.

God, yes! With those words, he knew that all was lost. He simply did not have the will power to say no. Not when she was standing right there in front of him—so tempting, so seductive—asking him to kiss her.

He closed the distance between them in three paces. "Nothing would give me greater pleasure," he told her as he wrapped his arms around her and lowered his lips to hers.

His lips were soft and tender as they pressed against her. Tightening his grip about her waist, he pulled her closer as he nibbled on her lower lip, reveling in the moistness of it. A small sigh escaped her lips as he glided his tongue across them. She trembled, like a leaf rustling in the wind, as sparks ignited from her head down to her toes.

Her need was as desperate as his own, he realized with

great satisfaction as he slipped his tongue inside the warmth of her mouth. And as their tongues tangled rapturously together, his hand came up to rest upon her breast. With skillful mastery, he kneaded that soft, round, pliable mound, then pushed it up to free it from the restraints of her bodice.

Breaking the kiss, he stepped back to look at her, his eyes heavy with a burning desire that excited Emily to her very core. Seeing the effect she had on him fueled her own hunger. She wanted to partake of everything he had to offer her, unleash the passion that she felt building inside her, and let him take her to places she'd never even dreamed existed.

Raising his other hand, he tugged at her dress to watch the other breast emerge. A look of devilish content settled upon his face. His lips curled upward in a wayward smile. "So beautiful," he murmured in a husky undertone as he let his fingers sweep across them. With expert ease, he teased her nipples, watching in reverence as they responded to his touch, perking into tight crimson buds.

Seizing her head with his hands, he drew her hastily toward him, his kiss transformed to one of fierce desire as he plunged his tongue inside her.

Matching his ardor, her arms flew about his neck, clutching onto him as though her life depended on it. Stars shone behind her closed eyelids while her body exploded in bursts of sensuality. Never in her life had she thought she'd feel so revered—it was nothing short of sensational.

Breaking the kiss once more, Francis trailed kisses down her neck—so soft, so sweet. "Beautiful—sweet—Emily," he murmured between kisses.

She ran her hands through his thick dark hair as he lowered his head to her right breast, then gasped as he licked her nipple with the tip of his tongue, coaxing it to grow harder still. His own manhood grew taut as it strained against his breeches, desperate to find comfort within the warmth of her body.

A small voice whispered to him from somewhere far, far away. He wanted nothing more than to ignore it, to tell himself that it was insignificant—yet he could not, would not. He stepped away, his breathing coming hard and ragged as he looked at her like a man who'd crossed the desert and finally found the water he'd been so desperately seeking. She looked equally affected, her eyes beseeching him to continue.

"Emily," he sighed. "If I don't stop now, I'm not sure I'll be able to."

He saw the immediate look of disappointment upon her face. She wasn't just a dillydally, however. She was his friend, first and foremost, and as such he had to do right by her. "You . . . you don't want me after all?" she asked carefully. She suddenly appeared to be on the verge of tears.

"Emily," he said, his voice full of incredulity. "How can you possibly think that I don't want you after what we just shared?" Her face was flushed as she focused on the pattern of the carpet. "Look at me," he beckoned. "Just look at me to see how much I truly want you."

She raised her eyes to meet his. Giving her a quick downward glance, she followed his line of sight only to find herself staring at the massive bulge at his crotch. "Oh my . . ." she gasped, her face instantly reddening.

"Indeed," he grinned, though his eyes were deadly serious. "Emily, I cannot do this to you, not like this. It would be terribly wrong of me to claim your innocence. As difficult as it is for me to do, I must not take what rightfully belongs to the man you will one day marry. You would be ruined, Emily, and your chances for a perfect match along with it. Do you understand?" He did not tell her that he intended to be the man she married—nevertheless, it was suddenly very important to him that he did everything according to the book. He sensed that, even though she might not realize it now, it would be important to her that she wasn't deflowered before speaking her vows.

She nodded, then looked at him with sheer determination. "I know we've had our differences, Francis, though I like to think that we're beginning to move past them. Whatever happens, I want you to know that nobody has ever had this effect on me, not even Adrian. With you, it's as if my soul is on fire." She paused for a moment, an inward struggle evident in her features, as if she knew not whether she ought to continue. "Though I lack the experience, I'm not as naïve as you might think when it comes to the art of lovemaking."

Shocked, yet somehow intrigued by this new piece of evidence, Francis urged for her to continue. "You know how I love to read—I always have. There was a book in my father's study that I happened to stumble across when I was sixteen. I'd been looking for something with which to pass the time; a novel or some poetry. But instead I picked this book from the shelf. When I opened it and saw what it contained, I immediately hurried it off to my room where I hid it until later that evening.

"The book contained illustrations of a sexual nature—explicit positions that left nothing to the imagination."

Francis was stunned. Never in a million years would he have imagined that Emily's father would have had such a book, nor that Emily would have been the sort to secretly read it late at night in the sanctity of her bedroom. The thought was a pure aphrodisiac.

"So, Francis . . . I know that there are ways to . . . to . . ." she trailed off, her embarrassment too great for her to continue.

"To what?" he asked her gently.

She was silent for what seemed like forever. He was about to ask her again, when she turned away. "Nothing," she murmured, her confidence nowhere to be found.

"Bloody hell, Emily!" He reached out, grasped her wrist, and spun her toward him. "For heaven's sake, lose your inhibitions and tell me what it is that's on your mind. I'm not about to judge you. Come on—out with it!"

Her eyes came to rest upon his in a deadpan gaze. She saw the spark of passion in his and it fueled her own. She sagged against him, her arms once again about his neck. "Touch me," she told him simply, her breath warm against his neck.

He knew immediately what she meant.

"Say no more," he replied in a strained voice that conveyed with unwavering certainty his craving for her. In one swift movement, he picked her up in his arms and carried her over to a chair, then set her down carefully on her feet. "Don't move."

She watched in silence as he unbuttoned and removed his waistcoat, flinging it carelessly on the bed. He then unwrapped his cravat, pulled his shirt from beneath the waistline of his breeches and seated himself on the chair. "Come," he told her as he reached out his hand and guided her toward him, pulling her in so that she stood between his legs.

Inhaling her scent, he slowly reached down—beneath the hems of her dress, her petticoat, and her chemise—to touch her calf. She stiffened, and drew a sharp breath. He looked up to find her eyes upon him, her face frozen with sudden alarm. "Are you sure that this is something that you want?" he asked with a hint of concern.

She nodded, her eyes never leaving him, not for a second. "All right then," he smiled. "Just don't forget to breathe, and try to relax. I intend for you to enjoy this, Emily."

At the sound of her sigh, his lips broke into a greedy smile. He allowed his fingers to make their gradual journey upward, swirling in gentle motions around the backs of her knees and over her thighs—so whispery soft it sent tingles cascading over her, skimming the surface of her skin. She gripped his shoulders as his hands clasped her buttocks, nudging her closer toward him.

"Turn around," he said, and as she did, a glimpse of alabaster skin that almost made him spill himself like an untrained youth. He cursed beneath his breath at the injustice of having the moral standing and sense of responsibility that he did. "Now help me pull up your skirts, as high as you can, then sit down on the seat between my legs."

Without questioning him once, she did as he asked, her bare bottom coming to rest against the smooth silk upholstery. He ran his hands down her thighs and back up again, then pressed faint kisses against the back of her neck, relishing the way she purred at his touch. Then, taking one leg at a time, he picked them up and settled them on either side of his own, spreading her wide. With a slight groan that heated his blood past the level of boiling, she relaxed against him.

Brushing his fingertips softly over her inner thighs in an ever-upward motion, he placed a line of kisses upon her shoulder. When he reached the outermost part of her most sacred place, he pressed his lips close to her ear. "Tell me, Emily," he whispered, so faint she could barely hear him. "Tell me again. What is it you want me to do for you?"

"Oh God, Francis . . . Francis, please . . . please touch me," she gasped.

Without further delay, he swiftly moved one hand to her still-exposed breasts, caressing each of them in turn. With his other hand, he gently brushed against her womanhood, sending ripples of ecstasy coursing through her veins. With unparalleled care, he parted those velvety soft layers that surrounded her, seeking the bud that would take her to the highest heights of exquisite pleasure.

He ran his fingers over her so gently that he barely touched her, yet the sensations it evoked within her were electrifying. With soft, circular motions, he rubbed his fingers lightly against her, then slid one finger inside her to feel her moist warmth surround him. She groaned from somewhere deep inside as she pressed herself forward against his hand, quietly begging him for something she did not yet understand. "Yes, sweet Emily, let me show you," he murmured in her ear.

Pinching her left nipple between his fingers, he withdrew his other hand, added a finger, and plunged inside her again. She whimpered with pure pleasure. "That's it, Emily, let me show you the stars." His voice was low and guttural, his breath hot against her neck. Feathering his fingers inside her, he pressed his thumb against her bud and felt her insides contract as she shuddered against him, crying out his name.

Emily soared through space while stars burst around her, showering her with fervent pleasure. Nothing had ever felt so good or so right. Her only regret, as she drifted back to earth, was that he had not been allowed the same release.

"Thank you," she sighed, resting against him, her body limp with sexual fulfillment. "That was magnificent."

"You were magnificent," he told her as he burrowed his head against the nape of her neck.

"Should I . . ." she began, then paused, unsure of how to broach the topic. "The way you touched me . . . couldn't I do something similar for you?" Her voice quivered with uncertainty and self-awareness. Never in a million years would she have imagined that such a question might leave her lips.

"No," he told her as he eased her back onto her feet and lowered her skirts around her. "It's not that I don't want you to," he added quickly, before she could feel slighted. "In fact, there's nothing I'd like more, but I don't think I'd be able to leave it at that. Do you understand?" His eyes looked up at her imploringly.

Damn the rules of society. How utterly unfair!

"Yes," she muttered with great frustration.

He stood up, kissing her gently on the lips. Though she did not look at it directly, she was only too painfully aware of the hardness that still protruded from the crotch of his breeches—a reminder of how little she'd been able to do for him.

"I think it's best if you get some rest now, Emily," he told her softly as he brushed his lips against her forehead.

"Yes," she agreed. "We have Lady Cunningham's garden party to attend to tomorrow."

"Oh, is that tomorrow—I had forgotten. Well then you'd better hurry off to bed." Turning, he headed for the door, then paused and looked back at her. "Emily, I want you to know . . . you matter a great deal to me. This wasn't something that will be forgotten in the morning. I hope you know that." Then, turning away from her once more, he opened the door and slipped away, leaving her staring after him.

Chapter Eighteen

Emily opened her parasol, twirling it slightly between her fingers as she scanned the lawn behind Cunningham House. Everybody worth knowing had shown up, and rumor had it that even the prince regent was expected to put in an appearance.

"I don't even recognize anyone," Claire announced from behind Emily's left shoulder. "It's all just one massive blur."

It was true, Emily agreed with a slight twist to her lips. Amongst all the parasols, bonnets, ribbons, and lace that blended together in one single hue of white, it was very difficult indeed to distinguish one person from another. She looked across at Beatrice, whose arm was linked with Jonathan's. What a handsome couple they made.

"Well, here is one lady who I daresay will never conform to the norm," Francis remarked, tearing Emily's thoughts away from her sister. He'd placed himself directly between her and his aunt Genevieve, who'd been determined not to miss this afternoon extravaganza for the world. And, having no desire for anyone to see her with her cane, for fear they might think her old—to be fair, she was only approaching her sixtieth year—she had latched on to Francis's right arm for support.

Turning her head, Emily immediately spotted the lady in question—it was of course Lady Giddington, hurrying toward them in a bright spray of pink, her straw bonnet overflowing with ribbons and roses.

"My, my," Genevieve remarked. "She certainly is a splash of color upon a blank canvas." Then, addressing Veronica more directly, she said, "If only everyone else would be as daring as you, Lady Giddington, then London might not be so dull and dreary."

"I cannot tell you how pleased I am to see you again, my lady. It has been far too long," Veronica beamed before turning her attention on Emily, Beatrice, and Claire. "And look at you—how pretty you are, and each with a different colored ribbon about your waists. My dears, there shan't be a gentleman here who won't take notice."

"Thank you," Beatrice replied, her cheeks turning rosy. "We did try to follow your advice."

"I daresay that Jonathan and I wouldn't mind a compliment, too, if you have one to spare," Francis muttered with a crooked smile. "It does take a fair amount of skill to tie a decent cravat, you know."

Emily rolled her eyes while the rest of the ladies chuckled.

"Why, Francis," Veronica continued with an exaggerated note of apology. "I think it goes without saying that you and Mr. Rosedale are the best dressed men here. You must forgive me—it was very thoughtless of me not to point that out sooner."

"Shall we remain rooted here for the remainder of the afternoon then?" Genevieve asked impatiently. "Or shall we go and mingle with the rest of the guests?"

"I must admit I'd give my left slipper for a glass of lemonade," Claire said, looking about for any sign of a refreshment table. "The heat is absolutely stifling."

"If I may make a suggestion," Jonathan put in, "let us wander down toward the pond over there. The shade from the willow trees will surely offer some measure of relief."

The plan was quickly agreed upon, and when Francis and Jonathan offered to fetch drinks for everyone, none of the ladies protested.

"Well?" Veronica suddenly asked Beatrice as soon as the men were out of earshot.

"Well what?" came Beatrice's guarded reply.

"Oh, come now, Beatrice, the whole world can see you've been struck by Cupid's arrow . . . and if I'm not mistaken, then . . ."

"I cannot imagine what you might be referring to," Beatrice said, looking away in the hopes that Veronica might disappear into thin air.

"I think *I* can," Emily said with a wide smile directed at her sister. "We've all seen the way you look at Mr. Rosedale."

"You're one to talk," Beatrice countered. "For someone who's recently had her heart broken, you certainly seem rather chirpy of late—one cannot help but wonder if it isn't because of Francis."

"Why ever would you say that?" Emily squeaked.

"I can't say . . ." Beatrice said, her resolve withering.

"If I may," they heard Veronica say. "I believe it's because you look at him as though you'd like to devour him—clothes and all."

"I do not!" Emily gasped, appalled by the fact that her thoughts had been written so plainly upon her face.

"Hush, ladies," Genevieve admonished. "We will not discuss such matters in public—especially not when the gentlemen in question are presently coming our way."

But as Emily turned her attention toward Francis and Jonathan, who were doing their best not to spill the tall glasses of lemonade they were carrying, she couldn't help but feel Lady Genevieve's sharp eyes boring into her.

"It may interest you to know," Francis said upon his arrival, his eyes turning to Claire, "that we just ran into Lord Camden. He inquired about you . . . seemed quite eager to discover which flowers are your favorites. I told him I hadn't the foggiest idea. Perhaps you ought to go and tell him yourself."

It was Claire's turn to look as though two giant hearts had just been slapped over her eyes. "Oh, please, can I, Bea? If you come with me it should be all right, don't you think? Oh, please say yes." By the time she finished talking she was bouncing up and down like a spring.

"I think it sounds like the perfect opportunity for us to better our acquaintance with his lordship," Beatrice announced. "I shall be happy to accompany you, Claire." The words were barely out before Beatrice was being dragged away by her sister.

"And I'll be right behind you," Jonathan called out as he marched after them, sending a lopsided grin and wink toward Francis as he left.

"Oh look," Genevieve suddenly said, craning her neck. "There's Lady Barkley—haven't seen her in ages . . . but who on earth is that exquisite creature she's with?"

"Oh . . ." Veronica remarked, noticing the couple that were just now crossing the lawn with one another. "That, my lady, is Mr. Fairchild's bride-to-be: Lady Kate."

Genevieve appeared to study her more closely. "Hmmm . . . upon further inspection I can only say that she's not as pleasing to the eye as I initially thought." Then, appearing to have completely forgotten about Kate, she turned her gaze on Emily. "You, my dear, are far prettier."

"I couldn't agree more," Francis muttered.

Emily wanted nothing more than to fling herself into their arms in appreciation of their loyalty, but the smile upon her lips and the blush in her cheeks was enough to convey her gratitude.

"Do you know—it looks as though they've spotted us. I do believe they're heading this way," Veronica suddenly said.

Francis's eyes grew instantly dark, his lips set in a tight line. He reached out and took Emily by the arm, drawing her closer as if to protect her. As for Emily, the smile she'd just given Genevieve and Francis still graced her lips, allowing her to look absolutely thrilled at the sight of Kate coming toward her. But on the inside, her stomach had begun contorting itself into all sorts of unimaginable shapes. After all, the last time she'd spoken to Kate, she'd said her piece and walked off with her head held high after slamming the proverbial door in her face. Whatever was she to say to her now?

Before she could gather her thoughts, the two women were upon them.

"Good afternoon, Lady Barkley," Francis greeted the baroness, planting a kiss on her outstretched hand. "You're looking as young and lovely as always." He flashed her his most dazzling smile.

"Oh, Lord Dunhurst, really . . ." she snickered in such a girlish fashion that she did indeed appear many years younger.

"Lady Kate." Francis greeted Kate with a formal nod, his smile fading. "I don't believe you've ever met my aunt, Lady Genevieve."

Kate made a polite curtsey.

"Though I do believe you're familiar with Lady Giddington," he added.

"It is indeed a pleasure to see you again, my lady," Kate declared.

"Tell me," Veronica said once they'd all greeted Lady Barkley as well. "How are your wedding preparations coming along? Have you decided on a gown yet?"

Kate cast a nervous look in Emily's direction. "As a matter of fact, I have," she admitted with a great degree of reluctance. "Aunt Harriet found a wonderful dressmaker for me. In fact, she's been incredibly helpful in all aspects of the preparations, though I do consider the gown to be her crowning achievement."

"Well done," Veronica cheered. "I've always subscribed to the notion that a woman should begin preparing for her wedding by picking the right gown. Once that is done, everything else falls naturally into place."

"I couldn't agree more," Lady Barkley said with a nod of approval.

"Yes," Kate added, her voice dropping to a mousy whisper.

"It has served as great inspiration for all the wedding invitations, as well as for the cake."

"Cake, you say?" A spark of interest appeared in Genevieve's eyes. "And what sort of cake will that be, if you don't mind my asking."

"Not at all—as long as you promise not to tell anyone—I don't want to spoil the surprise," Kate replied.

The older woman's eyes sparkled with curiosity. "You can count on us," Genevieve assured her. "Isn't that right?"

Everyone nodded, including Emily and Francis, their curiosity getting the better of them.

Pausing for emphasis, Kate finally told them. "It will be a rich chocolate and cream layer cake with a slight hint of brandy, covered in butter cream frosting and chocolate shavings."

"That sounds utterly delicious—I believe I shall begin saving my appetite already," Lady Barkley told her. She then turned an inquisitive eye on Francis. "And what about you, Lord Dunhurst?" she asked. "When do you think your wedding will be taking place?"

All eyes turned to Francis, who looked as if he'd just seen a pig fly. "My what?" he exclaimed, not even attempting to hide the shock in his voice.

"Your wedding—to Miss Emily, of course," the baroness insisted as she cast a sidelong glance in Emily's direction, as if Francis needed reminding.

There was a thunderous silence while everyone tried their best to come to terms with what the baroness had just said. None of them could quite figure out what to say, never mind find an appropriate expression to match the situation at hand.

It was Emily who, having stilled her fluttering heart, finally spoke up. "Pray tell us, my lady, what has given you the impression that I am betrothed to Lord Dunhurst?"

"Oh, I never said that you were betrothed. However, it has been the talk of the town that Lord Dunhurst is courting you. One naturally assumes that it is with the intention to marry, and I therefore deduced that the two of you must have discussed a date."

"Perhaps they are not yet ready to share the news," Kate said. She sent an apologetic look toward Emily. "Lady Barkley, it does appear as though we've caught them quite by surprise."

"Dear me," the baroness gasped. "I do apologize if I have ruined it for you. I merely thought . . . why, it's clear as day the way in which you look at one another . . . I'm so sorry." She unfolded a fan and began fanning herself profusely.

Emily wondered what on earth was going on. She turned to Francis, hoping that he might give her an answer, but his face had taken on a rather bland expression. Veronica and Genevieve, on the other hand, seemed to think that Emily would be the one to offer them an explanation, for they had both turned toward her, their eyes filled with curiosity.

"I'm terribly sorry, my lady," Emily began with an awkward chuckle that sounded more embarrassed than she'd hoped. "But Lord Dunhurst and I are merely friends . . ." Her words faded the instant she looked at Francis. Noticing the flicker of disappointment in his eyes, she immediately wished she could take them back.

"Well," Lady Barkley was now saying, "you've certainly had us all fooled then. Do you have any idea how much gossip you've managed to stir up?"

"I don't believe we do," Francis replied in a clipped tone. "Though I'm fairly sure that you're about to enlighten us."

"Well . . . as it happens, Lady Kate and I were just discussing this very topic when we happened upon you."

"Is that so?" Emily remarked.

"Well . . . er . . . the thing is . . ." Kate stammered.

"Hush, my dear," Genevieve told her. "I for one would very much like to hear what her ladyship has to say on the matter, and your sputtering is holding her up."

Everyone turned expectantly toward Lady Barkley and waited for her to proceed.

"You see, the *ton* is divided as far as Lady Kate and Mr. Fairchild are concerned," she said, cutting straight to the chase. "There are those who believe they've been secretly engaged since childhood, and that Miss Emily merely acted as a decoy. And then there are those who are of the opinion that Lady Kate stole Mr. Fairchild away from Miss Emily—that she and Mr. Fairchild had a prior attachment to one another which Lady Kate somehow managed to dissolve."

Emily felt as though she might faint. Had her relationship with Kate and Adrian really been dissected and examined by the entire *ton*? It was horrifying.

Kate must have felt much the same way, Emily realized, for she looked quite pale all of a sudden, while her hands appeared to have begun trembling. "Naturally, I couldn't imagine Kate or Mr. Fairchild treating anyone so unkindly, and I have therefore made my own hypothesis."

"Is that so," Francis remarked with a scowl in Kate's direction.

"Oh yes," Lady Barkley chirped, completely ignorant of

the strained atmosphere that had descended upon the small group. "And that's where you come in, Lord Dunhurst. You see, my theory is that Miss Emily refused Mr. Fairchild's offer of marriage, or perhaps gave him reason to believe that he ought *not* propose to her at all. And it is my estimation that Miss Emily did so in order to pursue someone else instead—someone of far greater interest to her . . ."

Emily cringed. She dared not even look at Francis for fear of what she might see. She'd just told everyone that they were merely friends. She'd publicly refuted any romantic attachment with him whatsoever. She'd seen the pained look in his eyes . . . but what else could she have said? That they were lovers? Her hand flew instantly to her mouth to silence the burst of laughter she felt coming.

"And who might that be?" Francis asked, feigning disinterest.

"Why, you, of course, Lord Dunhurst."

There was a slight tug at the corner of his lips. His eyes found Emily's. "And yet, Miss Emily has just told you that we are merely friends."

What does he want from me? Emily wondered, looking away in embarrassment.

"So she has," Lady Barkley admitted with a great deal of disappointment.

"Oh, look, Lady Barkley," Kate then exclaimed as she reached for the older lady's arm. "I see Adrian over there. You were asking about him earlier, remember? Would you not like to say hello to him? I'm sure he'd be very pleased indeed to see you again."

"Oh, absolutely, my dear," Lady Barkley agreed. "Well then, Lord Dunhurst, Miss Emily, Lady Giddington, and

Lady Genevieve—it was a pleasure speaking with you. Do let us know if there are any developments—of a personal nature—if you know what I mean." And before another word could be exchanged, Kate had as good as dragged the baroness off with her in a desperate attempt to save the situation from getting further out of hand.

Emily could do nothing but stare after them.

"I daresay one doesn't get a better performance at the theatre," Genevieve remarked, her eyes drifting from Emily to Francis and back again as if she half expected them to fall into each other's arms.

Francis was the next to speak. "Friends, ay?" His dark eyes hadn't left Emily for a moment.

"Francis . . . I . . . I have no expectations . . ."

Francis's eyes darkened even further. He lowered his head and whispered in her ear for only her to hear. "I thought a kiss was all you needed in order to think yourself attached, and you and I have shared so much more than that."

Heat swept its way over Emily until she felt certain she'd melt away from mortification.

"Dear me, Francis," Veronica gasped. "Whatever did you say to her? She's pinker than my gown!"

Francis sent her a coy smile. "Please excuse us, ladies. Emily and I have a pressing matter to attend to." And then he dragged Emily away, her feet increasing their pace to a near run in an attempt to keep up with his long strides.

"Where are we going?" she asked, dodging a footman.

"To find Beatrice."

"Why?"

"Because I am thoroughly annoyed with you, Emily."

Oh dear. . .

"For years you've thought yourself attached to Adrian—based solely on that measly kiss he once gave you—yet when it comes to me, I am nothing but a friend?" He stopped so abruptly that she almost crashed right into him. Instead, she skidded to a halt, her hand grabbing his arm for support. He turned to look at her. "If Adrian were to come running after you now, begging your forgiveness and asking you to be his wife . . . would you accept?"

She stared back at him, completely caught off guard by the question. "I . . . I . . ."

"Be honest with me, Emily," he told her fiercely.

Was that jealousy in his voice? Her stomach fluttered in response to it. She shook her head. "No," she replied.

Relief flooded his entire face. He leaned toward her. "Good, because in case you were wondering, friends don't generally take the sort of liberties with one another that we took last night."

A gasp was all she could manage as she stood there, her skin tingling all over. The worst of it was that she longed for him to take such liberties again. She wondered if he could tell. A wolfish grin and a pair of smoldering eyes soon answered her question.

"Come," he said, giving her hand a tug as he set off again. "It's about time that I made my intentions known."

Emily almost choked. "And what are your intentions, exactly?"

"To make an honest woman out of you," he said, throwing her a cheeky grin.

An uncontrollable joy erupted inside her the minute Emily permitted Francis to court her. She had reignited a friendship that she'd once given up on, only to discover that he might possibly hold the key to the true love that she'd always been seeking. Francis had always been right there in front of her very eyes, yet circumstances had led them apart. Thank God circumstances had also led them back together again.

She knew he had secrets; nobody could change as drastically as he had without there being a reason for it. She only hoped that he would one day share them with her. If they were to make it as a couple, trusting one another would be vital, and then perhaps she'd be able to help him through whatever it was that had pained him.

She knew that she loved him, and she'd always insisted that she would only marry for love. Of course marrying Francis would be a wonderful match. Even if he didn't love her in return, she knew that they had a solid foundation upon which to build a happy future together. Not only did they share the same childhood memories, but they had also discovered that they enjoyed each other's company immensely. Emily had had some of the most enjoyable conversations she could recall with Francis, and she had the distinct feeling that he shared her opinion. And then of course there was the passion. . . . Nobody else in the world had ever been able to make her feel what she felt when she was with him, and she knew that it was unlikely that anyone else ever would. Her skin prickled and her heart fluttered at the very thought of it.

Chapter Nineteen

At the sound of skirts rustling, Francis lowered his newspaper and looked up to find Emily entering the dining room. "Sleep well?" he asked.

"Oh, exceedingly so," she replied. "In fact, it seems as if it's quite impossible for me not to sleep well while I am here—I don't believe I've experienced such deep slumber before in my life."

Francis grinned slightly at her childlike gratification. "I'm sure you must have, at some point."

"If I did, then it was so long ago that I don't recall." She poured herself a cup of tea, then seated herself on the chair opposite Francis's. "Any sign of Beatrice and Claire?"

"Yes, they went out no more than fifteen minutes ago—something about an urgent matter regarding a bonnet."

"I see," Emily chuckled. "It would have to be something like that in order to get Claire out of bed this early."

"Well, my dear, it is after twelve o'clock . . ."

Biting her bottom lip, Emily looked over at Francis as

she took a sip of her tea, an apologetic look upon her face. "I know. I'm sorry, but we did stay up rather late last night."

"It's quite all right," Francis told her with a grin. "In fact, it's to be expected. Very few people I know get up before noon."

"Really?" Emily asked with relief. "I was beginning to feel as though I was wasting the day away in bed. Back home, in Hardington, I would always be up by seven at the latest."

"Well, you have your own house to run there—that's a full-time job in itself, even with your sisters' help. But here nobody expects you to do anything other than enjoy life, and if I have anything to say about it, you'll never have to do laundry again." He took her hand in his, turning it over to study her fingers. "All those years of hard work are still visible on your hands and fingers. I'm sorry it's been so difficult for you, Emily—for all of you." Bending her fingers into a fist, he brought her hand up against his lips for a kiss.

"In many ways I can't help but think of it as a welcome escape, following the loss of our parents. It was so sudden . . . so terribly difficult to get through. We were forced to busy ourselves with so many chores, many with which we had to acquaint ourselves for the very first time. It gave us something to do—a purpose—and something to take our mind off things. Then gradually it just became routine, so much so that I find myself missing certain aspects of it—though I doubt I'll ever miss scrubbing the floors." She sighed, then raised her eyes to meet his. "Were you sincere when you said that you wanted to court me?"

"I was," he told her earnestly as he held her gaze.

"Why?"

"Because I believe that we would both be extremely happy with such a union. We have so much in common, Emily, and though I realize I'm not the man you'd hoped for, I'm quite confident that I'll be able to make you happy." He paused for a moment, then added, "At the very least, I'll do my damndest."

He hadn't mentioned love, Emily thought, but why would he? She knew that he did not love her, but did that really matter? In time, she was sure that they would come to love one another in some way—even if it wouldn't be the kind of love that Homer had written of in the *Iliad*, the kind of love that people would happily give their lives for.

They had something else, though—something which was in all likelihood just as important, if not more so: they were content with one another, enjoying each other's company immensely. She'd never felt more capable of just being herself around anyone else before, other than her sisters, of course. What was more, she felt as if she could tell Francis anything. He respected her as an equal, something that was of great value to her. And then of course there was the passionate desire that they felt for one another. The air seemed to sizzle when they were in the same room.

She'd been willing to marry Adrian in a heartbeat, knowing full well that he didn't love her as much as she'd loved him—as it turned out, he hadn't loved her at all. And with him, she'd never experienced that spark that she felt each time Francis looked at her or touched her.

Francis had only one thing against him, Emily decided. He had secrets, dark secrets, but somehow he'd still managed to brighten in her presence these past few weeks. He'd opened himself up to her, even though he hadn't shared his secrets with her. She didn't want to press him, and yet, she didn't want there to be anything between them.

"All right, Francis," she told him. "I'll accept your courtship, on one condition."

He raised an eyebrow, waiting for her to continue.

"You know everything there is to know about me, and what you don't know, I will readily tell you if you ask. I refuse to enter into a marriage that's filled with secrets, and I know that you have secrets—unpleasant ones, if I'm not mistaken." He opened his mouth to say something, but she stopped him. She couldn't help but notice an ominous shadow flickering across his eyes, though. She shuddered, but pressed on. "You don't have to tell me now, or tomorrow, or even the day after that. But you must tell me before you ask me to marry you, for I will not say yes unless you tell me what it was that had such a dramatic effect on your life that it's still affecting you to this very day."

He sat in silence for a moment, a struggle raging within him. He longed to tell her—in fact, he'd decided to do just that when he'd returned to London from Dunhurst Park. But now that she was sitting there, asking him point blank about it, he lost his nerve. Later, he thought. *I'll tell her later.* He nodded slowly. "You have every right to know, and I promise you that I will tell you, just not right now. I'm not ready, Emily, and besides, I've no desire to ruin our chance to spend an enjoyable day together. So, since it's just the two of us . . . I thought I might take you to see the Dulwich Gallery. Would you like that?"

"Oh, you know that I would!" Emily exclaimed. "I haven't been to a picture gallery since . . ." she paused. "Well, in more years than I care to remember. Who do they have on display? Do you know?"

"Well, you know I'm not so good at remembering the names of the artists—I just enjoy looking at the paintings—though I do recall seeing a Rembrandt there."

"Really? Oh Francis, when can we go?"

"Why don't you have a little something to eat first—you've done nothing but sip your tea since you walked in here—and then we can be on our way afterward. We'll ask your abigail to come along and chaperone, so that Beatrice doesn't jump to any conclusions. And then perhaps, once we've had our fill of art, we can take some refreshments at Vauxhall Gardens."

Emily beamed with delight, all worries of buried secrets and impending marriage proposals forgotten. "It sounds wonderful, Francis—I can't think of any other way in which I'd rather spend the day."

"I can," he told her with a devilish smile as blatant desire flashed behind his eyes. "Unfortunately we'll have to wait on that a while longer."

Emily was sure that her entire body must be flaming red from blushing. "Unfortunately, indeed," she muttered as she reached for a scone in an attempt to quell the tightening in her belly and the rush of heat that had quickly spread to the place between her thighs.

"Oh Francis, do come and take a look at this. What you're looking at there is far too dismal."

"It matches the drabness of my soul," he told her as he

eyed the painting of the windmills, cast against the darkening skies of an impending storm."

"Are you not in the least bit happy then?" she asked with a twinge of sadness.

"Emily, I haven't been happy for so long . . . but I find that when I'm with you, there's still a spark of hope that happiness may one day be restored to me."

"Then come and look at this," she urged him brightly. "If you keep surrounding yourself with dreariness, you'll never be able to rid yourself of it. You have to try to let a little light into your soul, to battle the darkness." Moving away from the picture of his choice, he strode toward her. "Now, tell me what you see," she told him.

Francis studied the painting before him. "I see a number of ships at different distances from the shore," he told her. "And there's a rowboat, too, with some sailors in it."

"That's right. Now, tell me what feeling it evokes in you."

"I'm not sure, I . . ." he paused, a bit puzzled by her question. "Peace and tranquility, I think." His eyes widened in astonishment as he noticed the plaque that hung beneath it, carrying the title.

"That's right," she said. "It's called *A Calm*. It's by Van de Velde, who's especially famous for his seascapes. I've seen a few lithographs of his work, but they were all in black and white—the color makes a world of difference, don't you agree?"

"I never thought I'd find a painting of ships on the water to be so beautiful," he told her. "In fact, I must confess that I probably wouldn't have given it a glance if you hadn't drawn my attention to it. Thank you, Emily."

"It's the blues, you know."

"The blues?" he asked as he looked at her quizzically.

"The tones—the way in which he makes the sky glow with light and how the water shimmers. The title is so very apt." With a small sigh and a final glance, Emily moved on to look at the next painting while Francis remained transfixed.

Never in his life had he thought to enjoy a museum visit as much as he was enjoying this one. It was as if each painting had a story to tell, a story that he was incapable of reading without Emily's help. He felt as though he'd always been blind and that Emily had just now granted him the gift of sight. He could think of nothing to say to her that might accurately convey his gratitude.

He caught up with her a moment later. "Do you know, I don't think I've ever met anyone who's quite as appreciative of art as you seem to be," he told her with a gentle smile as he came to stand beside her.

"I believe that I appreciate it because I understand it. I think it would be difficult to appreciate something that one did not understand. Wouldn't you agree?"

"And yet, most people appreciate love, or the act of being in love, though it's often quite impossible to understand the logic behind it."

"Perhaps there is no logic. Perhaps that's what makes it so thrilling, and perhaps it's what makes love so much like art. Art isn't logical, Francis—it's emotional, irrational . . . it's meant to stir your soul and your senses. A work of art is not simply a depiction of a flower, a landscape, or a portrait of someone—it is rather an insight into the artist's soul, a window if you will.

"Take this painting over here, for instance, of the Immaculate Conception by Murillo. The artist clearly poured his heart into it; such beauty and perfection could never be attained otherwise. Look at the Madonna's poise, the light that surrounds her, and the attention to detail—one is tempted to believe that it's possible for her to step down from the canvas and into this very room.

"Art challenges our mind, Francis. It makes us question the world around us, and it allows us to view it in a different light or from a different angle—it's enlightening. In truth, I dread to think of what the world would be like without it. I believe our lives would be quite dull, indeed."

They both stood silently, looking up at the beautiful woman that stood amidst the clouds, surrounded by angels. "You've given me a great gift today, Emily," he told her.

"How so?"

He paused for a moment as he wondered how he might best explain himself to her. "I feel as though I've been hearing music around me all my life without actually listening to it. You've taught me how to listen, Emily." He took her hand in his and squeezed it. "Thank you," he whispered and was rewarded by a dazzling smile.

It was six by the time they left the museum and entered onto Gallery Road. The evening air was balmy, so they decided to walk for a while, taking Croxted Road up to Brixton, where Francis hailed a hackney to take them the rest of the way.

By the time they arrived at the entrance to Vauxhall Gardens, it was just past seven o'clock. They paid for their admission and entered onto the Grand Walk, where freshly raked gravel suddenly crunched beneath their feet. Emily sucked in a breath at the sight of the nine-hundred-foot-long walkway that was flanked by elms on either side. "Shall we?" Francis asked as he offered her his arm. "Supper generally begins at nine, so we can take a turn of the gardens until then."

Resting her hand on his arm, Emily allowed him to steer her forward between the gathering crowds. Never in her life had she seen so many fashionably dressed men and women gathered together in one spot—not even at Almack's. The sight was so spectacular that she could not stop herself from staring, her head turning from side to side so as not to miss a single thing.

Francis grinned down at her. "You seem to be enjoying yourself," he mused.

"Oh, I'm terribly sorry, Francis," she muttered, suddenly painfully self-aware. "I don't mean to act like a gawking imbecile . . . but . . . oh my goodness, would you look at that lady's hat!"

"Please tell me that you do not like that catastrophe," he said with apparent alarm.

"Oh no," she assured him. "But it's quite extravagant nonetheless—from an artistic viewpoint, of course."

"Of course," he concurred, trying desperately to stifle an impending burst of laughter.

He led her all the way down toward the bottom of the walk, stopping along the way to buy an ice for each of them. They found a bench on which to sit as they enjoyed their refreshment, watching the vast variety of people passing by, quietly commenting on their appearances from time to time.

Continuing on their way, Francis steered Emily right

toward the Southern Walk. Once again, Emily found herself struck with wonder and admiration at the sight of three triumphal arches that were spread out along the length of it. As they passed under the last one, Francis nudged her in the direction of the grove. "Let us enjoy the music for a while," he suggested. "There's still half an hour until nine o'clock."

Taking a seat on one of the many benches that lined the periphery, they allowed the music to waft over them. Neither of them spoke until it was over. "I could sit here forever," Emily told him.

"I know what you mean. However, I do believe that it's time for supper." He rose, reached out his hand, and helped her to her feet.

Passing a statue of Handel, they entered a semicircular plaza surrounded by twenty supper boxes, all painted in bright colors to depict children at play, adults' pastime activities, and scenes from the theatre. "They're so beautifully painted, Francis. And the way they're lit up . . . as if the murals are glowing . . . I must admit, I never thought to see a place such as this. I believe it's my turn to thank you."

"It's my pleasure," he told her as he turned his head toward her with a smile.

They ordered some thinly sliced ham, a selection of cheeses, and some sweetmeats. Francis asked the waiter to bring them a decanter of arrack punch so that Emily might try the specialty. "Come, try this," he told her once the food had arrived. He held a piece of sweetmeat up to her lips and slipped it into her mouth. Her eyes opened wide in appreciation. "Now follow it with arrack."

The rich flavor of the confection mingling with the liquor

made for an extraordinary gustatory experience. Emily closed her eyes, savoring every moment of it as Francis watched her with delight, happy to see the joy that she took in such a simple thing.

Her eyes flew open at the sudden sound of whistles blowing. She looked about to find the source. In astonishment she watched the gardens flood with light as hundreds of globe lanterns came ablaze. "Incredible," she sighed. "How many do you suppose that there are?"

"Well over a thousand, if I'm not mistaken."

Emily shook her head in wonder as she reached for a piece of ham. "This place truly is magical, I believe. It just continues to impress me."

"Just wait until you see the cascade," he told her.

"A waterfall?" she asked in astonishment.

He nodded. "Yes, you'd better hurry up and eat so we'll be ready when it begins."

"How will we know when it begins? Oh, Francis, we mustn't miss it."

He grinned at her. "There'll be a bell," he promised. "Now, how about a dessert plate with a selection of tarts, cheesecake, and some fresh fruit?"

"Sounds divine," Emily told him dreamily as she finished the remainder of her arrack. "Perhaps with some coffee?"

"I didn't think you drank coffee," he teased as he leaned toward her, brushing her cheek with his lips."

"Just because you've never seen me drink it, doesn't mean that I don't enjoy it."

"Hmmm . . . I can't help but wonder what else you might enjoy doing . . ."

"Francis!" Her cheeks filled with color as she glanced across at Mary, who was seated on a bench within a reasonable distance of them. The maid was paying more attention to the crowd passing her by than she was to either Emily or Francis, however.

There was no doubt in Emily's mind that Francis was extremely aware of this, for in the next instant, she felt his hand grip her thigh beneath the table as he fixed her with a heated stare. A sudden primal urge to let him ravish her there and then hit her like a blow, knocking the air out of her. "Oh God, Francis," she groaned, her eyes swimming with desire.

"I've never felt this strongly for any woman, Emily. Just thinking about you—and the evening we shared in your bedroom—makes me hard." She whimpered slightly as she felt his grip tighten. "Do you have any idea how much I want you, Emily?" he asked. There was an almost desperate tone to his voice as he posed his question to her.

"I'm barely able to think of anything other than your hands on me, Francis. In fact, I think you'll find that my need is just as great as yours." She swallowed hard, then set her mind to slowing the beat of her racing heart.

"For pity's sake, Emily."

She eyed him warily. "Do you intend to seduce me before our wedding night, Francis?"

His hand was gone from her thigh the moment the words left her mouth, and she couldn't help but feel a surge of regret, as if she'd lost something very dear to her. "No," he told her with a hint of severity, determination clear in his eyes. "Some things are sacred."

"Then why? For heaven's sake, Francis, why would you . . ." The disappointment she felt at his sudden righteousness was so overwhelming that she felt she might scream with frustration.

"I wanted you to understand that what I feel for you is more than a passing fancy. I want to share my bed with you every night for the rest of my life. And when we're out of bed, I want to spend my days talking to you, sharing my thoughts with you, and listening to everything that you may wish to tell me. I want to see you laugh, Emily, because when you do, the whole world seems to brighten with your happiness."

The sound of a bell ringing was followed by a loud bustling all around them as men and women rose to their feet, all intent on viewing the cascade. "Come, Emily," Francis urged her. "Let us hurry so that we can find a good vantage point before the crowd closes in around it." He quickly handed a wad of money to their waiter as he hauled Emily out of her seat and hurried her along at a brisk pace.

They pushed themselves forward until they stood at the very front, to find themselves looking at a miller's house standing next to a frothing waterfall. At the bottom of the waterfall, the churning waters drove a huge wheel attached to the side of the house. The color of the water changed from blue, to green, to red as different lights illuminated it.

Unable to tear her eyes away from any part of it, Emily looked on in wonder, not uttering a single word for the fifteen minutes that the spectacle lasted. Finally, the water slowed and the crowd began to disperse.

"It never would have occurred to me that watching water

flow could be so mesmerizing," she muttered as she turned back toward Francis. "Thank you for a wonderful day and evening."

It had been wonderful, he agreed, as he took her by the arm and began leading her back toward Vauxhall Road—unbelievably wonderful. And while he'd never much cared for the notion of marriage, he suddenly had an urgent need to cart Emily off to the nearest church. The sooner they spoke their vows the better, he decided—especially if she was going to remain chaste until her wedding night.

Chapter Twenty

"A letter came for you yesterday, Miss Emily," the butler told her as she arrived for breakfast the next day.

Beatrice and Claire were both enjoying a hot cup of tea and some scones with strawberry jam as she walked across to the table. "Thank you, Parker," Emily said, taking the letter from the tray that he was holding out to her. She then looked at her sisters as she took her own seat at the table. "I didn't see either one of you yesterday. Francis mentioned something about a bonnet. Did you find it?"

"Oh yes," Claire replied. "It's the most splendid thing in the world. Don't you agree, Bea?"

"It is lovely," Beatrice agreed. "And I'm sure that I never would have heard the end of it if I hadn't gone with you. Sorry we left you here alone, Emily, but your sister insisted that if we did not hurry, then someone else was sure to buy it."

"That's quite all right," Emily chuckled. "As it turned out, I had a rather splendid day together with Francis." It was impossible for her to hide her joy as the corners of her mouth edged upward into a happy smile.

"Really? Well, what did you do? Surely you weren't alone with him?" There was a mischievous gleam in Claire's eyes that told Emily that she almost wished it were so.

"Mary was with us, of course." Beatrice made an evident sigh of relief. Emily then told her sisters of her visit to the Dulwich, and later trip to Vauxhall Gardens and how spectacular she had found it.

"Though I'm sure that both these places are of great interest," Beatrice said with a smile, "I'm more inclined to believe that it's the company you kept that has you looking so giddy this morning."

"Oh, Bea, it was wonderful—he was wonderful. When the fireworks started . . ."

"There were fireworks?" Claire exclaimed, to which Emily nodded. "I should love to see them sometime."

"Perhaps you shall," Beatrice told her patiently, then turned her attention back to Emily. "And what happened when the fireworks started?"

Heat flushed Emily's cheeks. "He put his arms around me, pulled me close, and kissed me, right there in the middle of the gardens."

"Good God, Emily," Beatrice exclaimed.

"Bravo!" Claire hooted simultaneously.

"Settle down, Claire," Beatrice told her sister sternly. "This is a serious matter. Where was Mary while all of this kissing was going on?"

"I believe she was right there next to us, but the poor woman had never seen fireworks before, you see. One can hardly blame her for her lack of attention toward us."

Beatrice slumped back against her chair, a perplexed look

upon her face. She looked at Emily, her eyes suddenly narrowing as if she'd just seen something extraordinary. She leaned slowly toward her as she scrutinized every inch of her sister's face. "Oh my," she finally gasped. Emily averted her gaze with a growing degree of shyness, the sudden sensation of being under a microscope making her extremely uncomfortable.

"What?" Claire asked, noticing the look on Beatrice's face. "What is it, Bea?"

"You're in love with him," Beatrice stated, much in the same way that she would have done if she'd just solved a mathematical equation. "You're in love with Francis, the very man whom you've done nothing but complain about for the past ten years or more."

A heavy silence filled the room. Emily could feel the weight of it confining her to her chair. She had no idea what to say. In truth, she hadn't known that she loved him—really loved him—until that very moment. Her sister's words somehow confirmed what she hadn't yet had the courage to acknowledge. "I believe I am," she finally sighed. "Oh my God, I'm in love with Francis Riley." Without further warning, she burst out laughing. She was completely incapable of containing herself. How utterly wonderful. "This is probably the last thing I had ever expected to happen," she giggled. Before she knew it, Beatrice and Claire had joined in until the whole room was filled with the sound of their laughter.

"Emily," Beatrice said, her voice suddenly serious. "Do you know if he feels the same way toward you?"

Emily's laughter subsided immediately at that question. It was the one thing that she had no desire to think about. Trust

Beatrice to force her to confront it right there in the middle of her breakfast. Letting out a long sigh, she shook her head. "He desires me," she told them plainly.

Claire looked as though she might choke on her scone at that remark, whilst Beatrice appeared on the verge of collapse. "Emily," she managed to say with some degree of haranguing.

"Don't you dare lecture me on propriety right now, Bea," Emily said as she shot Beatrice an admonishing look. She could see Claire freeze out of the corner of her eye. "You are my sisters and I want to share all of my thoughts and feelings with you without constantly having to worry about being judged by you." She bit down on her lower lip as her eyes softened into an apologetic look. "I'm sorry, Bea, but we're too often too afraid of stating things plainly because it's 'just not done.' Well, to hell with that!" she exclaimed, as both of her sisters' jaws dropped like flytraps. "I don't think Francis loves me. I do, however, know that he respects me. I know that he enjoys spending time with me and I know that he yearns to have me in his bed."

"He told you this?" Beatrice asked, dumbfounded.

"He did indeed."

"Well, I certainly have newfound respect for the man," Claire muttered. "I wish someone would tell me something like that."

"Watch yourself, Claire," Beatrice scolded. "It's bad enough that Emily has taken to blatant honesty—however, I'd still like to remind you that you're a lady and that there are certain things that ladies simply do not discuss."

"I would never dream of saying such things in public, Bea," Emily said. "But like I said, you're my sisters. Who else would I say such things to?"

"Your confessor?" Claire ventured with a chuckle.

"Perhaps I would if I were Catholic," Emily agreed with a grin. "And be given a thousand Hail Marys to absolve me from my sinful thoughts."

"Ah, so Francis is not the only one thinking of sojourning in bed." Claire's voice was cheeky to a fault, her implication undeniable as she arched an eyebrow and challenged Emily for the truth.

"I must admit that there is nowhere I would rather be," Emily acknowledged with a dreamy gaze.

"Even if he doesn't love you?" Beatrice asked in shock. "And when on earth did you become so candid, Emily?"

Emily met her sister with a happy smile. "I don't know. I've felt a change come over me for the past few months . . . something just had me feeling so tired of all the presence, and I must admit that it's really quite liberating. And then with this whole thing with Adrian—I've just had enough." She paused for a moment to sip her tea. "So yes, Bea, even if he doesn't love me. Don't you see that everything else—his eagerness to share my company, his genuine respect for me, and his ardent desire that's forever in his eyes, all of that—is more than enough for me to be eternally happy? And perhaps in time, he will love me as our relationship grows."

Beatrice nodded thoughtfully. "I believe you're right, Emily. I believe you would be happy. But I must ask . . . why do you assume to know his heart? How do you know that he doesn't love you already? After all, he's known you for years—since you were children, in fact."

"There's something in his past, Bea," Emily said with a hint of concern. "I've still to discover what it is, but whatever it is, it's something that has consumed him to such a degree that there's been no room for love or happiness of any kind. Since coming to London, however, I've witnessed a gradual change in him. I've seen him smile and laugh for the first time since I can't remember when. So perhaps in time, the darkness will pass, and he'll let love in again. Until then, however, everything else will have to suffice—and it shall, for they are just as valid elements in a relationship as love. In fact, they are the building blocks upon which love might have a chance to grow."

Reaching for the envelope that lay beside her plate, Emily eyed the elegant script of her name, written on the front of it. She opened it carefully and pulled out a letter. "I'm sorry, but I have to go. It appears that I'm about to be late for an appointment."

"With whom?" Beatrice asked as her eyes followed Emily to the door.

"With Kate. She says that she would like to talk." Emily registered the apprehension in Beatrice's eyes. "I have no quarrel with her, you know—she and Adrian love each other, they're happy together, and the feelings that I had for Adrian are nothing compared to what I now feel for Francis."

"That doesn't change the fact that she hurt you beyond compare. Even if you're no longer suffering, she paid no heed to your feelings at the time. Talk to her if you must, Emily, but don't allow her to reclaim the position she once held in your heart by giving you an apology or an attempt at an explanation—she's not worthy of it."

"I know, Bea. I'll be back soon. Will you be here?"

"Jonath— Mr. Rosedale," Beatrice quickly corrected herself, "will be taking us to pick up our calling cards from the printers any minute now."

"I had completely forgotten about that," Emily said as she bit down on her bottom lip. "Would you mind picking mine up, too?"

"Of course not. In any case, we should be back in a couple of hours or so."

Emily decided to ignore her sister's use of Mr. Rosedale's Christian name. There would be plenty of time for her to ask questions about that later. Right now, she was running very late. "Very well, then, I will see you later."

By the time Emily crossed Piccadilly and entered Green Park, a faint drizzle had started up. She opened up her parasol and headed toward the tall and slender figure that stood sheltered beneath a large oak. "I was beginning to think that you wouldn't come," Kate said as she walked toward her.

"I'm sorry, but I only just received your letter this morning. How are you, Kate?" Reaching out her hand, she linked her arm with Kate's as they began to stroll down the Queen's Walk.

"I'm well," Kate told her, "though I do miss our friendship terribly. I'm so sorry for the way in which both Adrian and I treated you. It was most unkind and inconsiderate of us. I think we were both so caught up in our own happiness that we completely forgot about everything else. I'm truly sorry."

"You hurt me very badly, Kate," Emily agreed. "But I'm

so much better now— and stronger, I think—because of it. Coming to London has done me a world of good—I can see why you love it so."

"Have you been to the theatre yet?"

"No, not yet, but Francis took me to see Vauxhall Gardens yesterday and I must say, it was unlike anything I've ever experienced before in my life. It was wonderful."

"I believe that you and Francis have spent quite a lot of time in each other's company lately. Am I right?"

"I find myself enjoying his company more and more, Kate. I've spent so many years disliking him, yet now that I'm taking the time to talk to him, to get to know him again, I can't help but be drawn to him. In fact, he's largely to blame for my speedy recovery following my heartbreak over Adrian."

"So you've taken a fancy to him?"

Emily paused for a moment. "No, Kate, I've fallen in love with him." Kate spun around to face her friend, a look of grave concern upon her face. "What is it, Kate?" Emily laughed nervously. "Why the worrisome frown?"

"I'd hoped it hadn't come to this," Kate said. "Oh God, Emily, that I should be the one to break your heart twice is really more than I can bear." Her eyes welled until tears dampened her rosy cheeks.

"Good grief, Kate, whatever is the matter?" Emily asked in trepidation as fear ran coldly down her back.

"I've heard a lot of talk lately," Kate said, "about Francis. First at Lady Cunningham's garden party the other day, and then again yesterday when I was out to tea with some friends of mine."

"What kind of talk?" Emily asked with a growing sense of alarm.

"Emily, Francis has a mistress," Kate told her seriously.

Emily froze for a moment, then burst out laughing while Kate looked on in shock. "Are you serious, Kate? I'm sure there must be some mistake. Francis just isn't the sort of man to entertain a mistress. In fact it's completely preposterous."

"Apparently it's quite a well-known fact amongst the *ton*, Emily. So well-known, in fact, that I'm quite surprised we didn't hear of it sooner."

"Do you have some proof, Kate? Some form of evidence that might convince me? Because to be quite fair, I'm not particularly inclined to believe such a rumor—and it is a rumor, is it not? Or have you actually seen the woman?"

Kate didn't respond; she merely looked at Emily until her unspoken answer sank in. "Oh God," Emily muttered. "Where did you see her?"

"She was at Lady Cunningham's garden party. Miss Cartwright and Miss Howard, two new acquaintances of mine, pointed her out to me. Her name is Charlotte Browne."

A chill settled over Emily as bile began to rise in her throat. "Where does she live? Do you know?"

They turned about, heading back toward Piccadilly. "Not precisely, no. I've been told that she has an apartment here in London—paid for by Francis, of course."

"Of course," Emily heard herself say.

"But apparently he never meets her there."

Emily had no desire to ask the question that she knew must follow, but her mouth and voice seemed to have taken up a united front against her better judgment. "Then where do they meet?" she asked.

"At Dunhurst Park," Kate said quietly, sensing her friend's distress.

"And when did she last visit there?" Emily found herself asking, pressing the issue, though she feared to know the answer. In fact, to be perfectly honest, the whole conversation was more nauseating than the smell of rotten fish.

"Rumor has it that she was there just last week. I'm not sure of the exact days, however."

"Oh God," Emily murmured as she clutched hold of Kate's arm. She felt a dull pain growing in her throat and her breath caught as if something was constricting her lungs. "Francis was there last week as well . . ." Her voice was barely audible, but it didn't matter—she was no longer talking to Kate. Had he really gone straight from kissing her in his study to spending three days with his mistress, only to return and . . . she groaned as the images of what they had shared in her bedroom flashed before her. It was too humiliating to think of.

"I'm so sorry," Kate told her as she hugged her friend. "I wasn't sure if I should tell you or not, but I felt that it was the right thing to do."

"It was," Emily murmured. "Thank you, Kate, you've been a true friend."

"I'm just trying to make amends . . . in whatever way that I can. I hope that one day everything will be as it was, before all of this happened."

"I know you do," Emily said, her voice growing distant. "But nothing will ever be as it used to be; too much damage has been done. I'm sorry, Kate, but you and I will never be as close as we once were—it's simply not possible."

"What will you do now?" Kate asked her, her voice heavy with regret.

They had reached the entrance to the park once more, where Emily now stood as if transfixed. She felt numb and defeated. What would she do? What *could* she do? She had no desire to return to Francis's home—the mere thought of possibly seeing him again nauseated her. How could she have been so blind? She'd known he was incapable of love—nobody as depressed as he was could possibly fall in love—yet she'd allowed herself to be captured by his desire for her. She'd treasured his touch and his kisses. . . . She'd relished his courtship.

Francis Riley needed a wife in order to produce an heir—all men of his stature needed that—and who better than someone who fell in love as easily as she apparently did. Given enough time and the right explanation, he probably would have coaxed her into accepting his mistress as part of the package.

As she allowed this final thought to manifest, she suddenly reeled away from Kate to cast up her accounts all over the pavement.

"You're not well, Emily," Kate told her, stating the obvious as she put her hand on Emily's shoulder. "Let me escort you back to your house."

"I'm not going back there," Emily said, her eyes wide with despair. "I'm never going back there." Backing away, she stumbled slightly as her foot caught the hem of her dress—yet she quickly managed to recover her balance as she reached for the back of a bench on which to steady herself. Without another word, she turned on her heel and ran out into the street to hail the first hackney she could find.

Kate watched in horrified silence as Emily scampered on board, just managing to make out the word "Redding," as Emily called out her destination to the driver. The carriage then took off with a jolt, leaving behind a distraught Kate at the edge of Green Gardens.

The butler responded rapidly to Kate's incessant hammering on the door. "Yes?" he asked, arching a disapproving eyebrow.

"Are either of the Rutherford sisters at home?" she stammered. She had run as fast as she could to get there, only to find herself panting and wheezing quite shamefully on the doorstep of Francis's home.

"I'm afraid not," Parker replied in a haughty tone that gave Kate the urge to hit him. She restrained herself, partly due to decorum but mostly because he was the gatekeeper—he had the power to admit her or to turn her away.

"How about Lord Dunhurst, then?" she asked, gritting her teeth. "It's a matter of some urgency."

"His lordship is not in either." Kate's shoulders slumped in visible exasperation. She wasn't handling the situation well at all, she realized, to her annoyance. "They may return shortly, however. May I suggest that you wait for them in the parlor?"

With a sigh of relief, Kate thanked Parker as she hurried inside before he had a chance to change his mind.

It was well over an hour before Kate heard the front door open and close to the sound of prattling voices. A brief silence ensued as hats and gloves were undoubtedly being removed, and then there were footsteps approaching. A moment later, the door to the parlor swung open, and Kate jumped to her feet as Beatrice and Claire entered, followed by Jonathan and Francis.

"Hello, Kate," Beatrice said in a polite tone. "Parker told us you were here. Where's Emily? She said that she was going to meet you—did you not find one another?"

Kate just stood there, staring back at them all, wringing her hands, unable to find the right words with which to begin. "Are you all right?" Claire asked. "Here, why don't you sit down? You look thoroughly put out."

"I'd much rather stand," Kate said, her voice quivering. "If you don't mind."

"Very well," Beatrice said. "Why don't you have a drink, then, to calm your nerves, and then tell us what all of this is about."

Kate nodded anxiously, eager to have something with which to still her fidgety hands. She watched in silence as Francis poured her a small brandy, then thanked him as he handed it to her. She took a large sip, her fingers trembling as they held the glass to her lips. Then, steadying herself on a table next to her, she sank down onto the chair behind her and heaved a big, strenuous sigh. "I told Emily . . ." she began, but her voice faltered. "Oh God, I'm so sorry, I should have come to you first, Francis."

Francis's brows were suddenly drawn tight, his eyes grown dark—Kate shuddered. "Where is Emily, Kate?" he asked her sternly.

"She's gone to Redding," Kate whispered with downcast eyes.

"Dear me," Beatrice moaned with a pained look in her eyes.

"What the devil does that mean?" Francis asked, his annoyance growing by the second.

"It means she's gone to see Edward, our cousin."

"Why would she do that?" Claire asked. "I thought she hated Edward."

"She does, Claire, but you see, Edward has been supporting us since Mama and Papa passed away, and . . ."

Francis scoffed. "You call that *supporting you*? The blackguard has barely given you enough to survive upon!"

"Nevertheless," Beatrice said calmly. "We've had no choice but to depend on him. All of these years, he asked for nothing in return, but then . . . about two months ago a letter arrived. He plans to cut us off once Claire reaches her majority."

"That's next month," Claire gasped. "Why didn't you tell me this?"

"Neither of us wanted you to worry about it—after all, we were so sure that Emily would marry Adrian and that it wouldn't be an issue . . . but now . . ." Beatrice glanced across at Kate who was looking more and more forlorn. "In his letter, Edward made an offer for Emily, promising that if she married him, then he would continue to support us—even raise our allowance. She dismissed the offer at the time, but I believe she may have reconsidered, as distasteful as she finds it."

"Bloody hell!" Francis exclaimed.

"But he's our cousin, Bea . . . she can't possibly . . ."

"He's not our cousin, Claire, even if we've referred to him as such—you know that. We're not related to him by blood, so it is in fact quite acceptable for Emily to marry him."

"We can't allow her to do it, Bea—we have to stop her somehow. Emily mustn't offer herself up like this on the marriage altar for our sakes—I could never forgive myself if she did."

"What I'd like to know is what the devil possessed her to take off in such a hurry without a single explanation." Francis glared at Kate as he now stood waiting for an explanation.

"I believe she may have been significantly upset not to care about who she might marry."

"And why is that, Kate? Let's get to the heart of the matter, shall we? You met her, and you told her something. Now tell me what the hell it was before you become the first woman I beat."

"I told her about your mistress, Francis. She has a right to know, even if you're not willing to tell her," Kate yelled as she met his stormy eyes.

Silence flooded the room while her words hung suspended in the air. A look of shock was evident on everyone's faces as they all stared at Kate with open mouths.

"You what?" Francis roared. "Of all the stupid things you've ever done in your life, Kate. It wasn't enough for you to ruin Emily's happiness once. Oh no, you had to go and do it again. What kind of a friend are you? And why the hell didn't you talk to me about this first?"

"I . . . I . . ." Kate stammered as her eyes darted about the room in bewilderment.

"I don't have a bloody mistress, Kate. How dare you fill Emily's head with lies and insinuations? How dare you ruin her chances of happiness?"

"But I was told . . . I mean, Charlotte Browne . . ."

"Was my father's mistress," Francis sighed as he shook his head from side to side in incredulity. "You stupid woman. Trust you to listen to all the gossip mongers and to make a big old Banbury tale out of it."

Kate slumped back in her seat, utterly defeated. "I'm so sorry," she muttered, as if barely capable of believing the extent of her blunder herself. "You have to go after her, Francis."

"I daresay the woman's got a point, Francis," Jonathan added as he patted his friend on the back. "After all, it wouldn't do to watch the woman you love marry someone else, would it now?"

Francis shot Jonathan a disgruntled look, then turned back to find the three women staring at him in astonishment.

"Is it true?" Beatrice asked. "Do you love her?"

He nodded grudgingly, though his eyes were filled with anything but the affection they might have shown at the thought of his heart's desire. Instead, he looked incredibly worried. "Yes, I do. In fact, I have for some time."

"Well, what are you still doing standing about here then? Be off, this instant!"

At Beatrice's demanding tone of voice, he did reward her with a sheepish grin, then gave her a curt nod as he strode out of the door with Jonathan on his heels.

Chapter Twenty-One

"What a pleasure it is to see you again, Emily," Edward said as he took the seat across from her. "And you're looking just as lovely as I remember you—I knew I'd made a wise decision when I offered for you." He lit a cigar, sucked on it a bit, and then twirled it between his fingers as he watched the smoke rise. He was older than Emily remembered, and not as lean as he'd once been. His hairline had begun to recede, just as his father's had. She knew he'd only recently turned thirty, yet he appeared to be well over forty. He sucked on his lips, then smacked them together before taking another puff of his cigar. "As I recall it, you weren't too pleased with my advances in the past, Emily. Whatever caused you to change your mind?"

Emily's face was cast in stone as she looked across at the man that she'd despised for so long. She and her sisters had never been anything but kind to him, but even so, he'd taken everything from them at the first opportunity. "Let's just say that things didn't work out the way I thought they would."

He nodded thoughtfully at that. "Well, it's no matter

now—water under the bridge, so to speak. The important thing is that you're here, and I take it, quite willingly?" he smirked.

Emily shuddered at the thought of what he was implying. "I'm merely doing my duty," she said in a dry voice that lacked emotion.

"Hmmm . . . I hope you understand what that entails," he said, allowing his eyes to roam over her before settling on the rise of her breasts. Emily had to grip the arms of the chair she was sitting in to stop herself from running away as fast as her feet could carry her. Instead, she watched in apprehension as Edward put down his cigar and got up. "You must understand," he told her with a smirk. "That I am first and foremost a businessman. And like any businessman, I have every intention of sampling the merchandise before I commit myself to anything."

Her eyes flittered instinctively toward the door as he closed the distance between them. He moved around her chair until she felt him standing directly behind her, the sound of his breath alarmingly loud in her ears. She tensed immediately when she felt his hands upon her shoulders, and she gasped anxiously when he took the liberty of letting one of those hands slide down her chest until she felt him squeezing her breast in a rough, demanding fashion that chilled her to the bone.

"Please don't," she begged him as she tried to wriggle herself free from his grip. It was of no use. He held her down as he fumbled with her bodice, pulling on it until one of her breasts popped free.

"That's more like it," he muttered as he tugged on her nipple.

"Release me at once," she yelled, the tears stinging behind her eyes.

He leered at her menacingly, knowing full well the power that he held over her. "You came to me, remember? Did you really think that I'd make you my wife without having a little taste of what you have to offer? I've no desire to take on another man's discards, if you know what I mean. So, how about you make quick work of that dress of yours instead of just sitting there quivering about it? I promise you, it'll be quick. . . . Besides, you can't possibly be so daft as to think that you can marry me and deny me the carnal pleasures that will soon become rightfully mine."

Emily sat as if glued to the chair, tears streaming down her cheeks. She watched as Edward strolled back around to face her. Taking her by the chin, he turned her head toward him. "Now take off your damn clothes," he yelled.

With trembling fingers, she began undoing the buttons of her dress. Never in her life had she felt so humiliated, so wronged, so filthy as she did now. But what choice did she have? If she didn't marry him, she and her sisters would be destitute. They had nobody else to turn to, and they'd all failed miserably in their attempts at finding husbands.

It wasn't meant to be, however, and now Emily felt duty-bound to save her sisters from a life of poverty—she felt responsible for what would happen to them if she didn't marry Edward. But more than guilt, it was pain that drove her to what she would have considered unthinkable that very same morning. She never thought she would hurt more than when Adrian had told her he intended to marry Kate, but she was wrong.

Francis had charmed her. He'd made her heart go pitter-patter, for heaven's sake. He'd made her fall in love with him—and she'd been all too willing to let him. It was quite clear to her now that her feelings hadn't been reciprocated. What kind of man asked a woman to marry him, showering her with tender words and kisses, whilst keeping his mistress waiting on the side? A man like Francis, apparently.

Yet here she was now, ready to throw her life away by marrying Edward. Well, a sacrifice had to be made if they didn't want to end up without a roof over their heads. By marrying Edward, her sisters would still have a chance at happy marriages to suitable gentlemen. At least that was some consolation, small as it seemed at that very moment.

Slipping her dress from her shoulders, it fell in a puddle at her feet so that she stood, trembling in her chemise, corset, and petticoat, her arms hugging her chest. Edward's lips curled into a nasty grimace of lust as he now stood watching her. It was nothing like the way in which Francis had looked at her. Francis's eyes had been warm and . . . oh God! Had she made a terrible mistake? By comparison, Francis had looked as though he loved her . . . but that was impossible . . . wasn't it? She couldn't think straight. Her mind was such a muddle of conflicting thoughts and emotions that she knew not what to do. But she knew what she now faced: a cold, hard stare that told her that Edward planned on being anything but gentle with her.

She shrank away from him as a terrible fear descended

upon her, but he reached out and pulled her toward him so roughly that she stumbled against him. "Having second thoughts?" he sneered vehemently. "Am I suddenly not good enough for you after all?"

"No . . . no, it's not that . . . it's . . ."

"You and your sisters never liked me. I always knew I didn't belong—you made me feel so unwanted, Emily."

"That's not true," she riled. "We treated you no different than we treated each other. We never thought of you as anything other than our cousin—surely you must realize that."

"Oh, I beg to differ, Emily. I know how I felt growing up. Don't think I've forgotten your favorite game after all this time. 'Let's play hide and seek, Edward,' you'd tell me. 'It's your turn to count.' And there I'd be, searching for you all over the house, only to find that you'd run off to the lake in hopes of being rid of me. What a triumph it has been to take all that was once yours and make it mine—after your parents died. And to think that you're now willing to marry me and to give me your virtue to boot. Don't think for one minute that I'll let you change your mind, *cousin*."

Burying his head against her neck, he clasped his hands over her buttocks, squeezing them as she writhed beneath his touch. Leaning back, he slapped her hard across her face. "Be still, you little chit," he snarled, his words a clear warning of what he had in store for her if she continued to fight him.

"No, Edward, please stop," she cried, looking desperately for a means to escape the wretched situation. "I'm sorry. I can't do this." Tears were springing from her eyes in heavy sobs as he ripped apart the hooks on the front of her corset.

"What the blazes is going on here?" an angry voice bellowed with such rage that it seemed as if the whole room shook.

Emily gasped as her eyes darted toward the door to find a furious Francis pushing aside a befuddled butler as he barged into the room. She just managed to spot Jonathan entering behind him, shutting the door firmly to keep out the curious stares of the servants.

"Who the hell do you think you are, intruding like this?" Edward asked with a small degree of uncertainty. He wasn't an idiot, so he knew he would be outnumbered if it came to blows between them.

"I'm Lord Dunhurst, Emily's fiancé, and this gentleman over here is a good friend of mine, Mr. Rosedale." His dark eyes were stormy as they fixed Edward with a deadpan expression.

"Is this a joke?" Edward asked, his nervousness beginning to show. He had no desire to have a duel, least of all with a man who looked like he was ready to rip him to shreds with his bare fists. "Emily, are you engaged to this man?"

Emily stared at Francis. She could still feel Edward's hands clenched around her waist.

Though she longed for him to release her, she felt as if she might be leaving one hell in exchange for another—Francis looked far from forgiving at this point. Truth be told, he looked mad as hell. In fact, she was probably in for a very long coach ride if she decided to leave with him. And then, of course, there was still the small matter of his mistress, which of course, from Emily's point of view, was no small matter at all. She had no wish to share Francis with another woman. Yet, she knew that she wouldn't be able to stomach Edward for one moment longer . . . at least where Francis was concerned, they had been able to get along. It suddenly seemed as if the choice was obvious. "I'm afraid so," she sighed.

"Well, there you have it then," Francis said. "And isn't it true, Jonathan, that she is then rightfully mine, even if she did happen to run off, straight into this man's arms?" His eyes held Emily's as his words tormented her. It was very clear that she wouldn't get off lightly.

"Well, it is true that you had the first arrangement, so unless this gentleman would like to contest it . . ." Jonathan said in a bold tone that had a highly official ring to it.

"Would you?" Francis asked Edward as his eyes shifted to meet his.

For a fleeting moment, Emily feared that Edward might say yes and that the next step would be the choosing of weapons and seconds. No sooner had the thought entered her mind, however, than she found herself shoved aside, physically discarded. She watched with a growing sense of relief as Edward straightened his back and headed for the door. "I trust you'll see yourselves out, gentlemen," he told them in a gruff voice. "After all, you do know the way." And then he was gone without bothering to wait for a response.

Emily stood perfectly still, the sound of her heart pounding in her ears, as she stared at both Francis and Jonathan in turn. Her arms were clasped about her, trying to hold together her corset in a small attempt at some modesty. Her hair was a tangled mess, her eyes huge with fear, and her cheeks pink from crying. In short, she looked a fright.

Francis's heart clenched with pain for what she must be going through, yet he was so angry with her for what she'd done—for putting herself in such a precarious situation—that he couldn't help himself from adding to her misery. "For Christ's sake, make yourself decent," he told her in a rigid tone. "You look like a bloody harlot who's just had a tumble in the hay."

Still, she stood there, incapable of doing as he asked, but what he'd said had reminded him of just what might have happened had he not arrived when he did. It made his blood boil in fury—the mere thought of that vile man pawing his sweet, innocent, and good-natured Emily was more than he could stomach. "Put on your damn dress, Emily, before I change my mind and leave you here."

Like magic she snapped to attention, rushing to put herself back in a more orderly fashion. She picked up her shoes that had been haphazardly discarded in a corner at some point, putting them on as she hurried after Jonathan—Francis had already left the building. She spotted him again when she descended the front steps of Edward's home. "Get in," he ordered her harshly as he virtually shoved her inside the landau, so forcefully that she almost fell flat on her face. Regaining composure, and unwilling to aggravate him any further, she quickly sat down on one of the benches, as close to the window as she could get. Francis and Jonathan seated themselves opposite.

None of them spoke for what seemed like an eternity. Emily was sure that they must be back in London soon, yet neither Francis nor Jonathan showed any sign that this might be the case. "Where are we going?" Emily finally asked after three hours of silence. She didn't receive a response; in fact, they completely ignored her. Perhaps she ought to try and apologize first, she thought. "I'm so sorry . . ."

"What the hell were you thinking, Emily?" Francis snapped as he spun his head toward her, cutting her off before she had a chance to say anything more. "Have you any idea of what would have happened to you, had Jonathan and I not arrived when we did?"

"I . . . I . . ." she stammered.

"You would have been raped, Emily—that's what would have happened. And more than that, you would have had no choice but to marry the bloody bastard."

"I went there because I *meant* to marry him, Francis," she muttered.

"Don't you dare say that or I'll have you back there in a flash, if that's what you truly desire." He glared at her from behind his dark eyes, his jaw tight with anger.

She bowed her head to hide the fresh rush of tears that pressed against the back of her eyes. Never in her life had she felt more rejected. How could he be so cold and so cruel? "I was trying to save my sisters from a life of poverty. If I didn't marry him, we would be left with nothing. In fact, I suppose that is what will happen—none of us can possibly hope to find a suitable husband in so little time, and once the time has passed and we're left with nothing, nobody will want to have us."

"What about me, Emily?" he asked, his voice softening marginally. "Do you not wish to marry me?" He gazed at her with the same eyes that she had grown so fond of. Gone was the menacing fury—instead she saw his pain, and it wounded her like a knife to the heart to realize that this had been the consequence of her actions.

"You have a mistress," she heard herself say, shaking her

head in bewilderment as if she was no longer able to believe such a thing herself. Certainly he wouldn't look at her in such a way if what Kate had told her was true. But what reason would Kate have to lie to her? Emily just didn't know what to think anymore.

Francis stiffened at her accusation. "Would you rather marry Edward then?" he asked.

"No, of course not!" she cried.

"Well, those are your choices, Emily." His voice was once again fierce and menacing. "You can marry Edward, or you can marry me . . . or you can decide to live a life of poverty. The choice is yours." He paused for emphasis. "So what will it be? Will you marry me?"

"There's so much I don't know about you, Francis . . . I told you I wouldn't say *yes* until you told me what it was that caused you so much pain. I don't want there to be any secrets between us."

He watched her with a steady gaze, carefully concealing his true feelings from her. He loved her more than he thought it was possible to love, but her actions had still pained him. In truth, they had pained him *because* of how much he loved her. He was hurt by how easily she'd believed Kate's word over his—hell, she hadn't even *asked* him about Charlotte. And what if Charlotte *had* been his mistress? She'd still chosen a far worse fate for herself by going to Edward. He just couldn't fathom what the devil had possessed her to do such a stupid thing, but it angered him so much that he couldn't stop himself.

"Beggars must not be choosers, Emily," he told her. "And if I were you, I'd hurry up and answer, for I will not ask you again."

"So you've no intention of telling me until after we're married?" she asked in genuine surprise.

"Who knows . . . I may not even tell you then," he said with a grimace that told her just how unpleasant he found the whole situation. "You haven't been very trusting of me, Emily, though maybe I haven't given you enough reason to. Perhaps it's past time we both started. I will tell you this: I will love none other than you."

Her heart skipped a beat as she held his gaze, those dark eyes of his drawing her in. He hadn't said it directly, but he'd implied it to the best of his abilities, and she'd be a fool to ignore what had been right in front of her for so long. It was suddenly as if her mind's eye zeroed in on everything that Francis had said to her over the past few weeks—and everything that he had done. And then, in a heartbeat, as a warm heat spread to her extremities and her stomach flipped in that old familiar way, she knew without a shadow of a doubt that he loved her. How it was possible that she hadn't seen it sooner, she wondered.

She made a heartfelt decision. If he happened to have a mistress named Charlotte Browne, then so be it. Emily was, however, willing to bet her virtue that it wasn't the case—no man could look as besotted as Francis did at that very moment, whilst having a mistress on the side. Taking a determined breath, Emily reached out to clasp his head between her hands, then drew him toward her until their lips met in a perfect kiss.

His surprise was evident in the stiffness of his shoulders, but he did not push her away. Instead, he brought his hands up behind her head to push her closer, parting his lips, and thrusting his tongue eagerly inside her mouth to tangle with hers. Passion overtook her with such force that she paid little heed to the bumping and swaying of the carriage. It wasn't until she heard a loud cough, followed by a lighthearted "cut it out, you two," that she was reminded of Jonathan's presence.

Releasing her hold on Francis, she quietly settled back onto her bench and began straightening her dress. "I beg your pardon, Jonathan. I do believe that I got carried away a bit."

Jonathan met her smile with laughing eyes. "If that's what you'd like to call it," he said. "However, I'm quite confident that Francis has a soft and comfortable bed that will be quite up to that sort of behavior later this evening."

"Good God, Jon," Francis blurted out. "Must you embarrass the poor woman? That's hardly the sort of thing that one says to a lady."

"Well, for some peculiar reason, I'm quite sure that Emily wasn't offended by it in the least."

"On the contrary, I now have something to look forward to," she smirked.

"By deuces, she is a feisty one, if ever I did see one," Jonathan hooted.

Francis, on the other hand, was doing his utmost to stop from ravishing her there and then. "There's still the small matter of your answer, my dear," he told her in the calmest tone that he could muster.

She reached for his hand, taking it gently in hers as she looked him straight in the eye. "Nothing in the world would give me greater pleasure than becoming your wife, Francis," she told him with such sincerity that he thought his heart might burst with joy.

"And not a moment too soon," Jonathan cheered, as the

carriage drew up to a large mansion and the door was flung open by a footman.

"Where in the world are we?" Emily asked, her eyes scaling the walls of the imposing stone structure as she stepped down from the landau.

"Dunhurst Park," Francis told her as he strode past her to greet a middle-aged woman who'd come to meet them. "Hello, Mrs. Reynolds," he said.

"Good evening, sir," The woman replied. "It's good to have you back home again."

"Thank you." He pulled Emily forward to stand beside him. "I'd like you to meet my fiancée, Miss Rutherford. She will become Lady Dunhurst before sunrise tomorrow, so please ensure that everyone who needs to be informed is made aware of the matter, so that they address her in the appropriate fashion—we don't want anyone to embarrass themselves, now, do we?" he added with a smirk. "That said, I do encourage you to be discreet. We wouldn't want our friends and relatives to find out before we have the chance to tell them ourselves. Do you follow my drift?"

Mrs. Reynolds nodded assent, then made a quick curtsey without as much as batting an eyelid at the prospect of having a sudden mistress in the house. Emily couldn't help but be impressed, for she was certain that the woman must be the housekeeper. In her experience, such women often considered a house to be theirs if the owner happened to be a bachelor, as was the case here.

But Emily's mind had soon forgotten all about Mrs. Reynolds. In fact, it kept replaying *before sunrise* over and over and . . . yes . . . over again. In fact, Emily had been so surprised when Francis had said they'd be married before the sun rose the following morning that she couldn't help but let her jaw drop wide open. *Before sunrise.* That was very, very soon indeed. But instead of being worried or feeling as if she might be rushing into something that she might later regret, she was suddenly beside herself with nervous excitement.

"And have Mr. Beacham sent for posthaste," Francis added. "We'd rather not be delayed any further."

"Very good, sir—I'll see to it right away," Mrs. Reynolds promised. "It's a true honor to make your acquaintance, Miss Rutherford," she added before bustling away to attend to her duties.

"She seems very likeable," Emily said as they headed up the stone steps and entered the massive foyer.

"Couldn't wish for a better housekeeper," Francis admitted. "She gets the job done efficiently and with a cheerful disposition to boot. I couldn't be happier with her, and I'm sure you'll find her just as agreeable, my dear."

Emily found herself smiling like a love-struck schoolgirl at the sound of his verbal affection. "I'm sure the two of us will get on famously," Emily replied, already looking forward to sitting down with Mrs. Reynolds for a chat. "So who's Mr. Beacham, by the way?"

"The local vicar," Francis told her plainly, then turned to face her as he took her hands in his. "I know you would have liked for your sisters to be present, but we can have a big bash of a wedding one of these days in London. For now, I'm, just so damn eager to make you my wife that I'd rather not wait a moment longer."

His honesty cut straight to her heart, sending it soaring. How on earth this had happened, she wondered. She'd no idea how they'd ended up so captivated by each other, and in truth it didn't matter. She only knew that she'd never thought to know so much joy and happiness, and to see it reflected in his eyes was more than she could ever have hoped for. "The faster, the better," she grinned anxiously. "I'm sure my sisters will understand. But is it even possible? Don't we need a license of some sort?"

Francis looked at her steadily. "I took care of that while you were having your little chat with Kate this morning." He spotted the pained look in her eyes and hurried on in hopes of lightening the mood once more. "I've known for some time that I wanted you to be mine—even before I began courting you, I knew. And then we shared such a wonderful day together yesterday. . . . Emily, I never wanted it to end. I knew then that I wanted to spend the rest of my life strolling through Vauxhall Gardens with you by my side. I love you, Emily—so much that my heart aches when you're not by my side, and leaps with joy when you are near. So, I took the liberty of attaining a special license in the hope that when the opportunity arose, you'd marry me straight away."

"Well, we are indeed fortunate that you were so thoughtful and farsighted—good qualities indeed in a husband," she giggled as she drew him close for an affectionate kiss.

"Would you like a tour of your new home before the vicar arrives?" Francis asked her. "Or would you prefer a drink in the library?"

"Let us have a drink," Emily said decisively.

"What a splendid choice," Jonathan said with obvious relief.

"A woman after my own heart," Francis concurred as he led the way down a wide corridor.

Chapter Twenty-Two

Jonathan quickly made his excuses after dinner, saying that he had some reading to catch up on in the library. Francis couldn't help but grin, for he knew that Jonathan never read anything other than the morning paper. He appreciated his tact, however, as he now sat alone with Emily in the parlor. She looked radiant, though she'd been unable to change her clothes—married life apparently agreed with her. Nevertheless, he would have to have some of her garments sent for in the morning.

The ceremony had been quick and to the point. Still, the sound of her "yes" had gone straight to his heart, filling him with so much hope for a happy future together. He regretted that she hadn't had a proper wedding gown, and that her flowers had been hastily picked in the garden, but for some reason, he sensed that she'd been perfectly happy with that. In fact, it had seemed that all that had mattered to her was that she was now his, and that she didn't give a fig about what dress she wore as that came to pass. He regarded her for a moment as a warm feeling of comfort washed over him. She was his, and she would remain so. He suddenly had a desperate need to pamper her—to show her how eternally grateful he was for that simple "yes."

"Since you're without your abigail here, I've spoken to Mrs. Reynolds and requested that she send up a maid to assist you in the meantime." He walked across to the side table and picked up a crystal carafe, pausing with his hand on the stopper as he turned to look at her. "Would you care for sherry or brandy tonight, my love?"

"I was hoping for a glass of port, perhaps," she replied.

"Well, if you insist on being difficult," he countered with a crooked smile.

"Ah, my lord, I'm afraid this is just the beginning," she chuckled wryly.

"In any event, it is well worth it," he told her as he picked up a dark bottle and poured two glasses from it. He handed her one of them as he sat down beside her on the blue silk brocade loveseat. He clicked his glass against hers. "To a marriage filled with joy, happiness, and a house full of children."

Emily blushed at the thought of how all of those children were to come about, then lifted her glass to her lips and drank to his toast. She felt a nervous excitement wash over her as she watched his eyes roam over her like a hungry man surveying a vast feast. Tonight was her wedding night, and she knew intellectually what that would entail. But there was no doubt that she'd only sampled a very small part of what lovemaking might involve, and her stomach now tightened at the thought of what was yet to come.

Taking her hand in his, Francis turned it over, mesmerized by the slenderness of her fingers and the transparency of her skin. Placing his lips against the top of it for a kiss, he felt it tremble ever so slightly beneath his touch. It took so little for Emily to arouse him, yet he forced himself to keep his primal urges at bay. They had the whole night ahead of them, and before he took her to his bed, there was much that they needed to discuss. "Why don't I ask Mrs. Reynolds to have a bath drawn for you so that you can bathe before bed?"

"Oh that sounds like a wonderful idea, Francis. Thank you."

"My pleasure," he said as he went to ring the bell. A moment later there was a soft rap at the door, which opened at Francis's request to admit a cheerful Mrs. Reynolds. "My wife would like to take a bath before retiring this evening. Would you please see that it is taken care of?"

"Certainly, sir," Mrs. Reynolds replied. "I've sent Georgina up already to prepare her ladyship's bedroom. Georgina will also be acting as a temporary replacement for her ladyship's abigail—I trust that her ladyship will be pleased with this decision."

"Thank you, Mrs. Reynolds," Emily responded with a smile. "I'm quite certain that everything will be to my liking."

"Very good, ma'am," Mrs. Reynolds replied with a bobbing curtsey before closing the door behind her as she went to see about the bath.

"In the meantime," Francis said, his eyes suddenly more serious than Emily was comfortable with. "I believe there are some things that I must tell you."

"Francis," she implored him. "There's no need to do it

now—why don't we just enjoy this evening without letting our pasts interfere with our happiness?"

"Because," he told her gently. "I don't wish for there to be any secrets between us when I take your innocence later tonight. Such a sacred act must not be tarnished by anything. It's all but too easy to brush it off until later, and there will always be another excuse to do so again. In truth, however, there is no better time for it than the present."

Taking a deep breath, she steeled herself for what was to come. He could see the fear in her eyes, and understood only too plainly the source of it. "Don't worry, sweetheart. There are things that I must tell you about myself—things that are quite painful and difficult for me to talk about, but I trust you with my heart, Emily, and for this reason, you must know about them. Believe me when I tell you that what I am about to say can never change the way I feel about you—if anything, it will only bring us closer."

"I lost you once because of this, Francis. I don't want to lose you again," she whispered with downcast eyes.

He paused momentarily as he lifted her chin with his fingers to look her straight in the eye. "Take courage, my love, and have faith that what I am about to tell you will only strengthen our relationship. It is the not knowing that threatens to hurt us."

"Very well, then," she said with determination as she kissed him lovingly on the lips. "Tell me what it is and let me help you carry this burden."

Francis sighed deeply as he rose to his feet and strode across to the window, where he stood for a moment in silence, looking out onto the driveway. "Lady Elisabeth Riley, the woman I have always addressed as mother—and whom I have always loved as such—is not the woman who gave birth to me," he began.

Emily decided at that point that it was very fortunate that he'd turned away from her, for it prevented him from seeing the shock that surely must have been visible upon her face. Her mind was immediately filled with a flood of questions, but she forced herself to remain silent, having no desire to keep him from continuing. Instead, she took a deep sip of her port and allowed the loveseat to support her as she settled back against it.

"After many attempts and a series of humiliating doctor's visits, it was eventually discovered that Lady Elisabeth was unable to bear children. She and my father were, needless to say, devastated—she perhaps more so, as she continuously blamed herself for not providing him with an heir.

"She loved him very much, you know—more than he ever deserved, as it turns out." Francis turned back toward Emily after a moment of pensive silence. "In fact, it was she who suggested that my father should take a mistress—another woman to carry the child that she could not give him. Do you have any idea how hard that must have been for her?" Francis's eyes glistened, though his voice remained firm. "He refused to . . . at first . . . but he so desperately wanted what she could not give him. The temptation, coupled with her blessing . . . well . . . it was too strong for him to deny."

Francis's eyes clouded over again with sudden rage. "He was a weak man who wasn't satisfied with what he had—and he had a lot."

"But . . ." Emily said softly with a great degree of caution. "If he hadn't done what he did, you never would have been born."

"I often think that would have been for the best, Emily," he told her grimly. "You see, it was my mother —I mean, Elisabeth—who handpicked Charlotte for him herself. She wanted his mistress to share her features, so that any child she gave birth to would be likely to resemble her. But my father was reeled in by Charlotte's charm and feigned sincerity. He became enamored of her, and she gradually tightened her hold on him, latching on, and refusing to let go.

"The only commendable thing that she ever did was hand me over to Elisabeth the minute that I was born. I'm told that she didn't even wish to look at me. And Elisabeth showered me with love and affection—she was a wonderful mother. But, she wanted her husband back, too."

Emily was shocked to see a damp line form on Francis's right cheek. He didn't seem to register the tears himself, so caught up was he in his story. "I don't recall ever meeting Lady Elisabeth," Emily said, unable to think of anything else.

"You would have liked her. She was pure of heart, with nothing but goodness and the best of intentions. She wasn't as strong as she needed to be in order to fight Charlotte, however. And Charlotte's incessant haranguing—the way in which she taunted her, dangling the fact that my father had finally chosen his mistress over his wife—it ate away at her. Do you know, he even moved Charlotte into the room adjoining Elisabeth's—at Charlotte's request—so that when he would visit her at night—and he did so often—Elisabeth was forced to listen to the sounds of their constant lovemaking, even if she didn't wish to. And the house in London . . ." His words faded as if he couldn't quite bear to continue.

Emily took a sharp breath. "That's why they're joined?" Her eyes were brimming with sympathy for him. "She lived at number five, didn't she?"

Francis could only nod. "Charlotte is a cold, manipulative bitch who drove Elisabeth to the brink of insanity—so much so, that even I could not stop the inevitable outcome." His face was contorted with such fierce anger that the fine hairs on the nape of Emily's neck stood on end. The man that she loved looked as though he was spinning out of control on a downward spiral into a place so dark that she feared he was bound to unravel before her very eyes. Tears came in a heavy gush amidst choked breaths as he stumbled onto a chair. "It's because of Charlotte that Elisabeth finally lost hope, gave up on love, and killed herself by jumping off the roof." He closed his eyes against the images that appeared before him. "I was the one who found her, you know . . . her eyes cast open, her neck awkwardly twisted, and her head battered."

Emily's hands flew to her mouth as her gasp filled the silence. "Oh God, Francis," she muttered. "I never thought . . . I mean, I never knew . . . oh God . . ."

"Nobody knew," he continued as he stared off into space. "Elisabeth's maiden name was used in the report—everything was hushed up, and everyone was led to believe that she died of tuberculosis."

"I'm so sorry . . ." she whispered, her voice filled with emotion. She wanted to go to him, to comfort him and heal his wounds, but something stopped her. Somehow she sensed that there was more to come, so she waited, drowning in the silence that flooded the room.

"Even to this very day, she continues to haunt me," he said as he lifted his gaze to meet Emily's. "Both of my parents are dead, and still Charlotte harasses me—claiming that I owe her the right to enjoy a portion of the wealth that my father left behind. It's not enough that he left her five thousand pounds. She spent that money a long time ago, having grown used to a lifestyle well beyond her means. So she shows up at intervals, demanding whatever sum strikes her fancy," Francis laughed self-mockingly as he raised his eyes to admire the ceiling. "And God help me, I pay it. Why?" His voice was instantly loud and defensive. "Because the bloody woman has a letter in her possession—a letter signed, sealed, and dated by my father—in which my birthright, Elisabeth's suicide, and every other bloody piece of information that might effectively tarnish the family name is plainly stated for the world to see. It would be devastating if it got out." He sighed, downed the remainder of his port, and slumped back against his chair, raking his hair with his hands. "What am I to do, Emily?"

Rising to her feet, Emily swiftly closed the space between them, put her arms around him, and hugged him against her. She didn't say a single word until she was quite certain that there was not a single tear left in him. When he let out an exhausted sigh, she eased her grip, but held on still as she bent to kiss the top of his head. He had suffered such a devastating loss, she realized, and had endured it alone, keeping all emotion bottled up inside for more than ten years. Not once had he cried over the death of Lady Elisabeth. Not once had he let another person close enough for him to lean on. All those years of buried emotions had finally been released. Emily only hoped that it would set him free.

"I love you, Francis," she whispered into his hair. A soft scent of chamomile wafted over her, so enticing that she buried her nose deeper in his thick locks. "We're together now, you and I, and together we'll find a solution."

Moving away from him, she sank to her knees before him and pulled his head toward her. Their kiss was gentle at first, but soon turned urgent as his hands came up against her face in such a loving gesture that her heart swelled with hope for their future together as husband and wife. Nothing would ever replace a moment such as this, she thought as they eased away from one another, her lips bruised by his.

They looked up at the sound of a soft knock at the door. It was Mrs. Reynolds who had come to inform them that Emily's bath was ready. "Thank you," Francis said to her. "Lady Dunhurst will be up presently."

As soon as the door had closed again they turned to each other, and as their eyes met, they both burst out laughing. "I doubt she's ever happened on a more delicate situation in her life," Francis grinned. "I'm sure it must have taken a great deal of willpower for her to maintain a steady countenance. It's not every day that one finds one's master looking a fright because he's been bawling like a baby, and one's mistress on the floor with a look of passion in her eyes that most would consider quite sinful."

Emily chuckled. "You don't look all that bad, you know, and as far as bawling like a baby is concerned, I'm sure I don't know what you're referring to."

"Well, I applaud your tact, wife. However, you still look like a sex-starved wanton." He grinned teasingly as she gasped in horror, clearly embarrassed that her wants were so plain for him to see. "Don't ever hide your needs from me, Emily, whatever they may be," he told her thickly. "It's one of the things that I love about you. Now, hurry upstairs so that I may soon join you."

She needed no further urging to send her on her way, her skirts rustling about her ankles as she jumped to her feet and hurried out the door. Sparing a quick backward glance at her husband, she noted that her eyes were not the only ones that blazed with desire.

Chapter Twenty-Three

Georgina helped Emily disrobe, handing her a silk dressing gown that was intended for prospective guests. It was a soft, cream-colored garment that fell supplely over her shoulders and felt delightfully smooth against her skin. A dusty pink garland of roses skimmed its edges in a pretty pattern that imparted a sense of femininity to Emily as she now sat before a mirror. With long, even strokes, Georgina brushed out her hair, the black tresses falling lightly about her shoulders. "I hope the room is to your liking, ma'am," the maid said as she picked up another loose strand and ran the brush over it.

It was the only bedroom that Emily had seen so far at Dunhurst Park, and she was, indeed, quite impressed with the luxury of it. The ivory silk upholstery of the chairs, the gold brocade of the bedspread, and the heavy toffee-colored velvet drapes went together so harmoniously and tastefully that Emily could not think of a more appropriate color scheme. It also had a distinct feel of comfort to it—mostly due to the plush accent rugs and throw cushions that begged those present to relax and unwind.

"Yes, thank you, Georgina. It's a splendid room—meant for guests, I take it?"

"Indeed it is, ma'am. I'm sure you'll be comfortable in it while your permanent rooms are being readied."

"I will not stay here, then?"

"I'm sure his lordship will want you to take over the rooms that once belonged to Lady Elisabeth—they adjoin his own."

"I see," Emily said thoughtfully, wondering how Francis would feel about someone else living amongst Elisabeth's things, even if it did happen to be his wife who was doing so. She would have to discuss this with him at a later date. "Georgina, let us not make any hasty decisions. . . . Sometimes change can be rather shocking. I would greatly appreciate it if you would tell Mrs. Reynolds not to open up Lady Elisabeth's rooms just yet. Let me have a word with his lordship first, if I may, and I'll let you know what we decide. Besides, I rather like this room, though it may be smaller."

She saw the maid smile at her in the mirror. "I'm certain we're quite blessed to have you as our mistress," she said. "For someone of your rank, you're unusually sensitive toward the sensibilities of others. Most ladies I've met would have jumped at the opportunity to increase their living space."

"Well," Emily said, smiling back at the reflection. "I'm not most ladies."

"You most certainly aren't," Georgina happily agreed.

Steam wrapped itself around Emily when she entered the bathroom, where a large white ceramic tub stood waiting on clawed feet. A rush of warmth filled her lungs as she inhaled the vapor, dampening her mood to one of deep relaxation. "Would you please see that my garments are cleaned and ready to wear by noon tomorrow, Georgina?" she asked in a quiet tone.

"I'll attend to it myself," Georgina promised as she stooped to pour some lavender oil into the water. The potent scent wafted toward Emily, swathing her in its sweetness as it soothed her senses even further.

"There's a pile of white linen towels right here, close at hand," Georgina told her as she pointed toward a table standing next to the tub. "The soap is on the tray next to them. Will that be all, then?"

"Yes, thank you kindly, Georgina. I'll see you in the morning."

"Very well, ma'am. I wish you a pleasant evening."

The door closed and Emily allowed the silk dressing gown to slide off her shoulders—it drifted to the floor. Warmth hugged her naked form as she stepped forward to stroke the still water with the tips of her fingers, scattering ripples across the surface. The water was hot against her skin, almost unbearably so, as she dipped the toes of her right foot, then let them sink in as wet heat swirled about her calf. Bringing her other leg inside, she gradually submerged herself fully, easing her way into the water while her body adjusted itself to the temperature.

Closing her eyes, she inhaled the balmy air, and then let out a long, deliberated breath as she felt the tension ease from her shoulders and her muscles relax. What an unexpected end to a day that had been far from ordinary, she thought. A wry smile curved her lips as it turned to laughter. When she'd met her sisters for breakfast that morning, she certainly wouldn't have thought that she'd find herself married by nightfall.

How odd—sometimes life managed to unfold in the most unlikely way. Just little more than a month ago, she'd still believed that she would marry Adrian. She harrumphed at the notion. Considering what she felt for Francis, she could scarcely believe that she'd ever entertained such a ridiculous idea—not that Adrian wasn't pleasant enough or handsome enough, for he definitely was both of those things. But he would never be able to affect her the way Francis did. Francis turned her legs to jelly with a single touch. He made her heart flutter like the wings of a butterfly while molten fire flooded her from head to toe, igniting her senses.

Reaching for the soap, she cursed herself for having been so hard on him all of these years. There had been good reason for his dark mood. He couldn't have been more than fifteen or sixteen when Elisabeth Riley killed herself—to think that he had been the one to find her in such a state. . . . No child should be subjected to such horror.

She wondered what had changed. Perhaps time had healed a part of his anger and grief, or perhaps it was just circumstance that had brought them together again. It was odd, really, to suddenly know what she'd been missing all these years without it ever having occurred to her that her life had been lacking in any way. She let out a sigh. There was no point in sentimentalizing over the past—what mattered was that they'd overcome their resentment for one another, allowed their friendship to grow, and fallen in love. Ah, if only all people could experience such bliss—she pitied those who did not.

Lifting her leg, she ran the soap over it to form a trail of suds along its length. She put the soap aside on its tray, then worked her fingers against her skin, enjoying the slippery feel of the lather beneath them.

A faint sound stilled her as she cocked her head to listen. It came again, a small careful creaking of wood. Turning her head, she bit down on her lip as she watched the door ease open, firm fingers gripped around its frame. Her eyes rose along a sturdy form clad in a gray velvet robe until they settled upon a familiar face. "May I come in?" Francis asked with a small degree of uncertainty that warmed her heart.

She nodded in response. The amount of relief that showed upon his face eased the tightening in her belly. He was just as nervous as she, it seemed, though her nod had apparently renewed his confidence. He had closed the door firmly behind him, leaned against it now, and allowed his eyes to linger upon her for a long, unending moment.

She shifted uneasily beneath his gaze, suddenly intensely aware of her nudity. The water offered some comfort, though he could easily make out the shape of her breasts beneath it. "Will you let me attend to you?" His voice was soft with a hint of raw desperation. Again she nodded, this time dismayed by the flicker of light that filled his eyes.

Her bare alabaster shoulders were like a glowing beacon of light at the end of a dark tunnel. They tempted him with their perfection, forcing him to move forward until he stood as close as he could without entering the bath himself.

Such beauty was the stuff of only legends. Yet here she lay, bare before his eyes, his very own nymph.

One of her feet protruded from the water. His eyes flew to it in reflex as she wriggled her toes. Quick heat rose in the pit of his stomach as his gaze followed the arch of it down into the water. His belly contracted at the sight of the pink, shimmering flesh that could only be that of her thighs. Dear God, she's stunning, he thought as the heat curled into a fiery ball that, as it burst, sent blazing heat down into his groin. There it stiffened before becoming an undulant pulse filled with ravenous hunger.

Soon she would be his, but not just yet. He meant to move slowly tonight, savoring every touch and each response, intent on prolonging her pleasure to the verge of torment. Quieting his own needs, he settled down beside her to the sound of short breaths that quivered upon her lips.

He dipped his fingertips in the water, then dragged them down the side of her neck in a moist line to the rise of her collarbone.

She tensed with anticipation below his touch, her skin prickling as new waves of heat darted across it. "Relax, and close your eyes," she heard him say in a muted voice that sent frissons scattering down her back. His breath was warm against the curve of her jaw, his lips momentarily brushing against the lobe of her ear—so close that her heart started hammering forcefully against her chest.

Doing his bidding, she closed her eyes against the candles that flickered around her, then leaned back against the tub, letting out a deep sigh of gratitude. For a moment she remained thus, caught in a world of dark comfort that lapped against her from every angle, her mind easing into a lull as she settled into deep relaxation.

Her breath caught when she felt the gentle touch of his fingertips slide across her chest, followed by the soft feel of his cheek as he leaned his head against hers. Supple hands skimmed the top of her breasts as they surfaced and dove, bobbing just below the surface. He wrapped one arm around the other side of her, locking her in his embrace, silky hairs tickling her skin, and she realized that he must have shrugged out of his robe.

Knowing that he was in all likelihood just as naked as she stirred a tingling within her that rolled and swam through her body, dipping and diving, until it finally settled between her thighs.

She inadvertently whimpered as his fingers circled her nipples, her back arched to the deep throaty hum of his voice as he teased them until they perked. Casting back her head, eyes still closed, her back flexed like a bow to meet his caresses, so that her breasts climbed out of the water, shedding water as they rose.

His hand drifted down the length of her breastbone, then further still, to her belly. There was a splash of water as one of her legs lifted, her heel coming to rest against the edge of the tub. She knew what she wanted, he saw—with great satisfaction—as he watched her body succumb to her more carnal instincts. "That's it," he whispered, his breath a gentle breeze against her burning flesh.

Waves of heat coursed through her veins, exploding in tremulous bursts beneath his fingertips as he explored her further. A quickening pulse beat like a drum within her womb, spreading waves of pleasure to her groin. Why was he tormenting her so? She was more than ready to feel his touch between her legs, was on the verge of begging for it, when she finally felt his fingers stroke against her. "Oh God," she murmured as her body ignited in a blaze of flames.

His touch deepened, her sounds of passion spurring him on as he felt his own manhood tighten and stretch at the thrill of the pleasure that he stirred in her. "That's the way," he muttered against her cheek as one of his fingers slid inside her. "Let me show you." And he pushed yet another finger inside as she gasped and shuddered in response.

The fire within her built, higher and higher, consuming her so fiercely that she thought she was sure to combust. It mattered not, however. Nothing mattered at that very moment—nothing save the exquisite bliss that washed over her. Tension expanded in every sinew, taking her to such staggering heights that she knew release must come soon. She hoped and prayed for it, for if it did not, then she felt she would surely die. And then it came, in waves of shudders as she cried out, expelling the pressure that now had turned to thrilling bursts of light exploding behind her eyes.

"Come, let me dry you off," he told her a while later as she sagged against the back of the tub, lulling in the wake of the storm. "There's much more that I intend to show you."

She never would have guessed that passion could be rekindled so quickly—she'd thought herself spent, but the hunger in his voice flooded her senses with renewed vigor. Rising, she stood before him, allowing his eyes to feast upon her every curve. Sparks of light flashed behind his eyes, the corners of his mouth drawn up into a greedy smile.

With great care, he dried her arms, her chest, and her legs until her skin glowed with the freshness that followed a hot bath. Tilting her head toward him, his mouth closed over hers in a soft and tender kiss. "I love you, Emily," he whispered as he hugged her against him. "I love you so very much."

Her heart expanded with boundless joy at those words. "Oh, Francis, I love you, too." He drew back, his eyes searching hers, imparting everything he felt for her in that single gaze. Then his lips were on her again, more urgent than before, parting so his tongue could brush against hers. She yielded instantly, swaying against him as their tongues became one in a hot, wet mixture of erotic passion that knew no bounds. Scooping her up in his arms, he carried her into the bedroom and settled her carefully on the bed.

Candles flickered all around, casting dancing shadows across the walls in a blend of yellow hues that mingled with the darkness. Emily cast a look at Francis. Her breath caught as her eyes fell upon broad shoulders and tightly coiled muscles rippling down his arms. His chest was firm, his belly lean, and . . . God almighty . . . she sucked in her breath as her eyes took in his manhood, thick and erect—a clear indication of his need. He was magnificent—a fine specimen of masculinity, indeed.

Heat flushed her face as she raised her gaze to meet his, a sudden shyness at her own brazenness leaving rosy patches upon her cheeks. He must have noticed, for he raised an eyebrow and granted her a mischievous grin. "Don't be ashamed of yourself, Emily. Nothing stirs my blood more than to be regarded in that way. The fact that you want me is plain enough in your eyes, and it excites me, as you can see."

"I'm sorry," she blustered. "It's just that . . . well . . . I feel like a wanton, and some of the things we've done seem so . . . indecent. I don't want you to think less of me."

"Sweetheart . . . nothing that you and I do together in the privacy of our bedroom will ever cause me to think less of you." He gave her a cheeky smile before adding, "And as far as indecency is concerned—you haven't seen anything yet."

"Then show me," she told him in a husky voice that quickly wiped the smile off his face, replacing it with something far more . . . indecent, so to speak. Her eyes clouded with a sudden need to join with him, to feel the strength and vitality of his body against hers. Reaching out, she took his hand in hers and drew him toward her. "You're right, you know," she murmured as he sank down between her legs. "I want you more than I've ever wanted anything before in my life."

His eyes held hers fast as everything narrowed around them until it was just the two of them caught in a heated moment. "Dear God, woman, you drive me mad with desire."

Before she could form a response, his tongue was licking at her belly, lips kissing, and teeth nibbling. She gasped at every touch, her nerves so raw, her skin so sensitized. When his mouth crept lower, she clamped her legs together without thinking, so mortified at the prospect of what he intended. "Do not deny me this pleasure, Emily," he implored, his voice so needy that she trembled at the sound of it. "I mean to taste every part of you, and I promise that you will enjoy this very, very much indeed."

Heat surged as he carefully parted her legs with his hands, spreading her wide, then kneeled between them. Staring down at her, he looked for what felt like an eternity to her. But she could not dismiss the way his eyes gleamed like those of a pirate who'd just stumbled upon a vast treasure. Mesmerized, she watched as he licked his lips, then bent his head and . . . *good God*. She felt the warm velvety touch of his tongue slide over that moist part of her, and she thought she must have died and gone to heaven.

Parting the soft folds of flesh that guarded her entrance, he passed his tongue over her in long and lingering licks that sent butterflies soaring through her belly. Over and over until she feared she might explode. He then delved deeper until her rich fragrance surrounded his senses and she knew that he'd been right. She did enjoy this very, very much indeed—wanton that she was. A deep hum of satisfaction caught in his throat as he eased away. Looking up, he saw the muddled look of complete fulfillment mixed with utter disappointment, clearly visible upon her face. He grinned, rising over her and brushing a few loose strands of hair from her face. "I think you're ready now, Emily," he murmured as he bent to kiss her. "What do you think?"

Her voice quivered as she spoke. "I think I'll dissolve and fade away if you don't take me this instant, Francis."

"I must warn you, sweetheart, there's bound to be a little pain when I . . ."

"Stop talking, Francis, just please . . . for the love of God, please . . ." The rest of the words would not seem to form, but he understood without any shadow of a doubt the urgency of her plea, for it was as fiery as his own.

He eased inside her with gentle care as he felt the proof of her virginity, barring his way. She was warm and tight around him, sheathing him snuggly with exquisite fluidity. Covering her mouth with his, he kissed her fiercely as he plunged deep inside her with one quick thrust that shattered her innocence. If she cried out in pain, neither was aware of it, both wrapped up in the motion that settled over them—the instinctual rhythm of coupling that would outlast time.

Emily's heart raced and her breath quickened until it came in short pants. Beads of sweat gleamed like dewdrops, a soft mist against her skin. Heat rolled and churned until it rose from the core of her body, lifted her skyward toward the stars before plummeting back to earth in explosive bursts of light. She shuddered against him, crying out his name until she felt him shiver and tremble as he found his own release. Letting out a soft groan of contentment, he sank against her chest, completely satisfied and contented, his heartbeat matching hers as it slowed.

Chapter Twenty-Four

It was well after noon by the time they rose from the comfort of the bed. They'd made love twice more before sleep finally overtook them, and once again upon waking. Kissing her tenderly on the lips, Francis quietly snuck out of her room, but not before promising to meet her downstairs in one hour.

Pulling on the silk dressing gown that lay discarded in the bathroom, Emily rang for the maid. Georgina arrived promptly and in a cheery mood. "Good morning, ma'am," she said with a great big smile as she laid the clothes she'd brought with her on the bed. Emily recognized the dress she'd been wearing the day before, only now it was clean and crisp—straight from the laundry. "Did you sleep well?"

"Like a newborn baby," Emily replied, seating herself in front of the mirror.

Georgina immediately went to work, dragging a brush through Emily's hair until it gleamed. Pulling it tight, she braided the loose tresses, then bound them into a knot at the back of Emily's head. "There now, I think that ought to do it,"

Georgina said, admiring her work. "Now, if you'll please rise, I'll help you dress."

Standing perfectly still, Emily allowed Georgina to put her chemise over her head, easing the garment down over her hips until it fell smoothly along the length of her legs. The corset was next, followed by the petticoat, and finally her dress. "I see you managed to remove the small spot that was on the neckline—thank you for your efforts," Emily said, referring to a wine stain she'd noticed the previous evening.

"Nothing that a good amount of soap and hot water couldn't manage," Georgina grinned. "Will you be going out, ma'am?" she asked as Emily headed for the door.

Pausing, her hand on the door handle, Emily turned to look at the maid. "I'm not sure," she said thoughtfully.

"Well, if you do, you'll be needing this," Georgina told her as she handed Emily a beautiful straw bonnet with long pink ribbons attached. "It belonged to her ladyship . . . not exactly the height of fashion, but beautiful nonetheless."

Emily eyed the bonnet apprehensively. "I'm not sure that I should be wearing that, Georgina. Did his lordship approve of your taking it?"

"Oh yes," Georgina enthused with a sudden rise of color at the suspicion that fleeted across Emily's eyes. "It was he who suggested it."

Hesitating only briefly, Emily finally accepted the bonnet that was still being held out toward her. It really was beautiful, and would make for a pretty accessory to her white dress, she thought.

Francis was in the foyer waiting for her when she appeared at the top of the stairs, his eyes finding hers instantly. There was love in them as his lips curled into a smile of genuine happiness. Her heart beat a soft tattoo as warm waves of comfort washed over her. There was cheekiness behind his gaze, and she knew that the memory of what had passed between them during the night was still very much present in his mind.

"I thought perhaps we might take a ride," he told her, offering her his arm as she descended the last step. "A spur of the moment decision, really, but I . . . well . . ." He looked suddenly awkward and abashed. "I thought it more romantic to take a picnic on the moor, surrounded by heather, than to sit in a stiff dining room."

"Nothing would please me more, my love," she whispered. "It's a wonderful idea."

His eyes ignited with pleasure at her words; how easy it would be to make her happy. She was a woman who found immeasurable joy in the simplest of things, and it delighted him immensely to see it.

A large picnic basket sat beneath their legs in the curricle as two white horses—mother and daughter—leapt forward with a smooth gait. "It suits you," Francis told her as he glanced toward the bonnet, pink ribbons trailing in the breeze.

"Georgina told me it was your mother's—Lady Elisabeth's, I mean—I wasn't sure if I ought to wear it, but she told me it was your idea . . ." Emily felt as though she was balancing a delicate line when she spoke of Elisabeth Riley, constantly fearful of the pain her words might awaken. But he smiled at her instead, white teeth flashing. Nothing would bring him down today, she realized, and she grinned back at him with open enthusiasm as wisps of hair twirled about her face.

They followed a long, straight road—a remnant of the Romans. Lilac blankets of heather lay thick upon the ground on both sides, the wind tugging slightly at the sturdy little plants as it whisked across them. Francis directed the curricle toward an old oak whose majestic crown boasted of its years. Ages had come and gone in the time that it had stood there, a silent witness to lonely travelers, armored knights, and occasional battles. But there were no knights, nor the hint of any battle as Francis helped Emily down from the curricle.

Spreading a quilt upon the ground, the heather a soft cushion beneath it, they settled down with the picnic basket between them. "Are you hungry?" Francis asked, swatting away a bold fly.

"Ravenously," she grinned.

"How wonderful it is to find a woman with a healthy appetite. Let's see what cook has prepared, shall we?" He swung away the lid to reveal a bountiful feast of chicken thighs, ham, spinach pie, crab cakes, and cheddar cheese. There were freshly baked loaves of bread, a bottle of wine, and a pound cake for desert.

Emily's eyes widened voraciously as she took it all in. "I hope you'll leave some for me as well," he grinned. "You're almost drooling, my dear."

A sudden look of embarrassment came over her. "How terribly rude of me; it just looks so . . . deliciously appetizing. Please forgive me, Francis—I'll try to control myself."

His grin broadened into a laugh. "You did not do so last

night, sweetheart. Why start now? By all means, help yourself."

Heat rose to her cheeks at the implication, yet she wasted no time in picking up a piece of chicken and sinking her teeth into the tender flesh. "This was indeed the best idea ever, Francis," she told him a moment later as she looked out across the blanket of heather that wafted in the wind.

"I was thinking that we ought to send for a few of your things," he said as he picked up a piece of cheese and popped it into his mouth. "A change of clothes, perhaps, and any other personal items you may require for the next few days—there's no need for us to rush back to London . . . unless of course you wish to return."

She shook her head slightly, almost dreamily. "No, I do not miss the city, save for my sisters, of course, but they will be fine without me for a while. I should like to spend some time with you here, alone. We've earned a little honeymoon, I think."

"I shall provide a far better honeymoon for you than this, Emily," he told her apologetically. "We'll have a bigger wedding for our family and friends as soon as we can, and then we'll go away somewhere truly special. I promise."

She took his hand in hers, turning it over as she gazed down upon it, her eyes misting over with emotion. He would give her the world if he could, she realized, and the thought overpowered her to such an extent that she knew not how to express her own feelings. "This is truly special, Francis," she told him finally after a moment's silence. "This moment right now, here with you . . . I couldn't possibly wish for anything more." She raised her gaze to his, a soft fire kindling in his dark eyes in response to her words.

"Speaking of your sisters, Emily," he said, withdrawing his hand and reaching for the bottle of wine. "We ought to send them a letter to let them know that you are safe. They must be worried sick about you."

"Yes, I'll write to them as soon as we return to the house." She paused for a moment as she contemplated the issue. "Where should I tell them we are?"

"I see no reason why you can't say that you're staying at my estate for a while, now that we're married."

"That's just it. I'm not sure I ought to tell them that at all—they'll be terribly disappointed if they find out that I went ahead and got married without their knowledge."

There was a note of sadness in her voice that unsettled him. "Do you regret how hasty we were?" he asked her carefully, his heart twisting into an aching ball of nerves in his chest.

"Not for a minute," she exclaimed as her hand came up to caress his cheek, her eyes clear windows to her heart and soul. There was no need for him to doubt her love for him, or her happiness at that very moment. Her eyes sparkled and gleamed with such sincerity that his heart unwound and melted—all anxiety gone in a single heartbeat. "Marrying you was the best decision I ever made, Francis. I wouldn't change it for the world. But that doesn't change the way my sisters might look at it—I don't think they'll understand why it was done so quickly and without their knowledge."

A blackbird soared overhead, dipping and diving as it rode the wind. A pair of yellow butterflies fluttered their wings in a graceful dance, reminding them that summer wasn't quite over. "Is news of our union likely to spread to London?" she asked as she leaned back on her elbows, the sun bathing her face with golden light.

"If you're inquiring as to whether or not my staff can be trusted with a secret, then the answer is yes," he told her. "I've known Mrs. Reynolds since I was but a young stripling. She knows my secrets and has never betrayed my trust, and she keeps the rest of the staff on a tight leash. She knows that I have no desire to have my personal affairs hung out to dry. Nothing will be said about our wedding to the entire staff until I make a formal announcement with you at my side—it is the proper way of doing things. So for now, it is only those employees with whom you've had personal contact—Georgina, for instance—who have been informed. I'm quite confident that they can be trusted. Why do you ask?"

"I was merely entertaining the idea that we shouldn't tell anybody yet. On one hand, I rather enjoy the thought of keeping it to ourselves for a while, and on the other . . . well, it would allow us to plan a proper wedding where protocol is followed to the letter—nobody will be disappointed." She paused for a moment. "Perhaps it would be best if we didn't send for my things. . . . It will only prompt my sisters' curiosity. I'm sure I can find a couple of things locally to tide me over until we return. In the meantime, I can always say that we were detained in Redding on account of the weather. How are Beatrice and Claire to know that we weren't trapped by a thunderstorm?"

"Hmmm . . ." he eyed her carefully. "A small deception, with the intent of sparing your sisters' feelings?"

"Well, not quite. I do intend to let them know we're married—but only them, and not just yet. Right now, I simply want it to be our little secret—something for us to enjoy. Once the cat's out of the bag, it will become all about the wedding. I'm not sure I'm quite ready for that yet."

As surprised as he was to hear her say that, it also made him immensely happy. Most women couldn't wait to get a head start on planning their weddings. Then again, Emily wasn't most women. "I see no harm in it," he told her. "As long as it doesn't keep you from my bed."

"Nothing could keep me from your bed, Francis—not now that I know what it's all about." Her voice was so low that he had to strain to hear her, yet the affirmation of the needy passion he stirred in her was impossible to miss. She might as well have said *anytime, anyplace,* she was so cajoling.

Fresh heat surfaced within him. He was full to the brim with tasty food, but there was another appetite that now required sating. Emptying his glass, he looked across at her, the urge to throw her on her back so tempting. Well . . . why not? They were married, after all. "Have you finished?" he asked.

"Yes, thank you. It was delicious," she replied, licking her fingers after popping the last bite of cake into her mouth. There was a seductiveness to the gesture that sent blood surging straight to Francis's groin. Unwilling to wait another moment, he hastily piled everything back into the basket and set it aside.

With one fluid motion, his arm was about her waist, pulling her forward and down until she lay on top of him, giggling mildly at his rough handling. Tugging at her dress, he quickly found the hem and his hand dove beneath it to the warmth of her bare skin. A sigh of partial gratification escaped his lips—full indulgence was close at hand.

He felt her fingertips tangling in his hair as she pressed her lips against the crook of his shoulder, faint kisses boring into him. And then the palms of his hands found her buttocks, splaying across each perfectly rounded form as he squeezed her flesh to the sound of soft purring. One hand reached between the hillocks to run pliable fingers along her crevice. She trembled slightly with a heady groan as she parted her legs even further. Her back arched slightly, pushing her bottom up in the air—such a thrilling invitation that instantly found him stretched to his full length.

With tumultuous eagerness, she sidled back to make rapid work of the buttons on his trousers as he looked on with unabashed admiration. Her fingers were nimble indeed, he thought with a sly smile. He sucked in some air when he felt them surround him, pulling him free from his restraints as her eyes remained boldly riveted upon him. Yanking on her skirts, she soon had them up around her thighs and then . . . dear God, this woman was his every fantasy come to life. With a quick, fluid movement, she sheathed him, the moist warmth of her deepest cavern surrounding him so fully that he feared he would not last a moment longer.

And then they were moving to a beat as old as time, back and forth, his eyes small slits staring up at her as she rode him. On and on they went, all else forgotten as she swept him away from it all; his pain, his sorrow, and every worry that he'd ever had—all was left behind in that moment.

With bursts of dizzying light, he felt the tingles morph into delightful shivers that coursed through him until they exploded from his core with a power that forced a loud groan from his lips. No sooner had he drifted back to solid ground, than he felt her trembling above him, her scream of fulfillment bursting forth from the very depths of her being.

"Oh my," she panted shortly thereafter. There was sauciness about her. "I never thought myself a temptress, but I must confess that I immensely enjoyed that."

Heat still flickered behind his dark eyes as he reached out to brush a strand of loosened hair from her cheek. "And I must tell you, wife, that I found your boldness intensely arousing. You have my permission to tempt me any time with such talent as what you've just displayed." Hell, if only he could spend each moment of every day with her in bed, for the rest of his life, he would indeed be the most content of all men.

Rolling off him and straightening her skirts about her, he thought he heard the familiar sound of choked laughter. Catching her eye, he found confirmation. Something had humored her to such an extent that he found her biting on her trembling lip as tears pooled at the corners of her eyes. And then she couldn't hold back any longer and gave in to the bubbles of mirth that rose in her throat. "I'm sorry," she sputtered, her eyes validating her amusement. "I just can't help but think of how shocked Beatrice would be if she knew how lusty I am."

"Is she really that prudish, do you think?" he asked, clearly skeptical at the depiction of her older sister.

Emily gave him a disbelieving glance. "Beatrice took on the role of parent when Mama and Papa passed away. It's her job to be straitlaced." It was said in a loving, almost protective way meant to stop Francis from pursuing it further. "Though I doubt her mind is completely closed to the notion that one might be tempted to throw caution to the wind on occasion, however. Have you seen the way she regards Jonathan?"

Francis lifted an eyebrow. If Beatrice had paid any interest in his secretary, it had entirely escaped him. He pondered the idea for a moment as his eyes drifted toward the curricle. What a pity that they ought to be on their way so soon. "I think Beatrice would be good for him," he finally said. "He's getting to an age where he needs to put some thought into making a family for himself."

"He's not even over thirty, I'll wager."

"He will be thirty on his next birthday, but that's beside the point. It's my feeling that he's sown enough wild oats. He ought to make a serious attempt at forming a more permanent attachment."

"You make him sound like quite the rogue," Emily stated in surprise.

"Not a rogue, but a young man like any other. The thing is, he's also a close friend—it would mean a lot to see him settled."

"Well, perhaps we can help nudge things in the right direction," Emily smiled mischievously as she started toward the carriage.

"We mustn't meddle, Emily," he told her sternly. "You'll only get caught in the middle if things don't go according to plan."

"We'll see."

It was only half a promise that had him grabbing onto her wrist. "Promise me, Emily," he implored. His tone was gentle, but his eyes betrayed the severity that loomed beneath his calm exterior.

She shivered slightly at the notion that he kept his harsh voice at bay for her sake. How she could ever refuse him, she wondered. "I promise," she whispered, sincerity brightening her eyes as she looked up at him, stepping onto her tiptoes to press her lips against his. And she knew that it was a promise that she intended to keep.

Chapter Twenty-Five

Knocking gently on the door, Emily carefully eased it open at the sound of the beckoning voice from within. As soon as they had returned home, she had gone upstairs to rearrange her hair and freshen up while Francis had withdrawn to his study. They had declined dinner, being quite satisfied from their picnic, and had suggested to Parker that he leave a couple of plates of food for them in the kitchen in case they got hungry later.

Emily now spotted Francis, seated behind his Chippendale desk at the opposite side of the room. He looked up as she slipped through the door, closing it gently behind her. "Am I disturbing?" she asked.

"Not in the least," he replied as he looked up from the papers he'd been perusing, pen in hand. "I was going over the list of my investments." He leaned back in his chair, the leather squeaking as he adjusted himself, then propped his chin against his right hand. Waving his left, he gestured for her to sit down. "I've been investing in the East India Company for years and it has proved to be quite profitable. Jonathan suggests that I buy stock in *The Times*, and I do believe that it's a good idea. Then of course there are a few smaller ventures, some more lucrative than others, but I'd like to find something new . . . something with a dazzling future ahead of it." He let out a long sigh. "I'm sorry, my dear, I don't mean to bore you with business."

Her eyes seemed to grow in size at this last statement, though she remained perfectly collected. Her voice was cool when she spoke. "Do you suppose that I'm not interested in your affairs because I'm a woman?"

He checked himself, felt his skin prickle at his blunder. Emily was different from other women. She was well read and knowledgeable in areas where he was not. She had a desire to learn, and he realized that it would be a catastrophic error to brush her aside with the assumption that she paid no heed to how he made his living. "I'm sorry," he told her and her gaze softened. "Would you perhaps like to make a recommendation?"

Her lips twisted into a triumphant smirk. "I thought you'd never ask." Flashing him a brilliant smile, her eyes shining with excitement, she got up and circled the desk to stand next to him. She then took time to kiss him softly on the cheek—a sign of her gratitude. Most husbands would never allow their wives to become involved in their business. Emily felt her heart overflowing for the man who sat before her, so confident in her that he would ask for her opinion in regards to his affairs. One day, she hoped to find the right words to express how she truly felt about him—words of love and endearment simply didn't suffice.

"There's a Scotsman named Henry Bell," she said as she

straightened her back and walked across to the side table. "Have you heard of him?"

"He recently built a steamboat, if I'm not mistaken," Francis said, his brows furrowing into a contemplative frown.

"The Comet," she said, offering the name that had escaped him.

"Ah yes, the Comet."

"Well, it seems to have been quite successful. I read in the paper last week that it had just begun transporting passengers between Glasgow, Greenock, and Helensburgh three times a week." She poured herself a sherry, smacking her lips together as the sweet flavor swirled around her mouth. "Anyway, I thought it might be interesting not only as an investment, but as a business opportunity. Imagine such a boat on the Thames. It could easily transport passengers from London to Slough . . . even as far as Oxford, and without the need for wind."

Francis stared at his wife for a moment with a look of disbelief. "You certainly are a woman of vision," he finally stated.

The compliment flattered her more than any comment about her looks ever would. She smiled brazenly. "Do you like the idea, then?" she asked nonchalantly, knowing full well what his reply would be, yet enjoying the admiration that showed upon his face.

"Like it? I love it!" he exclaimed with sudden excitement as he leapt from his chair to hug her fiercely, the air squeezed out of her. "Oh, Emily, you've saved the day. Remind me always to consult you on matters of importance."

He sprang back and reached for the abandoned glass of

brandy that sat upon his desk. "Hell, I need as much money as I can get if I'm to stop Charlotte from bleeding me dry." He winced as he took a large gulp.

"That's part of the reason why I came to see you," Emily told him a bit skittishly. She was constantly wary of the threat any mention of Charlotte might have on their happiness.

Francis raised an inquisitive eyebrow. "Oh?"

"If I'm not mistaken, you were looking for a way to permanently rid yourself of her."

"Well, yes, but if murder is what's on your mind," he said, noticing the conspiratorial gleam in her eyes, "then I'm sorry to tell you that I shan't resort to such extreme measures—not that I haven't considered it, mind you."

"Honestly, Francis," she chastised. "You have far too vivid an imagination for your own good. Do I look like a murderess to you?"

He regarded her momentarily, her black hair knotted at the nape of her neck, her milky complexion, and her bright green eyes. He had no trouble at all visualizing her with a carving knife in one of those delicate hands of hers.

She didn't miss the slight shiver that raked his spine. "Good grief!" she exclaimed, clearly exasperated that his mind would entertain such a preposterous idea. "Intelligent people don't resort to such base actions. They come up with a plan instead, and that's precisely what I've done. Are you willing to hear it?"

It was impossible for Francis to hide his surprise. It moved him that Emily had gone to the trouble to find a way in which to save him from Charlotte's clutches. It was as if a small spark of hope came to life in the bleak recesses of his mind. "More than willing—please continue, Emily. You have my full attention."

"Right," she said with a determined look upon her face. "It means that we won't be able to tell anyone that you and I are married, not even my sisters. My plan will depend entirely upon Charlotte never discovering that we've been wed, so I really hope that you're right in your evaluation of your staff." She fixed him with a quizzical stare. If he had any doubts about his employees' ability to keep a secret, now was the time to voice it.

"I believe their loyalty lies with me and that I can trust them not to reveal anything that might jeopardize us."

"Very well, then," she said, emptying her glass and setting it down. "Then here's what we must do."

Chapter Twenty-Six

They returned to London three days later, confident that they had a bulletproof plan by which to remove Charlotte from their lives forever. It was true that it depended on some degree of luck, but they hoped that Francis's connections with the *ton* would serve them well.

Beatrice shoved her way past Parker as the aging butler opened the door. Without a second thought to how she must look—rushing down the steps toward Emily, skirts trailing behind her—she flung her arms around her sister's neck in a fierce hug. "Thank God you're safe," she murmured against Emily's ear. Then, with some remnant of decorum, she peeled herself away from her sister, brushing her hands over Emily's Spencer in hopes of straightening the ruffled garment. "I'm sorry, but I was so terribly worried about you."

"That's quite all right," Emily smiled, taking her sister by the arm and leading her toward the house. "I would have been quite disappointed with a lesser display of affection."

"That's precisely what I thought," Beatrice grinned with a hint of smugness.

"I'm the one who ought to apologize, Bea," Emily stated as she gave her sister a sidelong glance. "It was incredibly stupid of me to run to Edward. It was very fortunate that Francis came along when he did. I believe our dear relation had set his mind on forcing me to capitulate to his desire to wed me."

"Come now," Beatrice chuckled. "Surely you exaggerate."

"I'm afraid not," Francis told her. "Your sister's virtue was in serious jeopardy."

Thunderous clouds of anger filled Beatrice's otherwise tranquil eyes. Emily flinched; she'd never before witnessed such abhorrent animosity in her sister before now. "One day, I'll have the bastard's head on a plate," she fumed. "The amount of grief he's caused this family is more than I'm willing to endure."

"Calm yourself, Bea. I'm all right now. Come, let's go inside and have some tea." Emily shot a nervous glance at Francis as she urged her sister toward the door. Nothing good would come of Beatrice making a public spectacle of herself out in the street. The thought that that was precisely what might happen was greatly unsettling. Beatrice had always been so calm, a pillar of strength that her younger sisters had clung to in the wake of tragedy. But even she was threatening to unravel before Emily's very eyes.

And then the storm had passed as quickly as it had come and Emily was left with nothing but uncertainty.

"Yes, let's have some tea," Beatrice was saying. "And we'll tell you the good news."

Emily's eyes drifted toward Claire, who stood waiting in the doorway. "Good news?"

"Yes—very good, in fact." It was clear that Beatrice was

bursting to tell them whatever it was. Her eyes sparkled with the knowledge that she held a secret that was sure to delight everyone. Claire looked equally excited as she hopped from foot to foot, impatience clear upon her face as she waited for Emily to remove her hat and gloves.

Once seated in the parlor, Beatrice fought the urge to spill the news as she went about pouring tea for everybody. Emily eyed her sisters carefully with the odd glance in Francis's direction. He and Jonathan looked equally unmoved—how could they appear so indifferent when it was clear that her sisters looked as though they might tell them they'd discovered a way of traveling to the moon?

"Well?" Emily asked, unwilling to contain her curiosity for a moment longer.

"Shall I tell them?" Beatrice asked Claire.

"Yes, yes, all right," Claire replied, her voice bubbling enthusiastically.

"No, no, it wouldn't be right; you tell them, Claire." Beatrice sounded equally giddy.

"Oh, but I couldn't possibly, Bea. I think you should do it."

Emily's eyes darted from sister to sister as though she were watching a game of tennis. The animated behavior suited Claire's personality, but Emily was stunned to see her older sister acting like a young schoolgirl. "Whatever is the matter with the two of you?" she asked, suppressing the urge to laugh that rose in her own throat—the scene was simply too comical for words. "You look like snickering girls who've just discovered the existence of boys for the very first time. Now get a hold of yourselves."

The fact that Francis raised an eyebrow wasn't lost on

Emily. She knew the reason behind it the minute it happened and couldn't help but bite down on her own lip. She was the one that was usually prone to laughing at her own private jokes, yet here she was, acting like an old matron, beseeching her sisters to be serious. It must be rather an odd tableau for any spectator familiar enough with their personalities.

"All right, Claire will tell you," Beatrice remarked, folding her hands in her lap and looking expectantly at her youngest sister.

"No, I really think that you ought to do it, Bea," Claire replied.

"Oh, for heaven's sake," Emily gasped in exasperation, her patience beginning to wear thin. "Out with it!"

"There's no need to be so blunt with us," Claire muttered. Emily let out a sigh that did little to hide her annoyance, then took a sip of tea to smooth away her agitation, and sank back against her chair. She would just have to wait for one of them to say whatever it was that needed saying.

A tense silence spread throughout the room. Francis and Jonathan had wisely decided not to add to the conversation. They each sat in complete silence, watching the scene before them. Claire began nervously fidgeting with her dress, twisting the fabric that covered her lap between her fingers. Beatrice finally gathered her wits and spoke up. "Lord Camden paid us a visit this morning," she said, the hint of a smile tugging at the corner of her mouth. "He has made an offer for Claire."

Emily was out of her chair quicker than a hound chasing a rabbit. She threw her arms about Claire in a tight hug. "That's wonderful news, indeed," she said. She pulled away slightly so as to see her sister's face. "This is what you want, I take it?"

"What gave me away?" Claire asked in a teasing voice.

Emily just laughed, embracing her sister yet again. "I'm very happy for you. I remember you dancing with him at Kate and Adrian's engagement party—you must have made quite an impression."

"It appears that he is quite besotted with our Claire." Beatrice picked up a strawberry tart and took a small bite from it. "He has agreed to marry her posthaste—on her birthday, nonetheless."

"But that's only three weeks away," Emily gasped. "We can't possibly arrange for a decent wedding in so little time."

"Don't you see that we must?" Claire said as she reached for Emily's hand. "If we don't, then all we have, little as it may be, reverts back to Edward. We mustn't let that happen."

Realization suddenly dawned on Emily. An offer had been made—a very good offer, it seemed—yet she couldn't allow her sister to sacrifice her life as she had intended to do—especially when it was completely unnecessary. "Do you love him, Claire?" she finally asked.

"I . . ." a look of uncertainty flickered behind Claire's eyes. "I like him a lot," she finally said. "And I'm confident that I shall grow to love him."

Emily winced. This was not what she wished for her youngest sister. She wanted her to love the man she planned to marry just as much as she loved Francis. "I think perhaps you're rushing into this because of circumstance, Claire."

It was a statement that was brutally honest and had Claire's eyes flaring in an instant. She rounded on her sister with a mean look in her eyes. "Do I not look happy to you, Emily?" she asked from between clenched teeth. "I am overjoyed—to be fortunate enough that a gentleman such as Lord Camden—a viscount, no less—is willing to marry me in spite of how little I shall be bringing into such a marriage—it is fortuitous, indeed. I have nothing but my parents' name, my looks, and my virtue to commend me. There is no dowry, and yet he is willing to have me anyway."

Emily's eyes stung at her sister's statement. The truth in it only made it so much more difficult to accept. "But you . . ."

"Just because you lost the chance to marry Adrian doesn't give you the right to thwart my hopes of happiness."

Emily sank her head, her eyes trying to focus on the intricate design of the carpet. How she longed to tell her sisters that she herself was happily married, that Claire needn't marry out of obligation. She longed to throw Claire's words back in her face, declaring her everlasting love for Francis, but how could she? Not without jeopardizing Francis's hope for a happy future. There was too much at stake. Besides, three weeks might be enough time for them to hatch their plan against Charlotte. Or perhaps Claire might come to love Lord Camden just a little by then.

"That was unjust." She heard Beatrice's voice chastising Claire's last remark, and she needn't look up to know that Francis would be frowning. "Please apologize to your sister."

"There's really no need," Emily said, raising her eyes to meet Claire's. "You are a grown woman, and the decision about whom you marry is up to you. But if I may give you a small piece of advice, try to spend as much time with your fiancé as you can over the next three weeks. Get to know him well. I shall support your decision, whatever it may be."

The look on Claire's face was greatly apologetic. She looked as though she'd like nothing better than to retreat to the farthest corner of the universe. "I'm sorry," she whispered. "I didn't mean it and it was badly done of me to say such a thing."

"On a more positive note," Beatrice chimed in. "You must no longer feel obliged to make any unnecessary sacrifices on our account, Emily."

She was referring to Emily's far too hasty decision to marry Edward, but the comment struck a chord nonetheless. Emily's eyes darted across the room to where Francis sat, completely immobile, his gaze riveted upon her in expectation. As far as Beatrice was concerned, he was still courting her. How her sister had managed to say something so cruel and insensitive was beyond comprehension. Anger flashed like shards of glass behind her eyes as she straightened herself, fully intent on reassuring the man who had captured her heart that marrying him had by no means been a sacrifice.

Taking on a regal stance that seemed to dwarf the rest of those present, she said, "Make no mistake, dear sister, that when I marry, it shall be for love. I shall respect my husband beyond all others, and I shall be happier than I had ever hoped to be."

The only one who showed a hint of a smile was Francis, and even then it was from behind his teacup. Beatrice looked positively stunned by Emily's verbal attack. "Did I offend you in some way?" she asked.

"You cannot know how much," Emily replied in a pained voice.

"Then I must apologize, for I had no idea."

"When shall we have the pleasure of meeting this Camden fellow, Claire?" Jonathan spoke up, easing the tension.

"Tomorrow evening at the Marquess of Ailesbury's ball," Claire said, turning to Beatrice, who seemed preoccupied. "Is that not so? Bea?"

"Yes, of course." Beatrice quickly composed herself, whatever had distracted her seemingly forgotten. "It's the last ball of the season, it being the twelfth of August tomorrow."

"Ah, the Glorious Twelfth," Jonathan murmured. "The hunting season begins. I almost wish we could warn the red grouse against the wrath of Lord Barkley—you know he always throws away half of what he shoots."

"We shall be sure to be on our best behavior," Francis promised, honoring Claire with a playful smile.

"Even your aunt has promised to attend," Beatrice added.

"Is that so?" Francis couldn't help but smile at the idea. "How is she, by the way?"

"Very well, though she still insists on taking her meals upstairs."

Francis nodded before heading toward the door. "Now, if you'll please excuse me, there are a few letters that have arrived in my absence—I'd like to go over them right away." He turned to Emily with a blank expression. "Would you please join me in the study? I'd like to have a word with you."

Emily nodded. It was impossible for her to determine what was on his mind. Would he chastise her for her outburst?

From the corner of her eye, Emily saw Beatrice regard the two of them with increasing interest, surely wondering what

Francis could possibly have to say to Emily that he couldn't just as well say in front of everyone else. They would have to be careful or Beatrice was sure to discover something was afoot.

The door closed behind them and Francis immediately pulled Emily against him, smothering her mouth with his in a desperate kiss. Lips parted and waves of desire poured over them as their tongues mingled—hot, moist, and sensual. Gently easing her away from him, Francis took a step back, his breath heavy upon his lips. "If we don't stop now, we'll soon be sprawled out upon the floor," he said as fire burned in his dark eyes.

Emily stared back at him. She knew that he was right. What shocked her was that she didn't really care. Her need for him—to have him inside her and to revel in all the pleasure that he offered—was so great at that very moment that nothing else mattered.

He seemed to read her mind. "You know that we can't," he told her, attempting to feign a voice of reason that he did not feel. "We're not even supposed to be married. But even if we were, I do believe your sisters would have a case of the vapors if they were to happen upon us in a tangled mess of partial undress."

Emily burst out laughing, light dancing in her eyes as she clasped her hands over her mouth to stifle the sound. The image that he'd brought to life was too hilarious to be taken seriously. He must have agreed, for he soon joined her with a heartfelt grin. "We would in all likelihood be forced to send for the doctor to tend to them," he continued, in a hope to impress upon her the seriousness of the situation, but it had quite the opposite effect—Emily only laughed harder.

"What a spectacle it would be," she gasped between giggles. "Me with my skirts up about my waist, you with your trousers down around your ankles, and Beatrice and Claire in a dead faint upon the floor." She bit her lip to stifle herself. "You're right—it would probably be more than my poor sisters could handle."

He nodded convincingly—more for his own sake than for hers. "On a different note, I actually did have something that I wished to tell you."

She smoothed her dress, then perched herself on the edge of the chair closest to her.

"I'm glad that you said what you did in there. I was worried for a moment that you might regret marrying me once you discovered that it had not been necessary in terms of securing your sisters' future, now that Claire is to wed Lord Camden."

"Beatrice won't understand my outburst." It was said with a hint of regret at the way in which she had treated her older sister. "But I said it for your benefit more than anyone else's. I would rather hang myself than to have you believe that I regret becoming your wife."

Reaching out, he gently brushed his hand against her cheek. "I should have told you what happened a long time ago," he whispered. "To think of all the years we've wasted . . . but instead I pushed you away. I was jealous, I suppose."

"Jealous?" She looked at him quizzically. "Of what?"

He gave her a sad smile. "It all seems so silly now . . . pitiful, really. To begin with . . ." He paused, eyeing her carefully. "I couldn't bear to see you fawn over Adrian the way you did when I . . . it's taken me years to acknowledge this, Emily, but the truth is that I've always loved you. And then . . . when Elisabeth died . . . I felt as though my world had gone to pieces. I envied you for being so happy. I despised Adrian for having captured your affection. . . . I hated the world for being so bloody unjust." His words faded and his hand fell away.

She leaned forward to kiss him gently on his forehead. "I love you, too, Francis. I believe I've always loved you, but I was so blinded by Adrian's charm and attention toward me that I turned my back on the one person who truly mattered to me. As it turned out, Adrian was a poor substitute, but one that I desperately needed. I felt abandoned when you shut me out, and I lost hope. I'm so sorry."

Her revelation shocked both of them into momentary silence. Color rose to Emily's cheeks. She hadn't even realized how long she'd felt that way until just now when she'd actually said it out loud. A sense of longing flooded through her. How many years she'd wasted, pining over the wrong man and criticizing the right one. "I'm so sorry for the way in which I treated you—it was terribly wrong of me, and now that I know why you acted the way you did . . . I feel awful!"

"And so you should," he teased her with a smile, but rather than laugh as he had hoped, her eyes glistened with the promise of tears.

"Dear, sweet Emily," he told her as he crouched before her and pulled her head against his shoulder in a warm embrace. "Why do you torture yourself so? We were both at fault back then, but there's no use in fretting about lost time now. Let's just be grateful that we are finally together, in spite of everything." He pulled back to look at her. His heart clenched at the sight of a wet patch staining her cheek. "I love you, sweetheart. Never in my life have I loved anybody more."

And then she did give him that dazzling smile of hers that made his heart leap. He kissed the top of her head affectionately as he rose to his feet.

"I'm worried about Claire," she said suddenly. "She's rushing into a marriage that she needn't rush into—you and I are already married, but I cannot tell her that. I don't know what to do."

"I'm afraid that I must agree with your sisters on this matter," Francis said, to Emily's surprise. She had hoped that he would side with her . . . no, she had *expected* it, but she was glad of his honesty nonetheless. "The truth is that Claire will never find as good a match as Lord Camden. I never doubted that she and your sister would have suitors, but I expected them to be men without a title who had to work for a living. In spite of her name, Claire has no wealth to match that of an aristocrat. The fact that a man such as Lord Camden is more than willing to marry her truly is a blessing."

"But if she does not love him?" Emily looked thoroughly perplexed, yet Francis thought the concern for her sister's welfare made her even more stunning.

"You're a romantic, Emily, and I commend you for it, but every now and again, it's necessary to be a realist. Claire doesn't seem to dislike her young lord or the prospect of marrying him. Have you seen the man, by the way? He's strikingly handsome."

It was true that Emily had not yet met the man her sister

intended to marry. In fact, the only times she'd even heard the mention of his name had been at the Carroway ball and at Cunningham House—she still had to see him in person.

"You have to understand that what you and I have is rather unique," Francis was saying. "In fact, it's extremely rare. We've known each other since childhood. There's a link between us that takes years for most newlywed couples to develop. Don't discredit your sister's union because you want her to have what you have—it's unlikely that she will. But that doesn't mean that they won't love each other in the end.

"Lord Camden is a man of means. He will provide very well for her, showering her in everything that her heart desires, and from what Beatrice says, he's already smitten with Claire. It is a start—I daresay a better one than many are given." He paused for a moment before taking Emily's hand in his. "If I may give you a piece of advice, don't do anything to ruin Claire's chances or to change her mind. You would be doing her a great disservice, and I doubt that she would thank you for it."

He was right, of course, though Emily was reluctant to admit it. She would do as he suggested, however—step back and allow her sister the space she needed, to make the most important decision of her life on her own.

Chapter Twenty-Seven

Francis had assured Emily that once Charlotte discovered that he and Emily had formed an attachment, she would undoubtedly approach them all by herself. At least, that was what he hoped, for it was less likely to raise Charlotte's suspicions than if Emily tried to befriend her on her own. With this in mind, it was with some degree of trepidation that they set out for the Marquess of Ailesbury's mansion on Wigmore Street the following evening.

Even though the general outline of their plan was Emily's, she had become increasingly worried that a woman such as Charlotte would be able to see right through her. She was not accustomed to lying, so befriending someone whose life centered on duping those that she wished to benefit from was suddenly the most terrifying thing that Emily could possibly imagine.

A dizzying shimmer of light, bouncing off of jewel-bedecked women and crystal chandeliers, twinkled like fairy dust when they made their appearance at precisely nine o'clock. It was a sight upon which Emily's eyes luxuriated as they sucked in the opulence of Lord and Lady Ailesbury's ballroom and of their guests. Music rose to the sound of Haydn's *Surprise*, softly filling the air from the far side of the room, only slightly muted by the hum of voices wrapped in conversation.

The floor was polished marble—cream outlined by three borders in black, beige, and brown. The walls and ceiling were ivory white, richly embellished with moldings whose varying patterns had been highlighted in gold. A set of twelve doors led to other rooms, as well as to a terrace overlooking the garden, and above these doors was a balcony that framed the entire ballroom. Up there, sofas and chairs had been set alongside small tables, so that those who'd grown tired of dancing—or simply wished to sit down and rest their legs—could do so without secluding themselves from the rest of the party.

Emily was glad she'd opted for her white dress with embroidered rosebuds lining the neckline and hem in splashes of scarlet. A matching ribbon ran beneath her bosom, tying in a neat bow at the back, the ends of it trailing elegantly behind her as she walked.

Francis thought she looked particularly stunning that evening, and he longed for nothing more than to take her home again so he could have her for himself. Shaking the urge, he tried instead to focus on the task that lay ahead.

They didn't know for certain that Charlotte would be present that evening, but he hoped that she would. Following Lady Riley's death, Charlotte had accompanied his father to all such events, taking on the role of his wife rather than that of his mistress. Time had caused many people to forget that she didn't really belong. Or perhaps they hadn't forgotten, he reflected, but were either too polite or too affected by habit to do anything about it. It was probably the latter, he decided. The *ton* generally didn't mind shunning somebody that they didn't feel belonged in their circle.

Then again, he was in all likelihood the only person amongst them who'd ever seen Charlotte's true character. Whenever she went out in public, she immediately donned the appearance of endless kindness and concern for those around her. Never in a million years would anyone have cause to believe that this wasn't her true nature. Her smile appeared as genuine as that of an angel sent from heaven, and her words so sincere that Francis had always thought she'd make a formidable opponent at cards—nobody would ever call her bluff.

His eyes now scanned the room for her unwillingly.

"I'm glad you were able to come, Dunhurst," a bold voice spoke, drawing Francis's attention away from the crowd. It belonged to his host, Lord Ailesbury, who was strategically positioned just inside the main entrance to the ballroom. He stood with his wife upon his arm, greeting guests as they swept past.

Both were in their mid-forties. The marquess was a tall, slim man with reddish hair. His face was softly rounded like that of a young boy, but the creases in his forehead betrayed his age. His wife was a voluptuous lady with heavy breasts and wide hips—a stark contrast to her husband. Her eyes and smile were warm and inviting, making her the sort of person that people gravitated toward.

"Ailesbury!" Francis shook his host's outstretched hand. He then directed an elegant bow toward the marchioness.

"My lady. I trust that you remember Mr. Rosedale. And may I present some dear friends of mine, the Rutherford sisters: Beatrice, Emily, and Claire."

"It's an honor, my lord." Beatrice, being the oldest, spoke for all of them, then made a slight curtsey. Her sisters followed suit.

"Surely not Anna and James's children?" the marchioness inquired in amazement.

"Indeed we are, my lady," Beatrice told her.

"Well, then, I daresay it's about time you've come to London. It simply won't do for three lovely young ladies such as yourselves to remain hidden away in a small place like Hardington—not that it isn't a charming little town, but one simply doesn't have the same access to culture and potential husbands as one does in London. I'm quite sure that half the gentry must be fawning over you already!"

None of the three women could help but blush at the marchioness's remark. "We visited Hardington once, you know," she continued. "Your parents used to throw the most extravagant parties—people would gladly come from miles away to attend. Oh, but we were so much younger then and far more reckless." She put her hand gently on her husband's arm to draw his attention. "Dear, do you remember how Lord Tenant had to walk home in his unmentionables? He'd gambled away everything else."

"I do believe Lord Barnaby took pity on the fool and gave him a ride, but yes, I do recall it being quite a colorful event."

"Ah . . . to be young again," Lady Ailesbury sighed as she reminisced about her youth. She suddenly shook her head to rid it of the cobwebs, returning her mind to the present.

"What a pleasant surprise, indeed. Oh and you must call me Margaret—I absolutely insist."

They spoke for a few more minutes until another set of guests arrived, and Francis and Jonathan led the sisters toward a table filled with refreshments.

"Is that not Lady Barkley over there?" Emily whispered.

Francis cast a quick glance in the direction Emily was looking. "Well spotted, my dear. You'll also recognize Lady Cunningham—you'll recall that you attended her garden party a couple of weeks ago. The other lady in their presence is Lady Ingham, the Countess of Arundel." He handed Emily a glass of champagne. "All three are very influential women, and they're almost always seen together. They've been friends since they were young girls, you know—I think we ought to go and say hello."

Leaving Beatrice and Claire with Jonathan, they made their way toward the small cluster of women. "Lady Barkley!" Francis called out as they approached, causing the older woman to turn around immediately in search of the voice.

"Lord Dunhurst and Miss Rutherford. What a delight! I was hoping that I might run into you tonight."

Francis greeted the other two women before ensuring that they were all familiar with Emily.

"You've made quite a catch for yourself, Dunhurst," Lady Cunningham told him without any attempt at discretion. "Miss Rutherford's a beautiful young woman with a cheerful disposition. I quite enjoyed making her acquaintance." She cast Emily a warm smile. "And I do hope that we'll be seeing more of her in the near future."

"I'm sure you shall," Lady Barkley chimed in. "Young Emily here has become quite the talk of the town. It seems that she has singlehandedly tamed our young lord—apparently he's been nothing but smiles for the past fortnight, and we all know that Lord Dunhurst *never* smiles." She cast a sidelong glance at Francis, who was suddenly favoring her with his severest frown. "Oh, there's no need to look at me like that. You know it's true."

"Well, I for one am quite pleased to finally make your acquaintance, Miss Rutherford," Lady Ingham intoned. "Perhaps you can work your magic on my husband as well?"

Emily blushed at the compliment, but Lady Barkley didn't miss a beat. "Give it up, Laura. We both know that your husband is a lost cause."

"We used to think the same of Dunhurst," Lady Ingham pointed out.

"Yes, but he at least has the advantage of youth. Your husband, on the other hand . . . well, you know how the saying goes . . . something about old dogs and new tricks."

"I'm sure your meaning is completely lost on me," Lady Ingham remarked, pretending to be greatly offended, though her smirk betrayed that she was very capable of enjoying jokes that were made at her husband's expense.

"You're quite right, though," Francis told them. "My recent good humor is entirely due to Emily—especially since she has recently allowed me to court her." He smiled broadly, completely unable to contain his enthusiasm. He would have loved for nothing better than to have announced that she was now his wife, but for now, this would have to do.

Lady Barkley clapped her hands together in a gesture of sheer delight. "I knew it," she squeaked. "Didn't I say that the two of you looked rather enamored with one another? I believe I told you to let me know if there was any development."

"And I just have, have I not?" Francis asked slyly.

"So you have," Lady Barkley admitted. "Well, congratulations—I hope it ends with a proposal."

Emily was sure that "just married" must be written upon her forehead in bold letters for all to see. Heat had risen to her face so forcefully by now that she feared she must look like a beetroot. Even a blind person would know, based on the waves of heat radiating off of her, that something was underfoot. How in God's name was she ever going to hold up against Charlotte, who was sure to be more astute than these women? On the other hand, they didn't seem to have noticed anything, so perhaps her worries were unfounded.

"Francis, I must add you to my dance card," a smooth voice said from behind them. It was Veronica, who had approached them together with Lord Farringale. She was wearing a bright orange silk dress with a black velvet ribbon highlighting the empire cut of it. Black feathers had been stuck into her hair at the back, adding that dash of flamboyance that she was so well known for. In truth, the whole ensemble would have looked ghastly on anyone else, but in some peculiar way, it really suited her.

"It was my intention to dance *only* with Emily," Francis told Veronica, as he stooped to kiss her lightly on her outstretched hand.

"Come, Francis, even you know that's not done unless she is your wife—is that not so, Lady Cunningham?" Emily's knees went weak and she clasped hold of Francis's arm. How the devil was he managing to maintain such a calm façade? It was doing nothing but unnerving her.

"I must agree with Lady Giddington," Lady Cunningham said. "You mustn't monopolize any woman, except, as Lady Giddington correctly stated, your wife. As Emily is not your wife . . . for heaven's sake, the poor dear looks as though she's about to have a spell. Why don't you dance with Lady Giddington, Lord Dunhurst? I'm sure that Lord Farringale won't mind ensuring that Miss Rutherford gets some fresh air."

"*I'll* see that she gets some fresh air," Francis insisted with increasing annoyance. "I doubt Lady Giddington will mind a short wait."

"You're far too possessive, Lord Dunhurst. If you don't give the poor girl an ounce of freedom, she may decide not to have you," Lady Barkley chirped. "She'll be in good hands with Farringale—he's quite capable, you know."

"I know precisely what he's capable of—that's what worries me." Francis's eyes had lost all sense of cheer and taken on a thunderous look instead. Farringale completely ignored it, however. Meanwhile, Emily was becoming increasingly anxious to remove herself from the group's presence. Their comments had completely undone every shred of her composure, leaving her a nervous wreck.

"Come now, Dunhurst. I know the lady is spoken for," Farringale told him. "And if that wasn't enough to keep me at bay, then surely even you must know that I'd never make any advances on a lady about to swoon."

"Very well," Francis reluctantly conceded, mostly because he was unwilling to raise any suspicions. If he pursued the subject any further, Veronica and Lady Barkley were sure to discover that things weren't quite the way they appeared.

Charlotte spotted Francis the moment he arrived, and soon noticed that he and the lady on his arm appeared to be rather tense. She couldn't help but wonder why. She'd been told that the lady in question was one of the infamous Rutherford sisters whom everyone had been talking about that season. The one her son appeared to be most interested in, however, was apparently Emily, though Charlotte couldn't for the life of her understand why. But contrary to what all the gossipmongers had been telling her, the couple seemed far from happy. His fierce demeanor alone was enough to cast serious doubt on their relationship. Perhaps he'd already tired of her then? It was the only reasonable explanation that came to mind—Francis would never tolerate a weak woman like that. For heaven's sake, she looked about ready to cry as she stood there now, clinging to his arm. What a pitiful sight, Charlotte thought to herself as she watched them talk to Ladies Barkley, Ingham, and Cunningham.

It was then, at that very moment that Charlotte decided to find out what Francis's relationship with Emily Rutherford actually was. If he had mistreated the girl or perhaps given her false hopes in any way, then perhaps she could use it to her advantage—after all, Emily Rutherford was a poor woman . . . surely she'd enjoy the prospect of taking what she could get from Francis, particularly if something made her angry enough to cloud her judgment.

Weak people were always susceptible to persuasion. And as far as Charlotte could tell, Emily Rutherford was a very weak woman indeed.

An idea began to emerge inside her head. Clearly Emily was terrified of Francis abandoning her. But if Charlotte could somehow help Emily salvage her relationship with Francis . . . if she could somehow guarantee that Francis would propose to her . . . Emily would be indebted to her forever.

A slow, deliberate smirk slid its way across Charlotte's lips. She needed a means by which to gain access to Dunhurst Park and retrieve what was rightfully hers. Perhaps this Rutherford woman would prove to be her golden ticket . . . the ally that she required to get back inside the mansion. She would have to speak to her as soon as possible, she decided.

Lord Farringale helped Emily outside, directing her toward a bench where he urged her to sit down. "The fresh air will do you good, Miss Rutherford," he told her. "Would you like me to fetch you a glass of water?"

"If it's not too much trouble, then yes, I would greatly appreciate that."

He left her instantly to find the large decanter of ice water that stood on the refreshment table. Returning with a glass in hand, he found his path blocked by Charlotte. "Miss Browne. How do you do?"

"Quite well. Quite well indeed," she replied with a sweet smile. "I thought perhaps I might take Miss Rutherford off your hands."

"I . . ."

"She is clearly unwell and in need of a woman's touch. Why don't you run along and enjoy the party instead?"

"But Lord Dunhurst . . ."

"Will be most relieved to have a lady tending to her rather than the most notorious flirt in all of London." She tilted her head and gave him the most convincing smile she could muster. "Really, I insist."

"Very well then, by all means," he said, handing her the glass of water.

Chapter Twenty-Eight

"Miss Rutherford?"

The words were softly spoken—almost a whisper—yet Emily found herself startled by them all the same. She'd been thinking about the task that lay ahead of her, attempting to regain her composure. It simply wouldn't do to fall apart in front of Charlotte. Somehow she would have to find the means by which to play her part—her happiness with Francis depended upon it. Now, looking up, her eyes met those of a woman who appeared to be quite beautiful in spite of her age. In fact, her skin was still fairly smooth—it was only the crow's feet and the occasional dash of gray in her otherwise light brown hair that betrayed her. Her eyes were kind and her smile pleasant. Emily couldn't help but like her immediately.

"I don't believe we've met," the woman told her, handing her a glass of water and sitting down next to her on the bench. "My name is Charlotte Browne."

Heat rushed down Emily's back at the sound of that name, her skin suddenly prickling with edginess. She was thankful for the darkness that would hopefully mask the stunned look upon her face.

Remaining perfectly still, she made a stoic attempt to relax and calm herself. "I'm Emily Rutherford," she heard herself say—her voice far cooler than she felt.

"So I've heard."

"Oh?"

"Do you know who I am?"

Emily merely shook her head, worried her anxiety would be plain in any words she spoke. The moment had come, and she would not forgive herself for making a mess of it. No, she would just have to get a hold of herself and manage to get through it . . . somehow. Indeed, she was fortunate that Charlotte had approached her in the first place, for it was less likely to make her suspicious than if Emily had sought to befriend *her*, as had been their initial plan.

"I couldn't help but notice that you arrived together with Lord Dunhurst. You are his guest, are you not?"

"Yes, I am."

"Well, I used to be a close friend of his parents. I've known Francis all his life, in fact. He's a good man at heart, though it seems he has been through some difficult years following his mother's death." Charlotte feigned a look of such sadness that Emily could not stop her own heart from clenching or the tears from forming behind her eyes.

If this woman truly was as horrid as Francis had described her, then she was far more dangerous than Emily had thought. She was a master at sympathizing and at being empathetic. What a supreme performer . . . so genuine and natural. Emily cautioned herself not to fall under her spell.

She had known her for only a brief moment while Francis had known her his whole life. She would trust that what he told her about Charlotte was true, and she would do whatever she could to help him be rid of her forever. She braced herself before charging ahead—the battle of wits was on, and there was no longer any going back. If Charlotte discovered her true intentions . . . she dared not think of what a woman like Charlotte might do to those who betrayed her trust.

"Yes, I believe it very nearly destroyed him."

"But not completely, I take it?"

"Time will tell." Emily said no more. She did not wish to rush or seem too eager. Trust was something that was gained with time.

"I hope you don't mind that I—instead of Lord Farringale—brought you the water."

"Not at all," Emily replied. "To be honest, I don't know him that well—I've no idea what we might have talked about and I do so hate uncomfortable silences."

"My sentiment exactly. Besides, I could not help but notice that you looked distressed earlier. I thought perhaps you might like to talk about . . . whatever's bothering you." Charlotte's eyes met Emily's.

What was she getting at, Emily wondered. It seemed as if she was digging for something . . . but for what?

"It was nothing," she said after a moment's silence. She wished to add to Charlotte's curiosity as well as to satisfy her own. Hopefully her dismissive response would cause Charlotte to press the issue.

"Has he wronged you in any way?"

So that was it. Charlotte wanted to know about her relationship with Francis; did she love him or . . . "I thought perhaps . . ." Emily sighed deeply, then brushed at her eyes as if to remove the onset of tears. "I'm sorry, Miss Browne. How utterly inappropriate of me to burden you with my personal affairs. We barely know one another."

Charlotte gave her the most compassionate of all smiles. It was clear to Emily that her little performance had wetted Charlotte's appetite and she'd grown eager to find out more. "Sometimes it can be easier to confess your troubles to a stranger. I shall not judge you. On the contrary, I shall offer to advise you on the matter if you so desire."

Emily paused, pretending to hesitate with a sense of uncertainty. "I do not wish to betray his trust, but I cannot . . . oh, it's a terrible mess!" And without knowing how she managed it, Emily began to cry with genuine heaving sobs that shook her shoulders.

"Dear me, Miss Rutherford. Whatever is the matter?" Charlotte said as she put her arm around Emily to comfort her.

Emily wiped at her tears with the back of her hand. "I thought he felt the same about me as I do about him," she sniffed.

"There, there now. Why don't you tell me what happened."

Emily paused, allowing time for rising suspense. "He told me we would marry, that it did not matter if we waited until after the wedding or not . . . we were betrothed, and . . . oh God," Emily drew a trembling breath. "I've been such a fool."

Charlotte's eyes grew wide. "And here I was, thinking that I might be able to help the two of you resolve your issues . . . I'm so sorry, Miss Rutherford," she said, squeezing her shoulder ever so slightly. "It seems the young buck has robbed you of the only thing you had to offer a potential husband."

Emily stiffened—something which Charlotte surely took to be an appropriate response to what she'd just said. But the truth was that Emily was shocked by her callousness. *The only thing you had to offer.* Charlotte had in one swift move removed any illusions that she might have about somebody actually loving her for her. That is, she probably would have done so, had Emily not known her true nature. It was becoming increasingly clear to her that Charlotte was up to something. Her best move, she reasoned, was to remain quiet and wait for her to continue.

"You must be devastated. To think how carelessly he used you without ever intending to do right by you." Charlotte shook her head with sadness.

"I just don't understand why he would do such a thing."

"It's quite simple, my dear. You struck his fancy, he decided to have you by any means necessary, and once he was done, he went back on his word—hardly the mark of an honorable man. In fact, it sickens me to see situations such as this happening time and time again. You must not blame yourself, Miss Rutherford, for I am certain that the fault lies entirely with him. How upsetting it is, though, that men continue at this game without giving us women the respect that we deserve."

"Do you mean to tell me that my . . . ah . . . situation is not unique?" Emily asked with a hint of surprise. She was beginning to see Charlotte's plan unfold, and she could not help but marvel at her shrewdness.

Charlotte chuckled slightly. "Far from it, unfortunately."

Her voice grew serious once again. "If only there was something that could be done about it."

"What are you suggesting?"

"I daresay that an example ought to be made of one of these men." She fixed Emily with her clear blue eyes, and that was when Emily saw the malice that Charlotte had so artfully hidden until that very moment when the taste of victory had brought it to the surface. It was so repellent that Emily could not stop the gasp that escaped her. Luckily, Charlotte was too caught-up to notice.

Emily took a slow, steady breath. "And you think that man ought to be Francis?"

"Don't you think he deserves it after what he's done to you?"

Emily paused, appearing as though she pondered the question. She believed that everybody ought to have the chance to prove themselves, and though Emily did trust Francis's opinion, and Charlotte was beginning to show her true colors to some degree, Emily still hoped she wasn't quite as bad as she feared. "Wouldn't it pain you to see him suffer?" *After all, he's your son.*

"Why? Because I've known him all his life? My dear Miss Rutherford, he has wronged you most severely and ought to be punished for it, though I must admit—I never took him for the sort of man who'd ruin a sweet young woman such as yourself. Apparently I have misjudged him." She paused for a moment. "He and I have never been very close, you know. In fact, our relationship has been rather strained of late, but that's a private matter. Let us not stray from the main issue, however—an opportunity has presented itself and I think it would be wise of you to take it."

Wise of you to take it. Emily could not help but consider how manipulative this woman was, counting on the fact that she would jump at the opportunity to make a *wise* decision following her supposedly foolhardy one. But Emily had been stunned by what Charlotte had said. She'd made it quite clear that she didn't care about what happened to Francis. Not one teensy weensy tiny little bit. On the contrary, she wished him ill—*her own son*. It was unthinkable to Emily that such a woman existed, more so that she was sitting there quietly speaking to her. Emily felt the anger rise within her, an anger so fierce that her eyes darkened and her jaw clenched.

"Perhaps," Emily replied cautiously, from behind gritted teeth, as she quietly gauged her reaction.

"I know of a letter that would be devastating to Francis if its existence was to be made publically known.

"Your suggestion is to blackmail him?"

A slight smile tugged at Charlotte's lips. "It's sometimes necessary."

Emily's eyes widened in dismay. Had the woman no shame?

"I don't quite see . . ."

"The thing of it is . . . his father and I developed a tendre for one another after his mother passed away. It was so tragic the way she . . ." A small sniff and a dab at her eyes completed the performance. "Francis's father and I loved each other very much. We made promises to one another, and when he died . . . I know he left an inheritance for me, but Francis has done everything in his power to prevent me from getting my hands on it."

Emily could scarcely believe what she was hearing. This woman, who considered another woman to be the mother of her child, sat here and spoke of love. There was no doubt that she was a slippery snake who'd managed to blind Francis's father with her charms.

"But if it's in the will, then surely . . ." Emily's face looked clearly puzzled.

Charlotte looked more distressed than ever. "That's just it, I'm afraid. You see, George never put it in the will. He made a separate amendment so that Francis would be sure never to find out until after he was gone."

Emily's eyes narrowed. "He didn't trust his son?"

"No. He knew Francis didn't approve of me. But if I could only find the amendment . . ."

"Do you have any idea of where it might be?" Emily asked, purposefully taking the bait.

Charlotte gave her a weak smile. "Yes, but I'll never manage to get my hands on it. Unless . . ."

"Unless . . . ?"

She shook her head. "Forget I said anything. It was a silly idea, really."

Oh, she's good . . . really good. Emily placed a gentle hand on Charlotte's arm. "What he did to me . . ." She clenched her jaw, her eyes deliberately misting over once more. "If there's any way in which I might be able to help you . . ."

Charlotte stared back at her for a long moment. "Francis won't let me back inside Dunhurst Park . . . that's where the amendment is. Help me get in so I can find it and . . ."

Emily waited patiently for her to continue.

"And I'll help you destroy Francis."

"How?" was all Emily could think to ask.

"Years ago, I decided that, should I happen to fall on hard times, I might need some leverage to help me back on my feet. So I wrote a statement outlining the truth about Francis's birthright—a truth which would cast absolute scandal upon him if it became publically known." She gave Emily a reassuring smile. "If you help me, then I'll give you that letter, to do with as you please."

"There's just one problem with your plan." Emily looked quite perplexed. "How am I to gain access to Dunhurst Park? Francis and I aren't married . . . I doubt we ever will be, and now that the season is over . . . I believe he'll expect me to return to Hardington with my sisters."

Charlotte took Emily's hand and squeezed it slightly. "If you use your feminine wiles, I'm sure he'll take you with him back to Dunhurst Park."

"Whatever do you mean?"

Charlotte chuckled at Emily's apparent innocence. "Let him think that he can enjoy you for a while—without the complications of marriage."

Emily gasped with shock. "I couldn't possibly," she stammered. "Besides, it doesn't seem right. I've never done something like that and I can't help but feel as though I'm betraying him. Worse than that, it wouldn't be moral to do such a thing."

"He betrayed you, Emily," Charlotte told her softly. "He took your most precious possession. He does not love you or even care for you. In fact, he has no interest in you save for whatever momentary pleasure you provided for him. In short, you are a dalliance that will soon be replaced by another. The only thing that might save any shred of dignity that you have left is to prevent him from getting away with it unscathed."

Emily raised her eyes to gaze up at the stars. Everything was going as she had hoped, but there was still a little work to be done. She sighed, returning her eyes to look directly at the woman who sat before her. "Perhaps you're right," she said. "Very well . . . I'll do what I can to help you."

The corners of Charlotte's mouth edged slightly upward. She lowered her voice to a soft whisper. "There's a private staircase that leads directly from Elisabeth Riley's apartment and down to the back of the house. Leave both doors unlocked one week from today and I shall come to retrieve the amendment myself."

"And once you do, you'll give me the letter you spoke of?"

"I shall."

"And I have your word on that?"

"Absolutely."

Emily let out a deep sigh of relief that Charlotte must have taken as a sign of gratitude, for she quickly squeezed Emily's hand. "Don't worry," she then said. "We'll have our revenge." It was difficult for Emily to contain her enthusiasm. Her plan had worked. The letter would be hers. But first she would have to help Charlotte. "It has been a great pleasure talking to you, Miss Browne. You've reassured me immensely," she said. "I hope to see you again shortly."

"Indeed, Miss Rutherford, I shall look forward to it."

Both women rose and gave each other a knowing look before heading back inside.

Seeing that her sisters were engaged with their respective

dance partners, Emily made her way toward the refreshment table. She needed something to soothe herself—a glass of champagne was suddenly very inviting.

She'd barely picked up the glass when she heard Francis's familiar voice behind her. "Would you care to dance?" he asked.

His breath was soft and warm against her neck. Fresh tingles spread their way down her spine, but she made an effort to push them aside. Now was not the time or place for her to allow such an indulgence. "I don't believe I would," she told him coolly as she turned to face him.

He arched an eyebrow, his forehead suddenly creased with marked concern. His hand went to touch her shoulder but she pushed it away with contrived annoyance. "We are being watched," she murmured, riveting her unblinking eyes upon him in a stare that warned him against giving them away. "In fact, I believe I've had enough excitement for one evening. Please give my excuses to our hosts—you may tell them that I developed a headache."

"Claire shall be disappointed." He wore an expression that was hard to read. It was as if he'd retreated from her somehow, because of the roles that they must play in front of Charlotte. Emily could not help but feel a pang of regret. *I hope this is worth it. If I lose him now. . . .* She dared not consider such an outcome. But the tension between them was suddenly very real, and she could not help but acknowledge the danger in the game they now played.

"Please give her my apologies," Emily told him before lowering her voice to a whisper that only he could hear. "Pray that this is the only sacrifice that we must make."

Without another word, she turned and left him. He stood for a moment, staring after her, wondering what Charlotte might have told her. He would find out soon enough, he reckoned.

As he turned his head in search of Jonathan, his eyes caught Charlotte's from across the room. She smiled sweetly at him before returning her attention to a handsome young gentleman who appeared to be asking her to dance.

Chapter Twenty-Nine

Emily had purposefully gone straight to bed upon returning to the house. She had no desire to face the look of disappointment on Claire's face, nor was she in the mood to offer an explanation for her departure. In addition, her thoughts kept returning to her conversation with Charlotte.

She could not help but be impressed by her ability to deceive. Had she not been aware of Charlotte's true nature, she probably would have fallen prey to her. She shuddered at the idea of it. Charlotte was without a shadow of a doubt the most despicable human being that Emily had ever come across. She loathed the fact that she would soon have to face her again.

How was it possible for her to have been in such close proximity to her son all these years, yet want nothing to do with him? It was so much worse than that, though. Not only did she not care about what befell him—on the contrary, she wished to wrong him in order to serve her own good. If there truly was such a place as hell, Emily quietly hoped that there was a special spot reserved in it for Charlotte.

The sound of muffled voices rose from the hallway. Emily

cast a quick glance at the clock on her commode, the numbers made visible in the faint glow of an oil lamp. It was just past three in the morning. Her heartbeat quickened as the footsteps climbed the stairs. They paused for a moment in front of her door, but a soft male voice urged them on, and shortly after, the sound of two doors closing could be heard, followed by silence.

Emily drew a breath. She knew Beatrice would be anxious to check on her, but thankfully Francis had persuaded her not to.

Her door swung open a moment later and Francis entered, closing it softly behind him and locking it for good measure. He'd removed his black jacket and was presently in the process of untying his cravat.

Emily thought him the handsomest man in the whole wide world at that moment, and she wasted no time in throwing open the covers and beckoning for him to join her.

"Tell me—what did Charlotte say to you?" He asked as he pulled his shirt free from his trousers and began to unbutton it.

God—he truly was incredibly good-looking, or—to be more precise—jaw-dropping, head-spinning, heart-hammering gorgeous, Emily thought. In fact, at that very moment it was just about the only thing she was capable of thinking about.

"Emily?"

"Hmmmm?" The last thing she wanted was for somebody—anybody—to be interrupting her perusal of what was undoubtedly the most perfect specimen of a male torso in existence.

"For heaven's sake, Emily," Francis said with growing impatience. "Stop ogling me and tell me what happened."

"Why so terse, Francis? You're the one who just *had* to go and take your shirt off. You ought to know better by now than to think I can concentrate on anything else when you're standing there . . . like . . . *that.*" She waved her hand to indicate his naked upper body.

"Perhaps I ought to put my shirt back on until we're done talking," he said, realizing that he would be distracted, too, if the roles had been reversed.

"Erm . . . no . . . I mean . . . that's okay." Emily cleared her throat. "I'll try to focus."

"But . . ."

"Let's just say that I don't much care for the topic that we're about to discuss. You, however—the way you look right now—well . . . you'll be my reward for getting through it." Emily paused for a moment, considering how best to tell him everything that Charlotte had said. "You were right in your estimation of Charlotte," she told him. "She's not a kind person by any stretch of the imagination, and she does not wish you well. I'm sorry."

Francis's eyes darkened and narrowed. His jaw tensed and his nostrils flared. "Tell me everything," he demanded in a clipped voice.

Emily drew a quick breath before plowing ahead, leaving out nothing of her conversation with Charlotte.

By the end of it, Francis's face had grown ashen. He stood perfectly still for a moment as if paralyzed. "She's lying . . . she has to be," he finally said. His voice grew louder, his eyes now black with rage. "Father left her five thousand pounds in his will, and now you're telling me that there's an amendment? What more could he possibly give her?"

Picking up the closest thing within his reach, he hurled Emily's book across the room. It landed with a loud unsatisfactory thud that only served to enrage him even further. He needed to break something, to hit something—someone.

Emily stared at him in bewilderment. She'd no idea how to approach Francis, or if it was even safe to. He looked like a caged lion, bent on attacking anything within his reach. His fists were clenched, his shoulders tense, and his breathing was coming in hard bursts of anger. She watched with growing concern as his eyes latched onto a crystal vase on the vanity table. Within seconds, he had it in hand, and before she even realized that it had been flung through the air, she heard the splintering sound of glass shattering against the floor.

A moment later, there was a knock at the door. "Emily?" It was Beatrice's voice. "Are you all right?"

Emily darted a nervous look in Francis's direction, then raised a silencing finger to her lips before climbing out of bed and moving toward the door. Unlocking it, she opened it just enough to see Beatrice's worried face. "Yes," she said. "I'm quite all right, Bea. Thank you for checking on me, but it was just an accident. I was trying to find the laudanum and ended up knocking over the vase instead. I'm sorry if I woke you.

"Laudanum?" Beatrice's eyes narrowed. "Your headache must be quite severe indeed."

Emily nodded. "You know I wouldn't have missed Claire's big announcement otherwise."

"I do." Beatrice gave her sister a sympathetic smile. "Why

don't you go back to bed and get some rest, then? I'll see you in the morning."

Thanking her sister, Emily quietly closed the door, locking it once more. She paused there for a moment, the guilt of lying to her sisters nagging at her conscience. Pushing it aside, she slowly turned to face Francis. There was no longer any doubt in her mind. She had to help him, at all costs. Taking a deep breath, she calmly walked toward him. His eyes flickered a silent warning for her to stay back, but she persisted. "It's all right, Francis," she whispered. "I won't hurt you, I promise. I know you won't hurt me, either. You love me, remember?"

Something seemed to soften in his face—a slight change, but one that Emily noticed nonetheless. It urged her toward him. She saw that he was blinded by his fury, that he wasn't thinking clearly. There was a thunderous darkness that swirled behind his eyes as he glared at her. But he wasn't seeing her, she realized. He was seeing Charlotte, and every thought and feeling that coursed through his veins at that very moment was centered on one thing, and one thing alone: revenge.

She had to find a way to let some light into that darkness. "You have every right to be angry, Francis, but don't let it consume you," she whispered softly as she took a step closer, her hand reaching out to him. "We can solve this together, you and I. Let me help you. I love you and I would never do anything in the world to hurt you."

He flinched when her hand settled upon his arm, but the tension in him had eased significantly. She wrapped her arms around him and hugged him close to her. It took a moment, but eventually his head slumped against hers, and his arms settled about her waist. "You know I'd be lost without you, Emily," he whispered, but then he corrected himself. "I *have* been lost without you. I need you more than I've ever needed anyone. I love you and I shall always love you."

Without another word, he scooped her up in his arms and carried her to the bed.

Their lovemaking was quick and passionate. He had a desperate need to feel something other than the hatred and the pain that, though drastically diminished, was still very much present. But loving Emily served to banish the darkness that so incessantly wrapped itself around him—to the point of suffocation.

And Emily . . . well . . . Emily needed to feel that her love for Francis was strong enough to help ease his torment.

Afterward, they lay in silence for a while, wrapped in each other's arms, enjoying the quiet satisfaction that followed the rush of sexual fulfillment.

"We'll leave for my estate tomorrow afternoon," Francis suddenly said. The anger was gone from his voice, replaced instead by determination. "The season is over, anyway."

"Claire won't be thrilled to leave Lord Camden behind in London, and I'm certain that Beatrice will be sorry to be separated from Mr. Rosedale."

"Why don't we just ask your sisters to join us? Beatrice will remain close to Jonathan this way, and as for Claire . . . Lord Camden has expressed an interest in seeing Dunhurst Park on numerous occasions; I'm confident that he'd enjoy a visit—particularly if Claire is also there. We'll invite my aunt and Lady Giddington, too—for propriety's sake."

"Have I told you lately how much I love you?" Emily sighed as she nuzzled her head against his shoulder. "You are without a shadow of a doubt the most wonderful man I've ever known."

Francis grinned. "And I am fortunate to have found a woman who's so easy to please and who takes such joy in the simple pleasures of life—those that most would think insignificant." He kissed the top of her head so that waves of warmth flooded her body. Never had she felt so content, so happy, and so loved.

"Will you tell my sisters that we're leaving London, or should I?" she asked.

"What do you prefer?"

She thought about it a moment. "I just hate having to lie to them."

"I know." He ran his hands lightly through her dark hair, twirling a few loose strands between his fingers. "I realize that you find all of this extremely uncomfortable, and that being dishonest with your sisters is not something that's easy for you to do. Emily, you're a God-given gift, and I simply cannot find the words to tell you how grateful I am for you. Thank you for helping me."

"You're my husband, Francis; it goes without saying. Everything we do from now on, everything that we face, we face together. I love you and I'll do everything I can to ensure your happiness, for as long as I live." She kissed him lightly on his chest as she ran her hand across him.

"So far you've proved to be very good at that," he muttered as he felt fresh waves of heat spreading through his body like wildfire. His left hand found the round fullness of her right buttock and her immediate moan told him she was just as aroused as he.

Their lovemaking was slower this time—more deliberate somehow, as they each strove to show the other how much they cared. When neither was able to bear it any longer, Francis finally entered her with steady ease, kissing and nibbling, lavishing in her sighs of response. She wrapped her legs around him and together they allowed the tension to build toward a crescendo that sent them soaring over the edge.

"I love you with every fiber of my being," Emily whispered afterward as she lay curled up in his arms.

"As I do you," he replied softly while his fingers played along her spine.

"Promise me that this will never change, that we will always love like this."

"I promise you, Emily. With all my heart, I promise."

Without another word, they both drifted off to a well-deserved sleep.

Chapter Thirty

Emily woke the following Saturday with a sense of foreboding. She had enjoyed the past week that she'd spent at Dunhurst Park, familiarizing herself with what was now to be her permanent residence. Beatrice and Claire had both accepted Francis's invitation, as had Lady Genevieve and Lady Giddington, while Lord Camden had joined them a couple of days later.

Emily soon realized that her preconceptions regarding Claire's fiancé had been unfounded. He clearly worshiped the ground that Claire walked upon, and was eager to do whatever he could to please her. Claire, on the other hand, looked radiant with love, and would (to Beatrice's growing exasperation) continuously find ways in which to be alone with her fiancé.

Beatrice seemed very much at ease, too (when she wasn't worrying about what Claire was up to with Richard Camden). With the London season being over, and not having to tend to household chores herself, she'd begun embroidering again. She spent hours on end in the privacy of her room, working on what Emily suspected must be a wedding gift for Claire. Only two weeks remained until Claire's wedding, so there was much to be done in spite of the fact that both bride and groom wished for a simple event with only the closest friends and relatives invited.

But when she wasn't cooped up in solitary confinement, Emily couldn't help but notice that Beatrice favored Jonathan's company. The couple often went for long afternoon walks together, but whenever Emily would bring it up, Beatrice would simply smile and tell her sister that she was jumping to conclusions.

In the evenings, they would all gather in the dining room for dinner, and play a game of cards or charades. Emily particularly favored the latter of the two since it allowed for her imagination to roam free, and generally resulted in more laughter.

Once they were certain that everyone had retired to bed, Francis would invariably join Emily in her bedchamber for a few hours, before returning to his own room.

But that particular evening would be different. Francis and Emily waited in his study until everyone else had gone to bed, each trying to read their own book, only to find themselves reading the same page over and over again. Thoughts seemed to whirl through their heads, allowing them little peace of mind to think of anything other than their upcoming encounter with Charlotte.

"I think it's time," Francis finally told Emily. "Let's get on with it."

Without further ado, he led her quietly up the stairs and down a long hallway toward the three rooms that had once constituted Elisabeth Riley's apartment.

A chill settled over him as they walked. It was a dirty business, this, and as much as he looked forward to putting an end to it, he couldn't seem to shake the uneasiness that stalked him like a shadow. Charlotte was unpredictable; he doubted that she would allow something as important as this to depend on a virtual stranger. She wasn't the trusting sort, and he feared that she would have prepared herself for the eventuality of being betrayed.

They reached Elisabeth's anteroom and entered without hesitation.

Emily had seen it once before—right after their return—when she and Francis had gone in search of the amendment themselves, hoping that they might be able to gain the upper hand. Unfortunately, it had been to no avail—they had no choice but to let Charlotte lead them to it. Francis had been surprised—disappointed, even—that Charlotte had been more privy to his father's last wishes than he. But then, of course, his father hadn't known Charlotte for who she really was. No . . . the old fool had loved her, Francis thought bitterly.

The room was completely dark, save for the lantern that Francis held out to cast a yellow haze before them. He led Emily toward the far corner of the bedroom, where he handed her the lantern. A soft click told her he'd found the door to the stairwell and opened it. "Do you want me to go with you?" he asked.

"No, it's best if you stay here," she said, trying to sound more confident than she felt. "If Charlotte's waiting for me, as

I expect her to be, then seeing you will ruin everything, and all that we've worked for will be for nothing."

"What if she means to harm you, Emily? What if she doesn't trust you? All she needs is for you to unlock the door; once that's done . . ." He dared not finish the sentence. He loved Emily with all his heart and was suddenly paralyzed with fear for her safety. "This is a mistake, Emily. I cannot allow you to put yourself in jeopardy for my sake."

"You are my husband, Francis. If you and I are to have a happy future together, then this matter must be settled immediately. I won't allow this woman to torment us any longer. Besides, this is not something that you can do alone; and I am only too happy to be able to help you."

Her words went straight to his heart. What a courageous little thing she was, and the thought that she would do whatever was necessary to protect those she loved—to protect him just as he would do what he could to protect her—filled him with tremendous pride. "I will be here waiting for you," he whispered as he kissed her forehead, inhaling the sweet scent of her hair. "I love you, Emily."

"And I love you."

It was with much determination that she entered the circular stairwell. She was clad in her night shift and a velvet wrap, but the draft that drifted up and around her seeped under her skin anyway, and she soon found herself shivering. She held the lantern high in order to see as much as she could, but once or twice she still managed to miss a step, sending an awful jolt through her bones when she stepped down harder than she ought to.

Eventually, she found the large wooden door at the

bottom of the stairs, and setting down the lantern, she moved to unlatch it.

A sudden gust of wind threw it back with such force that it would have knocked her over, had she not darted out of the way. The doorway now gaped open, with nothing between Emily and the darkness that lay beyond the secure walls of the house. A darkness in which she was certain Charlotte stood hidden, watching her. Emily shuddered as she strained to see, but her eyes failed her, and besides, she had no desire to linger for a moment longer. Picking up the lantern, she hastily made her way back up the stairs to the warm embrace that awaited her there.

Charlotte waited in the darkness, just beyond the tree line that surrounded the garden, biding her time. Wrapped in a heavy wool cloak, the large hood drawn down over her head, she had no difficulty staying warm. Still, she found her patience wearing thin. She'd expected Emily to appear much earlier than she did, and couldn't help but wonder if she had made a terrible misjudgment. But when she finally did appear in the doorway, Charlotte knew that she had found a good accomplice. Her only regret now was that she hadn't thought of such a ploy much sooner.

She sighed with satisfaction, for it no longer mattered. Soon, Francis would have to give her everything that she'd worked so hard—for so many years—to earn. If he thought for a moment that she'd ever enjoyed his father's advances and lovemaking, then he was sorely mistaken. Nothing had repulsed her more than George's hands pawing her, but she had always considered it to be a means to an end, and that had made it bearable.

She needed the money he'd left her if she was to continue living the life of luxury that she'd grown to enjoy. And she had every intention of cashing in tonight. Nothing was going to stop her, not even that unwanted child of hers who now basked in everything that should have been her own. She could barely wait to see the look of shock on his face once he discovered that his father had left half of his fortune to her, including the London home.

Dunhurst Park stood before her now, shrouded in darkness. It looked eerie, silhouetted against the night sky, the wind tugging at the trees. Charlotte shuddered in spite of herself. Few things ever bothered her, yet for some reason, she couldn't shake the uneasiness that crept over her. Drawing the cloak tightly about her shoulders, she made her way across the lawn.

Once inside the stairwell, she closed the door against the hammering wind, and bolted it behind her, shutting out the worst of the cold night air. But the thin soles of her shoes were a poor barrier against the chill of the stone steps. Impossible hopes of a warm bath entered her mind, and she hurried up the stairs with renewed hopes that her task would soon be complete.

The door to Elisabeth Riley's bedchamber swung open effortlessly, and without the slightest sound. But Charlotte remained cautious, allowing her eyes to adjust to her new surroundings. She had a clear recollection of what it looked like in broad daylight, and as far as she could tell, nothing had changed since the last time she had been there.

It was shortly before George's death that he had taken her

to his late wife's room to show her where to find the amendment he intended to leave for her. He'd already been sick for a long time by then, and heaven only knew how sick she'd been of tending to him. But the promise of inheriting half his fortune had sweetened the deal. So, she had somehow managed to continue treating him with care and listening to him recount tales of his youth until she felt just about ready to end his life with her own bare hands.

The minute he'd closed his eyes for the last time however, Francis had swiftly escorted her off the property. She'd been furious with him for denying her the chance to claim her prize, and had made no further attempts at pretense. Then again, it hadn't mattered. He hadn't been surprised in the least by the torrent of obscenities she'd thrown his way; he'd already known her for what she was for years.

The vague outline of the bed filled much of the space in front of her now. She moved past it as she held out her hand to glide across the silk brocade bedspread. Her fingers wrapped around one of the corner posts, and she paused to listen—nothing but silence.

Circling the foot of the bed, she crossed toward Elisabeth's desk. Her hands settled upon the smooth cherrywood surface, resting there for a moment while memories of Lady Elisabeth, seated before it in lavish silk dresses, flooded her mind. How she'd hated her dignity.

She'd been so easy to eliminate. All Charlotte had needed to do was encourage George to indulge in his sexual fantasies with her. She shuddered as the faint taste of bile rose in her mouth. Thank God all of that was behind her now. The next time she took a man to her bed, it would be on her terms.

But Elisabeth had taken it all like a true lady. She'd kept her head held high and remained aloof toward Charlotte, forever addressing her in a manner that made it quite clear that she was superior to her in every way. Charlotte's eyes narrowed beneath the hood. It had been so very easy. All she'd needed was to get her alone. The pretext that she'd wished to make amends—to teach Elisabeth how to properly cater to her husband's needs—had been a lure that her ladyship had not been able to refuse. All that had remained was a little push.

Charlotte's lips drew into a tight smirk. She still recalled the look of surprise on Elisabeth's face as she fell backward, her golden hair flowing about her face as she plummeted to her death—her neck broken upon impact. And even then she'd looked pretty.

The incident had immediately been ruled a suicide. Everyone knew how depressed Elisabeth had been. All Charlotte had needed to do was compound the matter a little and mourn her loss for all to see. "*The poor woman—if only I had known, I might have been able to help her,*" she'd said. "*How difficult it must have been for her. I should have done more to earn her friendship. Perhaps then I might have been able to prevent this tragedy.*" She grinned in spite of herself, unable to fathom how easy it had been to get away with it.

Her fingers now opened the top drawer of the desk. It was empty, but that didn't worry her. What she sought lay beneath the fake bottom. Pushing down, she eased the bottom of the drawer backward, giving way to a small space that lay hidden beneath. She reached in and pulled out an envelope, her fingers lightly grazing the wax seal that carried George Riley's insignia. *Finally.* She let out a quivering sigh, her eyes closing with relief as her grip tightened around the paper.

"I see that you found what you came here for."

Her eyes shot open to find the room in the process of being lit. She spun around to face the source of the voice, her eyes settling on Francis, who sat comfortably in a beautiful rococo armchair as though he didn't have a care in the world. What caught her momentarily off guard was the fact that Emily sat beside him, her eyes flashing daggers. Clearly she had misjudged the woman. She gritted her teeth, ready for battle.

"Aren't you eager to read it, *mother?*" Francis asked as he waved his hand in a nonchalant gesture.

Her heart quickened at the thought of what she held. This would be her salvation, and her lips curled into a hideous snarl as she unmasked her true character. "Oh how I've longed for this moment, Francis." She fixed him with a cold gaze that sent shivers down Emily's spine. Francis seemed unexpectedly calm and reserved. "Do you have any idea how much I've suffered? How much I've had to endure in order to get my hands on this? To feel that man's hands all over me . . . to endure childbirth only to watch *you* indulge in everything that ought to have been mine. But no more, Francis. Today I get what is rightfully mine."

"And pray tell, what is that?" Francis asked, masking his growing concern with remarkable perfection.

"Would you care to guess?"

"I would much prefer it if you would just cut to the chase and spit it out."

"Very well then, why don't I show you what your father has written with his own hand? You know he revered me. Did you honestly think that he would leave me with nothing? Not a single token of his gratitude?" She chuckled slightly as her eyes fell upon the letter that she held between her hands.

"He left you with five thousand pounds," Francis stated.

"Come on . . . you don't seriously believe that I would have settled for so little, do you?"

Francis just stared back at her, a blank expression masking his true feelings of apprehension.

"Here you are, Francis. Why don't you go ahead and open it? After all, it's the least I can do, considering that I'm about to take half of what you own." Francis's mouth fell open in a blend of genuine surprise and disgust. "What? Didn't he tell you that he made an amendment to his will? It will be such fun to redecorate the London home; yes, that goes to me as well."

Unable to contain himself a moment longer, he reached out and snatched the letter from her hand. He sensed Emily's agitation as she shifted uneasily in the seat next to his. She hadn't said anything, but then again, there wasn't really much for her to say. The situation was clearly far worse than he ever would have imagined. It was difficult to believe that his father would have done such a thing.

Taking a deep breath, he broke the familiar seal and removed the letter from the envelope. His eyes focused on his father's handwriting as his forehead furrowed into a deep-set frown. He read the letter, and then he read it again to ensure that he had understood it correctly, but the message was quite clear.

Dunhurst Park, 1809

Dear Charlotte,

It is with great sadness that I now prepare to leave this world. My physician tells me that it is but a matter of days now, and I do feel that I am ill prepared.

In a way, I consider myself more fortunate than most, for I know what is to come, and have therefore been allowed some measure of time in which to put my affairs in order. Still, there is one issue that I have failed to resolve, and that is my relationship with my son Francis. My heart is heavy with regret for how much that poor boy must have suffered. I wish I could have done more to help, but in the end, this will have to suffice.

Charlotte, my wife and I brought you into our home to fulfill a dream, and you gave us the most precious gift of all. For that, we have always been eternally grateful. However, I am baffled as to why you wish for me to say that he is your son, when clearly he is not. Let there be no doubt in anyone's mind that Francis Riley is the son of Elisabeth Riley and myself. We have always loved him and have always had the best of intentions for him—something that you completely lacked. If you look closely, madam, you'll discover that the signature on the letter you have in your possession has not been written by my hand. It is a forgery and will never stand in a court of law.

You charmed yourself into our lives, never once failing to serve your own interests, selfish as you were. Elisabeth saw through you much sooner than I, and I do believe that she paid for it with her life, though it was impossible for me to prove it.

I am a man of principle, Charlotte, and as such, I would never stoop to murder a woman—not even to avenge my own wife. But I have no qualms with attacking you in kind.

It wasn't always easy to play the part, and I do fear that my sacrifice may have been too great; I lost my son's respect and affection in the process. My only consolation is that he will one day discover that you did not deceive me, but rather, that I deceived you.

I'm sure you must have realized by now that I leave you with nothing. Your selfishness destroyed my family. I pray, that this letter may serve to destroy you, or in the very least, the chance of achieving your goal.

George Riley,
The Earl of Dunhurst

Francis felt his throat tighten. This was in truth the last thing that he had expected to discover. He carefully folded the letter, hoping perhaps to gain some time in order to get his emotions under control. Tears pressed against his eyes, but he forced them back. He would find time to heal his wounds later. "This truly is a surprise," he said in a clipped voice as he handed the letter back to Charlotte. "I think you'll find it likewise."

Taking the letter from him, Charlotte read, her eyes clouding over with anger and dismay as the truth dawned on her. By the time she was through, her otherwise beautiful features were twisted and contorted into an ugly grimace.

Francis noticed Emily tense beside him as they watched Charlotte grow red with fury. He placed a reassuring hand upon her arm as Charlotte crumpled the letter between her fingers. "No," she said. "No, no, no! To hell with you, Francis. To hell with all of you."

Emily saw the flash of silver first. Instinct told her what it was, and without a second thought for her own safety, she rushed forward, flinging herself toward their nemesis. She had hoped somehow to disarm her, but a deafening bang split the air, and the pain that followed quickly overpowered her. She knew immediately that she'd been shot, but before another thought could surface, the room tilted and everything went black.

Chapter Thirty-One

She felt the throbbing headache before she even realized that she was awake. The muted sound of voices filled the air, but what they said was unclear to her. It almost felt as though her ears were filled with water.

Her head rested on a fluffy pillow, but it did little to ease the pain that occasionally tore through her skull. She slowly eased open her eyelids, her lashes fluttering slightly as her eyes adjusted to the light.

The quickening thud of approaching footsteps sounded. "She's awake," someone said.

"Thank God."

She tried to focus, but her vision blurred, and with a heavy sigh she drifted back to sleep.

"It's been two days already. Are you sure we shouldn't try to wake her? She needs to eat." Beatrice was distraught with concern for her sister and Francis couldn't blame her. He was equally worried, having kept vigil ever since the shooting, silently praying that she would soon recover.

"The doctor says we should let her be, and I'm inclined to agree. This has been a traumatic experience for her. She needs to rest in order to heal. Don't worry; she'll eat once she wakes—in her own time."

Beatrice perched herself on the edge of the bed and placed the palm of her hand against Emily's forehead. "She feels cooler today," she said hopefully.

The bedroom door opened and Claire entered with Richard in tow. "You look awful," she told them. "Both of you."

Beatrice gave her a reproachful glance. They hadn't slept more than a couple of hours since the incident, remaining awake to watch over Emily and tend to her wound. She'd been feverish for the first day, and they'd repeatedly had to wipe her down with squares of linen soaked in cool water.

"Richard and I have agreed that you need to rest. We'll look after Emily until you wake."

"I don't want to leave her," Francis argued.

"You won't be much good to her if you're too tired to respond, should she need you. Now go and rest—that's an order."

Beatrice realized that Claire had a valid point, though she was just as reluctant as Francis to step away from Emily's bedside. "I should like to be here when she wakes." She saw that Francis nodded in agreement.

"We will call you immediately if she does. And when she does, there will be much to see to. You will both be of more use to her if you're well rested."

Beatrice knew that Claire was right. She kissed Emily

lightly on the cheek and left, promising to be back in a couple of hours to check on her. Francis muttered another series of complaints, but finally did as he was told and went to find his bed.

It was late afternoon before he woke. He cursed when his eyes drifted toward the clock next to his bed and he saw the time. He'd slept for six hours. What concerned him the most, however, was that nobody had woken him in all that time, which meant that Emily still slept. He'd expected her to be awake by now, and the fact that she wasn't worried him.

"Any progress?" he asked Claire as soon as he returned to Emily's room.

She shook her head. "Perhaps that's a good thing," she suggested. "The fever hasn't returned, and when I changed the dressing two hours ago, her wound appeared to be healing nicely. I think we're out of the woods so I'm sure she'll wake soon."

Francis nodded. "I think you're right."

Richard saw that Francis fought to gain control of his emotions—that no matter how hopeful the situation appeared, he was sick with fear for Emily. "It was lucky that the bullet struck her shoulder and that it went straight through," he said. "And though she did sustain a nasty bump to her head, I'm confident that she'll be as good as new in another couple of days." He paused for a moment, knowing full well how little comfort his words were to Francis. "She's very lucky to have you by her side."

Richard instantly regretted his words as Francis knit his brow in response. "She wasn't so lucky two days ago. That bullet was meant for me. What the hell was she thinking, jumping at Charlotte like that?"

"She was thinking of you, Francis. Clearly she loves you very much—so much that she would give her life for you without a moment's hesitation."

"I can't bear to see her suffer like this." Francis muttered, his voice full of emotion. "Not because of me."

"Yet if she hadn't, would you still be standing here?"

"I don't know."

The truth was that he'd likely be dead. Charlotte had been quick on the trigger. He simply hadn't seen it coming and he blamed himself for it constantly.

The door opened and Beatrice stepped into the room. "I'm sorry . . . I can't believe I slept this long. I must have been more tired than I thought."

"It's quite all right," Claire assured her. "You needed to rest."

"I told Parker to bring us some coffee and Mrs. Reynolds asked the cook to prepare a fresh poultice for Emily's wound."

"What about some food?" Richard asked. "I'm starving."

That comment brought the first smiles they'd seen in days. Richard Camden was fond of food, but he hadn't had a decent meal since the night Emily was shot—and even though he'd been hungry, he'd realized that there were more pressing matters at hand. Now that Emily looked better, however, he felt no guilt over letting everyone know how much he longed for a hearty meal.

"I will tell Parker to have a proper meal prepared when he brings the coffee," Francis told him. "Now that you mention it, I'm quite hungry myself."

A knock at the door heralded Parker's arrival. Francis called for him to enter, whereafter the aging butler brought in a tray with four cups of steaming hot coffee, some milk, and some sugar.

"Thank you, Parker. You may set it down over there," Francis said, pointing toward the dresser. "And please tell cook to prepare a substantial meal for us."

"Do you wish to eat it in here or in the dining room?"

"You may serve it in the dining room. Miss Claire and Lord Camden will dine first. Miss Rutherford and I will wait until they've finished."

"Very good, my lord." Parker said. He hesitated in the doorway. "She'll be all right, won't she?" he asked, glancing toward the bed where Emily lay.

"I believe so," Francis assured him, touched by the troubled look on the old man's face.

With a brief nod, Parker turned and headed for the kitchen, eager to help in any way that he could. He returned an hour later.

"Dinner is served," he announced, moving aside to allow Mrs. Reynolds to enter the room. She brought the poultice with her, along with clean strips of linen for dressing Emily's wound, and some warm water with which to bathe it. A quiet settled over the room as she left, followed by Richard, Claire, and finally Parker, who closed the door behind him.

Rolling back the covers, Francis gently eased Emily up into a sitting position. He braced her with his arms while Beatrice moved to untie the bandage that swept over her shoulder and across her chest. Beatrice had been concerned about her sister's modesty and had therefore wrapped a wide strip of cotton around her chest to prevent her breasts from being on constant display when they tended to her.

"It looks as though it's healing well," Francis remarked as he watched Beatrice dab at the wound with a wet piece of linen to wash away the old poultice. There was no sign of infection, just pink and swollen tissue with the first signs of a scab that had begun to form.

A soft groan startled both of them. "Emily?" Francis whispered. She groaned again, louder this time. "You'd best hurry up, Beatrice—I think she's coming round."

"I still have to pack the wound. Perhaps I'd best wait until she's fully awake."

Francis cursed under his breath. They had been used to a passive patient thus far, but Emily was already beginning to struggle against him, and he knew that what they were doing was paining her. "Sweetheart, can you hear me?" he whispered. "I know it hurts, but if you fight us, it will hurt even more. You were shot, and . . ." It was no use. Emily's eyes flew open, wide with fear. And then she screamed, thrashing about like a madwoman.

Francis gritted his teeth together. "Do what you must," he told Beatrice. "I will hold her."

It took only five minutes to get the job done, but they were the longest five minutes of Francis's life. Emily's screams stabbed at his heart. He hated what they were doing to her and he suffered alongside her. Repeatedly he wished that it was he who had been wounded instead of her.

When it was over, he kissed her forehead, her eyelids, her cheeks, and finally her lips as he stroked her hair with his hand to soothe her. "I'm so sorry, Emily. I'm so, so sorry," he whispered.

She took a shaky breath as he eased her back down to rest

against the pillow. "What happened?" she asked as she looked from one to the other.

Francis's eyes met Beatrice's, and he knew that she waited for him to tell her. "You were shot, Emily. Charlotte shot you." He added softly, "you saved my life."

She was quiet for a moment with concentration, and then her expression changed, and Francis knew that she remembered. "I did, didn't I?" she smiled. Francis nodded. "I think that's the bravest thing I've ever done."

"And quite possibly the stupidest." Both Emily and Beatrice turned their eyes on him. "You could have gotten yourself killed," he explained.

"I had no choice, Francis. She meant to kill you, and I just know that she would have if I hadn't stopped her. I couldn't allow that to happen. I could never forgive myself for something like that—knowing that I could have prevented it, but that I did nothing. No, then I'd rather suffer a hundred bullets instead." She moved slightly, but quickly regretted it, wincing as a sharp pain tore at her wound.

"Are you all right?" Francis asked before Beatrice had the chance to.

"I'll be fine," Emily told him with a hint of a laugh. "I suppose a little pain is to be expected."

Though Beatrice was beginning to feel increasingly like a third wheel, she couldn't help but be pleased at how much Francis clearly cared for her sister. She bent to give Emily a slight peck on the cheek, then told them both that she would go to fetch a plate of food for Emily.

"I still can't believe that you would do such a thing," Francis told her once they were alone. "Do you have any idea how worried I've been? I thought I might lose you."

"Then you should understand better than anyone why I did what I did." She sighed as she reached for his hand. "I've only just found the love of my life, though you were right in front of me for all these years. You are the man with whom I look forward to sharing my life, the man with whom I wish to grow old. What we have is unique, and I'm not willing to give that up for anything. So if that means taking a bullet to the shoulder, then so be it. All I know is that I'll be damned if I'm going to lose you so easily. I love you, Francis, and I cannot wait to tell the world how much you mean to me."

Francis looked at her with wonder. How he'd managed to be so lucky was beyond him. Emily was such a rare gift, and he felt honored by the very notion that she was his. Gone was the heartbroken girl who'd pined for Adrian. Before him sat a woman of tremendous courage who'd fearlessly thwarted their enemy. His heart swelled with pride as he leaned over to capture her lips in a long, heartfelt kiss.

"I was brave, wasn't I?" she grinned.

"You were exceptional, Emily. I still can't believe that you're my wife. When should we tell the others?"

"Let's wait until I'm well enough to get out of bed," she suggested.

"All right, but not a moment longer. Agreed?"

"Agreed." She paused for a moment as she bit down on her lip. "What happened to Charlotte?" she finally asked him curiously.

"She was caught off guard by you, so . . . I managed to hit

her over the head with a brass candlestick before she had the chance to fire a second shot."

Emily's hands flew to her mouth to stop the sudden onset of laughter. "You hit your mother over the head with a candlestick?" Her eyes were beginning to water from the surge of giggles that exploded in her throat.

Francis's eyes darkened. "She's not my mother," he grumbled. "Elisabeth was . . ."

"Oh, I know, my love, and I'm sorry," Emily stammered as she gave way to her laughter. "But it's just so ridiculous."

Francis stared at her. Only Emily could find the humor in something as awful as what had happened. Her smile and her laughter were infectious, and he soon found it impossible not to laugh along with her. "Oh, I wish I could have seen it," Emily grinned, wiping at the tears that spilled onto her cheeks. "Was there a loud thunk?" And for some reason, the thought of a candlestick producing a loud thunk as it struck Charlotte's head made Emily laugh even more. Wincing at the pain her excitement had produced, she did her best to calm her amusement.

"Is she still alive?" she asked suddenly, realizing that such a blow to the head could have been fatal. "And the letter, Francis . . . what about the letter?"

Pushing Emily gently back onto her pillow, Francis gave her a slow nod. "Yes, she is still alive, though I'll wager she'd rather be dead right now—she'll be spending a great deal of time at Newgate instead of at my house in London. As for the letter—I retrieved it from her cloak pocket before anyone else arrived at the scene. It's been destroyed." His mind seemed to wander. "It surprises me that she never questioned the signature."

"Hmmm . . . perhaps in her eagerness to wish you ill, she simply failed to notice," Emily said thoughtfully. "In any event I'm just glad that she's finally out of our lives."

"Me, too."

Chapter Thirty-Two

It was five days since Emily had been shot, and with just over a week remaining until Claire and Richard were to wed, everyone was kept busy with the preparations. They wanted a small, private function, so when Francis had suggested that they use the chapel on his estate, they had immediately agreed.

The weather was still pleasant, and they all hoped that it would hold for the big day.

It was late afternoon, and Francis had asked Parker to bring some refreshments out into the garden.

"How do you feel?" Beatrice asked Emily as they all sat gathered around a wrought-iron table.

"Much better; I can move my arm now without it paining me to do so."

Francis took her hand and squeezed it. "She'll be fully recovered in another week—just in time for the wedding."

Claire smiled as she watched her older sister. She looked so happy and content. She never would have believed that

Emily would find the kind of love she'd always hoped for with Francis Riley. "So, when do the two of you plan to marry?"

"Claire!" Beatrice exclaimed. "Why do you always have to be so forward?"

Claire chuckled. "Honestly, Bea, sometimes even you surprise me. Look at them. It's obvious that they're head over heels in love with one another, so it's really only a matter of time. In fact, I'm certain that Francis has already proposed."

Emily smiled as she looked over at Francis, and then her smile broadened until both Claire and Beatrice realized that they were clearly missing something. "What is it?" Claire asked impatiently.

"Well, as a matter of fact . . ." Emily giggled. "We're already married."

Complete silence followed. In fact, nobody would have been more shocked if King George himself had just strolled by.

"What?" Beatrice managed to ask, her face filled with confusion. "When?"

"When Francis rescued me from Edward's clutches." Emily told them, relieved to finally share the happiest moment of her life with the rest of her family. "We were married that same evening—in the very chapel that's now being readied for the two of you." She looked toward Richard and Claire, who both stared back at her with unfeigned surprise.

"But why the secrecy? For heaven's sake, Emily, of all the things . . . don't you know how much we would have liked to be there?" Beatrice didn't look as disappointed as Emily had feared, but she *did* look as if she didn't quite know what to make of it all.

"It was a spur-of-the-moment decision," Francis said as he came to his wife's defense. "We meant to tell you immediately after, but then Emily devised the plan to ensnare Charlotte, and we thought it best if we kept it a secret until Charlotte had been dealt with." He gave a sidelong glance at Emily and when she nodded encouragingly, he continued. "We thought we'd have another wedding later—one where you would all be able to attend."

"I have just the thing!" Claire exclaimed as she clutched Richard's hand to show a united front. "We'll have a double wedding!"

"Well, I . . . I don't want to impose on your special day, Claire," Emily said.

"Why, that's nonsense," Claire remarked. "Don't you agree, Richard?"

"I, errr . . . I didn't realize I had a say in the matter."

"Well, I do wish you would at least pretend that you do, for the sake of appearances," Claire chuckled jokingly as she kissed her fiancé tenderly on the cheek.

"What say you, Dunhurst?" Richard asked in the hopes of diverting the attention away from himself.

Francis saw his intent and favored Richard with a scowl. "I have no desire to get myself tangled up in this conversation. I shall leave it up to the ladies to decide."

"It's settled then," Claire exclaimed. "Unless of course you'd rather have your own ceremony, Emily?"

"I already did," Emily reminded her before turning to Francis for reassurance. He shrugged his shoulders to let her know that the decision was up to her. "I think a double wedding would be a wonderful idea, Claire."

Claire immediately rushed out of her seat to hug her sister, who laughed in return. "We'll have very little time in which to have your gown made," Claire stated, her mind already brimming with ideas of how to go about the necessary preparations. And we'll have to send out invitations immediately to anyone that you might like to attend."

"Do you know," Emily said thoughtfully. "I believe that Mrs. Hughes would be thrilled to receive an invitation. I shall write to the old dear straight away. And, then of course, we simply must invite the Fairchilds. . . . Dear me . . . there really is a lot to see to all of a sudden."

"Actually, I already invited them," Claire told her as she bit her bottom lip. "I invited Kate and Adrian, too. I meant to ask for your opinion first, but then you got shot, and . . . I'm sorry, Emily—I hope you don't mind."

"I don't mind at all," Emily told her sister as she hugged her yet again. "In fact, I think it would be nice to have the opportunity to thank her."

"Thank her?" Francis asked incredulously. "She and Adrian broke your heart, Emily, and may I remind you that it was because of Kate that you ran straight to Edward." His voice grew angry as he reminded himself of what Emily had been through.

"Don't you see, Francis? If it hadn't been for Kate, then you and I might never have realized how we felt about each other." She wrapped her arms around him. "As for telling me that Charlotte was your mistress . . . well, I do believe that she had my best interest at heart and hoped to warn me."

"Still, she should have come to me first."

Emily sighed. "We all make mistakes, Francis. I think it's

important to look at the reasoning behind it, and in this case, I do believe that the mistake is forgivable."

"So if I were to take somebody's life because I 'mistakenly' believed that they intended to take mine . . . should I not be made to pay for it?"

Emily rolled her eyes, but couldn't help from smiling. "That is not only an exaggerated, but also a completely unrealistic example, and you know it."

Francis shrugged. "Sometimes it's necessary to exaggerate in order to make a point."

"Francis Riley, I do believe you're trying to wind me up."

He cocked an eyebrow. "Is it working?"

She refused to take the bait and rather looked at him as blankly as she could manage. "Not at all," she said.

"Then I have no choice but to . . ."

"Might I interrupt?" Beatrice asked.

Emily and Francis turned to her apologetically. They had been so carried away that they'd forgotten that they weren't alone. "Please excuse us," Emily said.

"By all means." Beatrice looked genuinely amused, but her expression soon turned serious. "It's just that . . . well, with all the excitement, I haven't yet had the chance to tell you that Mr. Rosedale has asked me to marry him, and I have accepted."

Claire and Emily both responded with a simultaneous, ear-deafening squeak while their prospective husbands clasped their hands over their ears.

"A triple wedding!" Claire exclaimed with unparalleled excitement as she bounced up and down, clapping her hands together. "Oh, this is famous!"

Hugs and handshakes were quickly exchanged as they all congratulated one another.

"You certainly caught me by surprise there," Francis told Jonathan with a wide grin. "I had no idea, although Emily did suggest that something might be in the works. But marriage? It seems we've all been leg-shackled."

The men laughed as they supportively patted each other on the back. "If I didn't know better, I'd say they were plotting this all along," Richard remarked. They all turned to look at the women.

"Who says we didn't?" Emily challenged before bursting into laughter along with her sisters at the befuddled looks on their fiancés' faces.

Francis reached for Emily and pulled her toward him. "I do believe I'll have to keep my eye on you," he teased as he kissed her fully on the lips for all to see. "You've become far too candid for your own good."

"Do you wish that I were less so?" She asked sweetly as she wrapped her arms around his neck.

Looking down at her, he favored her with a brilliant smile that instantly melted her heart. "Truthfully? No." He kissed her again with increased passion. "You are perfect in every way, Emily, and I love you. I've always loved you."

"I love you, too," she said as tears of joy threatened to spill from her misty eyes.

He tightened his hold on her as he pressed his cheek against hers. "How many children would you like, Emily?" he whispered in her ear for only her to hear.

She pulled back so she could look him straight in the eye.

"Lots and lots and lots," she told him joyfully, her eyes overflowing with love for him.

"Then what are we waiting for?" he asked as he scooped her up in his arms and started toward the house. "We are husband and wife, after all."

"But it's midafternoon," she giggled as she turned a pleading look toward her sisters.

"Don't look to us for help," Claire called after them. "We're eagerly awaiting a hoard of nieces and nephews."

"Traitors!" Emily shouted, her voice ringing with laughter.

"Promise me that we'll always have this much fun," she told Francis as he opened the door to his bedroom.

"I promise, if you will promise that we'll always love with as much passion as we do now."

"Always." And to prove it, she kissed him so thoroughly that all other thoughts abandoned both of them.

They savored that moment, for in and of itself, it held a promise for the bright and happy future that they had always dreamed of.

Acknowledgments

A special thank you to my friend and fellow author, Julia Quinn, for pointing me in the right direction.

To my wonderful editor, Esi Sogah, who patiently chipped away at all the rough edges, helping the story shine.

To my wonderful family for their words of encouragement and for their enthusiasm about my books.

A big thank you to my mother-in-law, who introduced me to the wonderful world of Regency-period romances.

And to all of you who have read the story, or are about to read it, thank you.

Keep reading for an excerpt from Sophie Barnes's next exciting historical romance

Prologue

Moorland Manor, 1810

Bryce stood on the neatly trimmed lawn, his feet planted in a solid stance, his hands clasped firmly behind his back. The wide stone building that constituted his home lay stretched out behind him with its neatly trimmed rose bushes lining its edges. Sir Percy stood at Bryce's side, yet neither man uttered a word. Instead they listened, their eyes riveted upon the gentle swell of hills that rose from the meadow just beyond the property line.

Any minute now, Bryce thought to himself as he drew a deep breath of crisp afternoon air. It was only mid-October—no more than a month since he'd last sat outside in the still warm afternoon sun. The days had now grown chilly and were more often than not filled with cloudy skies and showers of rain. But today was an exception. Today was one of those magical fall days where the leaves turned fiery red beneath clear blue skies while the air bit at one's cheeks.

Bryce cocked his head, and then he heard it—a faint rumble, off in the distance. He sensed that Percy must have heard it too, for it seemed as though his friend shifted almost imperceptibly by his side. "They're coming," Bryce told him.

Percy nodded, his eyes still fixed upon the hills in the distance.

Like the sound of approaching thunder, the drum of horses' hooves rose through the air as the first rider peaked out from behind the crest of the first mound. Bryce held his breath as he squinted his eyes against the sun. "It's William," he said.

"You're sure?"

Bryce nodded. "And here comes Ryan, right on his heels."

Percy let out a sigh, and Bryce couldn't help but notice the hint of disappointment in it. "Don't worry," he told his friend. "She hasn't lost yet."

Percy had always had a particular fondness for Bryce's youngest child, Alexandra. When Penelope had died four years earlier and Bryce had been left to raise his children on his own, Percy had disagreed with his methods. Bryce was after all a man, completely ignorant of how to raise a young lady, and had decided to raise his daughter just as he would his sons. Being a military man, this had included nothing short of learning to handle weapons to perfection.

Percy had been appalled to find Alexandra wielding a sword during one of his visits and had made a good attempt at persuading Bryce to let the girl's aunt take her under her wing. Eventually Bryce had agreed and Virginia had taken Alexandra to live with her.

Not a week had passed before Alexandra was back home again, having stolen a horse and ridden haphazardly through the night, returning to Moorland at dawn. She'd received a good scolding for her thoughtless behavior, just as she knew she would, but Bryce had never since suggested that she leave her home, and Percy had come to understand how wrong he'd been to suggest such a thing in the first place.

Over the years he'd warmed to the idea of a girl running around in shirts and trousers, handling weapons as well as any boy could. Perhaps it was because Alexandra was that girl, Percy mused as he finally spotted her in the distance. She never looked more comfortable than when she was tearing across a field on her horse or dueling with her brothers. *Come on, girl, you can do it,* he silently prayed.

"Quit holding your breath, old chap," Bryce told him with a grin. "Just watch her now . . . here she comes."

They watched in silent awe as Alexandra leaned forward against her horse's neck and spurred her on with a "yah, yah," that carried across the meadow. Her golden locks of hair streamed behind her in a wild frenzy of tangled curls as she leapt ahead of Ryan.

Dirt churned beneath the horse's hooves as a flock of pigeons scattered in their path, the ground reverberating as they approached.

"Now watch this," Bryce said with an edge of excitement as Alexandra rose from her saddle while her mount rose onto her hind legs in a jump that sent both horse and rider flying over the garden fence, passing William in mid-flight.

"She won," Percy said, his voice but a whisper of disbelief. "Good God, she actually won!"

"I told you she would," Bryce said with a proud smile as he gave his friend a hard slap across the back.

They watched as all three horsemen eased their mounts

into a walk, patting them gently on their flanks to praise their efforts. "You don't want to reconsider letting her train for a position with the Foreign Office?" Percy asked in a muted voice.

Bryce knit his brows in a disapproving glare. "You might as well suggest that I let her enroll in the army," he growled.

"Come now—it's nowhere near the same thing. The army is full of men . . ."

"And the Foreign Office isn't?" Bryce arched a mocking eyebrow.

"Well, she needn't be surrounded by them," Percy told him defensively. "Besides, this is Alex we're talking about. She can hold her own."

"I know what she can do, Percy. I trained her." They watched as the three youngsters dismounted, handing their reins over to the awaiting grooms. "But the Foreign Office is a dangerous place for a woman—especially for a stubborn woman with a mind of her own."

Percy regarded his friend for a moment. "Do you regret the choices that you've made?"

Bryce let out a heavy sigh as he ran a hand through his hair. "I've no regrets about the way I've raised her, if that's what you're asking. She's a strong girl and she'll make a fine woman one day, but just because she can handle a sword as if she'd been born with it in her hand, doesn't mean I'll put her in harm's way by encouraging her to live a reckless life."

"I understand your reasoning, old friend, but it's still a pity to let such talent go to waste."

"Listen to me, Percy," Bryce muttered from between gritted teeth. "I won't have you putting any ideas in her head. Do you understand what I'm telling you? If you so much as . . ." He glanced toward his approaching children. "It won't matter that we've known one another since we were in short pants—I'll still beat the living daylight out of you." He softened his tone when he noticed his friend's pallor. "I understand that you're actively looking for new recruits, but I'm asking you to please leave my Alex alone. This is not the kind of life I intended for her to have, regardless of her abilities."

Percy acknowledged his friend's wishes with a slow, pensive nod. He couldn't help but wonder if Alexandra's fate was entirely different from what her father truly wanted for her. Sometimes such things simply couldn't be changed, no matter how much one might want them to—particularly not when the ball had already been set in motion. What Bryce was, in fact, completely and utterly unaware of was that Alexandra had already approached Percy on her own. She'd wanted to know what working for the Foreign Office might involve—whether it might appeal to her or not.

Knowing full well how Bryce might react at the thought of his daughter riding off on a potentially dangerous mission for king and country, Percy had tried his best to supply her with nothing but plain fact. But Alexandra was an adventurous girl with a desperate need to make her own way in the world, so she had swallowed every piece of information that he'd given her with unparalleled greed.

It was true that she was turning into a young woman before their very eyes, but as of yet, she had more in common with a musketeer than she did with any of the young ladies of her own age. For one thing, she never, ever wore a dress, and was therefore by default completely excluded from ever attending any function where she might succeed in meeting a potential husband. But what point would there be in that, anyway, when she had clearly declared on numerous occasions that she had no desire to ever marry.

Well, she was still young, Percy thought. In a few years' time, her view on men was likely to change, and perhaps then—once she found the right man—she might do as her father hoped: settle down and start producing a hoard of babies.

It was at that very moment that Percy reached a decision. If in four years' time, Alexandra was still voicing an interest about the Foreign Office, Percy would do his damnedest to help her follow her dream, because what Bryce didn't seem to understand quite yet was that he was creating a woman who would one day have a very difficult time trying to find a place for herself in the world. She was different, and as fun as that might be right now while she still clung to her childhood, Percy sensed that it might one day be more of a curse than a blessing.

"I can't believe she beat us again," Ryan grumbled as he came to stand across from his father.

"Face it, Ryan—I'm a much more accomplished equestrian than you," Alexandra grinned as she sidled up next to her disgruntled brother, giving him a playful nudge in the ribs.

"Come now," William remarked in a playful tone. "You only beat me by two yards . . . I'd hardly say that that's a victory to brag about."

Alexandra let out a perplexed sigh. "Whichever way you look at it, William, I still won and you still lost." She poked a teasing finger in the middle of William's chest.

"That she did," Bryce concurred.

"But you must admit that she has a clear advantage," William stated. He didn't mind losing to his younger sibling, even if she was a girl. In fact, he was very proud of Alexandra's achievements, but he didn't want anyone to think that she'd won because she was more adept than he.

"Are you honestly going to hold my weight against me again?" she asked with feigned disbelief. "I can't help it if I'm as light as a feather while the two of you are making your poor horses sag in the middle."

Percy coughed into his closed fist as he tried to stifle the laugh that he felt rising in his throat. As agreeable as Ryan and William were about letting their sister compete against them, he wasn't sure they'd appreciate being laughed at.

"Never you mind," Bryce told his sons. "We all know that if it were a matter of fisticuffs, the two of you would win while Alexandra would most likely be beaten to a bloody pulp. She may be able to match you in certain things, but there are still those in which her gender simply can't compete."

Alexandra glared at her father, her blue eyes laced with frost. "There's no disputing that you have a talent," Bryce told her. "Just keep your feet planted firmly on the ground. Modesty is so much more becoming than haughtiness."

"But I'm not . . ."

Bryce raised the palm of his hand to silence her. "Don't argue with me, Alex. Just take it for what it is—a solid piece of advice that's sure to earn respect.

"Now, how about some of Rosemary's scones and a nice hot cup of tea?" Draping his arm around Alexandra's shoulders and squeezing her against him, he started toward the house with William and Ryan at their sides. Percy followed at a distance, still wondering what the future might hold for Lord Summersby's brood.

Chapter One

London, 15 May 1815

Percy took a slow sip of his single malt whiskey, savoring the rich flavor as it warmed his chest, and sat down in one of the deep leather armchairs that stood in his office at Whitehall. Lazily swirling the caramel-colored liquid, letting it lap against the edges of his glass, he regarded his friend with caution. "I'm sorry that it had to come to this, old chap," he told him quietly.

Bryce nodded, his forehead furrowed in a thoughtful frown. "Do you see now why I didn't want Alex to get involved?" He shook his head in disbelief.

William had joined the Foreign Office four years ago when he was twenty-three years old. He'd had a number of successful missions during that time and had been personally thanked by the Prince Regent for uncovering a Russian spy who'd managed to infiltrate parliament. Bryce was having a difficult time now believing that William was handing over valuable information to the French.

He'd gone to Paris in late March, as soon as news of Napoleon's escape from Elba had reached the British shores. Accompanying him on his mission was his longtime friend, Andrew Finch, who'd joined the Foreign Office a couple of years earlier based on William's recommendation.

Percy picked up the most recent letter that Andrew had managed to send out of the country. "It seems that Mr. Finch was completely caught off guard by William's behavior, judging from the tone of this." He waved the piece of paper with a casual flick of his wrist.

Bryce snorted before taking a swig of his scotch. He wiped his mouth with the back of his hand before setting his glass down on the table. "I'm just not buying it," he muttered, his eyebrows knit closely together above brooding eyes. His mouth was drawn in a grim line.

"Is that an objective statement or one based on the fact that William's your son?"

"Bloody hell, Percy!" Bryce glared at his friend. "Do you seriously believe that William has betrayed us—that he's a traitor?"

Percy let out a deep sigh as he leaned forward in his seat, his elbows resting in his lap as he studied the glass of scotch that he held between his hands. "I have to accept all possibilities." His eyes settled on Bryce's in a deadpan stare. "My position decrees it."

"Who are you sending, Percy?"

Percy paused for a moment. The only reason he'd sent for Bryce in the first place was because he considered him a close friend. He'd already shared the details regarding William's mission with him and was beginning to wonder how much more he ought to divulge. "I've settled on Michael Ashford," he said.

"Thomas's boy?"

Percy nodded at that, not at all surprised that Bryce was familiar with the Duke of Devonshire.

"Thomas is a man of great integrity. Hopefully the apple didn't fall too far from the tree."

"Would you like to meet him?"

"What's your plan, Percy?" Bryce asked, ignoring his question. "Are you sending this Ashford fellow to kill my son?"

Percy sighed. "My hands are tied, old chap. You know that treason is an unacceptable offense, but I'm not sending Michael to assassinate your son, Bryce. I'm sending him to bring William back home so that he may face the charges against him in a court of law."

"And if he resists?"

"Let's hope that he doesn't." Percy gave Bryce a meaningful look.

"Michael will assume that he is guilty of all charges and do what must be done by all means necessary. Is that it?"

Percy nodded reluctantly. "Yes," he said, in little more than a whisper.

"Then by all means, show Lord Ashford in so that I may meet the man."

It was a delicate situation—one that Percy wished to have no part of, but what could he do other than hope that it would soon be over?

He was inclined to agree with Bryce when it came to judging William's integrity. William had always been an honorable man. It seemed unthinkable that he might have turned traitor. Then again, Percy had seen it happen before. As he went to the door and called for Michael to enter, he sent a silent prayer that he would somehow manage to bring William home in one piece.

Michael strode into the room with a confidence that immediately told Bryce that this was no greenling he was being introduced to. Before him stood a tall figure of a man—well over six feet, with broad shoulders, a powerful chest, and strong arms. In short, he looked like he could slay a dragon with one hand whilst protecting a damsel in distress with the other. His hair was dark and ruffled, his eyes sparkling with boyish anticipation.

"Gentlemen." Michael followed his greeting with a polite nod of his head in first Percy's, then Bryce's direction.

"Ashford, let me introduce you to a close friend of mine—Lord Bryce Summersby, the Earl of Moorland."

Bryce rose to his feet and grasped Michael's outstretched hand in a firm shake.

"I've heard much about you Lord Summersby—from my father, in particular. He's a great admirer of your military endeavors—says you're quite the strategist." He released Bryce's hand with a wry twist of his lips. "He also says he's never managed to beat you at chess."

Bryce chuckled. It had been a while since he'd last seen Thomas, but he had fond memories of the poor man's numerous attempts at beating him at his favorite game. "How is your father?"

Michael shrugged as he reached for one of the decanters on the side table. "Do you mind?" he asked Percy.

"Not at all—help yourself."

Pouring a glass of port, Michael glanced over at Bryce. "Still going strong," he said. "He'll be sixty-two in another couple of months, but he's still running around like a young lad. Trouble is his limbs are stiffer than they used to be. I can't help but worry that he might hurt himself—you see, in his mind he's no more than twenty years of age."

"Just wait until you're our age," Bryce told him with a grin. "You won't believe your eyes when you happen to catch yourself in a mirror. You'll most likely draw your sword wondering who the devil that stranger is staring back at you." He raised his glass to Michael. "Enjoy your youth while you've got it, Ashford. Lord knows it'll be gone before you know it."

Michael grimaced. He had some inkling of how fast life was passing by—he couldn't quite believe that it was already ten years since he'd joined the Foreign Office.

"I briefed Ashford on his mission this morning," Percy said, deciding that it was time to get on with the business at hand. The sooner it was taken care of, the happier he'd be. Nothing was nastier than having to decide the fate of somebody's child—especially not when that child was like family. Responsibility weighed heavily on Percy's shoulders—but so did disappointment—and as he sat in his dark brown leather chair, he desperately hoped that Finch was somehow mistaken about William's actions. "He's ready to leave in the morning."

Bryce moved to the side table to refill his glass. "How long have you and William known each other?" he asked Michael.

"Well, err . . . actually, I . . ."

"Ashford has never met your son, Bryce—you know that we don't allow our agents to meet unless they're working on the same assignment. It helps protect their identities when they're in the field."

"Well, I certainly don't mean to point out the obvious," Bryce remarked, his voice laced with annoyance. "But how the devil is he supposed to find William when he doesn't even know what he looks like?"

"There are ways."

Bryce scoffed at that. "We both know that William is skilled at deception. He works well undercover—hence the reason you gave him such an important assignment in the first place." He looked at Michael as if to highlight the fact that *he* had not been selected, but Michael simply stared back at him with a bland expression. Bryce took a large gulp of his whiskey, savoring the potent flavor that filled his mouth. "I want Ryan and Alex to accompany him."

Percy's mouth dropped open like a flytrap. "But you always said that . . ."

"That was then and this is now. They'll be able to identify William."

"And you're certain that you want Alex to go as well?"

Bryce had no desire to let his daughter get muddled up in this mess, but on the other hand, she was a better horseman, a better swordsman, and a better shot than Ryan had ever been. In fact, the only reason he was sending Ryan at all was to act as her chaperone. "Quite certain," he said.

Both men turned to Michael. His expression was impossible for either of them to read as he quietly pondered the thought of Bryce's children tagging along. "It will be a perilous journey," he stated. "They'll have to hold their own—I've no desire to babysit anyone."

"You won't have to," Bryce grumbled. "Alexa . . ."

"Is the best swordsman you're ever likely to come across," Percy said as he cut off his friend. It would be a cold day in hell before Michael would ever agree to bring a woman along, no matter how much Percy might vouch for her. He'd likely quit first, but that wasn't a risk that Percy was willing to take.

"And if William is guilty of treason . . . if he fights back? What then? I won't have his siblings standing in my way if I'm forced to take action." He paused. "Do you think they'll be willing to stand by as they watch me kill their brother, or will they turn on me in a foolhardy attempt to save him?"

Bryce's blood ran cold at Michael's tone. He didn't doubt for a second that the man before him was prepared to carry out his orders to exaction. Would Alex and Ryan let him kill their brother, even if he was a traitor? Absolutely not, but they gave him hope that he might see William again, and for that reason alone, he was prepared to say anything to ensure that they'd be in a position to help their brother. "If they were to discover that he's been consorting with the French, then I believe they would."

"Very well, then," Michael acquiesced. "We leave at dawn. Will they be ready by then?"

Bryce nodded. "I've already told them to prepare themselves in the event that they would be joining you."

Michael nodded. "There's a tavern on the outskirts of town—The Royal Oak. Are you familiar with the place?"

"I am."

"Good. Tell your sons to meet me there at five. I don't plan to wait for them, so if they're late . . ."

"They'll be there," Bryce told him sharply. And you'll be

in for one hell of a surprise when you discover that one of my sons is a daughter, he thought smugly as his eyes met Percy's. "You have my word," he added, reaching out to shake Michael's hand.

"And you have my word as a gentleman that I shall act fairly," Michael told him. "Percy tells me that both of you find it unlikely that William is a turncoat. I will discover the truth of the matter, and I hope that you will trust me when I say that I would never dream of harming an innocent man. Furthermore, my prerogative is to bring him back alive, so if all goes well, you'll see your son soon enough, Lord Summersby."

"Thank you," Bryce told him sincerely. "I shall await your return. Godspeed," he added as he raised his glass in a final salute before gathering up his coat and heading for the door. "You'll keep me informed?" he asked as he looked back over his shoulder at Percy, his hand already on the door handle.

"You'll hear from me as soon as I have any news."

With a heavy sigh and a thoughtful nod, Bryce left Percy's office with growing trepidation. He wasn't a gambling man, yet here he was, willing to risk everything dear to him in order to save his first-born child. Though he had faith in both Alexandra and Ryan, he hated having to sit idly by in anticipation. If only he could go in their stead, but that was of course an impossible notion. He'd grown too old to be gallivanting about on rescue missions, particularly with his left leg paining him whenever he walked for more than five minutes. No, he had no choice but to send his children in his stead, and in spite of himself, he suddenly smiled. This was exactly the sort of thing that Alexandra had been dreaming about for years. Now he was finally ready to indulge her.

About the Author

Born in Denmark, SOPHIE BARNES spent her youth traveling with her parents to wonderful places all around the world. She's lived in five different countries, on three different continents, and speaks Danish, English, French, Spanish, and Romanian.

She has studied design in Paris and New York and has a bachelor's degree from Parson's School of design, but most impressive of all: She's been married to the same man three times, in three different countries, and in three different dresses.

While living in Africa, Sophie turned to her lifelong passion—writing.

When she's not busy dreaming up her next romance novel, Sophie enjoys spending time with her family, swimming, cooking, gardening, watching romantic comedies and, of course, reading. She currently lives on the East Coast.

Be Impulsive!

Look for Other
Avon Impulse Authors

www.AvonImpulse.com